Tor Books by Kathleen Ann Goonan

The Bones of Time
Queen City Jazz

The
Bones
of
Time

Kathleen Ann Goonan

A Tom Doherty Associates Book
New York

THE BONES OF TIME

Copyright © 1996 by Kathleen Ann Goonan

Cover art by R.S. Winter, NYC

Map by Ellisa Mitchell

Edited by David G. Hartwell

A Tor Book
Published by Tom Doherty Associates, Inc.
175 Fifth Avenue
New York, NY 10010

Tor Books on the World Wide Web:
http://www.tor.com

Tor® is a registered trademark of Tom Doherty Associates, Inc.

ISBN:0-812-55746-8
Library of Congress Card Catalog Number: 95-40994

First edition: February 1996
First mass market edition: March 1997

Printed in the United States of America

0 9 8 7 6 5 4 3 2 1

For Joseph, again

Acknowledgments

Mahalo to our friends in Hawaii who graciously allowed us to stay in their homes while researching this book—Kay and Daniel Susott, Dan and Keiko Formanek, and Carol and Craig Severance. I would also like to thank Kam Sung for giving me a copy of the Permaculture documentary he produced, which introduced me to the philosophy of primal societies.

Thanks to Ted White, George Andrews, Richard Moore, Dave Bischoff, and Steve Brown, who gave valuable feedback not only regarding the novella from which this book grew, "Kamehameha's Bones," but who immensely improved everything I put through the group. And I deeply appreciate Gardner Dozois and Sheila Williams for publishing "Kamehameha's Bones" in *Asimov's*.

Thanks to Wanda Collins and Pam Noles for critiquing this manuscript, Bil Click for the first-draft map, and John Gribbin for granting permission to use a quotation from his book *Unveiling the Edge of Time*. David Hartwell also deserves many thanks, for helping me envision the book within the original material and helping it come to light.

Thanks especially to my husband, Joseph, for our times in Hawaii and for the enthusiasm with which he has supported my ideas and this project.

And finally, thanks to my parents, Tom and Irma Goonan, for having the courage to move to Hawaii with three small children when it was a brand-new state.

I must have been born under an unlucky star, as I seem to have my life planned out for me in such a way that I cannot alter it.

—Victoria Kaiulani, Hawaii's
last princess, in a letter to a friend
Jersey, England, 1897

What matters is that there seems to be nothing in the laws of physics that forbids travel through wormholes.

—John Gribbin,
Unveiling the Edge of Time

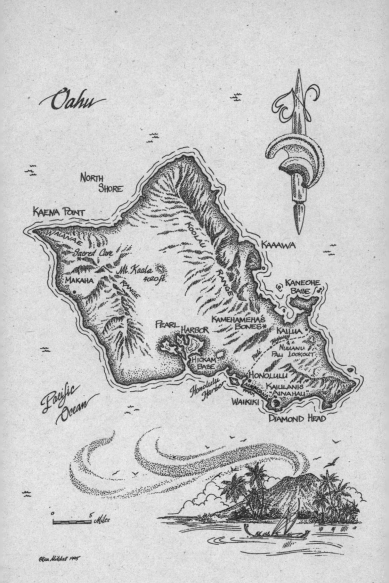

Prologue

The first thing Princess Kaiulani saw, as her eyes adjusted to the dim light in her mother's sickroom, was the old holy man. The kahuna.

Her breath caught in her throat as she paused in the doorway.

Thin as a barracuda, golden and dry as sand, he looked out of place, yet stood with grace and authority. Polished Victorian furniture crowded the large bedroom, a fit setting for the sister of the king of Hawaii, but the kahuna ignored a cluster of mahogany side chairs and carefully unrolled a mat he had brought with him onto the Belgian carpet. He sat cross-legged upon it in a single, lithe movement.

Kaiulani had watched the kahuna approach the house from her second-story window an hour ago. She had been staring across the tops of the blossom-laden mimosas at the brown, craggy slopes of Diamond Head, wondering why her mother had chosen to die. How could anything be more beautiful than the deep blue line of sea, the sweet scent of pink-spined mimosa fans, and the hush of surf beyond the narrow tidal swamp? Her mother had said something once, a few months ago, about old Hawaii vanishing. Eaten by the sharks, she had said. Who were the sharks? Kaiulani wondered, blinking against sudden tears, gripping the windowsill as hard as she wanted to grip the slender thread of her mother's life and hold it on this side of death.

Then the kahuna had emerged from the shade of the long green lane that led to Ainahau, startling Kaiulani.

He wore only a loincloth, and his white hair was short. His bare feet raised puffs of dust from the unpaved drive. In his outstretched arms he carried with obvious reverence a large, bulky bundle. As he passed the tortoiseshell carriage with gleaming silver fittings in which Kaiulani and her mother made their many obligatory social calls, he seemed a throwback to an ancient world, one which Kaiulani was young enough to have only glimpsed.

He stopped before vanishing beneath the porch roof. With fathomless eyes he had stared up at her as the white curtains snapped in the wind. She had stared back, wondering what he thought of her.

Now, on the threshold of her mother's room, she did not want to enter: not with him there. Her father gripped her hand more tightly when she balked in the foyer like a stubborn horse.

"What is it?" he asked.

"What is *he* doing here?" she asked. Her old Hawaiian nurse-maid told her many frightening stories about kahunas, but she had rarely seen one, and never close up. This one had been at her aunt Liliuokalani's house only two months ago, though. His look an hour ago had chilled her. Implacable, judging, *urging*.

"You *must* go in," her father said, voice hoarse from weeping. "Your mother has been asking for you. She loves you so."

Kaiulani felt utterly alone as she stepped inside; the door clicked shut behind her.

Neither the new electric light in the wall sconce nor gentle oil lamps illuminated the room, and the sun was likewise resolutely excluded. Princess Likelike's room had been darkened at her request since she took to her bed after Christmas, though a thin stripe of light leaked through the curtains and bisected the kahuna's thin dour face.

Kaiulani breathed shallowly, not wanting the camphor-laden air in her lungs. No wonder her mother was . . .

Dying. She said it to herself. Dying.

Likelike had cut herself off from the outside. From light,

from *air*. The constant birdcries and the rustle of the botanical paradise her father created in the Waikiki swamps were muffled by closed windows. The faint sea-tang that filled the other rooms of the house was replaced here by the close cloying smell of sickness. The old Hawaiian nurse turned and set an empty washpan on a table. Kaiulani jumped at the sudden clink. Open the windows, she wanted to shout. Let my mother breathe!

Her mother, a small, shadowed figure on the enormous four-poster that was swathed in lacy white bedclothes from England, twisted restlessly, then lifted her head.

"Come, my keiki," she said.

Kaiulani ran and flung herself at her mother, kneeling next to the bed. She could barely feel the weight of her mother's hand, light as a bird's claw, on her hair. Likelike hadn't eaten for weeks. It was as if she had simply decided to die.

The whispers and gossip of the palace and the servants filled Kaiulani's mind. For the past few weeks it seemed as if every Manoa stream bubbling over the rocks was filled with those whispery voices, as if each plant rubbing two leaves together in the wind spoke the same horrible, fatalistic thought: Likelike is being prayed to death by a kahuna. What else could it be? they asked. The royal doctors, educated in America and Europe, said nothing was wrong, and Likelike was only thirty-six years old. And just this morning word had come that a school of red *aweoweo* had been spotted several weeks ago off the coast of Hawaii. Her mother had once been Governor of that island, and the *aweoweo* was a portent of death for the royal family. Had she angered someone there, maybe by marrying a Scotchman and diluting the royal blood? But many Hawaiian royals had married haoles in the past fifty years. Kaiulani had asked her father about it and he had become angry, for he had no patience with Hawaiian superstitions. One careless servant had said that she should beware, for it was Princess Likelike's own brother, King David Kalakaua, who was behind it. Kind Papa Moi? Kaiulani couldn't believe *that*.

Kaiulani turned at a deep, hollow sound, almost like bells.

She rose slowly, wiping tears with the back of her hand while the nurse hastened to hand her a handkerchief.

The kahuna, leaning forward, was unwrapping his dank bundle, which smelled of cold dark earth. He had donned one of the Hawaiian masks that had always frightened Kaiulani when she was younger. This was a simple one: black on the left side, white on the right. No snarling teeth, no terrifying frown. The straightforward, inescapable gravity of day and night, life and death.

Kaiulani saw what *had* to be bones: a pile of enormous bones, overflowing the woven mat and spilling onto the priceless rug. Too large to be dog bones, the sacrifice of choice since Kamehameha forbade human sacrifice a hundred years ago. Her stomach clenched.

"What are you doing here?" she demanded, unafraid suddenly. She was heir to the throne of Hawaii; he was most properly her subject. "Are you the one who is killing my mother?"

The nurse turned, shot her a look of raw fear behind the kahuna's back, and crossed herself. Likelike opened her mouth, but no words came out. Kaiulani stood very straight and grasped her mother's hand.

"No," said the old man, his voice unusually melodious, yet studied and calm. He beckoned. Kaiulani stayed put.

"Go," whispered her mother.

Kaiulani took one step only toward him.

"Touch these," he said. "They are the sacred bones of King Kamehameha, from whom you are descended."

Kaiulani shook her head. Related, and only through Kamehameha's cousin. She knew her genealogy well.

"Do as he says," Likelike commanded, her voice surprisingly strong.

Kaiulani hesitated, then knelt, her full skirts billowing on the floor. She brushed one of the bones swiftly with her fingertips.

The kahuna caught her hand and yanked it toward him, pressed it beneath his onto the jumble of bones and held it down with surprising strength. The bones were neither warm nor cold to touch.

"*This* is your baptism, your initiation," he said. "Not the haole one, the Christian one. You are our last hope, the last hope of all Hawaiians. You are half haole, but you are our last *alii,* our last royal child. Our people have a life, which you are bound to preserve. Our people have a land, which you are bound to preserve for them."

Tears glimmered in his dark eyes and he seemed unashamed as they overflowed and traced glistening trails on his withered cheeks. The room stilled utterly, as if the ceaseless trades had stopped, as if time itself were holding its breath.

And then the cries of the peacocks that roamed the grounds burst forth, loud and dreadful, even in this closed room.

Mad, sudden dreams rose all around Kaiulani, rushed toward her, enveloped her. Foreign cities shimmered, color and sound like a blow, so strange that she barely grasped that each one *was* a city before it faded into the inevitable next: new streets, new canals, new rushing crowds. Flames, screams and horror; buildings crumbling, strange gray battleships exploding against the unmistakable background of the Koolau Mountains, and burning men leaping from them into the deep, crystal-clear harbor into which the Pearl River flowed. Festivals of gay music, grim hordes marching. Was this *her* world? For an instant a small girl lay gasping for life in her arms, a red gash in her side soaking her clothing. Small poor shacks were crowded with ragged beggars next to impossible glass towers. Between the carnage flashed scenes of sanguine beauty—billowing green forests, wide, slow rivers weaving through grassy plains, a small golden island topped with sparkling coconut palms across a brilliant blue lagoon. Kaiulani was filled with dazzling light as these visions passed through her one after another like waves, as if her body were made of light like them, permeable and fluid, frighteningly without a center, an ocean of time filled with images and pain without end, without a beginning. She cried out, but it was like the voice of someone else, falling on her own ears like the muffled bird cries outside the sealed windows.

The kahuna was still holding her hand to the bones when her mother spoke, and the swirl of images became shadowed. Likelike's words fell into the dark room like bright stones tossed into a deep pool, shimmering then receding into darkness while ripples spread endlessly outward. She spoke in a harsh whisper; the words were sharp and precise and offered singly, slowly, charged with inevitability. "You will live far away," Likelike said. "You will never marry. You will never be queen."

Shaking, struggling for breath, Kaiulani yanked her hand from the bones, from the kahuna's dry strong grasp. She took two steps across the ornate designs woven into the rug, strange abstract turrets and passageways that stood out for her somehow in the slowed and awful moment.

At her mother's bedside, she saw the sick woman's eyes were closed. Her chest—was it? . . .

Yes, it still rose and fell. Barely.

Barely. Kaiulani touched Likelike's cheek, but those dear eyes remained shut. She felt the itch of sweat rolling down her face. She grasped her mother's narrow shoulders with both hands. And shook her. Just a bit. Wake her up. It didn't work. She shook harder. "Wake up, Mama. Wake *up!*"

"Princess!" shouted the nurse, and Kaiulani struggled against the strong arm around her waist, hauling her backward. The door slammed open and her father rushed in, heavy boots thudding.

"What has happened? Is she . . . ?" He whirled to face the kahuna, shouted at him, "Get out of here!"

Kaiulani had never once heard him shout before.

The kahuna stood and chanted, in slow, beautiful Hawaiian.

It was a passage chant, words to build a bridge to the otherworld for her mother's spirit.

She ran from the room and rushed down the wide, polished hallway, through the great room cluttered with chairs and tables where her mother had so recently played cards with the German ambassador and his wife, her shining dark hair piled high and laced with flowers.

Holding up her long skirt, Kaiulani burst into the bright sunshine, ran toward the strip of bright blue ocean that shone at the end of the leafy lane, away from the terrible visions, the conflagrations, the barely glimpsed deaths of loved ones, each of whom went into the fearsome dark alone.

Princess Likelike, the sister of King David Kalakaua and Lili-uokalani Dominis, neither of whom had children, died at four o'clock that afternoon.

Her daughter Kaiulani, the sole surviving heir of the Hawaiian royal family, was twelve years old.

Lynn

Honolulu 2034

1

Lynn Oshima paced, then whirled, short-stepping within a larger rhythm to leap a pothole. Caught in the endorphin flow of running, she let every objection to the pain dissolve in pure white energy. She could forget, when running, that she knew too much about the illegal genetic work of Interspace—IS—because it was based on work that *she* had done. She could forget that she chose to do nothing about it. She could forget Nana's constant criticism of her Zygote Clinic embryo, implanted two months ago.

And she could almost forget, in the glow that emanated from everything after the first three miles, that despite her disgust with IS, she was nevertheless powerfully tempted by the completely off-the-record offer of her brother James, a top Interspace official, to fly to Hong Kong and be the liaison in a black-market deal to buy some of Mao's bone marrow. James was ignoring a month-old ultimatum from her that she was through with his shady deals. He knew that information was an even more powerful addiction for her than endorphins.

Downtown Honolulu was glorious this morning. Glass towers, bathed in golden sunrise, surrounded her. The deep green Koolau Mountains were suddenly revealed like a vision of paradise as the morning trades pushed heavy clouds past Hickam Spacebase and then out to sea. Lynn pulled cool pure air deep into her lungs. A silent, open maglev coasted past her, and two lawyers getting an early start stepped out onto the rain-damp street.

The Chinese flower woman smiled at Lynn as she ran past bright orange sheaves of bird-of-paradise set in tall black containers. That gloomy Nana, trying to make her feel bad about deciding to have a baby! *Let* her huddle in her ancient Japanese shack, taking her old-fashioned blood pressure pills instead of getting an implant, and mutter about how terrible the world had become, and her son—practically the head of Interspace—and grandchildren along with it!

She felt a brief stab of pain but ignored it. She'd feel better in a minute. She'd left the Zendo because she'd felt sick. She went every morning at 4:30 A.M., walking down dark Nuuanu to the corner Zen church, next to the Japanese Embassy. This morning, leaves had rustled and drops from a sudden shower spat through the screen next to where Lynn sat, eyes unfocused, erect, as in some utterly new atmosphere. The shower passed in minutes, and, as always, the birds took up their chatter ten minutes before the tropical dawn began to grow.

Lynn had not reflected on these events; they occurred and were noted. The old roshi knocked the wooden tima and the chanting began like some deep, remote, alien energy source and ran through Lynn's bones.

She remembered rising for kinhin, walking meditation, and stepping slowly around the room. Then her stomach lurched and she ran down the hallway and out onto the porch. She knew they could all hear her puking her guts out, all the old men in there who weren't even sure they wanted a woman in their midst but taking her because she insisted, because on community night she went to archery instead of flower arranging. At least she was entirely Japanese; probably the only point in her favor. Of course they thought "nothing," or else, "woman." "Not-married, disgraceful." Something like that, as completely old-fashioned as her father and proud of it. Then they forgot that thought, and the next, and the next. Lynn's thoughts stubbornly stuck to her like grease on dishes. Wiping sweat from her forehead she had walked over to the drinking fountain and rinsed her mouth.

And then had she walked the few blocks home? No! The sky was a brilliant, delicate deep blue, and dawn was so swift, so full, that she could watch it come and feel a part of full morning and there was no time for her attention to waver. There was nothing as stunning as equatorial light. Ignoring the pain, which seemed to be increasing, she had slipped her sunglasses out of her pocket and turned on her heel, started to run . . . *that* would fix it!

Was it getting worse? She wasn't sure. Lynn switched to a Two-Part Invention with a glance to the upper right quadrant of her sunglasses, skipping through traditional Japanese music and Billie Holiday until she reached the Bach, which blended with her stride. Salty sweat slid into her eyes, and she mopped her forehead with the bandanna she carried.

She drank in the scent of plumeria blossoms that were falling in a breeze-tossed flurry to vine-draped Nuuanu Stream. The stream roared in her ears, and two young boys zipboarded toward her, yelling at each other, and parted without a glance at her to pass her on each side. Nana's whispery old voice overrode the Bach: "You are crazy, girl, to run every day with a baby inside you. You were crazy to put it *in* you. You picked the father from a *catalog?* It can't be a *real* baby. Getting your doctorate only made you stupid, I think! Why don't you get married and have a real baby? A baby needs a father. You're not too old yet to find a man. Thirty-five is not too old." Every day, the same thing. But Nana's acerbity was probably why she'd lived to be over a hundred. Every day she sharpened her brain, as if it were a knife, on uncooperative shopkeepers, her family, and the world at large with absolutely no discrimination.

Two blocks from Nana's house, Lynn gasped at sudden, wrenching pain. She clutched her abdomen and bent over.

The world seemed to recede. The Korean restaurant across the street, an old Japanese man carrying a net bag of groceries half a block ahead of her, the sky-filling mountains rising sharply straight ahead, the shriek and clatter of the garbage truck were all blurred and distant. Drenched with sweat, she grabbed at a half-rotten fencepost next to her, which crunched and gave slightly as she leaned against it, breathing hard. The pain was like nothing she had felt before. She saw a line of dark blood running down the inside of her thigh, below her shorts; one drop fell onto the sidewalk.

Almost hidden behind thick mango trees was one of the tiny frame houses like Nana's, built ages ago for immigrant workers. But Nana's was utterly neat and trim, square and painted gray with glossy black trim. This one looked haunted—unpainted, with a crooked porch. The rest of the house was concealed by a tiny, private jungle. Red and yellow hibiscus rioted through vines that hung from mimosas, still wet from the morning shower. Not a patch of lawn was visible.

Lynn tried to straighten. She pushed open the gate hanging crooked from the decrepit picket fence and forced herself to walk up the overgrown concrete walk. She was on the first step when the screen door swung open and slammed against the house.

Dizzy with pain, Lynn stared. The Bach was still playing. Lynn yanked off her sunglasses and threw them down. They clattered on the steps.

The beautiful boy seemed so perfect he must be a vision. His skin was a deep golden brown. His eyes were large and intelligent, fringed with long black lashes. Curly dark hair framed his oval face. He wore a pair of loose white shorts and his feet were bare. His body, too, was perfect—smooth and unblemished, as lovely in proportion as a living statue, framed by yellow-flowering vines that wandered across the weathered boards around the door. She thought he must be fifteen or sixteen.

His eyes widened as he looked down and saw Lynn's shoes, now splattered with blood.

Her impressions took only seconds. The pain seized her again.

"Call an ambulance," Lynn said and sank onto the step. "I'm having a miscarriage." When the boy just stood there in seeming shock she yelled, *"Hurry!* Is there anyone else here?" She tried to stand, but could not straighten up and staggered to the door, shoving the boy aside. She shouted down the dark corridor, "Anybody *home?"*

First an old man, then a younger woman, emerged from different doors in the hallway. In the dim light, they looked at each other, at her, and then toward the front door where the boy still stood.

"Get in here!" the woman said, her black hair falling almost to the back of her knees, longer than her yellow muu-muu.

"What were you thinking of?" She rushed past Lynn.

The boy said, "But she's hurt."

"I need an ambulance," said Lynn. "Please."

The man nodded and went back in his room. He emerged in less than a minute. "It is coming," he said. "Let me help you out."

"I don't think I can walk," said Lynn. She was terrified and, to her horror, began to cry.

The man, though the hair on his broad chest was white, bent down and picked her up as easily as if she were a child. Lynn looked up and down the hall as she tried not to think about what was happening, what *must* have already happened, to her.

"Where is the boy?" she asked.

"What boy?" the man said.

"There was a boy here."

The man's stride was long and swift, and the scream of the ambulance grew. They were only a few blocks from Kapiolani Women's Hospital, where the baby was to have been born.

"Must have been a neighbor boy," he said. He laid her on the stretcher and she felt the cool, soothing sensor that monitored vital signs touch the back of her neck. The man left without another word.

As they pulled away the medic put an oxygen mask over Lynn's face, but she knew it was too late for anything that would help.

Against the loss of her fetus, whose name, at two months, had been Masa Elizabeth Oshima, who had been on the waiting list already at the exclusive Rainbow Keiki School, Lynn held the face of the golden boy steady as a long note of music. Like water in a swift stream her other future rushed away, the one where she magically changed from a Type A to a Type B personality, composed synthesizer masterpieces, raised Masa, and lived off the money she got from her dead mother's gene-scan patent—plus the sale of her Interspace shares when she completely and finally, bravely divorced herself from that corruption-riddled institution.

Yes. With the shot of pure oxygen to her brain Lynn knew

without a doubt who that boy was. His picture had burned into her years ago and had remained all this time.

She knew he would probably be dead soon, just as the others like him were dead. Dead like Masa. A wasted child, a wasted life.

She turned her head aside and felt the tears burn.

2

The old bamboo blinds buzzed in the night wind as Lynn kicked back in her chair, propped her legs on her desk, and bent over the pale screen of her small handy. She heard Nana shuffle toward her half-opened bedroom door past the faded old prints of Himage Island. Nana's father had brought them from Japan when he came, a laborer, in the 1930s, his picture-bride following a year later.

Nana stood in the doorway, tiny and stern. She would tell no one how old she was, but Lynn and her brothers had her pegged at about one hundred and two. Her eyes were black, intense in her sunken, weathered face. No enhancement for her!

"You've got to get proper rest, young lady," she scolded. "It's not good for you to stay up half the night after being in the hospital." Nana hadn't used the word *miscarriage*—much too bald.

Lynn felt something in her chest ease at her grandmother's voice. The old woman had been so gentle, never once reprimanding her—so far. Now things were getting back to normal. *This* was home, not the rarefied estate high on Tantalus Drive from which her father, a top Interspace executive, had ejected her years ago. She had insisted as a teenager on taking a job playing her own synthesizer compositions in the Waikiki San Bar, a roofless Tourist Zone nightclub atop the Princess Kaiulani Hotel. A disgrace to the family *and* a waste, he'd proclaimed.

Lynn still performed occasionally, but genetics, and the theoretical designing of humans to adapt them to long space journeys, had seized her imagination years ago. It was like an entirely new form of music, composing possible humans from the infinite combinations of the notes of potential physiology.

"You're right," she said, but pushed a few pads on her handheld. Her small desk holo projector beeped, and she gazed at a representation in light of a rat brain section from an obscure Czech study that had just arrived via the web. She touched another pad several times and watched as different parts of the section were revealed.

Nana clucked with disapproval before turning to continue down the hall. The curtain blew in the slight, fragrant breeze, bisecting the holo without disturbing it.

Lynn had always reveled in the freedom she had won and thought that her half brothers, twins a few years younger than she and firmly ensconced in Interspace, secretly envied her.

On her black enameled desk was the note from one of them, James. Arriving last week via snailmail, unsigned, and coded in a childhood code, it suggested that she go to Hong Kong and procure the genetic material of—it was claimed, at least—Mao. One of their typical black-market schemes. She couldn't deny she got a kick out of such transactions. At least she used to.

Just a week ago, it had been irritatingly tempting. With her retrieval of the material would come replication and study rights carte blanche, something to add to her genetic library, which already contained the DNA of the visionary president of China, Zhong Chau. She'd been assassinated in 2025. Lynn also had a collection of once-powerful ayatollahs, which had come in a bundle, various queens and kings both ancient and recent, Lenin, Indira Gandhi, Teddy Roosevelt, and a host of other politicians. She also had libraries of writers, artists, athletes, scientists; and also at her disposal was the vast computer-held information of the World Health Organization, in which a drop of blood from every person born since 2004 was analyzed and cataloged. Whenever anyone had any interface with the medical community more information was added. Many genetic problems did not manifest for years and now it was possible to begin to help those with potential problems when they were young.

Mao would be an interesting addition to her library, and one that was unique. As far as she knew no one had him.

Lynn pushed aside some papers on her desk and picked up James's note, studied it again, then tossed it back down. When she had first opened it, she had added the passport code he'd included to her passport—a thin blue pad filled with electronic identification and records. The code would be activated by the Hong Kong agent when she got off the plane, and it would tell him everything was fine.

Then she had put it into her wallet, proof of her indecision. This was an addiction, that was all, one she ought to break. Lately she had entertained the thought of slipping away to a remote Buddhist monastery somewhere in Cambodia or Japan.

Right, Lynn.

She reached across her desk now and picked up her passport, opened it, and scrolled through the entries. Bangkok. Kathmandu. Beijing. Narita, Narita, Narita. London. Cairo. Two, three trips a year. She had to admit that she loved the travel, *craved* it, no matter how sad she found the world. An image from Bombay often haunted her—a shimmering holographic advertisement of a white, blond family standing in front of a beautiful mansion casting faint rainbows upon a dark-skinned family begging on the sidewalk below.

Well. She couldn't just mope. It would be something to do. Mao! Hers, nearly exclusively, at least until she chose to release him to the public. Just the thing to cheer her up. She pulled her wallet out of her back pocket, slipped in the passport, returned the wallet to her pocket. She could give it up later.

Sure. Stop kidding yourself. But don't give yourself such a hard time. *Knowledge* is neither good nor bad—it's who uses it and how.

So who's using what you learn? How? What for?

She tried not to think of Masa Elizabeth and looked over at her hologram. Right now, she was studying the neurochemical mediators of intelligence in humans and in human development, linking them to various genetic markers. Or, at least, she *had* been, before the miscarriage, and publishing results quite regularly in various journals. She'd had as little as possible to do with IS in any direct way for several years, save for her trips. There were things that she just didn't want to know. She had IS stock, but she'd quit attending meetings years ago; her dividends were automatically reinvested. The less she knew about the murky inner workings on which her brothers thrived the better she felt. They could not understand her lack of loyalty to Interspace and blamed it on her mother, a Japanese scientist, who had died when Lynn was four, after infusing her with independence. That was a quality the twins couldn't fathom.

Worried about possible uses and ramifications of some of her research, she had lately filed many experimental conclusions away without publishing. Sometimes she despised herself for sticking her head in the sand, but really, what could one person do?

Nothing, she told herself.

But was that really true?

Her field was fairly new and covetously administered by the genetic engineering department at the University of Hawaii, for all intents and purposes a branch of Interspace. Her thesis was an exploration of the physiology of intelligence—whatever that *was*—and what that might mean in regard to future space exploration. One had to have an IS bias here; it was inescapable. It was impossible to earn a degree at UH without it.

Child development had come a long way since the gender-biased educational systems of the late twentieth century had been forcibly dismantled, administrators and teachers kicking and screaming. But in Lynn's opinion, worse things were afoot. While investigating schools for Masa, she had found that discreet inquiries were made concerning the addition of Strand X to her fetus's genetic code.

Called *bionan,* the manipulation of minute sequences in the genetic code was being fiercely litigated in many forms worldwide. If parents chose to bear a child whose physiology would manifest mentally or physically crippling traits that could be easily corrected, was that child abuse? Was it the state's responsibility to pay for any extraordinary care or education such children might require?

But for other children the definition of normality was becoming ever more finely shaded, as Lynn had found.

There was nothing written—of course not; but in the interview the administrator, sitting behind a desk made of opalescent material that Lynn recognized as the latest space-age breakthrough, said, "Of course, she's going to be a happy child?" Her tone of voice gave the phrase brand-name status.

"What?" asked Lynn. "I—"

"Oh," said the woman, whose myriad degrees and certifications caught the light behind her on the sun-dappled wall. "I'm sorry, I forgot if it's a boy or a—"

Lynn could forgive her that. But—"I don't understand. Happy? I hope so . . . " Then it dawned on her. "Oh! You mean—"

"Yes," said the woman. "I can give you a list of labs that are qualified to perform—"

Lynn had stood up, shaking. "That's completely illegal," she said.

"Oh," said the woman brightly. "Don't worry—we have close connections with the state legislature. I have it on the highest authority that it will be perfectly legal before the year is out." She whirled a screen toward Lynn, began punching buttons. "And then you'll be glad we insisted that *your* child got a head start. Look—you'll be so pleased with the results. Happy children are able to learn *so* much more quickly without all those ridiculous tantrums. Wait!"

Lynn had slammed out of the door, out of the school. She strode across the busy street to a cool, tree-filled park and curled up on a bench, feeling sick. Later that afternoon she'd filed a complaint with the board that regulated genetic engineering, but she heard amusement in the voice of the man who took it.

That night, she'd tracked down the so-called Happy Child strand. Carried by a benign virus as was most bionan, it stimulated the endocrine system to produce soothing hormones when subtle markers of rage and rebellion appeared in the blood.

No, Lynn thought, staring at the screen, flooded with despair, think I'll have *regular* kids, thanks all the same. She had a feeling that those inconvenient tantrums they were wiping out were necessary for the child to become separate from the parent, to learn about power and limits. And that was just on the surface. What other essential function might they serve, and how would the adults who had not experienced it be crippled later? Intellectually? Emotionally? Who could tell, now: no one, till they graduated from Happy Kid Preschool and, later, Happy Kid High School . . .

Down the hall Nana shut her bedroom door, bringing Lynn back to the present. She didn't have to defend Masa's genetic and developmental integrity now.

She stood, bent backward until her spine cracked, and stretched. She leaned on the windowsill and looked out over Nana's precise, tiny lawn, where no plant dared put out a single untoward leaf to disturb the otherworldly order. If they did, Nana was there with clippers instantly, frowning and snipping.

The dark branch of a plumeria tree slanted past Lynn's window, blossoms white in moonlight. Maybe she would climb up on the roof and look through her telescope for a few hours. She knew that she wouldn't be able to sleep. It might be a good night to digiscan the fitful progress of the generation ship, moving toward swift completion after a two-year hiatus with a new infusion of money from Korea. She had been at the ever-so-elegant party at her father's estate when Samuel, James's twin, finally finessed a firm promise from the Korean ambassador after laying the groundwork for a year. It was good that the moonbase was being used again for larger goals than pleasure jaunts.

She turned from the window. She didn't care about that right now. Silly to pretend that she cared about much of anything. She had rejected the hormone implant advised at the hospital, where the tech told her that it would take a while for her hormones to rebalance. She knew how to rebalance them.

Running could cure anything. No matter what Nana left unspoken, Lynn knew that running hadn't caused her miscarriage. She had been sick that morning at the zendo, sick in a different way.

Well. So? It would have happened anyway. Something must have been wrong with little Masa. Or her. She had blithely disregarded her tech's suggestion of various tests. Everything would be *fine*. Blind faith. Which was now revealed as stupidity.

Restless, she felt like running right now, stepping out into the streets and *moving,* but didn't dare. Downtown Honolulu was dangerous at night, filled with off-duty space-station workers, wild as any sailors had ever been in the port town of Honolulu.

She thought of the boy with the golden skin, as she had so often in the hospital. It was none of her business.

What *is* your business then, Lynn?

She tried to ignore the flashes of dread she felt at the thought of him, her concern for his almost-certain fate, her certainty that she knew *who* he was.

King Kamehameha's clone. A perfect genetic copy of an extraordinary man who had been dead for over two hundred years, even though human cloning was internationally banned.

So what? At least 50 percent of Interspace operations fell under the banned umbrella, as far as she could tell. Genetic manipulation, bionan, and the routine disposal of the inevitable unsuccessful experiments, animal or . . . human . . . could occur only within strict limits.

But those limits were a joke, and a worldwide joke at that. Many suspected that IS routinely violated the Genetic Conventions, but few had proof, and those who did were those who benefited most, through black market sales of genetic or bionan packages. The vast, enormous underclass of the world *wanted* perfect vision, *wanted* to be disease-free, *wanted* intelligence—however it was defined. Resentment against the scientific intelligentsia who had decided, in 2009, to formally withhold all such changes from humankind until more was known was strong, very strong. The world was divided more and more sharply into a tiny core of wealth—those who could afford, for instance, Happy Child modifications with the huge black-market surcharge—and a vast and primitive third world that had changed very little in the past hundred years economically or educationally.

Lynn touched off her handy. She felt as if the universe had taken something away, but in place of the lost child had given her the responsibility for something greater. A crazy thought, she told herself, jamming her fists into her pockets. You are hardly chosen one material.

But the fact was that this kid might be in trouble.

She turned abruptly and walked through the old house down the creaking hallway, grabbing a smooth silk sweater and pulling it on as she walked. She stepped out into the cool night, allowed herself a glimpse of the star-spattered sky. She turned left, away from Honolulu.

She crossed the street. It was late. In the silence, palm fronds clicked. Mimosas were black silhouettes against the stars, as were the condos that loomed two blocks ahead.

The Koolau House, at the top of the hill, was old, but superbly designed and maintained; the seventy-year-old garden enclaves of the fifty-story condo were mature, tropical jungles.

Lynn glanced at the retscan panel and the door buzzed open. She saw the back of David, the night guard, as he sat in his little office looking at screens. She raised her hand in greeting and without turning he waved back. She walked past the hissing fountain and summoned the maglift with a glance.

As she opened the door of her apartment on the forty-third floor, it was like walking into a dream from her high-tech childhood. She kept her real work here, away from the damp and clutter of Nana's old house.

Laid out before her were the lights of Honolulu, beautiful as stars through the smartglass that formed the condo's skin. She walked over and touched it; the place she touched responded with her personal preset preferences as to temperature and lighting. She touched the window icon a few times and all the windows opened.

Tourist skims with tiny colored lights cruised past Ala Moana on the dark ocean. The fireworks in the Tourist Zone over by Waikiki, silent and tiny with distance, were almost over. She was just in time for the grand finale—the familiar ritual of a solar-sailed ship disappearing toward the stars, the Interspace logo.

The vectored room, roughly a trapezoid with a kitchen at the back, was sparsely furnished: a computer, some pillows scattered across the carpeted floor, a low black table.

She dropped onto a pile of pillows in front of a wraparound blank screen; she preferred holo and used the screen for background. She touched on her computer and sank into what was the true joy of her life: information.

Interior information. The small things. The luminescence of the twining strands of DNA, the minuscule iota of information that flooded the electronic journals and the secret reaches of the IS web. Her screen was a 180-degree arc. She could holo any aspect of it she wanted, project it from the curve of the screen and make it pirouette.

Her fingers hovered over the glowing keys as if they were the keys of a piano that she was going to play, gathering the notes within her, letting the force of the entire piece fill her being, as her long-ago teacher had taught her, before her fingers even began to move.

She remembered the boy's face in perfect detail. She shivered, and considered how best to scramble her tracks in this night's work.

Then she began.

The first, and easiest, thing to do was something she had done since childhood, a game she had played with her brothers. She composited the face and told her computer to find it.

She was not surprised to find it three years ago in an old HV newscast. Perhaps as a warning to the Homeland Movement, Interspace had not suppressed the fact that this child—his body, *his,* the one Lynn had seen a week ago but reduced by Lynn now holographically to a six-inch-long body—lay sprawled on the road out on Hawaii's North Shore. His head was bent at an angle that sickened Lynn. Hit-and-run. He was dead.

Of course, it was not him. This boy, and the one Lynn had seen, were both clones.

She quickly moved to hypertext the news. Since she was very young she had moved through the intricately coded IS web like a fish through water. It was second nature to her. Lynn brushed her hair back and leaned forward, arms between her legs, tapping the keys, surprised when the time floating near her right hand blinked 2:00 A.M., then 3:00. She teased out layer after layer of information.

Many paths led to Kohala, the great northern peninsula of the Big Island, where Kamehameha had been born. The Homelanders had been awarded this land long ago as part of a legal settlement. Lynn hit a wall every time she ventured near; suddenly an old-time thatched longhouse would appear, or a brief icon-like movie of a woman pounding poi—something bland and traditional.

She caught a glimpse once of a high-tech corridor, and, disappearing out a door, someone wearing full spacewalk regalia. But that flashed white and vanished and she couldn't get it back. There was some sort of very effective gatekeeper, human or AI.

Well, anyway, she had other things to find out.

As her eyes grew heavy, she set up the search, pushed a final key, then shoved the pillows back on the carpet and lay down with her head on one of them.

Morning was wild with birdsong, which woke her, rising in volume as the dawn grew. Still lying down, she opened her eyes.

The air was filled with something gorgeous. The time elapsed note showed that it had taken two hours, forty-six minutes, and twenty-three seconds to find it.

Lynn sank onto the black cushions in front of the wraparound, hunched forward, tapped keys through the vee of her knees, long, slim brown fingers sure and mistakeless despite excitement. Smooth calmness enveloped her and was echoed in the ageless blue of the sea beyond a Honolulu muted by forty-three stories, silver-glitter toy city.

She enlarged a segment of genescan from a certain Bone Fragment #4283, Hawaiian, Male.

What was the marker for navigational capabilities? And, extrapolating from that, the marker for navigation of mathematical spaces as well? She switched to a statistical program that analyzed this pattern, the A,T,G, and C of him.

Few pure Polynesians left. Yet they were the ones who had traveled by star, for whom the earth, or sea, truly did stop, while the stars moved overhead in a time/space reversal that sprang not from reality but from their minds. In fact, she recalled that one of the old navigators had hastened to assure a professor doing research that the sailors knew *they* were moving, rather than all that was around them, but that they maintained this state of mind in order to navigate correctly.

Yes, here it was. She quickly made some tea, then sat again, lay one leg flat, bent at the knee, and leaned one elbow on her other thigh. Her tongue tingled from a sip of bittersweet anquela tea, and the heavy sweet scent of her neighbor's plumeria drifted across the open expanse of her lanai. And still she stared, holding her breath, as she made the DNA dance before her.

Why was the marker for creativity—for adventure, for great, open intelligence, like a solar sail netted and spread to catch the phantom photons—so often madness and depression?

For there it was, the drunken sequence, the one that had dissipated through humankind from some shaman source, the one that gave chimerical mad beauty; violent, self-inflicted death.

Her sadness was heavy. She saw Hemingway, after shock treatments at the Mayo Clinic, proving that he could find the hidden bullets and unlock the gun cabinet, always in control. Virginia Woolf, cool and somehow utterly rational, filling her pockets with rocks and walking into the river. The visionary African web poet Tunesia Mynen, who thought she might be able to fly from her window through the streets of Paris shortly after receiving her Nobel.

Lynn smiled, felt her mouth twist with bitter wryness. She flicked a few keys. There. See? She could fix him. Replace that unfortunate predilection. That, after all, was her illegal specialty.

Lynn could blot out the hunger for the stars in this fellow's genetic template cleanly, precisely, without wrecking the body. That was the Interspace way. He might be useless for navigation. He might be just a normal being, without special eyes, without incredible thoughts.

For all *they* would know, anyway.

She saved the true genescan on a personal sphere, which she labeled Music. She had a very old one just like it, she was pretty sure. Saved from several years ago, when she had first seen his face. Except it had not been the face of this particular child, but another, now most certainly dead. But maybe not. She knew, for sure, that one of them was dead, the one on the news. How many had the Homeland Movement managed to nurture? How many were frozen? How many had been implanted? Had the women known *who* they were carrying?

She had been barely twenty when the rumor of a live Kamehameha clone arose. She had electronically attended an Interspace board meeting where the child was discussed; she still attended them then, though she couldn't remember exactly when she'd stopped. Eight years ago? Ten? When had she realized that she couldn't make a difference?

At that particular meeting it was revealed that a high-level employee of Interspace, someone with considerable expertise and access, had added a clone of a human to the bank of animal clones on which experiments were being run to determine the effects of space travel on DNA. This was in a little-known in vivo lab, where creatures entirely spun from human imagination, for an infinity of reasons, were created in a test tube, then grown, tested, and killed once the information was stored. Before this human clone was retrieved, it was discovered.

It had been a clone of Kamehameha. At least, that was what the employee, when interrogated, eventually revealed.

Kamehameha was the first Hawaiian monarch to unite the Hawaiian Islands under one rule, in the late eighteenth century. His bones had been hidden at his death in the Hawaiian manner—probably in some cave high on a crumbly sea cliff.

King Kamehameha was deified by the Hawaiians, and rightly so. After uniting the islands through hideous—but typical—Polynesian warfare, he had calmly and rationally brought Hawaii into the then-modern age, and strengthened it against outsiders while engaging in trade and treaties. If *he,* or someone with his power and commitment to the Hawaiian people had remained in control of the Islands, they would probably never have been annexed by the United States, but remained an independent kingdom. Instead, his direct line had died out and a line of more distant relatives, eventually diluted by haole blood, had gained power.

If Kamehameha's heirs had been his equals, what might the course of history have been? At the very least, Hawaiians would have remained in control of their land and their government.

Rumor was that Cen Kalakaua, the legendary cosmologist who had mysteriously disappeared years ago, had found the bones and left them in the possession of the Homeland Movement.

Lynn leaned back, remembering snippets of the Kalakaua legend.

Like Ramanujan, the famous Indian mathematician, Kalakaua left behind dazzling glimpses of a world of thought still not fully fathomed by his international peers. The fragments available pointed to a deep understanding of spacetime, ideas that held their own with those of the greats of cosmology—Carr, the earlier Gell-Mann, Hawking, even Einstein—with strange and curious new twists on string theory and quantum reality. But Kalakaua himself had been both elusive and, if the tales were true, dissolute. He had disappeared well over a decade ago. For all anyone knew he was dead or living under a bridge somewhere.

She was ready, with another keystroke, to lose the true records, send a virus trace through the web. The boy would not change. But his image would, the record of a particular person.

She frowned, realizing: they were not really the records of Interspace anyway. There it was again—the Homelander symbol, a tiny fleeting icon of the *Hawai'i Loa,* a replica of the canoes with which Polynesians had populated the Pacific. These were the records of some unknown, anonymous user—but still, of course, not hidden from IS. Nothing was, ultimately. The originator was, she was sure, from the Homeland Movement.

Apparently there was a very recent entry concerning this boy. From *whom?* Something about Tripler labs?

But that tag end vanished. She tried to follow it, but hit a brick wall with every trick she tried. She decided that she must have imagined it.

Lynn stood and walked out onto her lanai. The tiles were cold beneath her bare feet. She leaned on the railing and stared out over Honolulu, straight ahead, and Hickam Spacebase to the west, *Ewa,* just as *Diamond Head,* from where she was standing, was the synonym for east. North was *mauka,* for the mountains behind her and to tell someone that the place they sought was *makai* would be to send them straight ahead toward the ocean. On the other side of the island, of course, *mauka* turned into south. She breathed deeply of the cool, clean air, still damp from the usual skein of cloud that brushed streets and billowing trees and left them to glitter in sudden sunlight.

The Pacific was steely blue in the early morning light, and the latest tiny portion of the generation ship, assembled baseside in increments, then taken to the ship for integration, was hidden inside an enormous blue warehouse with a tarmac-colored roof that was almost invisible against the sea.

Not content with Kohala and their other awards, the Homeland Movement claimed that they owned the land beneath the Spacebase. Lynn knew that it was true, but Interspace lawyers blocked progress on the forty-year-old behemoth case at every turn.

Interspace dreaded the fury of the Hawaiian Homeland Movement, which had more than once delayed progress on the generation ship by sabotage both subtle and overt, claiming racism kept them from being included in any level of the Interspace program. Interspace simply claimed that any Hawaiian who met their standards was welcome, but the quiet policy was to exclude any pure or even part-Hawaiian as a possible double agent. At this point, Interspace feared bad international press as well, which might endanger the constant, delicate negotiations that kept the organization solvent. Homelander leaders were methodically eliminated whenever possible—intimidated, or even murdered, Lynn, with her insider's information, knew. One of the many reasons Lynn tried to have nothing to do with Interspace. IS had managed to avoid implication so far, but it danced along a dangerous edge with an alliance of supersecret intelligence and good old-fashioned mobsters.

Not a bad idea for the Homelanders to clone Kamehameha. Keep a lot of backups handy.

What a world, Lynn thought, blinking; her eyes burned with tiredness despite her brief nap. She leaned forward against the railing; gripped it with both hands.

Why did she care about this boy?

How could she help him? And if she could help, how much was she willing to risk for him?

She dropped onto a lounge chair and stared down at the house where he lived. Only two blocks away, and she could tell which one it was because it was the only one hidden by a dense umbrella of mimosas.

If she knew about him, so did Interspace.

They were just biding their time.

She yawned again. No sense trying to think straight now. The chaise looked enormously inviting. She sank down on it, turned on her side, pulled a pillow beneath her head. Not even the swiftly increasing sunlight or the beckoning pocket of information that might soon yield to her probing could keep her awake.

But before she closed her eyes, she saw movement far below, through the lanai railing.

Two men were walking up Nuuanu. They were both wearing white—white pith helmets, white shorts and shirts. It was still so early, about six-thirty, that no one else was out.

She grabbed her binoculars from a chairside table; they automatically focused on the men as she looked through them.

The men's movements were purposeful. They walked quickly, clearly not just out for a stroll.

Lynn held her breath when one of them turned onto the half-hidden sidewalk that led to the boy's house. In ten seconds he rejoined the other man. They turned and quickly walked back the way they came.

Lynn stopped only to pull on her running shoes, briefly thankful that she had been so engrossed in her work that she had not bothered to undress. Rushing into the hallway, she glanced at the red emergency override scan panel that brought the maglift almost instantly. Once on the street, she began to sprint, ignoring the ache from the miscarriage, rushing toward the unruly jungle on the next block.

She halted at the crooked gate, in front of the narrow, shaded sidewalk. The rotting front porch was empty. The door stood ominously open and the interior was dark.

She paused, indecisive. Perhaps he had gotten out. If so, no sense in her risking her life. It was not like IS to be so unsubtle. They must be afraid. This was her fault, her work of last night. She had not mentioned an address. But maybe she hadn't needed to. They had known. It was the attention, that was all.

She had only seconds to do *something*—

The curtain moved.

She pounded up the steps, rushed through the door, and turned right.

The boy, next to the window, stared at her, a shadow in the dark room. "What are you doing here? I thought I heard something—"

She grabbed his arm. "Come on," she said. *"Move!"*

He looked startled, but followed her as she ran down the hallway toward the back of the house, out onto the back porch. A high palisade fence surrounded the yard. She looked around helplessly and he pointed to a gate at the *mauka* corner.

"What . . . " he yelled, as he panted behind her, but she did not pause. Once through the gate, she flattened herself against the neighbor's house and looked around.

Anyone could be watching, anywhere.

"Where are your parents?" she asked.

He stared at her, looked back at the house. "I—I don't know."

And then a wave of heat and sound ripped apart the fence

and sent ragged portions of it hurtling through the air. Smelling her own singed hair, she watched the wild flames leap.

He watched too, for about ten seconds, with tears in his eyes and stolid resignation on his face. Then he grabbed her arm.

"We'd better get out of here," he said.

Ten minutes later they were alone in the mag to the airport. Lynn did not sit, but held a pole, trembling. The boy perched on the edge of a blue plastic seat, his face thoughtful.

"Are you coded?" asked Lynn, stooping to look nervously out the window as they passed over blocks of small frame houses. Many people had a lifelong code embedded in their wrist when they were born—mostly the poor who were ignorant of their right to refuse, though they were supposed to sign a waiver for themselves or their children at the time it was implanted. "It can be removed later," they were usually told, and many believed that they would not receive any societal benefits without it. Not true; that was illegal, at least in the U.S.

But this boy?

"No," he said. "But I have a passport, if that's what you need." He reached into his back pocket and pulled out a flat green wallet, opened it.

The old-fashioned electronic passport was the only thing in it. No money, no game flats, nothing you would expect a regular kid to have. "If you don't like that one I have three others." They were in his other back pocket. He fanned them out and she took them, glanced through them.

"Who gave you these?" she asked.

"I'm surprised you asked." He gave her a long look. "Who are you, anyway?"

"My name is Lynn," she said.

"What happened to you last week?"

"I was pregnant, but I lost the baby." She scrolled through the first one he'd handed her as the mag took a measured curve toward the airport. "This says that you're sixteen years old." How *many* clones? she wondered.

"No. I'm thirteen."

"You look a lot older."

"I know. That's why they told me they had to make me older, so that people wouldn't wonder."

"How would you like to go to Hong Kong?"

His face had a grayish cast; his lips a blue tinge. He gripped the edges of his chair and took a deep breath. He appeared to consider the question, Lynn thought impatiently, as if he really had a choice.

Finally he shrugged. "That might be a good idea. I can't go back there, can I?" Before he turned away his eyes were full of unasked questions.

Lynn was sure hers were too.

The boy looked out the airport window at the Concorde. They were the last in the boarding line, behind a mob of Chinese tourists. The two hours of negotiating and waiting had been nerve-wracking for Lynn. Heat waves rose from the tarmac. A hundred yards away the blue Pacific shimmered, mesmerizing through the heat waves.

"That thing looks *ancient*," the kid said. "I don't know if we should get on it."

She didn't exactly blame him. But she wished he'd take a break. Every time he opened his mouth he complained and her headache got worse. Some mother *you* would have made, she told herself.

"Look," she said quietly, though she felt like yelling. "I've just spent forty-five minutes getting us seats. This is a tour plane from Mainland China, and they can't really afford the latest thing, but this group is stopping in Hong Kong and we were lucky to get on." Luck had nothing to do with it. Her bribe had been outrageous, but they couldn't stay in Honolulu and she needed time to think. And sleep. "Do you have any better ideas? Anyone you'd like me to call?"

"No," he said, frowning. "I guess not."

She had bought him a T-shirt and zoris in an airport shop. He looked pretty normal. She raised her hand to brush back his messy hair and caught herself. The line shuffled forward.

At last, they boarded. She let out her breath when the jet left the ground with a rush, and Honolulu fell away behind them.

The tourists oohed and aahed over the nearby islands the pilot pointed out, Molokai and Lanai.

Kauai, about seventy miles to the north, was not visible; neither was the Big Island of Hawaii, about a hundred miles to the south. Lynn had never been to the island of Molokai, though it was only about twenty-five miles from Oahu, the island they had just left. Forty miles long and ten miles wide, Molokai had remained "the friendly island," with a high percentage of Hawaiians, relatively undeveloped since the 1950s. She'd heard there had never been a single traffic light on Molokai. The residents had never succumbed to the temptation of pandering to tourists. A good portion of the island was National Park, another an International Biosphere Reserve. The rest of the island was just as low-key, some sort of model cooperative community based on Hawaiian tradition and the most up-to-date social theories.

Molokai was almost the opposite of the Kohala Peninsula on the Big Island, where the top-secret high-tech enclave of the Homeland Movement was ensconced. That enclave was the heart and soul of the Homeland Movement. The elusive leader, whose name no one could seem to pin down, had at various times been rumored dead. Lynn had seen a short video of him, years ago, his long, white-streaked hair blowing in the wind as he ran across a road in about ten seconds before disappearing behind a building.

Molokai was gone almost the moment she glimpsed it. There would be nothing out the windows for several hours except relentless clouds and ocean. Hawaii was the most isolated land on earth.

Lynn glanced over at the boy. He was asleep already. Poor kid.

His name was Akamu. Hawaiian, he had told her proudly, for Adam. One of the first things the missionaries had done when they arrived was promptly Biblicize Hawaiian names. Adam. Had the others been Adam too?

She waved away a drink, then motioned the man to come back and she took it: cheap whisky. She downed it in a gulp and choked. She looked out the window and tried to think. The waves were tiny wrinkles on the ocean far below.

Adam. No, Akamu, she reminded herself. That's the name he went by.

Lynn tried to stretch out in her cramped seat and hoped they'd bring something to eat soon. Of course he was big. Kamehameha was a giant. When Akamu was an adult, he would be almost seven feet tall.

Well, now you've got yourself in a corner, Lynn. What next?

One thing she had learned was that it was best to fight fire with fire.

She opened the phone holder on the seat back in front of her and was surprised at how old and grimy the headpiece was. The screen would not light and that suited her.

She touched James's personal code, the same since childhood. Few people had it. The call went to his Black Point home, and when the house answered and told her to wait she heard spider monkeys, his latest affectation, chattering in the background. She was surprised he'd let them live. On her last visit she and James had drinks on his lanai, which hung fifty feet above massive waves smashing onto sparkling black lava rock. When they went inside after sunset she had burst into laughter while James ran around the room yelling, arms flailing. The monkeys had methodically ripped apart his new couch and were throwing stuffing at each other.

Then she heard James's voice. "Hello?" He sounded surprised. "Lynn?"

"Yes." Her code was of course on his screen.

"Ah. No picture?"

Lynn forced a laugh. "I'm on an old junker."

"Oh." Puzzled tone. He had a private late-model *Silence 300*. She could almost hear him thinking, *Why suffer? But that's like Lynn.*

He cleared his throat. "Well. Nana called. She was wondering if you were with me. She told me that last week—"

"Never mind," said Lynn.

"But you didn't even tell us you were pregnant."

"No," she said. "I didn't."

"Well," he said again. "You're on your way to . . . " she knew he was looking at what his screen said " . . . ah, yes, Hong Kong. Lovely day to travel." He sounded surprised. "A sudden decision, though."

"Well, it was because of the miscarriage, James," she said, trying to be brisk though her voice caught in her throat. *Good.* "I guess I'm still a little upset. I just decided this morning that a trip might help." Was he *really* surprised, or just pretending to be? Had anyone seen her rescue the boy? Someone *must* have been posted, somewhere, but they might not know who she was yet, the woman who had run into the house just before it blew up.

"I hope it *does* help." He sounded sincere. He was very good at that. "It will certainly be good for—" He was thinking of Mao, and genetic leadership markers and modified cloning. Lynn could almost see his calculating smile. But he only said, "Lynn, happily, you have called when Father is visiting. He wishes to speak to you."

She opened her mouth to say no. So many harsh words had passed between them, and so many silent years.

Then her father spoke. "Lynn. I am so sorry to hear of your trouble."

The timbre of his voice, which she heard so rarely lately (and is that really *his* fault, Lynn?), the unmistakable concern in it, brought back days of childhood in a rush. Her eyes filled with tears and she blinked.

He continued. "Please visit me when you return. I know . . . " he was quiet, and static crackled. He left that thought unsaid and cleared his throat. "Please do. And also call the Colonel, remember? We visited him when you were six."

Lynn remembered. A glorious trip. Just herself and her father. Before he married the twins' mother. Before he tried to stop her from growing up. "He still lives in the same place, up on the Peak. You can easily find his code. Don't forget, now. He would be *very* glad to see you. You *will* call him, won't you? His name is Hawkins. Don't forget."

"I won't," she said.

He abruptly wished her luck and broke the connection.

How very strange. She had imagined he would have been

coldly disapproving at her choice to have a child without a proper father. Her mind filled with memory eddies, pictures and atmospheres that overlapped like ripples in a pristine, mysterious jungle pool. Yes, they had been happy, the three of them, before her mother died. Very happy. That core of happiness, she felt, saved her from being like her half brothers. Their mother was acutely aware of her exalted station as the wife of one of the most important men in the world, always pushing her sons.

A bowl of cold noodles with vegetables came. Akamu still slept. Asleep, his face *did* seem young, maybe even younger than thirteen. Suddenly her heart ached. What sort of strange life had he led? Did he know who he was? Did he know what had happened to the other clones?

She ripped the wrapper from her chopsticks. If she had just *left* and not told anyone where she had gone, they would have been enormously suspicious. It wouldn't have taken them long to figure out everything she had done the night before. This way, she had bought some time to figure out what to do.

She hoped.

3

"Passport."

Lynn's stomach clenched, even though everything was in order, cleansed and perfect. No connection to IS would show. She was not Lynn Oshima, daughter of one of the most powerful men in the organization.

She took her passport from her pouch. Akamu waited on the other side of the entry station. He had had no trouble, much to Lynn's relief, and had been waved through without a glance.

"What is your business in Hong Kong?" the agent asked, while running the passport through his handheld. He frowned and looked at her several times, then back at the picture. Agents were always annoyed when they got one of these.

"Tourist," she said.

"Oh? What do you intend to see?"

"The night markets," she said. "Museums. You know."

He visually appraised her, and she realized that perhaps she looked a bit too wealthy, as if she might be intending to exceed legal spending limits. Must be the haircut, she thought. It couldn't be the clothes.

He frowned at her passport again. She rubbed her neck with the back of her hand. Well, it was hot. It wasn't an admission of guilt to break out into a sweat. Technosmuggling was a serious crime. But information shouldn't be limited. It belonged to humankind, and besides, IS wasn't stealing it. They were paying a small fortune for it.

But they would not get it. She would take it. Somewhere. She knew that much. She hadn't even had to decide about it. Somehow, it would come in handy, when all the pieces came together, when her head stopped aching. Leverage.

She studied the agent while he mulled things over, and she wondered: How would one design a more perfect person for this job? What qualities were necessary? What limitations? A certain way of seeing information? And was that, really, what all her work and research was leading to? She had her own ideas of the possibilities, could see humans advancing, expanding, growing, moving quickly beyond her range of vision.

But that was not the only path this line of inquiry could take.

There could be orders rolling in to a particular lab for a hundred workers perfectly tailored for customs duty. For their entire life. That sort of thing would suit certain people. A very clean bottom line. No unexpected worker illnesses. No rebellion or choice. They could be patented, or FDA approved, or strictly black market. Beyond theory. The reality. And where had all those other grand technological dreams of the last hundred years gone, anyway? How little change, how little improvement there was to show for all those hopes. Because true change was too expensive, sometimes, for those with a vested interest in the present.

She usually pushed these thoughts aside. Someone else's problem. I must be tired, she thought. I *am* tired.

Finally he must have found the right code. His face lit in a cordial smile. "Sorry," he said. "Have a good time in the En-clave." He returned her passport and waved her through.

She grinned at Akamu and he grinned back. She was surprised. He looked excited. "This is a *weird* place," he said. "Weird." He seemed pleased at the thought.

So it *is,* she thought, gazing for a moment at the gleaming, overwhelming towers of smartglass. Much of Hong Kong was a gigantic enclosure of vast acreage, with atriums of every style from medieval Chinese to day after tomorrow blending into in-terior gardens stepped throughout, private apartments, shops, restaurants, all holding the buzz and excitement of one of the richest cities on earth.

Lynn hurried him to the head of a line of driverless taxis, pods iridescent purple, teal, pink. They slid inside; she pressed the picture of a hotel where she'd stayed before and it con-firmed a room for them, but the car would not move.

"Must be broken," she said, and opened the door to go to the next one back but as she did so a tall, uniformed woman got in on the other side of the car and nodded.

"Konnichiwa," said the woman. She tapped her thigh and Lynn felt the car silently vibrate beneath her feet. The car moved forward before Lynn closed her door. The woman did not steer; she just sat there. Lynn's door shut itself.

"What's the deal?" asked Lynn, apprehensive. "I didn't need a driver six months ago."

"You didn't hear?" asked the woman, switching to English. "Riots. The Human Union is very strong here." She pulled her cap down tighter over her long black hair and gazed out the window. Lynn surmised she had an implant in her thigh that activated the car. The car moved smoothly along the translu-cent smarttrack, gripping it from beneath, occasionally choos-ing another branch of track from the many options that sometimes glowed with faint colors to indicate which part of the city they serviced. Lynn relaxed. The hotel was in the Green Sector; the cab was making the right choices.

Advertisements glowed on every interior surface of their cab and chattered softly in both Japanese and English, the two languages spoken since the car was activated. The mute button was red. Lynn pushed it, but the voices continued. She saw that Akamu was staring through the window at the ads on the corridor of apartments through which they passed, some buildings only a foot or two from the side of the mag-way. The ads appeared and disappeared, sometimes overlapping, occasionally holoing outward for a few seconds so the car could pass through them, reminding her that they were approaching the major trade center of the world, which had played a huge role in the quiet crumbling of communism in China.

The people living in the apartments were oblivious to passing traffic. Lynn saw a family sitting down to eat, and then an old man undressing, for fractions of a second as they passed. This was the new workforce, the programmers of clothing, jewelry design, or legal—and illegal—information replication, those who fought to keep their jobs against the constant inevitable encroachment of artificial intelligence. The car released a small ad of intense scent and said "Nova!" and Akamu sneezed at the cloud of free perfume.

"I am sorry you have to see this," said the driver, as the car made another choice. "They are going to route around this any day. This sector is going to be demolished."

"I've seen it before," said Lynn.

Many of the windows they passed did not have any glass at all, only shards. Within the shadowy rooms were derelicts, refugees unable to find work despite the bright promise of Hong Kong. She caught a glimpse of a near-naked woman curled in a ratty chair, staring straight out the window and smoking.

Then the car took a line that forked to the right, upward, and for a moment Lynn had a dizzying glance of brilliant blue water between the mammoth buildings of glittering smartglass. They looped behind the third tower and swooped into a vast enclosure.

They debarked in a stunning, elegant lobby, made of smooth light blocks of marble, one wall a stepwise fountain that held her eye with visual paradox and soothed her with sound and mist. A bellhop came and looked for their luggage; she shook her head.

"Sorry," she said to the driver. "I haven't changed money yet." The woman smiled. Happy to get American cash, Lynn supposed.

The cab glided toward a membrane where the almost-invisible track exited the lobby and went through it.

The room was sybaritic with fresh shoots of bird-of-paradise and a huge tub. Web screens were everywhere, even the bathroom. She checked the window: good. It didn't look out onto an atrium, nor did it have lush smartglass visuals disguising no view at all. They had the most expensive option, an outside window with a view of the harbor. She got much too antsy without this.

"Come on," she said to Akamu.

Back in the lobby she chose a moving sidewalk from the map. In ten minutes they emerged from the layers of the human-made world onto a sunny street.

Lynn took a deep breath and relaxed, just for an instant. Behind them were towers of smartglass; in front of them, glimpsed through twisting streets, was the harbor traced with the vanishing white lines of jetcats heading to and from Mainland China. The scent of garlic cooking oil laced the air, mingling with the musty scent of junk stores and the chemical tinge of clothes fresh from the factories, heaped on tables that lined the narrow street.

She bargained and bought Akamu some cheap, anonymous-looking shirts and pants. "Silk," she said, letting the smooth cool shirt shimmer through her fingers before holding it up to him, gray with overlapping designs made up of triangles. "Like it?"

"It's okay," he said, glancing around the street as if he were searching for something. Suddenly afraid he might bolt she wanted to grab his hand but thought that might set him off.

"How are you?" she asked.

"Starving," he said.

They chose food from sidewalk braziers; she had it wrapped—skewers of grilled, aromatic meat, rice from a big tub. He wore a watch and she asked the time. He looked at it for a moment, frowned, then said, "Oh, yeah. It reset from satellite. Two-thirty."

"Well," she said, trying to ignore the nervousness tightening her stomach, "I've got some things to do. I'm taking you back to the room."

He looked like he was going to argue, then his shoulders slumped. He just looked weary, frightened, and very young, and returned to the room with her without saying a word, just gazing at the other people on the moving sidewalk, holding his bundle of new clothes under his arm.

He sat at the table by the window and unwrapped the food immediately when they got back. His was gone in about a minute.

Lynn said, "You can have mine too. And order more from room service if you want. I need to go out. You'll have to stay here alone for a while."

He didn't seem surprised and looked only the least bit disappointed. "Is it all right if I use the web?"

There was a small, light, flat screen on the bed table that could be used while sitting on the bed; another on a nearby desk. "I'd rather you didn't," she said and made a note to have it deactivated when she returned to the lobby. "How about a handy?"

He shrugged. "Better than nothing, I guess, if I have to sit inside all day." Lynn wondered, briefly, how long the shock of having been almost blown up would hold. He seemed too compliant.

Like someone at the end of his rope, perhaps?

"Tomorrow we can go out and really shop," she said. "They have the best of everything here. I'm going to need some equipment myself. That will be fun, won't it? For now I'll ask the concierge to send one up. What would you like? Some games, perhaps."

"Just get me SP Three and . . . I guess SP Five too."

"Uh, sure," she said, and called the concierge.

"Room eight-ninety-five. Could you please send a handy—"

"A flat," he said. Much lighter than an old-fashioned handheld, a flat was a flexible computer with a very thin keypad and screen that could be folded or rolled up.

"A flat," she corrected. "Um, a Kaiban four-point-three." The best. She saw the ghost of a smile cross his face and was pleased. "With everything, of course. And Standard Packages Three and Five." These were hard-core packages. Not for beginners, and not games; tools for high-level abstract thought.

She said to Akamu, "They only had Three. She said they'd have Five in two days. She was extremely apologetic, but she said that the upgrade was just released last Friday. You're pretty up-to-date."

His eyes asked *who are you?* He flopped facedown on one of the beds.

She waited until the flat was brought up, opened the door a crack, and took it.

"Don't return this," she said. She didn't want anyone to see what he might have done. "It's yours now. If you get hungry again before I get back, order anything you want to eat. Anything at all. I'll be back as soon as I can. And then we'll probably go on another trip."

"Of course," he said, and sat cross-legged on the bed. The flat beeped as he touched it on.

He didn't glance up as she left the room.

Lynn decided it was best to follow the agenda. She spent a suspicion-free day, what was left of it, set up originally to protect IS; now she did it to protect herself from IS. She shopped for jewelry, was measured for new clothing with a brief burst of light in a tiny crowded shop that smelled of wool and silk and displayed the Human Union logo. Strong teal silk shorts and a matching jacket would be ready in two hours, along with a dress and a few shirts, and a pair of light wool pants. A young man smiled and nodded, took her deposit, and got the cloth ready to feed into the cutting and sewing machines.

Lynn mulled over five brilliant natural emeralds in a hushed jewelry store that the shopkeeper, a stern-looking woman dressed impeccably in a black velvet evening gown, displayed in an unfolded sheet of white paper. Lynn pushed them from side to side, saw them magnified, smiled and said no. She bought a watch in another shop, then petulantly returned it an hour later, complaining that it didn't have some of the functions she'd been led to believe that it had. And finally she bought a single black pearl earring at Ocean Riches, a shop shaped vaguely like the inside of a shell, opalescent walls softly glowing, the crash and backwash of breakers and distant insistent gull laughs swirling round her ears, a delicate synthetic salt scent infusing the cool air. She picked up her new clothing. She didn't call the Colonel. She didn't have time for socializing.

It was the second day she feared.

She rose early. Akamu was still asleep, sprawled on his large bed. Where to next? she wondered, as she dressed. But she had a place in mind, the perfect place, the perfect refuge for them both. They could depart from here, once she had what she wanted, and vanish. They were no longer isolated on a tiny island by thousands of miles of ocean.

She ordered rice and miso soup to her room, then looked down at a park, tiny so far below, and watched the tai chi practitioners move in slow, balanced precision, part of their meditational mind-set. She moved with them for fifteen minutes, thinking herself back to Tantalus. The glimpse of blue bay through skyscrapers pinkened by dawn steadied her. She let the memory of North Shore surf echo through her mind and soothe her before she put on her black pearl earring, quietly closed the door, and stepped into the lift.

In ten minutes she was standing just outside the Walled City, a dangerous, exhilarating mixture of medieval streets and cutting-edge technology, outside the law. In here one could arrange brain implants, swallow the latest genetic trick, and wonder at the last second if it would perform as hoped or twist you unpredictably and irrevocably.

One moment she was moving with the crowd, and the next

she heard two faint beeps. Left turn, now, into a dark alley. Three beeps, down the stairs, that's right, down, down, through four metallic levels of shops. Right turn, an underground train, one stop only, then up and out into the blinding sun.

Tourists slipped in and out of here all the time, of course. Chinese thugees exacted high taxes from Hong Kong in general, and trade was so brisk that they got more here, in these few, intense blocks, than out of the entire regulated sector.

No record, she reminded herself, that's why you're here. Naïve, able to perhaps plead ignorance if something goes wrong, once you're in.

But really, only her own greed for Perfect Information fueled her steps now, on cobblestones that glittered from the morning hosing. Shopkeepers were setting wares on tables in front of shops. There were backrooms here, and backrooms to backrooms behind the awning-festooned streets, beyond the racks of silk ties, bins of off-brand computer crystals, smiling, round, bargaining men, and morning braziers fueled and evanescing the scent of roasting meat and black bean pastries warming in compartments above. Fortune-tellers sat at flimsy tables reading newspapers; she saw a small thin girl shove a pile of used newspapers into a recycling slot and wait a few seconds for the print to be removed, then take the extruded deposit chit and run into a tea shop. A black dog scattered a flock of chickens.

She stopped to examine some cheap ties, jumped at a touch on her shoulder, felt a rough hand caress the single black pearl. "Something to match, missy?" asked the man, and beckoned.

The room was dark; the window was almost completely blocked with heaps of ties and bolts of silk. Lynn stepped gingerly around a tower of cloth, afraid she would topple it, and followed the man as he parted a heavy brocade curtain for her.

The room was filled with opium smoke. "Sit," said a tall, thin woman with white hair. "It is all arranged. Have you breakfasted?"

Lynn nodded but did not sit. The woman had a Saturn tattoo on her left cheekbone. A member of a society Lynn knew little about, and that frightening. She straightened, stood tall as possible.

"The sequence," she said. "And the marrow sample itself."

The woman smiled. Shook her head. "Anxious, aren't we?" she said. "I would see your passport." Emerald silk swished against ruby silk as Lynn held it out. Her passport would yield verification to those with the correct way of looking at what James had given her. It would also, she knew, electronically transfer whatever amount of money had been agreed upon. That was of little interest to her.

The woman took it, put it into the handheld, frowned. "It is enough," she said, "But—"

"I will give you the activation code when I check the sequence," Lynn said. It was just a word James had mentioned in his note. She tried to keep her mind on what she would do with this—add it to her growing store of genetic information, aid the world, send humans to distant galaxies, save Akamu. As if he wanted to be saved. For a dizzy moment, breathing the opium smoke, she was afraid. I need air, she thought. How is Akamu doing? She would be back within an hour. And then they would fly.

The woman turned and unlatched a small rosewood cabinet. The double doors opened outward, revealing an interior lined with gold. She took out what looked like a black pearl earring, then paused. She bowed her head briefly, held it out to Lynn, who bent her head sideways, removed her black pearl, and inserted the other.

Then the shooting began.

Lynn woke coughing, choked by acrid smoke and a sickening jolt.

She was hot, sweating, lying in a tangle of sheets.

And, she realized, she was on a bullet train. A very old bullet train. She glanced up at the speed panel but it was dark, long broken, she suspected. Whoever was in charge of this train system had probably bought it used.

A wide, dirty window was bisected by a strip of metal where the top had been lowered to reveal clear blue sky. Hot wind rushed in, making her feel sticky rather than cooled. One hundred kilometers per hour, no more, she guessed. Painfully slow, for a bullet. She raised up on her elbows and glanced away from the window.

The tall, thin man who was watching her was smoking a cigarette; an elbow rested on one crossed leg. He wore black pants, sandals, and a thin white cotton shirt that stuck to his chest in patches of sweat. His nose was narrow and slightly hooked; his eyes were slanted and black. He smiled at her and irony filled them, as if he, she, and the train were some grand joke. He was bald, and his eyebrows were white.

Lynn stirred and realized that her right calf was wrapped in a thick bandage, and that it ached.

"More opium?" asked the man. He reached over to the wall behind him, where what looked like a bottle of soda sat in a metal drink holder, unscrewed the lid, and handed it to her.

"More?" She tasted the thick, bittersweet liquid, grimaced, handed it back. "How much have I had?"

The man shrugged. "I don't know."

She saw rolling dull brown hills outside her window, punctuated by green fields. Distant mountains edged the horizon. On a road parallel to the track, two huge trucks lumbered along behind a bus where people rode on the roof. She raised herself up on her elbows, chilled.

Where was Akamu?

And who was this man?

He reached into a bucket next to him and pulled out a white cloth; wrung it. "Lie down and rest some more," he said. He rose and she felt the cool rough cloth on her forehead and cheeks. "You've been very ill," he said. "I was able to find a doctor in the New Territories to staple the bullet wound, and he gave me some antibiotic patches and opium for your pain. Things are still very primitive here, of course. Not like other parts of the world to be sure. Definitely not like Honolulu! I was able to bribe this private room and they decided that it wasn't essential to see your passport." He grinned.

"Who are you?"

"I've told you before. I guess you've forgotten. Not surprising, though. Well. You know that your father flew contraband for the Cambodian underground when he was young."

"Supplies. Not contraband." This man must be as old as her father, eighty. And fairly wealthy, because he didn't look it.

The man smiled once again, and she saw an ironic gleam in his eyes. "Supplies. Yes. Actually, I was more of a liaison between the suppliers and the next person on the chain, but I had occasion to fly with your father more than once."

"Colonel Hawkins!" she said. "But—"

He continued. "He is like a brother to me. We are still very close. I am honored to see you again. You were such a pretty child, and he was so unhappy to lose your mother."

He reached down, picked up an open bottle of whisky with a Chinese label from the filthy floor, and drank. He set it back down.

"There are channels through which your father informed me of your coming. You didn't call. I found and followed you. I owed it to him. You knew the danger, of course."

"Yes," she said. "I guess I didn't really believe in it though."

"Just as well," he said. "Apparently you were trying to get something quite rare and valuable."

"Yes," she said. He waited, but she didn't say anything more, wondering how she would get back to Hong Kong, and wondering if Akamu was lost forever. *He* was infinitely more valuable than her silly insistence on Mao. Darkness filled her heart and mind, despite the brightness of the day. How foolish and selfish she had been. She should have simply taken him and run. Now it was too late. China!

Beijing, she knew, rivaled Tokyo in sophistication and London in size. But since 2002, when Communism broke down for good, China had lurched through several phases. Years of mob-run exploitation of fragile new businesses, internal wars between this or that ethnic group, until visionary Zhong Chau united the country in 2019. She was midwife to a new level of education and scientific endeavor until her assassination in 2025. Despite that tragedy, the fruits of her work, the manufacturing and education and trading infrastructure, were finally beginning to flow across the land. But not quickly. Bicycles were still the vehicle of choice.

She smelled a toilet somewhere. Her stomach heaved, but there was nothing in it. She fell back into the aching edge of pain once more, realizing that it was pain that had wakened her. She dimly remembered swigs of opium-laced pop, vivid dreams of brightly colored helixes swirling through dark space, flames, and beautiful music. My vision of Mao's DNA, she supposed wryly, raising her hand involuntarily to brush the earring.

"My father didn't say it was important to call you. I thought it was just social. I was going to call you later."

The Colonel bent over and fumbled in a bag, pulled out a plastic bottle of water. He uncapped it and handed it to her. "I think he knew that you might think so. I have some food here. Some fresh black bean pastries. An apple."

Lynn took a drink of water and settled back. She really wanted some soothing miso. Her head was splitting, but she didn't want any more opium. She needed to be able to think. "Any soup?"

He laughed. "There is a problem. I'm afraid that a lot of what you find to eat here might make you sick. We're in the middle of China, my dear. Your stomach is not exactly adjusted to locust and black dog stew." He glanced at his watch. "We'll be pulling into a small village in an hour. I can get off then and try to get some sort of broth. Maybe some noodles, eh? How does that strike you?"

She nodded and wiped sweat from her face. "Where do I pee?" she asked.

He pointed to a curtain fluttering in the wind that cordoned off a corner.

Pain shot through her leg as she sat up and shifted to the side of the narrow bed. She stood with care and found her leg would bear weight. She felt grateful and with a hobbling step lurched across the compartment and pulled the curtain aside.

When she came out, the Colonel was taking another sip of whisky. "Have some?" he asked.

She shook her head, then her hand shot out.

It was rotgut stuff, and she took two swigs that heated her chest and made her cough. She pushed herself across the cot, leaned against the wall. She could see the vast, hot plain; the dust-laden wind tossed her hair. "Is all of this necessary?" she asked. "I mean, wasn't there any way to just take me somewhere else?" She still wasn't sure if she had been rescued or kidnapped.

"Let me show you something," he said.

He rummaged around in his bag again, setting an apple, then a melon, on his lap, frowning. He finally pulled out a battered handy and opened it. He hit a few keys, then turned it to face Lynn.

Her specs and parameters were there. Name, age, weight. A picture. Kill on sight, it said.

"What?" She handed it back to him. "That's crazy."

"Set it there, in the sun," he said. "It needs to charge." He lit another cigarette; Lynn shook her head when he held out the pack to her.

"There was some informant in your organization, I think," he said. "But who knows. Maybe someone on this side. Anyway, the Chinese government does not feel inclined to share genome information with any other nation. They hardly want to admit that such research is going on. I know that much, you see, about what you were doing. Of course, that is your father's branch at IS, isn't it? The work is done at such great expense that—well, who is selling it, anyway? A traitor from one of the Chinese government labs, eh? Someone very high up, right? You have become part of a web of conspiracy, my dear. If possible, you might try considering it fun. I do. I always have." He coughed, once, and his face creased with spasms. He glanced up.

"But," he said, grinning now like a Cheshire, "you were successful." He nodded and looked right at her left ear.

She let out her breath. He knew—at least something.

She sat back and looked out the window. They passed a dirt intersection where three skinny men waited on bicycles to continue their journey.

Her father and her brothers differed quite a bit as to goals

and means. Her father often seemed blind to the obvious mis-
doings of his sons, preferring to be obliviously proud of them.
They were Good, they hewed to the family mission. Their
wives were quiet and dutiful and had produced children. Her
father, though, was really a straight arrow when it came to le-
gality. She remembered his rage at finding out about one illegal IS program . . . but she knew, now that she was grown, that
he hardly knew anything about what was *really* going on.

But she did know one thing: No matter what, her father
would strive to protect her, never mind how angry he had been
with her in the past. She trusted him.

She did not trust her brothers. She was useful to them, that
was all. And they were useful to her.

She studied the Colonel, wondering how to find out his
agenda—which might or might not depend on her father's
agenda; and that would depend on how much *he* knew. Had
he known about Akamu? Had her brothers known?

It was all too late anyway. Even if she returned to Hong
Kong immediately, would he still be there in the room, working on the flat? Not likely.

"The borders are being watched," the Colonel told her.
"Most certainly you would be apprehended if you weren't with
me."

"So where are we going?"

"Tibet," he said, and smiled once more, this time quite happily. "My favorite part of the world. So high, so grand. So very
sad and poor. Long sacred horns blowing at each meditation.
Where there is electricity, the prayer appears on computer
screens in the corner of homes. It is bizarre, it is wonderful.
And eventually I will be able to put you on a plane to
Bangkok, and you will have absolutely no trouble once you
are there."

She looked at his face again and saw broad cheekbones and
coppery skin. His face flashed with some odd glow, like a fire-
fly, a chimera, in tangent with his smile.

"I see," she said. "Give me another sip of that whisky,
please." She settled back, and the broad plains clacked by in
the hot Mongol wind. Maybe when he went for food at the next

station she could slip off and catch the next train back to Hong Kong. But she would need money . . . and a new passport . . .

"I have something to show you," he said. He opened the door to the other compartment. "Come in," he said. A shadow stirred, then someone filled the doorway.

Akamu.

Cen

Honolulu 2007

4

It was just eight in the morning, but down at Honolulu Harbor next to the Aloha Tower, eight was hot.

Cen, wearing a neon green bathing suit and zoris, was covered with sweat, and his arms hurt from loading crates of iced squid and mahi from a boat into the back of Lu-Wei's van, which was more rust than car. He stopped, wiped his forehead with the back of his hand, and looked around for a Coke machine.

Lu-Wei, a short, fat man who spent most of every afternoon mah-jongg gambling in the seedy Chinese park on Nuuanu, said, "Hey, boy, I pay you good you do this work not laze around. My customers pay extra for wild. But not if it ain't fresh."

"Fuck you," Cen muttered, but went back to get a crate of yellowtail, still thirsty. Like hell these were wild, anyway. He could tell farm-grown even if the customers couldn't.

He turned; stopped short. A young girl stood on the dock next to the boat. She hadn't been there before.

She wore a frilly white cotton dress with a large bow tied at the side of her slim waist. Her chest was still flat, and many fine pleats ran from her high, lacy collar down to her waist. He'd gone shopping with Mei once or twice and had never seen anything like this, not even in the most expensive department in Samson Brothers.

As he approached, the girl looked at him directly, seriously, with wonderful, enormous brown eyes, as if taking his measure. Her long black hair was held back in a ponytail. It frizzed slightly around her oval, olive-complected face, which was shaded by a parasol held in her right hand. She wore unscuffed black patent leather shoes that shone in the brilliant sun. Cen blinked. She looked distinctly old-fashioned against the backdrop of the generation ship in Hickam Spacebase across the glittering harbor, the latest abandoned Interspace project.

"Hello," she said. "I've been watching you. You are *alii,* aren't you?"

He laughed with conscious bitterness. "Sure I am. Royal blood, that's right, a real prince. My dad, he was a prince too. A great man." He rubbed his forehead with his hand as if he could wipe away the web of red and black that suddenly enveloped him.

"You remind me of my uncle David," she said, and he saw sunlight sparkling on the water once again and clear blue sky above.

"What you stopping for now, lazy son of bitch," Lu yelled across two docks and rapped the side of the Forerunner with his ivory cane. "Gotta get this stuff to market. Late already."

Cen jerked his head back toward Lu-Wei. "Yeah, I'm special. That's why I work for that asshole." Then he was ashamed of saying *asshole* in front of this weird girl. He bent and picked up the yellowtail, walked over, and shoved the flat into the van.

He wiped his fishy hands on his trunks and turned to wave at the girl before leaving.

But she was gone.

He looked down at the fish he would soon have to gut. Shimmering red blood would swirl down the drain beneath his spray; one fish eye would stare at him as he yanked out the guts. He swallowed bile and climbed into the driver's seat.

A young woman from the Marquesas Islands, Mei, had taken Cen in two years ago, after he'd kicked around Honolulu for a month, sleeping in doorways and avoiding the cops. She soon stopped asking him about his past, because he would say nothing. She got him a job and saw that he kept it, because he helped pay the rent on their tiny apartment on Hotel Street, where the tall old windows opened onto the wildest street in the city.

The first night there he'd lain in bed and tried not to hear what went on below: shuffling footsteps, "I'm gonna cut you till you bleed"; the music of smashed bottles blending with the buzzing of the midnight trades through the pulled blinds.

Whores had most of the rooms—Mei was one, he soon found out—and they looked out for him. Mei said he reminded her of her little brother.

In the can Cen had taken the night he left home was a photograph of his great-grandfather.

The massive, dark man stood erect. A few palm trees cast shadows across the sand where he stood. He was naked, but his tattoos—delicate, tiny geometric patterns that didn't go far above his hips—gave him a clothed look.

Cen took the picture to an old-fashioned tattoo artist over on Queen Street. He gritted his teeth once a week, for months, in that tiny, hot room that smelled of whisky, until it was complete. That was how he spent his first money the year he turned thirteen.

At first he was afraid his father would find him, but after a while he decided that he wouldn't even take the trouble to look. After all, Cen was on the other side of the island now, several hours away by car. And to most residents of Hawaii, "the other side of the island" was usually about as close, for some reason, as the other side of the moon. Certainly Cen's visits to Honolulu before fleeing there were fewer than five in twelve years: a field trip to Iolani Palace, a shopping expedition with his mother, once, and maybe one or two others that he didn't remember. The Honolulu side of the island boasted a population of three million, not an easy place to find someone who wanted to disappear.

And soon he was able to forget why, exactly, his father might be looking for him. The night he had left home had become a blur of terror for him, something he couldn't remember very clearly.

He saw his mother's face at night when he closed his eyes: her dead face, covered with blood. He wondered why he never could remember her alive, but only that last, horrible vision.

Of the rest of the day, he remembered nothing. The emptiness did not bother him, because somehow he felt that remembering would have been worse.

And everyone had told him he'd be sorry about the tattoos, but they were wrong. They anchored him to something beyond his own life. He'd been very pleased with his decision.

Until now, when he was fifteen.

He was pretty sure this girl wasn't the type who liked tattoos.

Cen was proud of the old brass key he used to get into the two rooms he shared with Mei. All his friends lived in run-down high-rises with mag keys, pieces of signal-embedded plastic. The weight of the key felt good in his hand, cool in evening's heat that was held in the high old hallway. Wallpaper peeled next to the door, and the ceiling was narrow latheboards painted countless times, the last time tired gray. A plaque downstairs read Mark Twain Slept Here, and Cen believed it.

But when he turned the knob, he smelled a difference. Later, he told himself there was no smell, but he stopped and took a deep breath and fear held him for a second before he stepped forward and touched on the light.

Mei was sprawled across the bed, wearing a white silk nightshirt. The wide window behind her was fully open, and long curtains fluttered in the evening trades. Down the street he saw the lights of the ships in the harbor, heard tourists walking below, slumming before they would desert the quarter and leave it to the natives around midnight. The smart ones left a lot sooner. Across the harbor, the glass tower topped with the IS logo ubiquitous in the Islands shimmered on the still, dark water: nineteen stars, one for each participating nation.

Cen wondered as he took the few steps toward the bed why he was worrying. She could be napping, sleeping off some sort of weird binge.

But he touched her cheek and it was too hot. Her face was flushed. He shook her and she moaned; he turned her on her back and a bubble of saliva formed over her mouth and burst and he felt a little relief. Alive, okay, she's alive, now what? He shook her. "Mei," he said. "You okay?" He shouted at her, then slapped her face in desperation, dismayed at the red mark it left on her cheek. "No," he breathed. "No." He ran to the window.

Huang Po was leaning back against his storefront, as usual, waiting for a sucker of one kind or another to pass by.

"Call an ambulance," Cen yelled out the window. "It's Mei."

A moment later he heard steps pounding down the hallway, and Huang burst in. "What's the problem?"

"Did you call the ambulance?"

Huang said, "Don't know if that's such a great idea. Saw her with two Interspace people today. A woman and a man."

Cen didn't ask him how he knew. You just did.

"They were walking her back home, one on each side. I wondered about it but thought maybe she was just drunk. You know she's been doing stuff for them over at the Tripler Lab." The big pink hospital on the flank of the mountain, infamous now as the site of rumored illegal experiments.

"No," said Cen. "She didn't tell me." She wouldn't. She knew what he thought of IS and their biotech experiments. "How long?"

Huang shrugged. "Couple weeks, I guess."

Cen turned from Huang, ran downstairs and punched the white button, told them the address, heard computer keys click over the line. "Sorry," he heard. "No clearance for that person. Mei Fossant."

"No," he said, "it's not for her, it's for a Huang Po, a neighbor," but he heard a click and knew it was true.

Huang left muttering "Bad business, bad business," and Cen cooled Mei for half the night with wet washcloths until she shivered and moaned. Then he tossed a sheet over her and nestled close, hugging her tight, trying to be the bed full of brothers and sisters she'd grown up with, though she'd never allowed him to touch her before. "I love you, Mei," he said over and over, hoping it would get through to her, hoping that something would pull her back from whatever edge they'd pushed her to.

Mei had come to Hawaii, she had told Cen, in hopes of working for Interspace, the international space consortium that leased the old U.S. military facilities—more than half of the Islands landwise. All of the nations that had space programs had agreed in the year 2000 to pool their efforts in one place. By that time grass had overtaken most of the mainland U.S. facilities, as they were used only to launch and land the shuttle. Mir too had stagnated. Hawaii lobbied hard to be the locus of all operations—physical and scientific—and won. The goal, breathtaking in scope, was interstellar travel. Hawaii was ideal—the most isolated land on earth, so that failed launches were less of a liability and microwave interference was very low. Most important, a vast military infrastructure had mushroomed since World War II. Hickam Air Force Base had even been designed and built in the late 1950s with the landing and launch needs of the future space shuttle in mind, and that level of planning made the crossover ideal. Top secret control centers, state-of-the-art communication wonderlands, vast underground facilities, and sophisticated hardware were all up for lease since the U.S. military had shrunk, wrecking the economy of the state. Few people knew that tourism and agriculture ranked below the military economically in Hawaii, but it was true. Hawaii hailed the surge of Interspace money into the economy, as well as the influx of scientists from around the world. Interspace was multifaceted: visionary, though unrealized, engineering of space stations and colonies proceeded apace. Nor was the human side of the equation ignored. Genetic engineering (including, it was rumored, internationally banned aspects of genetic engineering as well as bionan) had a strong place in the IS agenda.

Fuzzy goals, such as intelligence enhancement or the adaptation of humans to long-term space travel, allowed for a wide range of research. The dust from a recent genetic engineering scandal within IS was being energetically swept under the carpet just now. These illegal experiments were attempts to bypass the internationally agreed-upon conventions that had been developed to protect humanity from various hypothetical disasters. Here, the envelope was pushed. And often, it was suspected, broken.

Cen himself had sometimes felt a pull toward the wildly speculative cosmological studies of time and space in which IS scientists took advantage (unfairly, nonaffiliated astrophysicists complained) of the Mauna Kea observatory; at least it excited him to read about it in the paper.

Only locals felt the unvoiced hysteria that had lately infected Interspace. Their charter was to be reexamined in two years—every two years, in fact, from now on—and little actual progress had been made since the tragic failure of the embryonic Moon colony in 2005. Shadow cartels within the organization apparently dealt with the Hong Kong and Japanese underworld, selling information; the percentage of profits available for reinvestment were thereby reduced.

Mei's had become an old story. The Asiaslums of Honolulu teemed with people like her: people who flocked to Hawaii hoping to become a part of Interspace, to get their children on the generation ship, to benefit from rumored medical and genetic breakthroughs, to be near the source of illegal experimental informational nans. To live near the steam vent of Information. They became cheap labor. The highrise lanais of Honolulu were draped with their laundry, filled with the cooking smells of chili'd sesame oil, lemongrass, noodles, steamed fish. Downtown, the Oriental Market was open twenty-four hours a day. Tropical sunlight drenched the crowds by day, and at night the Chinese computerized tortoiseshell fortune-tellers set up their tables and waited with high-res screens that employed the algorithms of complexity theory to foretell the grandeurs of transtime travel, which would carry their client's grandchildren to worlds of wild beauty where there was always plenty to eat.

Mei's enormous brown eyes were dull the next morning as she sat up in the bed sipping strong, steaming Vietnamese coffee he'd run out for. She tried to smile at Cen, but tears welled from her eyes and spilled onto her thin, aristocratic face.

"I'm okay," she said, and motioned Cen back into the chair where he'd been watching her take each sip.

"What happened, Mei?" he asked. "Drink a couple bottles of tequila or what?" Give her an out if she wants it.

"Nothing but ass*holes* up there," she said, her French Polynesia accent giving even the word *asshole* charm. "But I was a fool to think I could get that bionan for free. Well, it's done now," she said, and looked at him with a glimmer of triumph in her eyes.

"Mei," he said. "Why?" He imagined her tilting a vial of bright-colored, sweetened liquid, eyes narrowed in shrewd anticipation, and tossing it down. The bionan, as far as he knew from the sketchy information available to the general public, piggybacked into various parts of the brain or the rest of the body quite precisely. Or at least, that precision was what they were trying to achieve.

She just stared at him. "Don't you want it?"

"No," he said, and that single word was tinged with horror.

"Ah, it is because you are *ig*norant," she said. "But not as ignorant as many, believe me. You are actually a smart boy, very smart indeed, I think. But me, I am not, not too really. You live on a small faraway island, you hear about the wonders of enhancement and you want it for yourself, I guarantee it, all my brothers and sisters wanted it but only I was brave enough to come and get it."

"Get what?"

"Information," she said. "Learning. Wisdom. Ha!" she said, folding her thin brown legs under her. "It must seem that I'm just a common prostitute. But I have plans, Cen. It's just that I need this *in,* this doorway. First I'll probably go back and teach again. I'm a teacher, you know. Now maybe I'll have something to teach. It will be so easy for me to *learn,"* she said. "I'll pick things up just like"—she snapped a thin, brown finger against her thumb—*"that!"* Her eyes hooded, and Cen thought she was drifting back to sleep.

"I hope you're right, Mei." He'd heard too many horror stories to believe that Mei might be a success.

First she might get an odd twitch, stumble and seem drunk when she was not.

Or perhaps she might get to seeing things that weren't there. The brain could do funny things. One side of her vision might go, or it might all reverse so that she could no longer read. And she loved to read.

She could possibly develop insights that would leave her

stranded, without tools to express them—without the language, the mathematics. And go crazy with frustration.

Cen's memories of school were fleeting now, but they were good. He'd found that he knew much, much more about the world, about literature, mathematics, about the *possibilities*—than anyone he ran into down here. He was jeered at for watching the news on Janelle's TV instead of "the stories" everyone else seemed to lap up. Every day when he bought a newspaper he pressed the science button, which gave him a paper, on thin recyclable material of some sort—he knew not what—that he could slip back into a slot to be reused. Sometimes he itched for a computer, for web access. He'd had a taste of that too. Maybe when he'd saved some money . . .

Some people said that there was safe bionan that cost a lot of money. Cen felt nothing but contempt for IS when he considered that. Why were they doing things like *this*, if it were true?

"Your tattoo, you know," she said, opening her eyes again. "These are not so rare where I come from. Many of the old ones have them. There's information in them."

She leaned toward Cen, who was still sitting next to her, reached over and traced one of the squares that climbed the side of his waist; he shivered and pulled away. She usually treated him like a little brother. He didn't want that to change. The thought scared him. He stood up.

She laughed softly. "Yes, information, you know?" she said. "That's what everything is. Beautiful patterns. It . . . it seems to come and go. This way of seeing. Like everything is upside down, or drifting apart, like what it used to mean to me is gone so that I can really *see*. I'll master it more later, of course. That's what they told me." She set the coffee down on the table next to the bed and yawned. "Have you ever heard of wormholes?"

"Go back to sleep, Mei," he said. "You'll feel better later."

"No," she said. "I mean it. Wormholes. Gateways between different times. IS didn't tell me this, of course. One of the girls who cleans the lab is from my island, we found out once when we were alone there, and she tried to stop me. So frightened!"

Mei laughed, but her laughter had a kind tone. "She told me about these *wormholes* she'd heard them talking about. Like she thought that might keep me from going through with this, as if I would be somehow pushed right into another universe! She said that only the Old Ones had *that* information, about how to get to the next universe after death. She still believes in *that* nonsense. Me, I believe in science. There is nothing after death. Wormholes! What an ugly word. Couldn't they think of anything more beautiful? I already traveled out of a different time, a different *age,* when I came here. Where I am from is fifty years behind."

Cen felt chilled, thinking about the strange girl he had seen, then dismissed the thought. Nonsense. Wormholes were something that happened in virtual arcades. A great *whoosh,* then the challenge of navigating its swirls, held open by something called exotic matter, and emerging in another universe, one— what was that word?—one *contiguous* with this one.

But that was just a game and it cost a bunch of yen and you came back alive even if your ship was crushed.

"They paid me a lot," Mei was saying. She leaped out of bed, long brown legs flashing, and went to her bureau, pulled open the top drawer, rummaged beneath her underwear, and pulled out a stack of yen, tossed them into the air, laughing and laughing as they settled, fluttering in the breeze from the window.

Then she carefully picked each one up, stacked them neatly, and buried them again. A fine sweat stood out on her forehead as she bounced back onto the bed, crossed her legs, and picked up her coffee cup.

Cen wondered how he could feel so much older than her, so weary, so very sorry.

"I can bring my sisters here now, if I want," she said. "Or if I go back, I can put a down payment on a house big enough for all of us. Because of their silly idea, I am able to have this information. That's all everything *is! Information!* Oh, Cen, it is all so lovely! The colors are so bright! And the window. Look! All the light coming in, spreading out so that everything looks so—so *white,* and . . . and coming apart . . . " Her voice weakened for a moment then continued, though tears welled in her eyes. Cen could tell she was trying to make her voice normal and firm. "I'm supposed to tell them what happens to me, that's all. Once a week, I go for tests. That's all. I . . . "

The hand with which she held the coffee stiffened, and then the cup was flung across the room. Mei's eyes opened wide, and she slumped back in the bed.

5

Even on the welfare ward, the corridors at Queen's Hospital were broad and white, shining. Cen's nose stung with the antiseptic tang of hallways where knee-level bots meandered from wall to wall, endlessly cleaning the floors.

Somewhat miraculously, they had told him at the front desk that Mei was in intensive care. After he found his way there, he was told by the Samoan nurse that Mei wasn't allowed any visitors.

He said, "You just mean you won't let *me* in! You don't like the way I look? What is it? I'm the one who put her in a cab and got her here." Then they hadn't been able to refuse her. It was against the law.

The nurse hesitated, perhaps seeing the steely defiance he felt.

"It's not that," she said, crossing her hefty arms across an even heftier bodice.

"Then what?"

"First of all, only next of kin are allowed."

"They're thousands of miles away. She's alone except for me. I'm her next of kin."

Her face softened a bit. "I did see that she's from the Marquesas . . . but you're too young anyway."

"I'm fifteen," he said, with what he hoped was quiet authority. "So let me in. I *have* to see her. Look. I brought her some rice candy." He pulled the bent cardboard box from his pocket. "She really likes it. Even the silly prize. I thought it might cheer her up."

But when he looked into the deep, grave eyes of the nurse, he was chilled by what he saw.

"How—how is she?"

"She's in intensive care."

"I know that—"

"She's not conscious," said the nurse. "It wouldn't do either of you any good. In fact, she's in a totally restricted room—"

"*Please,*" he whispered, surprised at the pleading in his voice, something entirely new for him. "She's all *I* have . . . "

Something seemed to click in the nurse. She straightened to her full height, about six feet.

"We'll have to wait till the charge nurse goes on break," she said.

When she slipped him into the room, he could only stare.

A large tube entered Mei's mouth. The breathing tube. It pumped her chest, tiny beneath the sheet, up and down, up and down, relentlessly, in an even, dull rhythm. Several IV's looped around her, filled with clear liquid. Digital feedback blinked.

"See?" whispered the nurse. She looked around nervously.

"Mei!" he cried, the word bursting from him. He stepped to her side, touched her face . . .

She didn't respond.

"What's *wrong* with her?" he asked, but knew. If not what, then *why.*

"Come on," said the nurse, and her hand clamped over his arm like a vise. "I don't want to lose my job, kid."

As she led him out the door, he felt with his other hand the crumpled box of candy in his pocket. The jellied squares of bland sweet candy were wrapped in transparent paper that dissolved in your mouth. He wanted to toss it onto her bed. She might wake and see it, know that he'd been there. The nurse was looking up and down the hall. He could do it.

He didn't. It would have been childish. It would only get the nurse in trouble, and no matter how many corny stories they aired on TV, the box of candy wouldn't somehow magically wake the thin, kind, beautiful woman whose head now swam with forbidden nanotechnology. That thing attached to her head . . . was that something sticking into her ear? Was that her *blood,* pulsing slowly up one tube, then down another? God!

The nurse yanked him around the corner. "Satisfied?"

He didn't realize he was crying until she shoved a wad of tissues into his hand.

Cen stood at the window of a Thai carryout pouring sweet condensed milk into his iced coffee. He felt dazed; maybe the coffee would help.

"Hey that's enough, you greedy pig," the woman told him, and snatched the can from his hand. She slammed the window shut.

Cen smelled the strong, sweet scent of ginger and turned.

"People are very rude here," the girl said, but smiled. Her eyes were mischievous. The sun was directly behind her head and her face was dark, but the wisps of hair that stood out around her face were lit like a nimbus.

"Do you want some?" he asked, confused. Who the hell was she?

She took it and drank. "Good," she said, and drank more.

Cen wished he hadn't been so generous.

"Don't worry," she said, as if she knew what he was thinking, and handed it back. "Do you want to go for a walk?"

What does she want? "Sure."

He started to walk toward the deserted pineapple plant, where the squalor of the streets reminded him of the punk virtuals down at the arcade, scumworlds where you had to keep your wits about you to keep from getting offed. A few Filipino boys had a cockfight every afternoon in the Mongoose's packed-dirt backyard; he had a few hundred yen to blow.

"No," she said. "This way."

He shrugged. He'd probably just lose his money. "Okay." They started to walk toward Diamond Head instead.

She was wearing the same white dress. You'd think that

she'd be hot, but she looked cool as the white clouds that hid the mountaintops. "It's so strange here," she said.

"It is?"

"I'm getting used to it. I'm not so sad, here. I'm so tired of being sad." And she laughed with such hysterical abandon that Cen was afraid that she was one of Interspace's bionan crazies and didn't press her. He found, to his surprise, that he wanted only to protect her, give her a feeling of safety.

To keep her from vanishing as she had before.

Cen stopped and looked at her. She returned his gaze with the same intense, liquid, intelligent expression he remembered from the other time they had met.

"Who are you?" he asked.

"My name is Kaiulani."

"Where do you live?"

"My father has a big house down at Waikiki. He would be very angry if he knew that I was coming over to the harbor. He wants to keep me all locked up. Safe. But I need to know what my people are like."

"Your people?"

Serenity and composure blazed from her, yet she answered a bit impatiently, "Yes. King David Kalakaua is my uncle, and Liliuokalani Dominis is my aunt. After her I'm next in line for the throne." She raised her chin and stared at him.

"What are you *talking* about?" And how did she know his last name, Kalakaua? He had given Lu-Wei, the only person who ever asked, the name Cen Smith. Panic filled him. Had his father found him, sent her? No. Impossible . . .

"I guess you don't believe me."

He took a deep breath. "Believe *what?*"

"That I'm going to be the next ruler of Hawaii."

A nut. But a rich nut, obviously. She was very beautiful, frail, fine-boned. He relaxed. Kalakaua was not an unusual name, after all. He felt sorry for her. She wasn't a tourist. She looked Hawaiian, which was about as rare as the o-o bird. And yet—

"Your father is right," Cen said. "You shouldn't be over on this side of town. Let me walk you home." Even if his own father did find him, what could he do? Cen was almost six feet tall now, and very strong. He'd beat his father to a pulp and then—

She frowned. "I can get home by myself, thank you," she said. "It's almost time for tea, anyway, and they become upset if I miss it."

Tea? He was so dumbfounded by the whole performance that he let her walk away. By the time he thought to follow her she had turned the corner, and when he rushed around Huang Po's and looked down King Street, it was empty of people, as it often was this time of afternoon.

The street vibrated with her absence.

His breath came short with terror. "Don't leave me," he said, gazing at the old buildings, suddenly afraid that they might vanish too and leave him alone in a dark, frightening void with flashes of red, the nebulous place of his recurring nightmares where nothing was real, but that was all he had and all he ever would have.

Score some pakalolo, he told himself. Forget about this girl. Be stoned all night—you got to work anyway.

His side job right now was loading dishwashers with the greasy dishes of rich tourists who stuffed themselves on fish covered with macadamia nuts, macadamia nut pie, and washed it down with about ten Blue Hawaiis. He wished he could afford to leave his job at the fish market. It physically sickened him; he rushed from the flopping fish and rivers of blood at least once a month to puke in the bathroom, but Lu-Wei paid surprisingly well, valuing his dependability, and Cen had vague dreams of going to school. Or something.

Stoned, he could dream of it being winter, when the surf would be big over at Makaha. Life was real then. Lots of dumb tourists came out there and locked their cameras and wallets in the trunk of their car, thinking that would keep their stuff from being stolen. Cen could break into a trunk and be gone with the goods in about ten seconds flat. Yeah, sure—if he tried, maybe even a street kid like him could do something besides clean fish and steal. Someday.

But right now, maybe the Mongoose could help him out. He usually had a little extra.

She was back the next day. She just showed up next to him as he sat in the park, trying out his pakalolo. The cops didn't care; this was a park for bums. He felt like a bum. Maybe he'd *be* a bum. Why not? Earlier he had walked to the hospital, stood at the door while people brushed past him unseeing, then turned back. He hadn't gone to work. What did it matter? What did anything matter? The world was a crazed, dark place, and the fear that he always carried with him, that his father might suddenly show up, seemed like a beast ready to uncoil and overwhelm him. Nowhere to run. No safe place. The park was bright, shot with brilliant hot sun that lay across his shoulders like a soothing protective shield.

"Have you ever read Robert Louis Stevenson?" she asked.

His heart beat fast as he turned, recognizing her voice instantly. Be cool, he told himself. Don't scare her away.

"Who's that?" he asked, only a slight tremor in his voice. He found he didn't want to admit to her that he didn't read much. Reading reminded him of his mom.

She smiled at him, her face only inches away. She had a lovely smile. Her eyes were the kindest he'd ever seen.

"He's my friend. He reads with me—Shakespeare and Plato, and he's even teaching me Latin. He's a *haku mele.*" A poet. She looked grave again. "You have to know a lot to be a ruler. You have to know just about everything there is to know. Especially you have to know a lot about politics and the world and everything. And foreign languages—French is my favorite. I hate German, don't you?"

He liked this crazy girl. "The only foreign language I know is English," he said.

"You mean Hawaiian is your native tongue?"

My native tongue. "Yeah." Sometimes, like whenever he went up into the Waianae Mountains, or rode Jake's dirt bike around Kaena Point, where it was so wild, or when he was out on somebody's borrowed board, he thought in Hawaiian. "How did you know?"

"I told you," she said. "I can tell you're *alii.*"

"That's crazy," he said.

Then he realized: it was not.

His mother had taught him to recite his genealogy back to the days of the ancient chiefs, but he hadn't even remembered that until just now. Funny what you could forget. If you tried. It had mattered to her.

But it was bullshit. It wasn't important. Not these days, when they were trying to rebuild the Moon colony and the shuttle roared in every Wednesday from the space station, where the generation ship was being built.

But what could a little pretending hurt, especially in a world where you could talk to a ghost? He thought of her as one, though she seemed solid enough. It was the way she dressed, the way she just appeared. The mind could do funny things, and what did it matter? She made him *happy*. Shouldn't that be enough?

"Yeah," he said, "and I know where Kamehameha's bones are."

He thought she would say, sure you do.

Instead, she jumped up from the grass and stood in front of him. Her face had a wild look.

"Don't ever, *ever*, tell anybody," she said, and kissed him quickly full on the lips.

Everything seemed real, though intensified in color by her presence—especially the touch of her lips on his.

And what was that about Kamehameha's bones? It had just popped out of his mouth. Weird things happened when she was around.

He did dream about bones sometimes: yellow and pitted. Scary. Giving off the awful energy of death. He feared those dreams most of all. Sometimes he felt that dark power struggling to come into his world, to leak through the bright buildings of a not-real Honolulu and sweep him into everlasting night.

Anyway, Kamehameha had died over two hundred years ago. He was the first king to unite the Hawaiian Islands. Nobody knew where his bones were. They were hidden by kahunas—priests—as soon as he died. But she was right: bones were sacred to Hawaiians. They had much *mana,* much power. If your enemies got hold of them, your bones became fish-hooks. It was the ultimate insult.

He didn't know why he dreamed about them. He figured he'd seen them on TV when he was little, or something, and they made a big impression. He could even *hear* them, in his dreams. Smooth, dark, long-fingered hands rolled them into an old piece of tapa cloth, and they made dry, distant tones as they clanked together and went back into darkness.

He could tell already that Kaiulani was nothing like death. She was like the sun in the park: bright, lifegiving.

He looked at his joint, tossed it in a far arc across the park. You never knew what the Mongoose might be lacing through his stuff. He steeled himself to ask her questions. He didn't like to think that he might be crazy, like an old drunk ranting to the air.

"Why shouldn't I tell anyone? Who are *you?* What makes you think you can tell *me* what to do?"

In response to his question, Kaiulani stared at him, and turned pale. She picked up a ripe mango and threw it right at him. It splattered against his arm, its overripe tang exploding in his nose. Well, *that* was real enough. He watched, amused, as she whirled and ran, hoisting her long white dress. Then he broke into a run.

Cen was surprised at how fast she could dart across the broad green lawn splotched by the short midday shadows of coconut palms.

Still, he got close enough in a minute to catch hold of her sash. It ripped from her dress and she turned, eyes blazing.

"You don't do that to a *princess,*" she said, and slapped him.

His cheek stung. Angry, he said, "Just tell me about the bones, then, *princess.*"

She stared at him. "You believe me."

"Sure," he said. Maybe.

"Sit," she said.

They sat together and watched surf breaking out on the reef.

But she was oddly quiet. Finally she spoke.

"I've seen them before. They are *kapu*. Very bad luck." She laughed. "I was cursed, by the power of the bones." She laughed again, her voice light and unconcerned. "Silly superstition!"

She was quiet for a moment and then said, "But still, *I* need to see them."

"Why?" he asked, in a whisper.

She stood up and turned to look out at the ocean. A narrow strip of it was visible through the trees, with its distant edge of white. Green till it turned deep blue, suddenly, at the reef line.

"To see . . . " her voice broke, but she recovered and went on. "To see if they are real. To touch them again. To know more. Because *I* am to rule this land. And bring justice to it again. They will . . . *remind* me."

If anyone else had uttered these words so seriously, he would have laughed in derision. But she brought dignity to everything she said. It was easy, very easy, to believe her.

He felt his whole mind and being spin, then expand, into *her* reality, *her* life. So much more bright than his own. The red and black heaviness always pressing upon him, and the vision of Mei in that awful room, dropped as he listened and watched her beautiful, earnest face. He realized that he had to help her in any way he possibly could. Nothing was more important than her dream of justice for Hawaiians. All around he saw his disenfranchised brothers and sisters, many of them filled with deep, debilitating anger at the descendants of those who had taken their land and their country. Still unwilling to adapt, after all these years, to a life they saw as less holy and less pure than what had been stolen from them. A hereditary dream handed down to them through the generations, one that he had always rejected, though he had nothing, really, with which to replace it. There were at least eight factions of Homelanders, all with slightly different agendas, all rabidly sure of their goals. Each claimed to have the true needs of Hawaiians at heart. He had had some slight contact with more than one and found them vaguely repulsive.

Kaiulani stared out at the waves breaking on the reef. Her

long dark hair swept back from her face in the onshore wind. "They're talking about sending me to Europe for my education," she said. "I'm not supposed to know, but I hear things. I was always supposed to go, but not until later. But apparently there are all kinds of things going on downtown." She frowned. "There are so many crazy haoles here in Hawaii. And they all manage to get into my uncle's cabinet somehow." She turned and looked directly at him. "Was that opium you were smoking before?"

"No," he said. "That didn't come from poppies." Don't ask her anything. Keep her talking, remember what she says, use it for clues . . .

Keep her *here*.

"That's my uncle's latest trouble," she said. "For a long time it was illegal for Hawaiians to drink or to smoke opium—*only* Hawaiians. It was all right for everyone else. But now he's sold a license to a Chinese merchant. That's a crime in itself, you understand. I believe he was paid about seventy thousand dollars. And then he sold the same license to someone else, and told the first man that it was too bad, but that he was keeping the money! So the first man went to the papers . . . " she sighed. "Now it's coming out that my uncle—he's the king, you know—signed the affidavit because the annexationists paid him to do it, which discredits him even further. Well, it's true that he doesn't seem to have any sense of responsibility at all. That's what my father says. Uncle David is my mother's brother, of course! He's like an overgrown child. He sits there on his houseboat drinking cases of champagne with *my* friend, Louis—Mr. Stevenson, that is. Louis isn't very healthy! But at least he acts like a grown-up. I have a lot of work to do, Cen. I have a lot to learn. Everybody complains because Hawaiians don't work. Of course they do! How do people think we got along before they showed up? This is our land! Before the Europeans came, everyone got along fine. We worked hard when we had to and we played just as hard. That's what my old nurse told me, and my aunt Liliuokalani. If the businessmen want to make a fortune selling sugar, why should the Hawaiians be serfs on their own land?"

She turned to Cen, her cheeks red. He didn't know what to say. She was so much more passionate than him. He thought of Lu-Wei. Lu's family had owned the stall in the fish market for over a hundred years. He didn't want to think about his own family. He couldn't. It was like a wall.

"You're going to Europe?" he asked gently, wondering why the words of a ghost could fill him with such desolation. He reached up and felt his stinging cheek. His brain refused to function. It didn't make sense. And what did it matter? She was dead anyway, if the strange things she was saying were true.

But it *did* matter.

When she was here time was intense, bright, causing the rest of his life to seem meaningless in comparison. Everything about her was the opposite of himself, as if they were two sides of the same mask, dark and light. Why care about *why* he could see her? It only mattered that he *could,* didn't it?

No, he was surprised to find himself thinking. It mattered, quite a bit, *why.*

And now she was leaving.

"I don't really want to go so far away," she said. "But it's for the good of my people. Yet, to help my people, I need to know everything about *them.* Their beliefs. My life is very civilized. I sit in the great room in the evenings, listening to queens and kings from my own and other countries speak. The windows are always open and the breeze blows in from off the sea and rattles the banana trees. All the foreign ambassadors are friends with my father. They come and drink gin and play cards. I'm very quiet so they don't chase me away. It seems that everyone wants Hawaii—the British, the Americans, even the Japanese. But we need it for ourselves. After all, it is ours."

She turned to look at Cen. "You are *alii,* like me. If you know where the bones are, you must show me. It's not only the things in Europe I need to learn. My father is Scots, and that's what *he* thinks—but I think he might be wrong about that. My old nurse said that the bones give life to the land. Perhaps if I saw them—*touched* them—" he saw her shiver "—I would understand things—my land—better. I would know what it is that I have to do. They have . . . information."

Cen felt very cold. *Information.* The same word Mei had used. "I haven't seen any bones," he said. Why had he ever said such a ridiculous thing?

"I don't believe that," she said, looking straight at him. "I don't believe that you would lie to me."

You don't know much about me then, he thought.

"If you're really a ghost," he said, "why can I see you? Touch you?"

She reached over and brushed his arm with two fingers. "Because you are special. Maybe that's the reason I can see you. We must be *uhana make.*"

Friends of the soul. A Hawaiian phrase. But he was shaken. What was a soul, anyway? Did he *have* one? *What is it like to be dead?* he wanted to ask, but was afraid.

The genealogy chant his mother had taught him came back to Cen whole that night, after he woke from a nightmare, in a rush of bright, linked words. In the torrent of names, he found hers: Kaiulani. The last princess of Hawaii. Her real name was Victoria Kawekiu Lunalilo Kalaninuiahilapalapapa Kaiulani. Her claim to the throne was through her mother, Princess Likelike.

His hospital visit the next morning was brief and painful. He wore his most respectable clothes and carefully combed his hair. He took the nurse a box of candy, which she accepted with bemusement. She shrugged. "It's okay, I've cleared you. Said you were her brother. But it's weird, let me tell you. I guess they don't know what the hell's wrong with her. They seem to have some unusual procedures. Think you're up to it?"

"Sure," he said, but his voice cracked. He followed her down the hall to Mei's room.

"Wait," she whispered, catching him just before they went in the door. "I thought he'd left."

Mei was sitting up in bed, wearing a pale blue hospital gown. Some sort of wire helmet was on her head, like an upside-down basket. She was looking at a card she held. A man wearing a white coat sat next to her. Cen couldn't hear what they were saying, but they talked; Mei nodded, and the man took away one card and handed her another. She was too pale, too thin.

Cen stepped back and from his new angle saw a screen, and on the screen was a colorful vision of—a brain?

Mei's brain. Filled with shifting colors, blossoms of light that grew and shrank. She looked up, suddenly, perhaps feeling his eyes on her, and her mouth opened. She smiled; dropped the card, reached for him—

"Come on," said the nurse, who had watched with him. She pulled him down the hall so fast his feet dragged. She yanked him into the next doorway, and Cen heard a door slam.

They were in a room with two empty beds. "Who was that?" asked Cen. "What were they doing?"

"Don't ask too many questions," she said, and told him to try again the next day.

Later on at work he was so nervous he cut himself badly. He felt completely helpless. Was Mei a prisoner? He knew who those people were. Or he thought he knew. The same people who had taken her to Tripler, seduced her with the dream of becoming supersmart. Now that something was wrong, they didn't want her associated with Tripler. If you asked, those people would probably say they were social workers trying to rehabilitate her or something. Maybe he should call the police?

Right. *He* should call the police. That would be a good move, after these years of hiding. The first thing they'd want to know was *his* name. He wouldn't do Mei any good if he was in jail. Besides, those people in there—they were more powerful than the police anyway.

That evening he walked through dark streets and went to the Bishop Museum, a vast repository of Hawaiiana. He felt aimless, anxious. This was something to do, at least.

The showcases, filled with ancient tools and artifacts of various Pacific Islanders from prehistory on through the history of the last Hawaiian royal family, reminded him so much of his mother that he almost left. *Fuck you,* he thought to the people he thought were staring at him as he rubbed tears from his face. He didn't know why he felt this way but he hated it.

He had to ask for help. And after he got it, he hesitated before opening the faded pictorial of old Hawaii.

In the index, he found her name. Princess Kaiulani.

Trembling, he turned dry pages until he came to the right one.

It was eerie how much the same she looked.

The photograph, in sepia tones, showed her on the lawn of a mansion. Ainahau was built by her father, Archibald Cleghorn, at Waikiki, and everyone ridiculed him for building so far from town in the middle of a swamp. The tops of a few palm trees were visible behind the house, and the front yard was deeply shaded by a massive banyan and lots of mimosas. That would be just about right; she reminded him of those odd pink flowers, fans of soft, bright pink spines that floated to earth when the trade winds blew, filling the air with sweetness.

Two peacocks strutted in front of her, and she was bending toward one, laughing, her long black hair loose around her face as she directly faced the camera.

"Robert Louis Stevenson, King David Kalakaua, and Princess Kaiulani," the caption read.

He got the feeling that, in the picture, it was almost time for tea.

He leafed through the book. He found another picture of Princess Kaiulani. She was a child, standing next to her aunt, Queen Liliuokalani, on the steps of Iolani Palace. They were watching the coronation of her uncle, King David Kalakaua, and his wife, Queen Kapiolani. It was 1882. Her face, even at seven, was grave and certain.

That was all. But it was her. Beyond a doubt.

How?

The librarian was very helpful. "Kaiulani is quite a favorite," she said, and gave him white gloves he had to wear when reading the fragile letters in which Kaiulani wrote to her papa about her European studies. He realized that in the museum there were touchscreens and virtuals that could only be accessed by a library key. That—the ability to do deep research—cost money. And even if he had it, the shadowy fear that always hovered around him would have asserted itself: he had to remain invisible. Outside whatever system there was. He didn't want his father to find him.

He found a cheap little book in the gift shop about Hawaiian ghosts, and another about Kaiulani, and took them home. He read them that night in his lonely room, to keep from falling asleep and having nightmares about what they might be doing to Mei. Kaiulani had never put in an appearance as a ghost in the old legends, but after all, she had died after the time of old Hawaii, when they were so prevalent in the lives of the people.

Perhaps, he reasoned, she was a new one. They seemed to have plenty of powers. Traveling through time was only one of them. They gave advice and warnings. They could envelop people in dreams and thus influence them. They could transport anyone they pleased from place to place as easily as the police moved their "missing" holos around. Pele the volcano goddess was the most famous, but there were hundreds.

And, most important to him, they seemed to be strongly associated with *place*. As if they were manifested by the land, encountered by people who happened to walk the same path, perhaps fifty years after the last spotting, and the ghost would be there, ageless.

He threw the ghost book on the floor, feeling stupid, and picked up her biography. The worst part was that she had died so young. Why did everybody have to die? he thought angrily. He remembered some of the recent rumors on the street, that an immortal nan-person had been created, somewhere, in some dark lab. The thought made him furious. Give me some of that stuff for Mei, he thought. Some for Kaiulani too . . . I can slip it into the past and . . .

But the more he thought about that, the stranger the idea became. *If I could make her live . . . what might have happened instead? Mei might be fine. Or . . .*

It was too much to think about. And silly anyway.

It struck him to the heart to turn the last few pages. While she was in Europe attending expensive schools, all sorts of political shenanigans went on. Hawaii was up for grabs, too small to defend herself against greedy haole business interests. Almost all the land was finagled from the Hawaiians. Kaiulani finally went to Washington when she was eighteen and met with Grover Cleveland and his wife in a last-ditch effort to keep the United States from annexing Hawaii. A self-styled "Provisional Government" composed of rich American businessmen had ousted Kaiulani's aunt, Queen Liliuokalani, but as long as Cleveland was president, Hawaii remained a kingdom. In January, 1895, there was a small rebel uprising that was quashed by American troops.

Once Cleveland was out of the White House, the Annexationists had their way. On August 12, 1898, Hawaii ceased to be a sovereign country. In January 1899, Kaiulani, while staying at the Parker Ranch on the Big Island, went for a horseback ride with friends. Instead of putting on her raincoat during a sudden cold storm, she said, "What have I got to live for?" She loosed her hair and galloped off into the tempest. She took cold, worsened, and within weeks was dead. She was twenty-three years old. There was talk of a kahuna's curse.

Her last years were filled with proud heartbreak and the desolation of knowing that she was not to fulfill her destiny.

Kaiulani was so young and beautiful, so full of life and hope. Like Mei. How could this terrible thing, this untimely death, have happened? It almost seemed foretold, like the birth of Kamehameha had been foretold: the kahunas had decided before he was born that he would be the one to unite the islands.

The Hawaiians seemed to have a fascination with prophecy, and with death. Apparently, at the time, people thought that Kaiulani had been prayed to death like her mother before her. Her mother had been only thirty-six when she died, after mysteriously taking to her bed. She had foreseen not only her own death, but had predicted all the major events in Kaiulani's life: that she would live most of it far away, that she would never marry, and that she would never be queen. What was this terrible vision that Hawaiians had?

How could he change things for her? If he could *see* her, *touch* her . . .

You fool, he told himself. She's a ghost, and there's no such thing as ghosts.

And yet . . . He wondered when he would see her next.
If ever.

Stevenson had written a poem for her. When she was thirteen, she was sent to Europe to become educated as befitted a future queen of a kingdom, and this was his going-away present.

> Forth from her land to mine she goes,
> The island maid, the island rose,
> Light of heart and bright of face,
> The daughter of a double race.
>
> Her islands here in southern sun
> Shall mourn their Kaiulani gone,
> And I, in her dear banyan's shade,
> Look vainly for my little maid.
>
> But our Scots islands far away
> Shall glitter with unwonted day,
> And cast for once their tempest by
> To smile in Kaiulani's eye.

Pretty hokey stuff, as far as Cen was concerned. He could probably do better himself. At least it made him sleepy. The book dropped from his hand.

The next morning Huang Po had the nerve to stop him on his way out and demand the rent, since it was the first of the month. Cen stalked upstairs, opened Mei's box of neatly kept papers, and showed Po the receipt.

"We're paid up for the next two months, according to this," Cen said, waving it under Po's nose, pointing out his signature on the bottom.

"Oh, yeah, I forgot," said Po.

"Right," said Cen.

He hurried over to the market. He had overslept. The world was like a vague skein before his eyes, as if it were a shimmering curtain he could rend, almost transparent. A wave of dizziness swept over him as he handed the first bag of mahi to a customer, and he dropped it and grabbed the counter to keep from falling. Lu-Wei rushed over, scolding in Chinese, waving his cane. He apologized to the customer and served her. When she left Lu-Wei turned to Cen and hollered, "Useless today! Get out! I don't pay for no sick time."

"Fuck you!" said Cen. "I'm not sick!"

"I think I fire you," said Lu-Wei. "Here's your last pay. Get out."

Dazed, Cen didn't argue. He stood while Lu-Wei counted out the money. Fine. Nasty job anyway.

Once he was out on the street, the strange brightness took hold of him again. What was going on? His life was falling apart. Did he have a fever? He raised his hand to his forehead, but it felt normal. He realized that he was heading back to the park. *She* would be there. *She* would make everything . . . fit.

But she didn't come, and he fell asleep in the park. When he woke he hurried to the hospital, but visiting hours were over.

Heartsick, Cen went out into the evening. He walked slowly, then faster, until he realized with a start that he was heading back to the Bishop Museum.

Why not? He started to run. Toward Kaiulani.

Once there, he wasn't sure what to do. He *had* to see Kaiulani again; he was possessed of a weird, frantic energy he'd never felt before in his life. The catalog said that the museum had created a single virtual of her, based on photographs. It ran for three minutes.

He carefully watched how the booths were used. There was a virtual arcade in Waikiki where he'd dropped too many yen. He was there so much that he could almost tell what virtual somebody was in just by their dance. But this was more complex: the virtuals were hypertexed and even getting into the system required some computer expertise. He'd used computers in preschool, sure. What was that—ten years ago? Things had changed.

He jumped at a tap on his shoulder.

He turned and found himself looking into strange gray eyes. The man's hair was short, light brown with lots of gray.

"I've been watching you," he said.

Cen tensed. I'm not doing anything wrong, he told his body, but years of sneaking and stealing bound his muscles. His heart was beating fast.

"You know, it's not hard to learn the virtuals," the man said.

"Who are you?" asked Cen, upset that he sounded so tough and belligerent.

The man smiled. "I'm Ross Benet. I'm a mathematics professor at UH, but I come over here pretty often. It's a good place to think. You were here last night, I noticed."

Cen didn't like his searching look. "So?"

"So I'm impressed. Not many kids are as interested in learning as you."

Not many kids have a *uhana make*.

"You're really missing out on things without the virtuals. I'd like to teach you how to use them."

Cen didn't trust the guy, but what the hell. He wanted to know how to hype. He let the guy lead him over to a booth and sat in the extra chair he pulled up. Ross slid in his key, a flat plastic card with a magnetic strip, watched as the screen told him it was accepted, then returned it to his shirt pocket.

"Helmet," Ross said. "Gloves."

Yeah, and I'm four years old. Cen put them on.

"Judging by your reading material, you're interested in Hawaiiana."

Nosy old coot.

Cen forgave him in the first rush of virtuals.

Later that night, Cen was in Ross's living room shouting at him. "Find yourself another whore," he yelled. He threw his beer across the room; it smashed against a black-and-white photograph on the impeccably white wall. Glass shattered; beer foamed down the wall; it had arced from the bottle's mouth while in transit and darkened a chair covered in a delicate shade of lime green silk.

"Cen, my dear," Ross began. He stood in the doorway to the hall that led from the living room to the bedrooms. Outside, the night traffic of H-4 in downtown Honolulu a few blocks away was like the sound of surf; up here on the lower flank of the Manoa Valley, crickets hummed and the breeze rattled the blinds.

"I'm not your *dear,*" yelled Cen. A part of him stood apart, amazed at his fury. He wondered if this was how his father used to feel.

"You knew, of course," said Ross, his face settling in lines of ironic amusement. He went to the kitchen and came back with a towel, began to wipe down the wall.

"I'm sorry," Ross continued. "You are very attractive, and I thought—"

"You thought that since I live on Hotel Street that that's how I made my money. I know. You must have followed me home last night and thought you had it figured out, right? Or maybe tattoos turn you on?"

Ross's silence as he knelt and cleaned the wall answered Cen.

Ross stood and turned around. "I mean it," he said. "Forgive me. You are a very gifted boy—"

"Yeah," said Cen. "I'm gifted, all right."

Ross sat in the green silk chair and held the wet towel in both hands, twisted it into a knot. "Look," he said. "I don't need you for sex, Cen, even though you *are* attractive to me, in many different ways. In fact I have a steady lover who'd be pretty pissed off if he knew about this. But it's true that you're very bright. I teach. Believe me, I can tell bright from dull pretty quickly. You deserve to have the opportunity to learn. To get ahead. To become educated. I can help you with that. No strings. I promise." He smiled wryly, shrugged. "I really *am* a teacher at heart, Cen. That's what I've devoted my life to. Working in a fish market—that's no life for someone like you. What's next? Now you don't even have that."

Cen stood in the living room, hands on his hips. He'd told this guy too much, rattled by everything that was happening—Kaiulani, Mei—everything. He continued to stare at the man and was impressed that his eyes held no hint of shame, though apology was there. He'd lived on the streets for a long time. Nothing was 100 percent right.

He was tempted to stay. He should take advantage of the situation. He had to go to school because Kaiulani had. She couldn't know more than him! He felt that something had been arranged, that there was something straight about this weird man and this weird chance, and that he couldn't just run from it. "I don't know—," he said, trying to shake the memory of being pulled toward Ross, and that sudden, searching kiss.

Ross's smile was rueful. "I guess I know."

"It's not that I think it's wrong," Cen said slowly. "I'm just not interested. I don't think I'll change my mind."

He turned and left the house, letting the door slam shut behind him. The air smelled of sweet plumeria in the dark garden in front of Ross's house. It was a very nice place. Idiot, he thought. You have a few weeks of time left at the hotel and then where will you go? He had no job. But what the hell did it matter? He hated gutting fish, hated the demanding customers. The only thing that was ever good about it, he realized, was making Mei happy that he was making money.

He felt again his impotence. Maybe he should just steal her from the hospital.

The more he thought about it, the more sense it made. Except that it was completely ridiculous.

With a great effort he shook the image from his mind and fixed on the present as best he could.

"It's not that I mind," Cen said to the air, or Ross, as he walked downhill through the dark campus. "It's not that."

He allowed Kaiulani to fill his mind, drowning out his inability to save Mei.

Kaiulani. She was dead. Yet he'd seen *her*.

You nut, he told himself bitterly. Sometimes he wished he had imagined Kaiulani.

But he knew that she was very real indeed.

"Kaiulani," he whispered, as he stood next to a flood of traffic waiting for the light to change, "it's not fair, you know. I can't see *you* when I want."

When he thought of her it seemed that he ought to be able to make time move, to flow like a liquid, like the rush of sparkling turquoise water in reef pools, ebbing and flowing. Kaiulani was like the little islands he kayaked to in the Hawaiian virtuals sometimes, ones he couldn't see when he started out but could only feel, guess at, and then they appeared, small dark lines on the horizon, moving toward him as she had. She was like them, pure and timeless. *There,* in the trackless ocean.

He knew that she couldn't see him when she wanted to, either. Otherwise she would come. She would. Of course she would.

But she didn't.

6

Cen stepped up to the intercom and said, "Doma." Today's password swung open the blue, peeling, wrought-iron gate. As he walked down the rutted driveway, Cen heard it clang shut behind him.

To his right was a cinder-block wall. To his left, an ancient house sagged, probably a hundred years old. A kapuna— old-timer's—house. Wide front porch, tiny parlor, obsolete kitchen. Cen had been inside and he knew how trashed it was.

He smelled the stink of the chicken houses before he came around the house, heard the metal clang of cages being pulled from vans with no windows. He rounded the house, squeezing the roll of yen in his pocket. It was all he had left. And he wouldn't consider touching the money for which Mei had paid so dearly.

Haleakala was there. The fighting cock's brilliant green-and-gold plumage was set off by red patches around his bold yellow eyes. Sunita, the owner, set his cage next to the pit, a sheen of sweat on her brown back and arms, and went back to her van to get another. Haleakala flapped inside his cage, excited. He knew where he was; he was eager for the kill.

Cen remembered exactly how the betting had gone the past ten times he'd been here—every bird, all the odds, every win, every loss. He hadn't been back since Mei had gone to the hospital, since he'd begun to see Kaiulani, since he'd met Ross. He breathed in the familiar smells. At least *something* was the same.

He'd never been so nervous before. Before, it had just been a game, one that Mei hated, even when he gave her pretty little presents with his winnings—a beautiful handmade rice bowl; a pair of jade earrings. The other guys just didn't seem very bright when it came to betting. They seemed to get so emotional and didn't take any of the facts into account.

Well. Fuck Lu-Wei. Like he'd said. At least he didn't have to gut fish anymore.

He felt someone next to him and turned.

The kid was tall, his lithe body brown and oiled. He looked about Cen's age. He wore only black trunks and a headband that held back a cascade of thick black hair on the right side of his face. His hair had a white streak in it; Cen wondered if it was fake. A Homeland symbol was razored from the left side of his hair, which was very short: the curving lines of Kamehameha's feather crown. In physical appearance he could have been Cen's cousin. Probably was. Pure Hawaiians were rare and closely knit.

He was looking straight at Cen.

Cen felt uneasy. He remembered, now. This guy had come to the last cockfight he'd been to and had stared at him the whole time. Some of the guys said that he'd been asking questions about him. Cen thought he'd even seen him at the virtual arcade he usually went to.

The sun was hot and high in the sky when the fighting began. Cen started yelling with the rest of them, and a frenzy built up around the ring. Cen doubled his money on the first fight. He was folding it, relieved, when someone touched him on the arm.

Cen whirled, knowing who it was. "What do you want?" he asked.

The kid regarded Cen steadily with liquid brown eyes lit by

amusement, but Cen saw hardness beneath, or thought he did.

"You look like you're *alii*," the kid said.

"Crap," said Cen and stared at him, wondering what he wanted.

"My name is Maui," he said.

"Pleased to meet you Maui," said Cen. "Nice name. I suppose you think you're some kind of god like Maui, eh? Pulled any islands out of the ocean yet this month?"

"My mother gave me my name," said Maui in a level voice, "and I love it dearly. I do my best to live up to it."

"Fine," said Cen. "So what do you want with me?"

"What's your last name?"

"None of your business," Cen said, looking at the guy more closely. Was he from IS?

"Look," he said, "what's the big deal? It's just that you look like *alii*, that's all. It's nothing bad."

"Why do you keep saying that? What difference would that make? Are *you alii?*"

The boy smiled slightly. "Kind of," he said. "My family is a line of kahunas, as a matter of fact."

A kahuna.

The cockfight receded, the sounds and the smells, Cen's newly fattened roll of yen that he held inside his pocket, the too-bright sky. He broke out in a sweat. He wanted to run. Why did that word bother him?

"What's your mother's name?" Maui asked.

"My mother's dead," Cen said after a long pause. It was very difficult to think about her, to be reminded of her. This Maui was really starting to piss him off.

"I'm sorry," said Maui. So why did his eyes change? Why did he get that weird eager look, like he'd just scored big? "We just like to know who everyone is."

"Sure. So does IS," Cen said.

"Naa, brah, don't be haole. Don't be stupid. You know where I'm from and who I answer to."

Cen saw Maui's eyes go distant, and he knew the thoughts that ran through the other's head: the glory days, of ancient splendor, when Hawaiians ruled the islands. He answered to the Homeland Movement; they had his head branded with their mark, and he thought they would return the islands to an Eden that Cen was sure never existed in the first place.

"Ever seen the Bishop Museum virtuals?" Cen asked. Forget reading. This guy probably didn't know how. Too haole, and even among a lot of haoles, reading was considered a passé form of information exchange. He was feeling more and more like at least there he could find a little bit of the truth instead of the tourist and Homeland Movement fairy tales that pervaded Honolulu everywhere you looked. Except in the Asiaslums—that's where the IS fairy tale of other, perfect worlds had its teeth in the throat of the poor Thais, Burmese, and Laotians.

All the people like Mei.

"The Bishop Museum is just full of IS propaganda," said Maui, and Cen knew that Maui believed it. He didn't believe that there had ever been hunger. He didn't believe that women and commoners had chafed, suffered, and often died under the absolute rule of petty chiefs and black-hearted kahunas—Maui's own ancestors, most likely—kahunas who prayed people to death if they felt like it, chiefs who indulged in frequent war games using their warriors and villages as meaningless markers.

No, Maui believed in placid sunny fishing villages, hukilaus where the village raised its voice in polyphonous song, strumming ukuleles no doubt. Probably didn't even know they were a Portuguese import.

Cen was surprised when Maui bowed, ever so slightly.

"See you around," he said, with that same unsettling look of gloating success on his face, and left through the iron gate.

Cen gambled some more but lost heavily, quickly. Disgusted with himself, he left, banging the gate behind him. Damn that Maui.

He walked back toward Honolulu on hot, bare sidewalks, past immense rusting warehouses, through decrepit neighborhoods where white houses were flanked by scraggly hibiscus. Hot places with tin roofs where the old folks were hard put to pay their soaring taxes, but where the new Interspace elite—

Germans, Koreans, Japanese—who forced values up had no intention of buying. He was grateful when a storm flowed down Nuuanu valley, a gray mist, and washed the dust from him in a five-minute torrent before receding once again to wreath the Pali peaks.

He let himself into his room. Again he dressed, combed his hair, went to the hospital.

The regular nurse was not there but they let him in anyway because he was Mei's brother.

Mei was asleep. Her temples were blue and bruised.

"Oh, Mei," he said, and touched one of the bruises lightly. Her eyes fluttered open and she looked up.

"Cen?" she whispered. She propped herself up on her elbows. "Cen, get me out of here, please." Beneath the covers, she started to shake. "Everything is so crazy. I just need to go home. Then everything will be all right. Yes! It will all go back together again like it's supposed to."

"Mei," he said, and helped her sit up, pushing her back toward the headboard, fixing the sheet. "You're better!"

She laughed, but it was a sad shadow of her old spirited laugh.

"Oh, of course, Cen. Much, much better. Look in that closet. Are my clothes in there? Good! Now, you'll have to help me." She swung her thin legs over the side of the bed, tried to stand, and fell back onto the bed. "Whoops," she said.

"Mei, I can't steal you from this hospital," he said. "Let me go tell them you're better—"

"No! No!" she said, her voice rising in terror. "Look," she said, breathing hard. "I bet there's a wheelchair out in the hall. You go get it. Take your time. Don't let anyone see you. I'll get dressed. Then you come back—"

The door swung open.

A woman wearing a white lab coat was standing there. She did not look like a doctor to Cen. She looked too strange, with her hair cut in a funny way, like she'd gone to a street-punk place to have it done. Only a very expensive street-punk place.

"Hello," she said. "Who are you?"

"I'm Mei's brother, Fred," said Cen.

"Oh? I didn't know she had any brothers."

"Well, she does. And I'm taking her home. She's better now."

"No," said the woman. "She's not ready to go home yet."

"I *am!*" said Mei, and stood up. She walked unsteadily across the room, holding on to the bed as she moved, and pulled open the closet. "I'm going home with Fred. You can't keep me here. I'm signing out."

The woman looked at Cen, and Cen felt very uneasy. But what could she do? What?

She could find out who he really was, for one thing. The police would probably like to know.

Well, he'd just have to risk it.

"She's going home with me," he said, and handed Mei her clothes. "Here you go. Get dressed and I'll find a wheelchair." He went over and pressed the intercom button. "We need a wheelchair, please." There was no answer, but he pretended it didn't bother him.

Mei emerged from the bathroom looking even more pale, but dressed. She'd even tried to comb her hair. The woman looked uncertain. Cen put his arm around Mei and said, "Let's go, sis."

The woman wheeled and walked out of the room in front of them. Cen saw her stop at the nurse's station and point to them.

"Hurry, Mei," he whispered. She sagged against him, and he turned to scoop her up when two security guards approached.

"You'll have to leave, sir."

"That's what we're trying to do," said Cen.

"Without her," said the other.

"She doesn't want to stay here." Cen said. "She wants to sign out. She's afraid of that woman," he said, pointing to the woman in the lab coat.

The woman walked up to them and stood there with her arms crossed. "Nonsense," she said. She looked at Cen with amusement in her eyes, and Cen hated her deeply.

"Cen," said Mei, as one of the guards reached for her. "Please help me. Don't let them do this." She backed away.

The man took Mei's arm and, as he did so, Cen whirled and punched him in the face. Then he staggered backward, surprised at the pain in his hand.

Blood spurted from the man's nose. "You little *shit!*" he said, letting go of Mei and staring at Cen. He raised a heavy fist.

"Kill him, Cen, kill him!" screamed Mei.

"Mei, *run!*" yelled Cen as he ducked.

Mei turned and took a few running steps toward the door to the stairs. The other guard moved to follow her, and Cen tackled him; with that, the injured guard let out a roar. Cen's heart sank; out of the corner of his eye, he saw the woman grab Mei by the arm. In the melee he heard Mei scream, "Let me go, you fucking bitch," and had a fleeting glance of people standing in their doors before he felt the slam of the guard's fist on the side of his head.

The next thing he knew his ears were ringing as he skidded on his side across the rough sidewalk in front of the hospital. The guard kicked him in the back and he gasped at the pain.

"Don't fuck with me again, you little prick," the man said, and spat. He kicked him again. "I think I lost a tooth. You're damned lucky I don't have you arrested." Cen heard footsteps recede.

He lay on the hot sidewalk and felt tears come, not for himself, but for skinny, frightened Mei, trapped inside.

He stood slowly, then waited for a wave of dizziness to pass. He wiped his face and his hand came away bloody. People walking down the sidewalk gave him a wide berth. The guard was gone.

He went back through the main doors into the cool, bright reception area and went to the woman at the information booth. She had short, frizzy hair and big glasses.

"Please, can you help me?" he asked.

"The emergency entrance is on Kuakini Street," she said.

"No. My sister wants to leave the hospital. They're keeping her against her will."

The door on the far side of the room swung open. It was the guard. "Call the police," he yelled.

"Please don't," Cen said hoarsely.

"The police will help her if that's true," the woman said primly, and pressed a button.

"It's Interspace," Cen said. "They're keeping her. Don't you *understand*? The police won't listen to me."

"Oh," she said. She looked confused.

Distant sirens began to wail. Black terror surged through him.

"Her name's Mei Fossant," he said. He turned and ran from the lobby.

At the end of the block he stopped running and turned. Two police were in front of the hospital, braced on mopeds, and the guard pointed at him.

He ducked down an alley and ran.

7

The Hai! Virtual Arcade on King Street was one of Cen's favorite haunts. He burst into its coolness, covered with sweat, and looked around in the dim light to see if he could find an unoccupied space.

He pretty much knew what he craved, just at this moment: old Hawaii. Maui's dream visions. A world that wasn't real anymore, if it ever had been. He didn't want to think about Mei and his inability to help her. He didn't want to think about being fired. He didn't want to think about anything. Not anything.

Cen realized, despite what he'd said to Maui, how satisfying it was to believe that royal blood ran in one's veins and that that made some sort of difference.

He was ready to get lost.

He ran through the pictographs at one of the few slots where a helmet still hung inside the clear door. Reading was a skill not assumed; all was done via icons and touchscreens.

Palm tree. Modified by spear; that meant old-time. Beginning-of-the-universe time, legend time, time that his aunt used to chant to him on Molokai as they picked pineapples in dull green fields that ran down to the sea while the wind rushed by on its way to China, kicking up red dust.

He punched it up, the programming lights lit, and the door slid open.

Cen put on the helmet and the gloves that hung next to it. He'd been in this one before, and he particularly loved it.

The canoe they'd made was almost finished. Cen caught the eyes of his brother, Aanani, and they both grinned.

They bent to lash the outrigger on. The coconut hemp was rough and hot in his hand; his back was seared by the sun. Surf crashed a few hundred feet away, beyond the expanse of bright gold sand unmarked by footprints.

For several months they'd been hacking out the center of the big felled koa tree—burning it, chipping away, tending the slow fire that they lit in the widening groove. Then they'd polished and burnished, shaped the long upturned hull into an elegant curve. Cen was proud of the lines of the boat. A fishing net rested on the floor of the canoe, along with some coconuts for drink, an ax, and a knife. The kahuna had already blessed the boat.

When they were finished, Aanani and Cen walked up the path to the taro field. Five of their brothers and cousins were cultivating lush rows of broad-leaved plants with pointed sticks; when Cen waved, they threw the sticks down and ran to the beach.

As a team, they launched the canoe. Cen's feet dug into the sand as they ran and pushed, then he and Aanani jumped inside, knelt, and grabbed the waiting paddles. Their relatives gave a shove, and the canoe surged forward. They paddled as hard as they could toward a cresting wave; they had to pass through at just the right instant. Cen broke their speed at the precise second by turning his paddle flat, and as the wave curled just behind them he and Aanani looked at each other and whooped. Then they headed for the break in the reef.

Once out on the sea, Cen was lost in the glory of the swells, the rhythm of the waves. He wished, as always, that he could just paddle on and on, island to island, stopping only long enough to kill a few pigs and pull some taro. Aanani was his brother, and they were of one mind.

He activated the island-hopping program by moving his eyes within the helmet, which he'd practically forgotten he was wearing, and as they paddled the sun set in a swift flare of pink and gold and the stars of the southern hemisphere unveiled themselves.

Suddenly a new program kicked in. He went with it, surprised. Maybe the machine was broken, giving him a little extra.

The canoe was larger, this time, like the huge sixty-foot canoes they had models of at the Bishop Museum. A claw-shaped sail was raised high, majestically filled with wind, so high that he could not see where it ended. The sky behind it was black, brilliantly starred. Chanting filled his mind, beneath a woman's soft voice saying, "Welcome to the *Hawai'i Loa*. We are going to travel from Tahiti to Hawai'i. The journey will take six weeks."

An older man stood next to him. "Our *etak* island now is Lamotrek. An *etak* is a reference point. This system of navigation is polydimensional, involving time as well as direction. It is not static, but dynamic. I will teach you the *kavenga*—the star path—that we will analyze as Lamotrek moves past us."

Cen let the immediacy of the experience wash through him. He relaxed into it, understanding that fixed point, the dynamical system with which the Polynesians had navigated the vast Pacific. Why not? This was pure Homelander stuff. He remembered when he was younger, how eager he had been to win a place on the *Hawai'i Loa,* the great canoe that replicated those fit for ocean voyages—sixty feet long, with a highly sophisticated sail.

The old man pointed at a low cluster of stars in the sky, and then punched his arm.

"You're in my goddamned space," he heard someone say.

It was the cheapest of the cheap, this arcade. Most places had individual booths.

"Sorry," Cen muttered, but his time was about up anyway. He took the helmet and gloves off and put them away. The plastic door slid shut.

He looked around before leaving.

There were about twenty martial-arts virts, and Cen could practically tell which one each of the dark dancers were in by the way they whirled, kicked, and crouched. Most boring were the pilots of space vehicles, provided with cheap chairs. Their arms moved with predictable jerks, accompanied by self-satisfied nods as another nuke burst was avoided, another time warp traversed.

Damn. Why couldn't he just have fun like those idiots? That intruder program brought back memories and, like all his memories, they were painful.

He remembered the lift of imagination he'd had when he was a keiki of six or seven immersed in educational virtuals of navigating the huge seagoing canoes that sailed the South Pacific along the old routes. The hunger he'd felt for the stars, for the lift of wind against the massive woven sail, the satisfaction when virtual land was sighted after six virtual weeks of sailing. The naïve hope that he, Cen, might one day be chosen for the privilege of actually being one of the crew; that's what all Hawaiian children hoped for then. The virtuals were based on reality; since the late nineties the Bishop Museum had sent such canoes across the Pacific regularly. The first had as navigator an old man, Tevake, a Santa Cruz Reef Islander from Nufilole, a tiny island. Illiterate, he was trained as a navigator when young. His information, tracked down painstakingly by scholars and snatched from oblivion at the last moment, had been a powerful catalyst for the Homeland Movement. The ancient Polynesians had not used sextants or compasses, but a concept called *etak,* in which the navigator imagined himself as a still point, while all of time and space moved past him. The stars and information read from swells, currents, birds were melded into something as precise as a computer program or radio fix. Everything was memorized.

An entire generation of Hawaiian girls and boys, himself included, had vowed not only to make the final cut for one of the voyages, but to become qualified to navigate a solar-wind-powered generation ship. The logo for this dream was a vast canoe with a South Pacific claw-shaped sail, designed to gather or spill wind with ease. The Southern Cross stood low on the logo's horizon. This was when IS was just coming to the islands, amidst the hubbub and excitement and hope, when it seemed actually possible that the Polynesian model for traversing vast distances might serve as the template for multi-generational space travel.

Then numb disbelief set in and grew when almost everyone associated with IS was imported. Hawaiians could, of course, work as janitors, maintenance people, or secretaries. But no matter how highly educated, it seemed that no Hawaiian ever got an entry-level position leading to work on the moon, starship design, or crew status. They were considered trouble-makers. And the great canoe program became a quaint laughingstock. What good was pride in past achievements, or the self-sufficiency gained during such a voyage? Sailing thousands of miles across the ocean without compass or sextant was fun, but that was all it was, a sop for Hawaiian children.

"You're a bunch of idiots!" Cen yelled, but in the din no one seemed to hear. Cen turned to leave, painfully aware that he was no longer able to ignore the darkness of the world just by putting some money into a machine.

When he emerged into the sunlight, he blinked.

Was that Maui on that motorcycle, gunning his engine? That was gutsy of him. Private vehicles were banned in the city. He must have slipped through the market zone—so crowded and so full of refugees that the police rarely bothered to go there anyway.

It *was* Maui, and he grinned. "I was hoping I'd find you here," he yelled. "Hop on. I got something to show you."

This guy didn't give *up*.

"Like what?" Cen asked, hoping Maui couldn't see how he was itching to get on that machine. He looked it over. Kawasaki. Vintage. He was cheered in spite of himself.

"You'll see. Out past Makaha. Come on, man. You won't regret it. What happened to your face? You must have been in one hell of a fight."

Cen shrugged. "Let me drive?"

Maui smiled faintly. "I knew I'd get you."

Cen followed Maui's directions and they safely left Honolulu. Then they roared Ewa, the direction opposite Diamond Head, past Hickam Spacebase, where the Space Hotel Shuttle landed once a week. Soon the green cliffs of the Koolaus changed to broad, dry yellow slopes covered with houses so close together you couldn't even see the ground. Cen knew their decks stuck out over the roofs of their neighbors', and that the richies that lived there sipped drinks and watched the sun fall into the ocean every night from those decks. The last of the private houses, and they'd banned high rises out here with the 2005 construction moratorium. Now that Interspace controlled most of the islands, including all the bean counters in local government downtown, only IS got building permits. And IS only built the spacebase, barracks, and labs.

The road dipped into the saddle between Oahu's two halves and then the sacred Waianae Mountains were on their right. Maui's arms gripped his waist tighter as Cen slipped between two cars at a hundred miles an hour.

At Nanakuli, at a traffic light, Maui said, "I'll take it from here."

Cen shrugged and they changed places.

The blue Pacific flashed by on their left through gaps in the old shacks, the proud and only possessions of the Hawaiian community. Palms shadowed lots of old rusting cars and barefoot children ran down the short, unpaved streets. Even IS didn't mess around out here, Cen had heard. They were as likely to get offed as not. Hawaiians were pissed, mostly, always had been, and hated outsiders.

"Why you going in here?" shouted Cen when they turned into the Japanclub. "I don't have the right genecard to get in, brah."

Maui laughed, and the laughter was left behind. Just before the main entrance, he veered off onto a narrow paved path that wound up one side of Makaha Valley. About a mile up the path became dirt.

Maui stopped. "We walk from here," he said, and pushed the motorcycle into a little alcove and leaned it against the side.

They climbed several miles along the edge of a sheer cliff. White birds wheeled around them, and far below custodial robots scooted over the green smooth turf of the Japanclub. Cen could just make out the white line of surf down at Makaha, and the sea was a deep, even shade of heart-piercing blue. He stopped and washed his face at a place where water flowed down the side of the rock; it burned, and Cen remembered his failure.

After another mile Maui touched his shoulder and they turned right onto a tiny unmarked trail made muddy by rivulets of water. They ascended through a forest of majestic koas that stirred in the wind, lit by shafts of light like an undersea scene, followed a cliff for another mile, and came to a cave mouth.

Maui nodded. "You first," he said.

Cen searched his face for a derisive grin or the intent to kill but saw nothing but an odd reverence there that made his face solemn. Cen shrugged his shoulders and walked inside.

He stopped in the dark to let his eyes adjust.

And because he was astonished.

The cave was spherical and utterly smooth, a womb of black, polished glass, about forty feet across. The inside of a huge lava bubble.

Two feet from the floor, which was covered with bamboo mats, a row of petroglyphs ran around the cave in a wide border like the decoration on the rim of a bowl.

A candle flickered within a single white skull, emitting light through hollow eye sockets, jaw, ear holes, and sinuses. The spaces where information had been gathered now gave off light that flickered across the floor. A kukui torch burned in one corner, lighting the woman who sat and watched him.

Her body looked young, supple, with none of the saggings of age Cen had seen breaking down the bodies of Mei's friends. Her breasts were beautiful, full and upturned. She was tall and majestic: pure Hawaiian, Cen thought. Like his mother.

She wore a tapa skirt and sat straight upright, legs folded beneath. Her hands rested in her lap one in the other like stacked bowls. Shimmering black hair flowed down her back and pooled on the floor behind her.

As he stared, he felt that he also was examined, tested, weighed.

Maui bowed before the woman. Cen did not, even when Maui kicked him in the ankle.

He studied her and she watched him with an amused look in her eyes. But more than amusement was there.

"Welcome, Cen," she said, and her voice was deep, grave, and formal. "We have been waiting for you."

"For me?"

"Sit," she motioned. He hesitated, then lowered himself onto the straw mat. Maui had stepped outside; Cen could see him sitting and gazing across the valley. Lush ferns fringed the mouth of the cave and the wind was constant, rushing inside occasionally with a blast that shook the torch's flame.

Cen noticed the mask at her side, a typical Polynesian mask, ferocious and tattooed. She saw he did and smiled.

"I want to ask you something. About some bones."

Her question hit him like a punch in his stomach. Suddenly he couldn't breathe.

"Kamehameha's bones," she said. "Where are they?"

"I don't know," he whispered, his voice tight.

Her face became very earnest. "We know who you are, of course. At least, I am pretty sure. I think that your mother was Poea Kalakaua."

Cen was aware that tears were rolling down his face, but he didn't blink. She blurred in front of him, and for an instant he saw his mother instead, royal, a princess—a *priestess*—

"I don't know anything about any damned bones," he yelled, and the viciousness of his outburst surprised him. He wiped his face with the back of his hand and got up. He was trembling. "I don't know who you people are or what you want, but leave me alone. Just leave me alone. I don't want anything to do with being Hawaiian."

His fists were clenched. He turned toward Maui, standing in the doorway of the cave, remembered how strong Maui's arms were around his waist on the bike, and didn't care.

"Please forgive me." The woman came up behind him, laid her hands on his shoulders and spun him around so quickly that he had no time to resist.

She embraced him.

He was tall, but she was taller. Her breasts pressed against him, but he didn't feel the desire he felt when he saw Mei's friends half-clothed.

A memory of his mother holding him rushed through his body. He began to cry, his sobs ragged and rough, and couldn't stop for a very long time.

She helped him sit again when he was through and went back into the darkness of the cave and brought out a box of tissues. This struck Cen as funny, and he began to laugh. Maui laughed with him, and the woman smiled at both of them. He took a deep breath.

"It's just that we're among the very last of the Hawaiians," she said, settling back down. "The bones—well, I won't say anything more about them. For now. They could be an important totem for us, but perhaps you were too young. Perhaps she was waiting for a daughter—a priestess—to pass them to. I don't know. She was one of the *papa alii* kahunas—chiefly kahunas who were *alii* as well as priests, the highest melding of bloodlines. She had very special duties, a high responsibility. Her death saddened me very much. What happened? The police report says very little."

"I don't know," he forced out, his whisper harsh. For some reason he did not trust this woman still, did not like her curiosity. "I—I ran away." He was ashamed that he knew so little, and even more ashamed that he didn't want to know, didn't want to even ask her any questions. He tried never to think about that night, and really couldn't, he had found, if he wanted to. There was only a queer, sick, empty feeling, one of horror. His memories of what he thought of as his childhood were becoming more vague, more far away, each day, and he was glad.

He felt a strong desire to leave, yet he did not. Who were these people?

"Your father flew to Las Vegas the night she died, and then he vanished. I don't think he'll ever be back. So we haven't been able to get any information from him. But we know that you're all alone, Cen."

He tried to hide his deep gasps of relief. Thank god, he thought, thank god.

"How do you know about my father?" he asked.

"It's our business to know," she said. This was not satisfactory, but something in her tone of voice precluded further questions.

Nevertheless, for some reason, he believed her. What would it be like, to live without being in constant fear of his father finding him?

She held up the mask. "I want to show you something."

He saw, when it caught the light, that the ritualized patterns on the face were biocircuits, not tattoos.

She rose, fluid as a dancer, and handed it to him. "Go sit on the ledge, in the sun," she said. "It's solar."

He stood and walked outside. Maui was nowhere to be seen.

He walked up the foot-wide trail a quarter of a mile, making sure not to slip on the crumbling volcanic pellets, which could easily turn into a thousand wheels beneath his zoris. The sun struck his left side.

The valley curved in and out in lovely undulations, a green lush wave turned sideways and held still by time's slow geologic velocity. A thousand feet below, the floor of the valley lapped at the foot of the cliff and widened out to meet a brilliant gold fringe of sand, and then the blue Pacific. The valley had been shaved of trees, though, and the ovals of sand traps and the cunning little Japanese bridges and koi ponds of the golf course marred it.

He thought of his mother briefly: warm brown face, loving brown eyes, her black hair like this woman's, loose and beautiful, comforting when coiled around him as she held him before he fell asleep at night.

He sat on the trail next to a tiny waterfall grotto where a million wild pink and red impatiens carpeted the ground between protruding rocks. Then he donned the mask.

The fine web inside it clung to his face lightly as a moth wing. Synthesized music stirred as if from far away, easing his transition with a whale call symphony overlaid by deep chanting. The breeze touched his face through tiny holes that permeated the mask.

He reached up and felt the raised tattoos with his fingers, pressed the portion over his cheekbone.

He was walking through a village where the sandy road was flanked by thatched longhouses. In the shade, three men were weaving something from a stack of palm fronds at their side. The moist steamy smell of roast pig drifted from an imu just ahead.

Five brown, naked children ran past him, screaming and laughing, followed by a skinny, barking black dog. Pigs nosed and grunted in a nearby pen. Cen walked on and saw a green, lush field of wide flat taro leaves and felt his mouth water at the thought of poi. There was a feel of lonely wilderness here, despite the people, of impossible distance like an unheard resonance deep within the sunny, open scene.

Enough. I get the picture.

He pressed the chin section.

Crouched behind a wooden barricade, he waited. The burned smell of his destroyed village made him want to retch, because he smelled cooked meat as well. The horde from Molokai had feasted on his cousins' flesh after the battle. He was only six, but he had one large rock with which to crush the head of a single enemy who chanced to walk below. He felt its hot, rough surface beneath his outstretched hands.

He brushed the portion over his eyelid.

And released the constellations to his mind.

He was the navigator. Soundlessly he repeated the chant, handed down by his master in Tahiti, that would lead him to new land. It had been cloudy for two days and nights. They had been warned not to start in winter but they had no choice: leave or have their vast canoe, their readied stores, their cages of pigs and dogs burned too, as their village had been. The marauders had heard of their plan but their warriors who now lay weeks dead behind them had battled furiously while the ones now with him had hurriedly loaded whatever they could. They'd risked a stop at one outer island for water.

They had been at sea one month.

Cen willed the clouds to part, and then they did.

He became lost in the voyage. He found it contained sophisticated hypertext circuits. This was his calling, what he had been born for: to steer toward unknown landfall with only memory as a guide. No sextant, only that dry ancient voice describing the way like the layers of a complex equation, shooting the information into his mind like a drug.

He felt a touch on his chin, and the story changed.

It was hard to follow because it jumped from scene to scene. The Hawaiian woman was in an operating room, her head shaved, eyes open. Calipers held the flesh back from her skull above her forehead.

Schematics, which he recognized as DNA helixes, flashed quickly before his eyes. The voice-over came and went like the voice in a dream and then he thought maybe he was dreaming.

The visions that came next were much more fleeting. A voice explained something that he didn't quite catch, something about doors in space, about research that touched on the very nature of time; Cen passed through membranes toward increasing light, each time seeing things he did not at all comprehend, each time in the company of Hawaiians, always the same faces, but engaged in different tasks, scientific in nature. Probing the edges of information as they had once pushed the limits of oceanic exploration.

Groggy, he felt his head sag, and then the mask was removed.

He saw that it was true night.

Infinity stretched before him.

"We wish to go there, too, Cen," the woman next to him said, gesturing at the intense stars of the tropical night. "The stars are the logical extension of our explorations, of the migrations of the Polynesians. I was worried about you. You've been quite a long time. I think you fell asleep."

Cen opened his mouth and closed it without saying anything. She handed him a bottle and he drank. It was guava juice.

"Who are you?" he asked.

"It doesn't matter. I am here. Our organization is larger than you might suspect, but we are your ohana, your family."

"My family lives on Molokai," he said, a stubborn sullen edge to his voice. His mother's family—aunties, uncles, cousins.

The moonlight lit her smooth, lovely face and again he thought of his mother. But his mother he could trust. He didn't trust this woman. He didn't even know her name and knew it wouldn't be given if he asked.

"We would like you to join the Homeland Movement," she said. "And—we need the bones."

He shivered and his throat tightened. "I don't want to join. And I don't know where they are. You say she was the guardian. That may be. But I *don't know where they are.*" He felt the certainty, the anger, the darkness, shooting through him again like a big wave about to drown him, kill him. He *didn't* know where they were. "Why do you keep asking me?"

She frowned as she sat next to him, her back resting on stone next to his, her long brown legs stretched out and crossed at the ankles. Her long hair hid her breasts. "You were really too young when she died for her to tell you. A child might tell others about it without realizing the sacredness." She sighed. "And yet, we hoped."

"What would you do with bones?" he asked.

She looked away, out into the valley, and said, "Perhaps they could move these stolid people, fire their imaginations. Remind them that once they were great. And also," she glanced at him, "we are gathering genetic information."

"You don't have the capability."

"No," she said, "but IS does."

He stared at her outright, shifting his butt and leaning forward. She was being very frank with him and he wondered why. He was just a street kid from Honolulu.

"What are you saying?"

"Nothing," she said.

"Something," he said. "Like you have members of your movement inside IS."

"I *said* nothing of the kind," she replied. "But Interspace is an international consortium—basically, many factions working together to promote space travel. Each of these groups has its own special interests, of course, and information isn't necessarily completely shared among them."

"These virtual biofeeds are complicated and very new," he said. "You must have money."

"Oh yes," she said. "We do. And we are looking for ways to get more."

"Like what?" he asked.

"No need to go into it very much," she said. "But of course everything in Hawaii was portioned out to the people by Kamehameha II in an effort to keep it in the hands of the Hawaiians, rather than the haoles whom he realized were stealing everything."

Cen shrugged. "I thought that most of them didn't really understand private ownership and sold it cheap to the haoles anyway. Or the Chinese, or the Japanese."

"Much of it was sold," she said. "But not all. We are very busy tracking down deeds. All we need is a strategic acre to be able to shut down their operations until they guarantee us ten full Hawaiians on the generation ship."

Cen was aware that many people, inside IS and outside, here and abroad, thought the generation ship project an impossible and absurd money-sucking chimera. But most of the island economy was based on building it, so the grousing wasn't too loud locally.

"Do you believe they'll really finish that?" he asked.

She was silent for a moment. "There are many things happening—technically, scientifically—that most people aren't aware of," she said. "Right now, to be realistic, it does seem impossible that humans will ever be able to get very far from the earth. But to be Hawaiian is to believe in the existence of what has not yet been found, Cen. The abstract promise of a place that might not even exist at all is what pulled us here in the first place. It may not take long at all to get to other stars, Cen, once time is better understood."

Time. Had he not wondered about time? He stared at the woman's profile, pale in the moonlight, as she gazed at the beauty that was spread out before them. How much did she know about him, about Kaiulani? But she couldn't know about Kaiulani. He had told no one. No one at all.

She stood and gestured outward, into the dark void that was Makaha Valley, where vertical wilderness rustled in the trades until the land leveled. The wide sandy beaches at the mouth of the valley were lit by tiny pools of light; rows of high-rise condos lined the shore. Brief flashes of white appeared in the darkness beyond—the mountainous Makaha surf, high now in winter.

"This is *our* land," she said. "Our heritage. We found it. We settled it. If it is to be used as a springboard into space, then we deserve to be a part of it, too. Instead, our children remain uneducated, and we are simply poor laborers, once again aiding, if we choose to work at all, in the construction of something that will be of great benefit only to others. We need education. We need a new vision. Come," she said, and he followed her down the moonlit trail.

Maui was waiting by the cave mouth. "He will lead you back," she said. "Please let us know if you ever need any help. We will keep in touch with you. Aloha." She kissed him briefly on both cheeks and went inside.

"She's really beautiful, isn't she?" asked Maui, as Cen followed him carefully down the moonlit path.

"Hmm," said Cen, trying to concentrate on keeping to the trail.

"She's eighty years old," Maui said.

"Sure," said Cen. "And I guess she's been living up here in a cave since 2000."

"No. She doesn't live here. She's a lawyer. Works for a big Japanese firm in downtown Honolulu. Made a lot of money, spent it on lots of experimental gene treatments. Nanotech, too. So far so good, I guess. It seems like she's really on the edge of something big. But she doesn't tell me. She was pretty glad I found you, though."

Cen felt uneasy as he picked his way down the mountain. These people knew his name, knew more about him than he knew about them; maybe more than he knew about himself. What were they up to, really? She hadn't really said what she wanted, except that she kept harping on those goddamned bones, insisting that his mother had known where they were.

"How do you know she's eighty years old?" he asked.

"She's my grandmother," said Maui.

It was chilly by the time they returned to the motorcycle.

On the way back as cold wind buffeted him Cen suddenly realized: these people have power.

Maybe they could help Mei.

When they stopped in front of his place, Cen told Maui, quickly, about Mei. "Do you think you can help her? Get her out of the hospital? If you could, I'd do anything. I'd join."

In the streetlight, Maui's eyes narrowed while he listened to Cen's story, seemed to fill with anger. His lips got tight.

"Of course," he said. "Maybe we can do something tonight." He squeezed Cen's shoulder. "That's what we're for, brah. Exactly."

He roared away, and Cen felt infinitely relieved. Two wonderful things in one day. News of his freedom from his father and help for Mei. He started for the stairs and Po came out of his room.

"Cen?"

Cen stopped on the stairs.

"Mei is back," he said. "She didn't have a key. Just showed up wearing a robe and no shoes. I let her in. Wanted you to know it wasn't *them*—"

Cen flew up the stairs and opened the door.

She *was* there, lying small on the bed.

Something about the way she was so still filled him with terror. Before he reached her, he knew.

He touched her cheek and it was cold; her eyes were staring outward.

"At least you made it home, Mei," he whispered, and closed her eyes. He went to the window and stared out. Too late, he thought, too goddamned late.

A few minutes later he was outside, in the suddenly alien night.

He started walking, aimlessly, gradually moved faster, then shifted gait and was running downhill, and into Honolulu's red-light district before he turned toward Diamond Head.

Images of Mei flowed through his mind, mixed with a trail of neon lights and the blur of smiling tourist faces as he struggled to breathe through the pain closing his throat. Stores, restaurants, bars, milling crowds, block after block after block. It took him twenty minutes to get to Waikiki and he veered makai; heard surf hiss as he ran past; saw hotel lights gleam wave breaks in black ocean. He passed the zoo, where the raucous descendants of Kaiulani's peacocks were silent beneath the click of palm fronds. Tears wet his face and he didn't wipe them away. "Let us help you," he heard Maui's grandmother say as he ran, but he didn't want the HM to help him, didn't want their imprint, their mission, their fanaticism, their superstition.

Or their strange demands.

They were the flip side of what had killed Mei.

Instead, as he ran, a single thought emerged: he wanted to *know*. *Everything*. But not with nan, as Mei had thought necessary.

He wanted to know with the power of his *own* mind. And nobody would tell him what he should and shouldn't know or what to think about it. He wanted to know everything about time. Time—the ocean that separated himself and Kaiulani.

Turning mauka, toward the dark mountains that hid the now-starry sky, he headed up the Manoa Valley. Where? Up this street, around this corner, farther, farther, his legs like rubber now and his heart pounding as he gradually realized exactly where he was heading.

A small but elegant house, trim tropical plants lit with small, subtle spotlights, the door standing open with only the screen door shut.

He ran up Ross's front steps and pounded on the screen door.

"No sex," he said, when Ross came out of the kitchen to see who it was, wiping his hands on a towel. Cen's voice was rough and hoarse. He coughed a few times.

Ross looked surprised for only an instant, then he nodded firmly. "No sex," he agreed. "That's what I said."

Cen looked past Ross into the beautiful, austere room, floored with thin polished koa, furnished in a way that said *this is a different world.*

"Well, then, come in," said Ross, his face suddenly filled with concern. "What's wrong?"

Cen stepped over the threshold into the well-lit room.

He bent over, covered his face with his hands. Rough sobs rose and shook him.

8

First, the books in Ross's library caught like wildfire in his mind.

Gamow, Bohr, Gödel. On through Einstein's explanation of relativity for lay people and then all the old popular books about chaos theory and everything Stephen Hawking ever wrote or said. And beyond. Inflation, and the theory that there are universes within universes within universes. And what about the many-worlds theory? Vilenkin, and his principle of mediocrity, in which Earth was just one of an untold number of planets that had evolved almost identically. Maybe *he* would sometime discover the exotic matter that would hold worm-holes open. So he could *stay* with Kaiulani, *save* her. He felt fierce excitement with each new idea. Others had thought of these things! Ross's library sparked weird hope and helped him want to learn how to explore the basis of such outrageous speculation. Outrageous for most people, he perceived.

Not for him.

Ross was a kind mentor, never pressuring him for sex after that first time. After all, he had told the truth: a physicist named Michael, Ross's lover, dropped by quite frequently.

Ross's computer library access had Cen on-line constantly for the first few weeks, until Ross got the bill, then he told Cen gently that maybe he ought to do his research on-site. After six months, Ross tried to send him to school, but Cen refused to have a genescan. But he passed all the academic tests with flying colors. One day, while he was pouring juice in the kitchen Cen heard Ross say to someone on the phone that there was really no reason not to award him his high school diploma here and now.

"You know just as well as I do what we have here," said Ross. "The kid's a genius."

Silence. Cen left the refrigerator door open and tiptoed closer.

"Yes, I know he's Hawaiian. Need I remind you of the anti-discrimination laws? No, he's not enhanced in any way. I can vouch for that."

Not that they hadn't tried, Cen thought. Interspace had labs that played with strays like himself and Mei, the ones so hungry for the new hormone washes or endorphin shots that they'd let themselves be mice for the mongoose. That's how he thought of IS, a slinky mongoose, an import that struck and killed the native wildlife, a furry thief that overran the land in hidden ways, in dark places. Striking like lightning.

No, they'd not laid a hand on him. But *Mei* . . .

His chest ached and he blinked back tears.

He heard Ross hang up the phone and was closing the refrigerator when he came into the kitchen.

"I assume you heard that little conversation?" Ross asked. "They want a genescan. It's standard, apparently, now, in all schools in Hawaii, public and private."

"No," said Cen. The sweetness of guava exploded in his mouth. He took another swig.

"It's a gross violation of rights," said Ross. He sat down at the table and picked up an apple, tossed it thoughtfully in his hand. "I wonder why they want them."

"I'll tell you why," said Cen. "I can't believe that you don't know. They're trying to get a fix on all the pure Hawaiians. It's because of the Homeland Movement. They're afraid of it."

"Why? They seem harmless enough. Demonstrations now and then. So what?"

"Well," said Cen, "what if the Homeland Movement could prove that their members owned the Spacebase, instead of the U.S. government?"

"That seems far-fetched to me, but if so, then I suppose that the HM would get that lease money—but Interspace has to pay someone, so why would that make a difference to them?"

"Lease money would make the HM more powerful all the time, don't you think? Next case. What if the Homelanders could prove that international laws against biological and nanotech experiments were being violated?" asked Cen.

Ross was quiet a minute. Finally he said, "Then the HM could bring the whole thing down on their heads, couldn't they?" He looked thoughtfully at Cen. "You're not involved with them, are you?"

"No," said Cen. "I'm not."

Ross gave up on public school, but without a past, Cen couldn't attend UH either. Ross solved the problem by arranging for him to sit in on a wide array of classes at UH without registering. At first it was just the intro classes, and Ross patiently brought him up to date in areas where he was weak. One day Cen looked up from his screen, as they sat at the kitchen table, to see Ross staring at him, a puzzled look in his eyes.

"You have a very good grounding in basic math. You're incredibly intuitive when it comes to geometry, algebra, trig. I have third-year students who have a hard time with calculus, but you're breezing right through it. Why?"

Cen shrugged, planted his elbows firmly on the table, and bent his head over the tilted screen resting in front of him. He hit a few keys.

Glimmers of memory shot through his mind when Ross talked like this. He knew he'd been to school when he was young. It had been a very good school. A large, open-air room, with showers pattering down on the wide banana leaves in the garden several times a day, making walls of water. The latest in educational equipment, he was sure. He remembered having to be careful to always shut the door to the air-conditioned room where the computers were kept, and that the screens were embedded in low translucent desks and that there had been huge windows looking out on blue Kailua Bay. He remembered other kids, vaguely, a few his friends; others, when he got older, snubbed him because he was Hawaiian. His parents had argued bitterly about the expense, often . . .

He frowned at his screen.

"Sorry," said Ross. "Here, let's see what you've done with that new quantum tutorial that came in the mail last month. It's good to have a guinea pig to test all these things on at last. I never knew whether to let my students loose on them or not."

Cen nodded, letting the visions Ross had called up blessedly recede. He knew that Ross was puzzled and sometimes angry about his insistence on letting his past be absolutely closed, but he'd told Ross flatly that he'd leave if Ross ever pestered him about it. If Ross had turned up anything with his snooping, he hadn't told him. And that was just fine with Cen.

The small frame house seemed empty without Ross. He was in San Diego at some meeting. It was Saturday morning, and the light lay long and lonely across the floorboards when it wasn't raining. Every once in a while the banana leaves in the yard would register the patter of drops, then the cloud would blow on down the valley.

Century sat Zen-style on the pillows Ross kept in front of his terminal. He touched it on, touched it off, then touched it on again.

He was awed at the power beneath his fingers. What he could do with such a system! Through the university, it connected to an entire world of information. But he was strictly forbidden to log on when Ross was not there. He'd been working on creating small virtual segments in his spare time; he'd told Ross that he hoped to make money, perhaps, creating virtuals for the parlors downtown. Ross had been amused, but let him play.

Now, he caressed the keys. He put his hands down at his sides, took a deep breath.

Then he reached over and donned the helmet.

He thought awhile about how best to disguise his path. It wasn't too difficult. He felt a twinge of guilt—Ross had taught him everything he needed to know in order to do that.

He was soon composing a world of swirling cloud, open sea. The surge in his mind was as nothing compared to the loosening of his heart as he worked, but he only realized that later. For now, there was a path that he could follow, direct, entire.

He had to find Kaiulani.

He worked on her for the better part of the day, although time passed without his realizing it. Her straight nose, her level eyebrows—he took and discarded a thousand possibilities for each before he was satisfied, then balanced and rebalanced them as she took shape.

He paused when doing her body—he had known her so long, ever since she was nine, flat-chested as a boy.

But now, she was almost a woman, and he formed her as such.

There wasn't any clothing like hers in the standard icon library, so he slipped on-line to the Bishop Museum and browsed through the photos of royalty. Through UH, he accessed a fashion history course and got her an appropriate wardrobe, down to the underwear.

His heart was pounding when he saved her and he lifted the helmet from his head.

It was evening. He felt a little dizzy when he stood; he went out on the lanai and sat on the floral chintz cushion of Ross's prized antique wicker chair.

Hard to believe that this glittering modern city, alight in the swiftly darkening sky, hadn't even been here a hundred years ago.

The trade winds cooled his face, arms, and chest.

In the darkness, he grinned.

He had charged the entire web bill for accessing Paris and New York to an enormously busy IS interchange.

"Where are you, Princess Kaiulani?" he asked. The churr of crickets and the skitter of geckos across the ceiling were his only answer as the stars became visible in black, ever-beckoning space.

He ascribed the glimmer of an answer that whispered through his mind to imagination. The world, the stars, the city lights all pulsed with her presence, and he fell asleep curled on the porch chair, and his dreams were chaotic and troubled.

He went back many times after that. Ross brought home a system that the university was discarding, with an old-style helmet, and set it up for him. Cen felt better when he was able to modify his pathways and leave Ross out of the picture. The helmet was a bit of a toy, not entirely necessary, yet it enabled him to test out new ideas using three-dimensional models. Slightly lazy, but fun.

After that first day, he did not bother with creating images, though he kept what he had made as the intro to his system when he logged on.

Instead he wanted to create pathways through time, to somehow link what he was learning with what he knew was possible. He could feel when something formerly abstract to him suddenly clicked, became usable. Gradually he could understand more of what he read in cosmology and in quantum mechanics. He wasn't working blindly, thinking only for the sake of thinking. He had a target, a vision of someone very dear to him, who was on the other side of a vast, raging river.

All he needed to do was figure out how to build a bridge.

Or find, again, the bridge that had once been open.

Kaiulani was his *etak,* his reference point, for all that he was learning, pulling it into a focus that no one else had.

Cen was sitting on the lanai bent over his handheld.

The gray posts framed a tropical garden that moved in the gentle breeze, shot with sun and shade. His favorite gecko, Lizzy, skittered up a post and vanished on the other side of it.

The plumeria tree was in full bloom and the sweet, heavy scent made Cen sleepy.

"Cen!"

He jumped.

"Be a dear boy and bring us some lemonade, please."

"Who does he think I am, his servant?" he grumbled to Lizzy, but he stood up and ambled into the kitchen.

As he was taking the glasses out of the cupboard—the best ones, this was the new guy occupying the rotating chair in the astronomy department sitting out there in a brand-new stiff aloha shirt—he listened to them talk.

"This quadrant shouldn't be empty, according to my figures," Hellman said.

Cen took the water-beaded pitcher from the fridge and poured sweet lemonade over the ice. He knew exactly what Hellman was talking about. Ross had mentioned the problem that a recent viewing at Mauna Kea had brought up concerning gravitational lenses—one that he'd been called about, and Cen had thought about it for two weeks.

"It isn't," said Cen, as he brought the tray in and set it down on the table. Hellman was a heavy, pale man recently arrived from Germany. He was sweating slightly as he sat on Ross's exquisite bamboo furniture. "Here," Cen said, and handed the fat man his lemonade.

"What do you mean?" asked Hellman.

"He doesn't know what he's talking about," said Ross. "Thank you, Cen."

"The hell I don't!" Cen said. He ran out onto the porch through the French doors and grabbed his handheld.

"I found him about a year ago," he heard Ross explaining.

Cen rushed back into the room, so eager he almost tripped over his own feet. "Now, take a look at this."

"Sir," said Ross, acknowledging defeat.

Cen ignored him. "I used Guth's Constant for these calculations."

As he spoke, he could almost feel Kaiulani at his elbow, drawing his thought further and further on. If only he could get to *her*, was always his thought when he approached these problems, as if *she* was the problem, her existence, her reality. His files were named after her, Kaiulani1, Kaiulani2, and his memory of their meetings was always the springboard from which he departed.

After twenty minutes, Hellman said, "Why didn't you tell me you had a genius on your hands? I thought he was your, ah, I mean . . ."

Ross laughed nervously. "He's just a fanatic, that's all," said Ross, looking proud and worried at the same time.

"Are you enrolled at the university?" asked Hellman. "You should really attend my seminar. You look rather young for that, but . . ."

Cen glanced at Ross, aware he'd been something of an idiot. "Uh—" was all he could manage. He shouldn't have said anything. But he'd just been so excited.

"Well," said Hellman. He stood and slapped Cen on the back, hard. "You've given me a lot to think about. Talk to Ross about it." He gathered up his papers and left.

Ross sat on the couch. He leaned forward, crossed his legs and stared into space for a few minutes. Cen didn't interrupt him.

"Where did you get that information?" Ross asked, finally.

"I don't know. I just . . . thought about it."

"You haven't been talking to anyone? You haven't accessed the work I've done on it?"

Cen started to feel annoyed. "What do you mean?" he asked. "Are you saying that you think that wasn't my own work?"

"Keep cool, young man," said Ross. "I'm just saying that it's stunning and excellent, and yes, that I don't really see how you could have thought of it. Bright as you are. It's quite a leap. One more thing," said Ross, as Cen grabbed a glass off the table and swallowed the last of his juice.

Cen looked at him.

"It's about Kaiulani."

Cen choked on his drink, gasped for breath. He ran to the kitchen sink and coughed until tears ran down his face. He turned on the faucet, bent his head, and splashed his face with cold water. Ross followed him into the kitchen, sat in one of the painted wooded chairs by the table, and draped his arm over its back.

"Mean anything to you?" he asked.

"What's it to you?" asked Cen, leaning against the sink, speaking in a whisper because his throat was raw. "You think I stole it all anyway."

Ross sighed. "I don't. Not really. It just seems the most sensible alternative, even given the fact that you're rather extraordinary. I really think that's the approach to take if anyone talks to you about it. You need to be more discreet. I'm sure that I told you that everything on my system is open to Interspace. I've spent half my life trying to stay out of their way. Everything has changed since they came. Everything's more tense. Nothing here is separate from them. You're either in or you're out. I got tenure by the skin of my teeth, and there's no reason why it had to be that way. I had good offers elsewhere—but Michael is here. IS has a good thing going. And who can criticize them? They have everyone in the world here who knows what's going on. The best and the brightest in the world. Like—oh, like Los Alamos in 1944. Like the complexity and chaos theorists in the nineties. And they *know* that nothing's happening, that everything is stalled. That the best minds in the world can't get them out of the solar system. And they've got a hold on every one of those people, one way or another. They keep us from organizing. They have ways of letting you know what might happen to you. Who's going to risk that?"

Cen felt sick. "Why doesn't everybody just stand up to them at once?"

Ross continued, but the anger had gone out of his voice. Cen knew Ross was just laying out the facts, as if he were a little kid. "It's hard to know who to trust. Ah, well, I think it's going to blow, eventually. It can't go on like this forever. I know that you put all kinds of protection on your work about—what's her name? Kaiulani?—but who do you think you are? Don't you know that wormhole travel is the hottest thing going right now? It's their last resort. If they had any hard information, they'd be on easy street."

Wormhole travel. He'd never even said it to himself. But that was what he was thinking about, working on. If Kaiulani was real, if their meetings were real, and he thought that they were. "I think I'm nobody, that's who," said Cen, feeling tired and defeated, yet curiously angry at the same time. "Who cares what I think?"

"Apparently Interspace does," said Ross. "They've been around, asking about you. They want to know who you are, where you're from. If you're affiliated with the Homeland Movement. It's well known that the HM limits their membership to pure Hawaiians. But what am I going to do now that you've got Hellman interested? He's one of their biggies. Anyway, I decided to look into this stuff in your files they're so interested in."

"You didn't ask *me!*" shouted Cen.

"Sorry," said Ross.

"No, you're not."

"Look," said Ross, "these are really very strange things for someone your age to be thinking about, much less render into mathematics."

"No, they're not," said Cen. "Most mathematicians do their best work before they're thirty."

"You don't actually *believe* in this stuff, do you? I mean, even if wormholes exist beyond theory, how could they actually be manipulated? What kind of engineers are you going to find to build a gate, hold it open, make travel predictable? The old thought was that it took some sort of what they called exotic matter to hold it open—a form of matter that might possibly be created by an advanced civilization in the far future. But if IS—or anyone—could do something like that *now,*" he said quietly, almost to himself, "it would be more dangerous than atomic energy. And if you knew anything about it—if you could give them just one of the many bits of information their think tank could use even in the most peripheral way . . . you *don't* believe in this, do you? And Cen . . . " Here he hesitated. ". . . these are not nice people. Who do you think brought Hellman to Hawaii, anyway? What do you think the University of Hawaii is all about, now? He invited himself over here—and maybe he got what he wanted. Well, I should have known better. If by wildest chance you *do* believe in this, you'd give it up, wouldn't you? They could twist your whole life, don't you see?" He sighed. "What have I gotten you into?"

Cen could *see* the concern on his face. Ross had been good to him, very good. He wanted to say, no, I know nothing, and yes, I could give it up. Just for an instant, he wanted to.

But it would be like killing her, killing Kaiulani. He could feel her sometimes, *needing* him, *counting* on him to get back to her. No matter how long it took.

Suddenly, as he looked out the open windows at the mango tree, and the bright orange birds of paradise massed below, he realized what he was trying to do, despite the careful distance he'd built the past few years between what he had experienced and what seemed sensible.

He was trying to—he *wanted* to—change the course of her life. His breath came short as ramifications filled his mind, like flowers blooming and dying in accelerated motion, as if he could look down corridor after corridor of possible times and see death at the end of every one. At the thought of her death (but she's already *dead,* repeated that part of his mind that he hated. Dead!), his chest contracted and tears began to burn in his eyes.

As he turned to run from the room, Ross rose more rapidly than Cen thought possible and grabbed his arm, spun him around. He stared into Cen's eyes for a long minute.

"Yes," said Ross. "I think you do believe." He let go.

Cen staggered backward and slammed into the door frame. The pain shocked him and he started to cry.

"I'm sorry," said Ross. "I didn't mean—"

I know, thought Cen as he ran from the house, I know, I know, I know.

9

By the time Cen was eighteen, he didn't remember when he had first begun to wonder whether Kaiulani might be a manifestation of some sort of time displacement. He only knew that there seemed to be no spells, no frame of mind, no stance of being that would call her back to him. He just kept on reading, studying, until all that energy was used, transformed. Ross had made him the son that he had never had. Cen still felt cut off from himself, but he accepted it now. He was somehow incomplete. Kaiulani was missing. He hadn't seen her in years. Years!

One afternoon, Cen climbed the twisty streets that laced the flank of Punchbowl crater.

He entered the cemetery with its rows of American graves and knew that beneath them were the lava rocks of scattered heiaus, the sacred platforms where kahunas had killed people to please the gods. The ground was riddled with bones.

Bones.

He remembered what Kaiulani had said about Kamehameha's bones and smiled. What a serious girl she had been. He shivered and something dark ran through him, thinking about bones. He turned instead in thought to her, who was so very bright.

He was no closer, he realized, to figuring out who or what she was than he had ever been. He seemed to butt up against mental barriers whichever way he turned. It was like the Name of God, only worse. His only hope was to study the limits of time and space wherever those were—in astronomy, mathematics, physics, cosmology. And if *place* had anything to do with it, there was a simple explanation for why he had not seen her in years. She was in school in Europe. She was in Berlin, being proposed to by a rich German count, and turning him down because she didn't love him. She was in the south of France, "flirting," as said in a letter—"better to have my fling now than later!"

Looking down the white stepping-stone rows of rectangular markers set flat in the ground, Cen felt the energy that gave the site its real name, Hill-of-Sacrifice. The gods had to be appeased, the gods of the moment, whether they be the gods that lent fury to Kileauea in fountains of flaming lava or the gods who whipped the entire world to fury and claimed these rows of bodies as their snack, their obviation, their very proof of existence. He had lately been studying history. It made him very sad.

He gazed over the rim, down the steep brambled hillside, past the Spacebase at Hickam. At the end of vision, he could see faint Barber's Point, a gray blur on the horizon, hallowed ground believed by Hawaiians to be the soul's departing place. The blue Pacific ceaselessly caressed the beaches at Ewa, Nanakuli, Makaha.

The heat-released scent of ginger and garlic drifted upward as someone prepared dinner in one of the tiny frame shacks that snugged together below on the steep hillside and were inhabited by Asians who couldn't speak English. He wished there were no gods, but knew there always would be, however they might disguise themselves. Their horrific grimaces and gaping maws lined with dog teeth may have found more graceful forms in other cultures, but Cen thought that maybe the Polynesian expression was in the end pretty honest after all. Give them all they want, stuff food into their mouths, keep them off your own back.

As for him, he had a goddess, one whose civility more than countered the savagery of centuries spent satisfying the greed of the Hill-of-Sacrifice.

He sighed and started back down.

With Ross next to him in the silent, slow electric jeep, Cen turned down the fork in the road that would take them to Haleiwa, the sleepy town that they had to pass through on the way to Oahu's North Shore.

The road was two-lane blacktop; the high golden grasses around them were occasionally specked by green, waving cane, a remnant of days gone by, and hummocks of trees were scattered across the plains that sloped down to the blue sea. To the left, the dry Waianaes arched over the saddle where eons ago two lava flows had met. The Koolau Mountains, laced with clouds, were to the right.

By law, nothing was allowed to change here—to keep it pristine and old-timey Hawaiian for tourists.

Until, of course, IS came up with a use for it.

"Isn't it a little late in the season for this?" asked Cen.

A brief smile flitted across Ross's face.

He was unusually pale. He'd been sleeping too much lately. "There must be something wrong with me," he said now.

"Yeah, like maybe you should eat more. Maybe you should use a little common sense. Maybe you should just sit on the beach today."

"No," said Ross. "Wavesporting is one of the things I'm truly good at. You don't understand. A good run will be the best thing for me. I mean, most people my age have been married for twenty years. Dave and John, Will and Ben—"

"They don't seem like the happiest people in the world," said Cen. Ross had seemed oddly regretful about his life lately.

"Well, then maybe I should just have my sequences checked. I'm tired of living this way. I'm tired of people hating me for no good reason."

Cen shrugged. "It's your life," he said.

"That's right," Ross said. "It's my life."

They stopped in Haleiwa for espresso. The sun strengthened. Red, green, and yellow kites fluttered on the porch of the little store, along with a row of T-shirts on hangers. Ross wandered next door and examined a wavesuit. "They've really improved the jets on these new models," he said.

"It's a stupid sport," said Cen. "Give me an old-fashioned board any day. I hate to think of you playing with tons of water like that. I mean, I haven't even *surfed* in three years. Not since I saw Kino die. You kind of lose your nerve."

Ross gazed out at the wind-roughened bay. He set his jaw. "Let's go down the coast," he said.

When they pulled into the parking lot at Waimea, Cen felt relieved. "The warning flags are up. They won't let you out." He got the cooler full of beer and ice out of the trunk. "Gorgeous day, though, isn't it?"

"They let the surfers out," said Ross, with resentment in his voice.

The row of bobbing people sitting on their boards was tiny, half a mile out in the bay. Whenever a wave swept in, they were briefly hidden.

"They're idiots to go out," said Cen. "I think those waves are at least twenty feet."

He saw Ross glance at his neon green suit, neatly folded in its clear bag, wrapped around the aerodynamically powerful fins, the set of tubes running to the sleek mask.

The suit used water for its jets, compressed it and squirted it out in a way that a skilled sporter could manipulate quite finely by minute flexings of various muscles, the way a surfer flew up and down across the face of a speeding wave just by a slight shift in stance. It was an advanced form of bodysurfing. Kids used the suits in still water or on small waves. People like Ross moved into ever-heavier surf, seeking the thrill of mastery when they slipped through a million tons of roiling water in stunning acrobatics.

Now, the offshore wind kicked spray from the tips of the waves; it streamed seaward in frail white banners. "I bet some of those surf idiots are going to signal for a heli pretty soon," Cen said. "I wouldn't want to come in through this mess." The wide golden beach, which slanted steeply down to the place where the powerful waves sucked at the shore, was filled with spectators.

"It's a great day," complained Ross. They took mats and the cooler and carried them past the lifeguard stand, where three guards watched the surf nervously with binocs, radios at the ready.

They drank beer for about two hours. Cen read, but Ross kept looking out at the surf, silent. Cen had fallen asleep when he heard Ross jump up. "They took the flag down," Ross said.

"So?" asked Cen.

Ross was already gone.

Cen watched him walk down to the shorebreak fully suited ten minutes later, about a quarter of a mile away. "Idiot," Cen muttered. He jumped up and ran down the broad golden slope awash in deep, surging foam, its pull even here so strong that Cen had to fight hard to keep his footing. The lifeguard whistled at both of them. Ross, small in the distance, just smiled, waved, and plunged into the water. He jetted beneath a run of three and Cen watched anxiously. Then Ross bobbed up and waved before he turned and jetted, flowing over the waves like a tiny green fish in the deep blue sea, cutting across the face of high, translucent waves just before they broke, crouching, at last, on his heels and hands before standing as the white breaking crest of a wave chased him across its face. He then somersaulted in a gorgeous triple spin, head tucked, arms holding his knees to his chest.

Cen glanced back and saw that quite a crowd was watching the show.

Ross kept it up for forty minutes, dazzling, in top form. When he finally bodysurfed in on the third giant wave of a set, Cen's heart was in his throat as his friend vanished beneath the deep, turbulent shorebreak that was even more sudden than that of Sandy Beach, known to bodysurfers as The Back-Snapper.

Then he saw the green suit.

He waded into the surf, let it pull him right to Ross, helped him stand and lurch, half running, up the beach. Ross pulled his mask off and flopped on his back, breathing hard, laughing.

"Have fun?" asked Cen.

"What does it look like to you?"

Cen looked up the coast. Kaena Point was steely gray, shielded by clouds that swept over it without leaving rain. He felt the menace of the winter sea in his bones, drifting into his mind again and again like a series of endless waves.

"It looked—wonderful," said Cen. "Let me help you get

your suit off. You shouldn't go out again until summer, I think."

"Summer! It's flat then," laughed Ross.

He went out again the next week, and the next. Once Cen refused to go with him and felt dismal all day as he waited for Ross to return. He knew he shouldn't worry. Ross was championship material.

When he did die, it wasn't from lack of expertise.

The police found a clogged jet when they examined his suit. That explained why he'd lost control at a crucial instant on a mammoth wave and tumbled beneath the tons of roiling water that broke his back. They ruled it "accidental death."

Ross's affairs were in such disarray that Cen knew that he had no intention of killing himself.

When it was all settled, the house went to a sister from Kauai that Cen hadn't even known about. She came herself to take possession, a golden-haired tight-lipped woman with a dark tan and little to say to Cen. "I'll give you a week to get your stuff out," she said. "The voiceprint people will come next Tuesday to change the locks."

Cen was a few months from completing his bachelor of science degree, but he let it drop.

He found himself taking the magrail out to Makaha more and more often. Once he even searched for the beginning of the trail up the mountain but could not find it.

To his initial surprise, he began to drop into the Pantheon, an old bar a few doors down from the place he'd lived with Mei. He was not too concerned when he started to drink, or even when he started to drink too much, or when he blacked out.

But the second time that happened he woke up at a trailhead just below the Pali. It was dawn. He dimly remembered hitching a ride up here the night before.

Groggy, he walked into the concealing jungle a few yards, stripped off his clothes, and soaked in the chill stream until he was numb. He put his clothes on, looked up the trail, and walked a quarter mile. But an odd, dark dread overtook him, stopped him like a wall. Dizzy and covered with sweat, even in the chill morning air, he turned back, crying.

That evening, he was back in the bar, nursing his fourth beer. By the second his lingering headache had been cured. He was going over some new virtual ideas in his mind while a tourist disdained to use the correction mode on the karaoke. Onstage, three life-sized male Tahitian virtuals shimmered. The two women who had activated them sat on one side of Cen, laughing, with a huge pile of tokens. Cen looked at the tokens and sighed. It might be a long night.

Someone on his other side said, "Buy you a beer?"

Cen shrugged. Then he glanced at the man, took in the IS look of him, then said "No thanks."

The man ordered it anyway, and it sat at Cen's elbow getting warm. "You know who I am," he said. His head was shaved, and he looked unnaturally neat and clean.

"Not interested," said Cen.

"Look," the man said. "You really can't pass up this deal."

"Try me."

"We'll pay for your Ph.D. Anywhere. Anywhere you choose."

"Fair exchange for a brain?" asked Cen. But his heart jumped all the same.

"Look," said the man, and Cen could tell that he was making a big effort to be reasonable, "Your friend Ross really kept us at a distance for a long time. You really don't know that much about us, but we can really help you out. Make your career. He was pretty damned stubborn about your work, believe me. He wouldn't tell us anything, and then he got that lawyer on our case, but—"

"What?" Cen's voice came out in a whisper. "What do you mean, wouldn't tell you anything? About what? *What* lawyer?"

"Come off it. You know what I'm talking about. Your math. He was the most stubborn person in the world—"

Without even looking, Cen moved his arm and pushed the beer into the guy's lap.

He shoved his own stool back. He walked across the dark wood floor, past smiling faces. What the hell did they have to smile about? What the hell did anyone have to smile about?

Had Ross died for *him?*

He waited impatiently at the Aloha Tower stop for the mag-rail to Kailua. He thought he saw Kaiulani appear next to him for a minute, in one of her white dresses. "You leave me alone too," he said, and stepped onto the open train.

He leaned back in his seat, feeling dreadfully sick. When would this nightmare end? When would this horrible blackness vanish? How could what *he* knew, each wild hypothesis about the parameters of what he had begun to call the Kaiulani problems, be of interest to anyone except himself? It was all so absurd, the craziness of a kid who smoked too much pakalolo. Why should Ross—good, kind, intelligent Ross—be the victim?

His sobs were harsh and echoed in the empty car.

He got off at the Nuuanu Pali stop and walked a hundred yards down the Kailua side. Just inside the trees, he found the trailhead. It was narrow, unmarked, overgrown, and faint.

Yet he knew it was the right one.

He wondered how he had forgotten for so long. He knelt and dunked his head in the cold, rushing stream, and when he lifted it, his mind was absolutely, painfully clear. Clearer than it had been in years.

He had been ten, and his mother had walked in front of him, very quickly.

Cen took one step, then another. Soon he was moving at a good pace.

As he walked he remembered it all.

Rain swept in a great sheet across the windward side of Oahu and pattered suddenly on the leaves of the koa forest all around Cen as he and his mother continued to climb. The gusting wind chilled him and he hugged himself, keeping a close eye on the slippery rocks of the trail.

The shower passed swiftly, leaving the air cold and smelling of damp earth.

"When will we be there, Mom?" he asked, panting.

She walked ahead of him, slim in her khaki thrift shop

shorts. She had knotted her plaid cotton shirt beneath her breasts; her back, between shorts and shirt, was brown. Her long, straight black hair was loose and moved with every gust of wind; a few wet strands stuck to her back. She seemed not to hear him.

"It's getting late," he said, more loudly. His legs ached, but she was starting to walk even faster. "Won't Dad be worried?"

She stumbled, said, "Damn," then resumed her stride. "No, sweet kukui, he won't be worried."

But Cen knew that they fought a lot, shouted after he went to bed almost every night. After he had a few beers, sometimes Dad hit Mom. At least, Cen was pretty sure he did. Where else did she get those bruises? Dad never painted like he used to, either—paintings he had once sold through small galleries in Honolulu. Not since some haole woman critic made fun of him, called him a "primitive Hawaiian" in the paper, and made people afraid to invest. Cen had watched him light that paper on fire and toss it into the air, had been afraid when the wind wafted it skyward spread-armed, a ghost that whitened to fragile ash then fragmented as it tipped the banana tree fronds.

"We don't have to go," he said. "I'm getting cold." He didn't know what she was up to.

She took a narrow trail that forked to the left. Cen snagged a ripe yellow guava as he walked and rolled the sweet pink insides around in his mouth, munched the seeds. He picked a second.

"Don't eat too many of them, Century," his mother said over her shoulder. She was the only one who called him by his whole name. "You'll get sick." How did she always know what he was doing?

They walked along the crumbling knife-edge of the peak for almost a mile, and Cen became terrified he might slip, fall to the floor of the deep green valley, almost a mile below. Wisps of cloud floated halfway down the face of the near-vertical ridge that curved around ahead of them, cloaked in dense green rain forest.

He concentrated on his breathing and on what he saw so far below, trying to calm himself.

The valley below the Nuuanu Pali was crowded. Subdivision roads etched minute black paths between squares of the plain white housing where Interspace workers lived; where he lived. A blue tile roof caught the sun next to Enchanted Lake, where rich Interspace execs lived.

Not so scary. Beautiful. Interesting.

The path dipped and they entered a clearing.

They were only a hundred feet below the top of the ridge; Cen decided that rain alone kept a narrow waterfall splashing into the rocky pool before them. A blast of chilly air bent the ribbon of water for a moment; then it fell straight once more.

"They're back here," his mother said.

"What?" he asked, but his question was drowned by the hiss of water washing stone.

Cen scrambled after her to a narrow, slippery indentation behind the waterfall. The scent of cool damp stone mingled with moist, earthy smells. He copied her handholds as she angled up, ten, twenty feet, terrified that he would smash into the shallow pool below.

He was bleeding from many small lava cuts when she reached a narrow ledge, sat back on her heels, and pushed aside a thin slab of stone about a foot high. She reached into the revealed cavity with both hands and pulled hard; a long, narrow bundle emerged.

She set it between them.

It was wrapped in crumbling tapa cloth, made from pounding bark until it was supple and flat. Her long, brown fingers untied the gnarled vine that held it together, and unfolded the tapa with great care.

Cen's breath stopped.

"Bones?" he asked.

"Go ahead, touch them," she said. "After me, you'll be the last one to know where they are."

He stared, uneasy. "Are they *human?*"

"Kamehameha's bones," she said.

Cen touched them. They were rough and yellow. He felt kind of empty and dizzy. It was weird to think that they were once wrapped in flesh and blood like his.

"Why do *you* have them?" he asked. He knew, of course, from the genealogy chant, that he was descended from Kamehameha on his mother's side. Sometimes, when his father was yelling at his mother, Cen heard him shout "princess," then laugh, as if it were a joke.

"Your grandfather was a kahuna, a priest," his mother said. "At least one person has known the secret all these years. These bones have much *mana,* much power. At least, that's what they thought at the time." She smiled slightly and glanced at him. "They still do," she said. "Someone must know. Later."

She was quiet as she enfolded the bones within the tapa, a bundle more than half as tall as she was. The man must have been a giant. His bones clunked together in a hollow way. Cen saw that she tried not to make any new creases in the tapa, because every time she did, the cloth, which was like fine brown paper covered with tiny, precise geometric designs, would break.

She wrapped the old vine around it again and tied it. She shoved the bundle into the long, dark hole, slid the tall stone back in front of it, and piled several smaller rocks against that. A bank of ferns drooped over the place, bright green in the gloom of the rain forest.

"That's all," she said.

It was a long walk back to the trailhead where they'd left the car, but she was as quiet as ever. He asked, "What do you want me to do with them, why did you show them to me?" a couple of times. She just said, "It's a sacred duty."

His dad was in the tiny kitchen when Cen pushed open the screen door, rattling jars in the refrigerator and muttering. He pulled out a beer. The picture of Queen Liliuokalani, some regal-looking old Hawaiian that his mom kept on the wall, jumped when the old man slammed the refrigerator door.

"Hi," said Cen, and smiled. Sometimes it worked.

Today it didn't. "Don't 'hi' me," the old man snarled. "I want to know where my dinner is. Where the hell have the two of you been?"

"We went for a walk," said his mother, right behind him. "Don't worry, it just has to heat up." She pushed back her hair, started up the mic, and took some plates from the cupboard.

"A walk, my ass," he said, leaning against the doorjamb. "You've got a pretty soft deal here. All you've got to do is cook and clean and spread your legs once in a while. Once a month, if I'm lucky, if you feel like it. While I'm out fixing those fucking robots every day." His dad upended the beer and swallowed half the bottle. Cen wondered if he should go to his room or just leave the house.

"I used to work," his mother said, so quietly that Cen could barely hear her, "before Interspace brought in the Japanese teachers for the Japanese, the Korean teachers for the Koreans, the Czech teachers for the Czechs. You always forget that *you* didn't have to have a job for years. And you don't seem to remember that I sent you to tech school, too, and pushed you to *get* that job. Otherwise all you'd do is surf and paint and live off my teaching money. Ha! Do I have the only clear memory around here?" She turned to him, her hands bristling with chopsticks. Her chin lifted. Her eyes were very black.

"It must be great to be so good and so very smart, too," his father snapped back.

Cen's stomach felt funny. It always started this way.

Maybe if he just acted normal, got some juice out, tried to joke around, they'd stop. He went to the cupboard and got out a glass. But he couldn't think of anything funny to say. His mind always seemed to get stuck when they fought.

Cen jumped as his father slammed a cupboard door his mother had left open. "I guess that's what you *think* I did, anyway. Maybe it's good you don't have a job. You spent all the money you made sending this lazy kid to a fancy school." His dad's voice was rising. "I don't see what difference it made. He's pretty dumb, if you ask me. Nothing special about him. He's a little hoodlum. Have you seen that crowd he hangs out with? Smoking pakalolo already."

"I wonder where he gets that from?" she asked, setting a dish on the table with odd care.

The chill in her voice made Cen feel very bad. He couldn't deny the pakalolo. He took a cold bottle of juice out and started to pour it into the glass he'd set on the counter.

"And why do you teach him all that stupid Hawaiian stuff anyway, all those superstitions," his dad continued, in his low, grating voice. "No matter *who* he is, they're useless. Why don't you face it? He's a bad kid."

A vision of Kamehameha's bones flashed in front of Cen's eyes. "Those old superstitions." Dad would really be mad if he knew what had made his dinner late. Nervous, he turned too quickly, bumped his elbow against the counter, and tried to grab the slippery bottle of juice.

It smashed on the floor.

"You stupid bastard!"

Cen bolted out the door into the rain, ducking under the up-raised arm of his father.

He cried as he ran down the road to the beach, zoris wet and slick and slapping his feet, fists clenched. He was only ten, but tall for his age, and his father was just a little shrimp, living on Primo beer, dark sweaty quarts of it every day after work, then picking these fights.

When he got to the beach park, he was glad the rain had kept everyone else away. He dived beneath warm small waves and surfaced further out, lay on his back and kicked hard, staring at the black hole in the mountain across the bay that was going to be the maglaunch. He rocked on the gentle swells and rain pecked at his face. Salt water leaked into his mouth, tasting like tears.

It was after dark when he started to walk back home, and he shivered in his wet clothes. Dad would be passed out by now and Mom would be sitting in the kitchen reading.

But as he got closer to the house, he heard more shouting.

The grass he walked across was rough and wet. Cen climbed up on the cinder block under the kitchen window and peered in through a crack in the blinds.

His mother was standing next to the door to the living room, beside the kitchen table. The glass top was littered with the remnants of dinner—chunks of rice, a bottle of soy sauce, a few scattered shreds of bok choy and bean sprouts. The exhaust fan pushed air out next to him and it smelled like garlic and beer.

"I've been working all these years." His father. His mother

laughed bitterly, but his dad overrode it. "That's right. Paying for the little *bastard* and you."

"Don't call him a bastard. He's yours, and he's *alii.*"

"That old crap. Wake up. That means nothing now. Nothing. Less than nothing. I thought so, and I was wrong. You think it makes a difference that you're from a line of kahunas? Oh, sorry, the *papa alii* kahunas," he said, his voice mincing. "The *chiefly* kahunas, the *royal* kahunas. So close to Kamehameha." Then his voice became menacing. "So *what?* What does it matter? You're dumb as a post. Why do you fill him with all those superstitions?"

She laughed gently, but something in her laugh made Cen shiver even more. Or maybe it was the desperate look in her eyes, which he could see even from across the room.

"It *does* matter," she said. "It means everything."

Her face looked different in the fluorescent light. She looked older, more regal, her long black hair flowing around her fierce face, the face of a warrior, he thought. The face of someone he didn't even know. Her hand on the table was shaking.

"You're crazy," said his father. "You've ruined my life with this Hawaiian crap."

"You believed in it once," she said. "When we were young—remember? We believed *together.* Until you started drinking—"

"Yeah, sure, it's always my fault, isn't it?" Cen couldn't see his father's face, but he knew the sneer—the curled lip, the terrifying, cold eyes. "I'm sick of you hounding me!"

He shoved his wife in the chest with the flat of his hand; slapped her face so hard that the sound hung in the still night.

Call the police, said the voice in Cen's head, but he couldn't breathe. He tried to shout, but his throat squeezed it to a low, hoarse sob.

"Stop it," she said, her voice ragged. "Stop, I'm warning you, I've had *enough!*"

Instead, he took another menacing step toward her.

She stared at him, her face twisted, tears running down it, and fumbled in the pocket of her smock.

Hand shaking, she pulled out the dull black gun they kept in a dresser drawer.

"No!" screamed Cen.

He jumped down and tore around to the front of the house. He tried to yell for help as he ran, hoping their Russian neighbors would hear, and that they would understand, but his voice sounded far away, like somebody else's.

He slammed through the screen door and rushed over to his struggling parents. He leapt onto his father's back, screaming and pounding with his fists, then shifted and reached for the gun.

He managed to get his hand on one of theirs, he didn't know whose, and he started shaking it hard, trying to loosen its grasp on the gun.

His arm was twisted, then felt as if it had been wrenched off as the gun exploded.

His father roared; turned, and with one arm sent him flying across the room. Cen's head hit the edge of the table and he lost consciousness.

When he opened his eyes, his head hurt like hell and his entire body ached. Especially his arm. He reached up and felt where it hurt: sticky.

He jerked upright.

His mother was crumpled onto the floor. A halo of blood was splattered onto the wall around her head.

He sat up and vomited onto the floor until his heaves brought up nothing, then leaned back against the cupboard, exhausted, not looking at his mother but at a pattern on the floor tile—white, crisscrossed by pink lines that formed diamonds. Blood had puddled in one of them, and his eyes began to follow the narrow, twisty convolution of red that led into it.

Then he hunched forward and hugged his knees.

He wondered why he felt so calm, and where his father was. Maybe he thought Cen was dead too. Maybe he'd come back to make sure. He should run. Now.

But he didn't seem able to get up, not just yet. A slight, slow trembling moved through him, peaked and subsided as if he had caught a sudden chill.

He finally rose, covered with goose bumps, and turned on

the faucet. He looked at the water for a minute, trying to remember why. He flared the stream with one finger.

Slowly, he washed the place on his head that burned, and his face until the red rivulets no longer swirled across pitted white porcelain.

Face dripping, he reached up and took his mother's tin box from the windowsill. She kept a little money in it, and a few other things. He stared out the window.

There was no reason to call the police. There was nothing they could do now.

The memory of the gun's coldness flashed through him, and he realized he didn't know whether or not it was still there and that he didn't care.

He turned, looking very carefully only at the chipped blue knob on the screen door. Night sounds filled the house. The ragged banana trees outside the window clicked in the wind, sounding like rain. He reached up with his left hand and turned off the light over the sink, still staring at the doorknob.

He walked toward it, holding the tin to his chest.

"Damn you, Kaiulani," Cen said, his legs aching. He raised his eyes from the trail and gazed about. He was high on the mountain, and he didn't even remember getting here. A cold, misty breeze ruffled the treetops. He lifted his hand and brushed his face. It was wet from the last quick shower. Or tears.

He shivered. His chest hurt. He began to walk, but his legs felt very heavy. He trudged upward, *knowing*.

Knowing that he had killed his mother.

And knowing that Kaiulani was not real.

She was not even a ghost. He had made her up entirely, perhaps from stories his mother told him, perhaps from something he'd learned when he was in school so long ago. Couldn't people do that, split their mind, hallucinate?

And why should the bones be real, either? He had made that up like he'd made up Kaiulani, to make himself feel better, to have one good thing in his life. He couldn't trust anything he *thought* he remembered, could he? He meant to laugh, but it was a harsh sound, pulled away by the wind: funny how his mind could twist things around. Yeah, pretty damned funny.

Except the blood was real, and he had killed his mother.

All that stuff his father had said, about him not being *alii,* about it not mattering—that was what was true. He'd invented that bone story and hugged it to him, to keep himself from thinking about the truth. He had made the whole world into a ghost to keep from remembering. This mountain, this gentle rain, the sweet smell of hidden jungle flowers—all phantasmas, like old Hawaii. Unreal as his imagined destination, or all his crazy ideas about time and space. When he was a kid he'd run around on these mountains like a wild goat with gangs of childhood friends, playing Hawaiian, playing Chiefs, playing the Olden Days. That was the only reason he knew where this trail was, and it led nowhere special. It was time to go back. Time to get real.

Then he rounded the bend and stopped.

A delicate waterfall drifted down the face of a high cliff and shattered to foam in a tiny pool. White flowers bloomed, fairy-like, from black lava rock.

He wanted to turn and run.

What he saw was a shimmering curtain that he could easily rend. It would all turn to dust if he dared to look too hard, a fragile and ephemeral decoy of beauty sent by the darkness in mockery of what he, Cen, really was: a murderer.

Yet, he realized as he stared, he did remember. For some reason. This was the place he could come to at night, after he woke sweating from dreams of blood, and hug to himself. If he dared to go further, could he bear to lose this solace, this idea that somehow he was *someone?*

Why not?

He might as well lose everything at once.

He walked across the clearing and leaned against the wet stone, pressed his body against it, raised his arms.

His fingers entered hollows that seemed to reach out for them. He moved like a spider across the face of the rock.

The rock was real. He could feel it. Just like he had felt the cold steel of the gun just before it killed his mother. If only he hadn't fought with them—

He sagged against the rock, nestling himself on a shallow shelf, and cried.

He saw his father, cross-legged on the lanai, painting, cursing when the mimosa flowers littered the air like pink butterflies and landed on his work. He remembered his proud presentation of money to Cen's mother, not once, but for several years. Cen felt the darkness and alcohol to which he'd retreated when that big shot New York critic laughed at him and his Hawaiianness, even when his wife had told him that it was nonsense.

A sensitive man, Cen realized, his face wet, his cheek pressed against the rough lava. A bitter man, caught between his wife's idealization of old Hawaii, his own artistic dreams, and the necessity of living in the present the haoles and changing times had made. Alcohol and ignorance had killed his mother.

"Not me," he whispered. That was the darkness that had always lurked, ready to spring, he realized. Not the fear of his father finding him. If he had been capable of thinking about it, he might have realized that his father had known that he'd be quite rightfully blamed, and vanish.

No. Cen's fear had been that, in the melee, it was *his* fault that the gun went off.

It was a thing impossible to know.

"Not *me!*" he shouted, and it echoed through the small clearing and rolled down the mountain into the misty rain forest.

Cen reached fiercely for the next hollow in the rock. "Not real?" he muttered, panting. "Just a ghost? Just stupid superstition? We'll *see,* Dad. We'll see."

Excitement and fear filled him like a fluttering of tiny yellow o-o birds in his stomach as he reached the shelf. The large rock grated as he pulled it across the stone shelf. The waterfall roared in his ears. His hands shook as he pushed the rock aside and reached inside.

"*Alii,*" he whispered and slid the rough package out.

The last hands to touch it had been his mother's.

Cen sagged back against the rock, pulled his legs up to his chest. Gladness filled him like light, and he gasped with laughter and shook with tears.

"You were right, Princess Victoria Kaiulani. I did know."

He felt as if she were next to him, watching.

But was it Kaiulani?

Maybe, instead, it was his mother.

Maybe she could rest now.

He unfolded the old tapa cloth and revealed the bones that had haunted his childhood dreams.

Time became for him so fluid, and so very beyond anything that he could possibly comprehend, that he may have stood, holding the bones as tightly as one would hold one's last—or first—shred of reality, for maybe minutes. Maybe hours.

Perhaps he felt the power coming from them just because they were real. Maybe it was just that they validated him, made him strong in a way he never had been before. The past slid in behind him as if it were an alternate past: the past he had tried so very hard not to see. Perhaps so hard that it had made him crazy.

No. For the first time, he thought not.

For the first time in his life, he felt utterly real.

He told IS he wanted to study in London. He was not surprised when they said no problem and made everything easy. He knew he was going to play a dangerous game. But he didn't care.

He only knew that he had a responsibility toward many people now. His mother. Ross. Maui's grandmother. She had asked for the bones, but Cen still thought they should be left in peace, and left them so, in their ancient place.

And he knew one other thing. He had to find Kaiulani once again. Find her and save her. He might even be able to fulfill, eventually, her childhood demand to *see* the bones, to *touch* them.

He didn't know how. He just would. And he knew he would see her in England. He knew it.

Crazy? No.

He was whole, now. Anything was possible.

Lynn

Asia 2034

10

Each jolt of the bullet train shot curiously distant pain through Lynn's leg, and that part lasted forever, and then the jolts shook her entire body. "Wake up!" she heard in her dream. "We have to get off here!"

She did not like waking as that brought the pain closer. She rolled over to escape the troublesome dream but someone yanked her from the berth along with the sheet, which was pulled from her roughly and tossed to the floor.

"Hold her up, will you?" she heard hissed next to her ear as she sagged back onto the hard berth and blinked as a pencil flash caught the side of Akamu's face; she was suddenly fully awake. Akamu's arm came around her awkwardly and steadied her.

"I'm fine," she whispered, breaking out in a sweat as nausea twisted her stomach. "Let's go."

The lev shuddered and hissed to a halt; she reached up and grabbed a metal bar. In the dim light she saw wiry Hawkins, wearing a green jacket with many pockets that all bulged. He bent and hoisted a large straw basket from the marred floor. Lynn had no idea where they were. It was night; the lights outside the window were irregularly placed, illuminating a phantasma of jumbled shapes and a crooked brick-paved street where dim lights burned.

"Come on," said Hawkins, and opened the door to their compartment.

They moved through an aisle where people dozed upright on both sides. She stumbled into a wire box holding two chickens and the birds woke, squawking. Baskets overflowing with lumpy garments and wrapped packages dangled from overhead hooks. Parcels were jammed everywhere. One woman, hair tied back in a scarf, stared at them as they made their way down the aisle.

Lynn tried to ignore the pain in her leg and the gnawing desire for more opium. Hawkins touched the platform access button and machinery whirred. The door stuck halfway open but it was quite wide enough for them to slip out to where the chill night air woke Lynn fully. The door slammed shut as if glad to have leave of them. She'd never seen such a run-down train in her life. It was a far cry from the modern levs she was used to riding in the sleek rich Pacific Rim cities where she usually did business.

As she stepped down to the platform, supported by Akamu, she leaned on him much more heavily than she had intended because her leg threatened to buckle. She wished she could go to a clinic, but if she really was on some sort of high priority wanted list, as Hawkins claimed—outlandish as that seemed—all it would take was a drop of blood to identify her.

So Lynn set her jaw against the message from her troublesome leg as it briefly bore her entire weight, angry at her helplessness. Dependent on an old man and a boy and unable to communicate with anyone else.

"That's good, sit her down," she heard Hawkins direct Akamu over the vibration of the lev as the boy led her across the concrete platform to a bench by the wall. Stars flecked the thin slice of sky between the station overhang and the lev; she shivered and saw her breath puff out. She hated cold!

Hawkins hurried over to the lev and said something she couldn't understand to a man standing there. Her father's friend scowled, then fished something from one of his pockets and handed it to him; the man nodded and grabbed the metal rail next to the lev steps and jumped aboard as the lev pulled away from the station. A motion caught Lynn's eye. A shade pulled up—someone looking out the window at them. The woman who had stared at them as they passed through the aisle.

"Hawkins—," she said.

"Ignore her," he said tersely. He looked around the empty platform. "Don't talk."

Then the lev was gone and she saw the town more clearly.

Across the tracks was a mixture of crooked brick and wooden buildings, clumped together like town houses, some with four stories, some with as many as six. The windows were small and dark. In the streets small tables piled with various goods alternated with fortune tables, their glow illuminating the faces of those bent over them. She did not know what time it was but perhaps it was not yet midnight. She wasn't sure how big this town was; it looked fairly small from here. And ancient—settled and lived in since long past forever. She stirred, nervous, looking around. That woman on the lev—she could have easily sent some sort of message to someone by now.

"What are they doing over there?" whispered Akamu. Hawkins walked up and down the unlit platform, glancing back and forth with quick jerks of his head.

"Fortune-tellers," she whispered back. Like on the streets of Chinatown in Honolulu—the tortoiseshell, the coins—though now chaos-based algorithms generated the cracks in the holographic turtle shell or the arrangement of the holographic yarrow straws that appeared after the customer paid to activate the program. The fortune-tellers usually carried their light tables to a park at the foot of Nuuanu every evening and did excellent business until after midnight. She was a bit surprised at Akamu's question. It meant that he probably didn't get out much. But then, many people from "out country" didn't venture into Honolulu.

She jumped at the roar of an engine shifting gears and then out of the night swung two bright headlights. In their glare she saw Hawkins's face soften in relief.

The truck continued past the station, and she was struck by irrational disappointment. If she didn't know herself better, she would have said she was on the verge of tears. There was nothing she could do and that was the frightening thing about it all. She calmed herself in her usual way; she watched her breath, not the puffing white external breath but the path of her interior breath, and turned it golden as it went up and down her spine. She noticed her surroundings dispassionately: long black shadows cast by the two streetlights across the tracks; green sign telling the name of the station, she presumed, in Chinese. What did it say? She squinted at it. Chinese kanjis looked the same as Japanese, but sometimes had a different meaning. She felt a pang of sadness remembering that she'd planned intensive language skills for little Masa; her own inability to master foreign languages had always made her feel stupid. Well, it looked like the kanji for house, in Japanese, and the population was 2,723. Or was that the elevation? An old man and young woman across the tracks conferred for a minute. The woman gesticulated earnestly; the old man shrugged. She smiled widely, then they pulled up folding chairs at the table of a fortune-teller.

Now that the lev was gone the air smelled fresh and calming. Lynn tried to recall some of her journey and remembered only vivid colors and that life had seemed quite wonderful, despite the minor details of sickness, injury, and the need to flee for her life. Great stuff, that opium. She felt her forehead—hot; did she have a fever? She remembered her mother, long ago, laughing at her—"You can't tell yourself, sweetie."

After about five minutes Hawkins motioned to them; she tried to stand by herself and Akamu caught her before she fell over. "Shit," she said, and caught Hawkins's frown and clamped her mouth shut. He was right. The less people heard them speak English, the less trackers would have to go on.

She hobbled around the side of the station to the back, leaning on Akamu. Relief spread through her as they rounded the corner, and she saw the large, ancient truck waiting, lights killed.

Hawkins looked both ways and motioned to them. He boosted her up into the cab and shoved her over toward the driver. The seat was big enough for all four of them and, after a word in Chinese from Hawkins, the driver shifted into a low, laborious gear and they rattled into the night.

They were on a hard-packed dirt road and vibrated along roughly at about forty kilometers an hour, Lynn guessed, because the speed panel was just an occasional flash when they went over bumps. Its flicker illuminated a blank satmap screen, set at an angle for the driver, pocked with melted-looking black spots and half-filled with cigarette butts. The truck had started out smart, probably twenty-five years ago, but had been effectively dumbed down.

But it still ran.

The driver was Chinese; he glanced at Lynn once but she couldn't read his reaction to her obvious Japanese background. She felt even more helpless; the traditional enmity between Chinese and Japanese was very old and very strong—not on her part, certainly, but out here, who could tell? He wore a flat-looking hat with a short brim and was not as old as Hawkins but older than she was. He wore some sort of work jacket and heavy laced boots caked with mud.

He and Hawkins exchanged a few more words. Lynn looked at Hawkins, pointed to her mouth, and raised her eyebrows. He shook his head slightly.

After they left the tiny town behind, the only thing that kept her awake was the constant pain of her leg. Hawkins reached into his pocket and handed her a patch in a packet across the sleeping Akamu. She wanted to ask him what it was and looked at it. She didn't want to take any more pain medication, opium or not; she was already disoriented enough. But she definitely needed some sort of antibiotic. She tilted her head questioningly; he pillowed his head against his hands and closed his eyes—she shook her head and slipped the patch into her pocket. He shrugged.

She almost smiled when she thought of all she was doing without—even the irrelevant detail of her sunglasses, which seemed magical in this environment. What the hell time was it, anyway? How could people live like this? The truck sounded as if it might fall apart any minute; she slipped her hands into her sleeves and longed for simple heat. The driver glanced at her and pulled a knob at the dashboard. It came off in his glove and slipped onto the floor, littered with old newspapers and empty pop bottles. A blast of hot air hit her in the face. She tried to lean over and find the knob, but the man touched her shoulder, shook his head, shrugged, and smiled.

The Milky Way was amazingly intense, dusted across the sky

without any interference from cities. She could see no glow on the horizon that might indicate the presence of one. She glanced at Akamu, thought of the sophisticated flat she had bought him. Did he still have it? Perhaps, using it, she could get some inkling of where they were, if Hawkins wouldn't tell her. It probably had lev schedules in it. Some geography programs.

She pushed her hair back; it felt matted and greasy. How long had she been out? How long had they been traveling? She thought of the sleeping pills and wondered how necessary they had been for her—perhaps they had just been a convenience for Hawkins. And how had he found Akamu? Was Hawkins simply her father's friend, with only her welfare at heart? Or was he to preserve the life of Akamu so he could be used by IS? But for what? Hadn't IS tried to kill Akamu a few days ago?

Well, who else?

She realized that though that was the most obvious explanation, she was uncomfortable with it. She had no proof. She was limiting herself by believing that was the only possibility, and thereby limiting the chances of their survival. *Someone* had tried to kill him, and *someone* had probably, but not necessarily, tried to kill her in Hong Kong. That was about all she knew. That and a mixture of possible motives. She knew nothing about Hawkins's motives either and did not know whether he was communicating with her father. And if Hawkins was in touch with her father, was her father passing information along to IS or not? It would, actually, be best to be rid of Hawkins, if possible.

She stirred, trying to relieve her pain. Now she was drenched in sweat. She had a fever for sure. And she was starving. What the hell had she gotten herself into? Nana would surely laugh . . .

They were heading north, because to the right, the horizon was lightening.

Although the road was a straight line on land flat and relatively featureless, she saw distant mountains etched in black. She glanced at Hawkins, but he was sleeping. Where was he taking them? And why?

The sunrise was magnificent but immensely different from

tropical dawn. It seemed to take forever, gradually coloring the horizon with a glow of brilliant yellow that for some reason reminded her of her mother, long dead. Lynn was surprised; the second time she had thought of her mother today, when she hadn't thought of her for years. Must be getting light-headed. The yellow intensified for ten long minutes, then flushed to pink as the sun emerged, a bit of orange that soon was blinding. There were no clouds to the east, but she saw a front line of high dark cloud splitting the sky, now a powerful clear blue.

The driver pulled a thermos from a pocket in his door and opened it. Steam bore the delicate scent of hot green tea. Her stomach rumbled. He handed her the thermos and she took a gulp. He gave her a greasy, crumpled bag, and she opened it. Black bean pastries, her favorite. She smiled at him and took one, bit into the sweet, sticky bun. Great. Enough carbohydrates for a whole day—of sitting in a truck, anyway. Akamu stirred next to her. She thought he might wake, but instead he settled back to sleep. She jerked her head up once or twice, then slept herself.

Lynn was filled with dismay as a great jolt woke her. She saw that they were entering a disheveled village composed of a row of—yurts? Yes, yurts. She rubbed her eyes. Was this possible? Yurts—and prayer flags.

Akamu was wide awake, staring with his great brown eyes. Hawkins leaned forward, holding onto the battered dashboard with both weathered, thin hands, his eyes searching and eager.

She felt like a child at a carnival, enwrapped in a mad swirl of color. She gazed in wonder at a million prayer flags, iridescent silken rainbows, strung between yurts and flying from freestanding posts, snapping in the wind. The aftermath of the opium seemed a state where colors were intense and glorious, yet somehow distant. She rather liked it, except that she still ached all over, and the jounce of the cab on the rutted dried-mud road did not help.

Atop a small hill to her right, a geodesic dome perched on a gleaming foundation of smooth beige plast, pale green hexagons shimmering like opalescent glass, with small satellite dishes affixed at the intersection of struts. A path through short golden grasses went straight up the hill to the dome.

From the double row of ten or so yurts, which formed a sort of road between them, emerged people, pointing and waving. Beyond them, across an expanse of grassy plain, was a permanent village, of sorts—a brief row of two and three story buildings, glowing white beneath the midday sun.

And above those buildings, as incongruous as a great white whale beached on a mountainside, was an ancient temple that seemed to radiate energy from its many gilded roofs, emerging from a cliff as if carved from it. It took Lynn's eyes a long time to travel across it, for it was a behemoth, a legacy of the age when lamas ruled Tibet with their exotic blend of Buddhism, superstition, and raw power. It seemed quite as splendid as pictures of the Potalaoma in Lhasa, her archetype of Tibetan architecture. Vast verandas jutted out here and there, and rows of tall, dark windows like the rectangular hollow eyes of an immense and powerful god drew horizontal lines across the temple.

Sunlight ran along great swooping expanses of electrical lines in the village, but the lines did not reach the yurts. As the truck jolted to a halt, she saw that the yurt roofs incorporated photoelectric cells.

With a last grinding of gears the truck lurched to a halt. The driver leaped from the cab, leaving the door open so that in the new silence the prayer flags seemed more insistent, and the cries of excited children filled the dry air. He went to the back of the truck; Lynn looked through the small grimy window and saw giant straw baskets filled with shiny red apples, some sort of hard-looking green fruit or vegetable she did not recognize, many baskets with lids, and several large cardboard boxes. Beneath all this she glimpsed a small stack of lumber and some plywood.

The driver pulled some ropes free with long backward motions of his arms. Hawkins yanked on his door handle and heaved at the door with his shoulder before it popped open; he got out and stretched. Two men and one woman emerged from the dome and went to help the driver. They all looked Chinese. The woman and one man were wearing western clothes; the other man was wearing a padded silk jacket.

"I think we're in Tibet," said Akamu. "I figured out some vectors on the lev." The expression on his face was one of ecstatic absorption, completely open, all sullenness and confusion gone. He wants to learn, Lynn thought, with admiration. Where some children might be terrified and need reassurance, he was excited. She felt great pity for this intelligent, strange boy. How must it feel to know that someone had tried to kill you? Well, he seemed to be coping all right.

"Tibet? Does Tibet exist?" But of course it must—Hawkins *had* said that was where they were going. Lynn realized that her fever must have broken; she was rather weak, and everything she saw looked dazzlingly bright. The stage before you die, she told herself sourly.

But looking out of the window, she lost her bad mood. The wind blowing through the cab was chilly but exhilarating. It indeed looked as if they were on a high plateau. Blue mountains fled downward toward a distant plain behind them; ahead was a wall of jumbled peaks faceted brown and white. She must have been exhausted to have slept while the truck arduously climbed to this height. The troubles of Interspace, of her brothers, even of her own obsession with collecting famous DNA, seemed far away. For a timeless, floating moment, anyway. Then she reached up and felt the earring. Still there. Her attempt to obtain it had been meant as a decoy to cover her flight with Akamu; according to Hawkins, it was the reason that they were being followed.

She wondered.

"Well, the *Tibetans* think Tibet exists," Akamu said, in a tone of voice that told her just how uninformed he found her, bringing her back to the present. "Just like Hawaiians still want the rights and property stolen from us. I guess it could be confusing. Tibet almost regained its status as a sovereign country during the Pacific Rim Alliance Summit in 2007. But China withdrew from the alliance before the negotiations were complete. Anyway, I think that's where we are. We went through two villages this morning, and it looked to me as if the names were in Tibetan. Old Hawkins doesn't talk much. He wouldn't answer any of my questions. At least he let me keep my flat. Look, I have the Dalai Lama's speech here, the last one he gave before he died—but there are other *kinds* of lamas, too—" he pulled out his flat.

"I believe you," she said. "Better put it away for now." More things she didn't know. Little things, like world history. How daunting. To know so much and yet so little. How limited one person was. She sighed and closed her eyes. Her sustaining vision of humanity exuberantly cascading into a future where knowledge and connections endlessly expanded shrank into a small isolated dot. Then Tibet morphed inside her eyelids from a tiny country on a map into a man who stood up and stepped on the dot. She opened her eyes with a start.

Akamu shoved his flat back into a yellow-and-purple pack and started walking toward the yurts. She looked at him more closely. The pack and jacket were new. She looked at herself. Her clothes were new, too. She hadn't even noticed before.

"What day is it?" she asked. But he was too far away to hear.

Lynn slid gingerly from the high cab and began to follow the strange entourage down the twisted narrow dirt lane—bulky Akamu wearing a too-large green jacket and clutching his high-tech treasure bag, thin mysterious Hawkins of unclear motive, and three huge black barking mastiffs. But the bobbing of the dogs as they hurried ahead upset her stomach somehow and then the blue of the sky overwhelmed her with simple brilliant intensity and she fell. Or fainted.

At least she thought, lying a moment later hands stinging, head ringing as the buzzing dots she saw resolved once again into the strange yurts, that must be what had happened. Chagrined, she tried to rise and felt several hands grab her and others dust her off. Clucks of sympathy filled the air. Akamu stared at her. Remembering how they had met, she decided that he must think her a rather weak specimen.

Testing her leg, she realized that she had simply been too bold and that lack of sleep and food and whatever was wrong with her leg had combined to cause her embarrassment. *"Help* me, if you don't mind," she snapped at Akamu and was then ashamed when he did not grin sardonically but with gravity stepped forward and took her arm. "Like this?" he asked.

"That will do," she said, relieved that Hawkins, who had turned at the commotion, did not seem alarmed that they were speaking. "Thanks."

Hawkins vanished into the door of a yurt near the dome, then emerged leading a tall, thin Tibetan woman wearing jeans and a jacket composed of beautiful wide bright stripes, yellow and red. The high leather boots she wore were dark and well-worn, soft-looking, with a fur cuff at the top. Her long black hair flew loose on the wind; seeing the long tendrils wave wildly Lynn almost expected to hear them snap like prayer flags, matching the energy and intelligence Lynn saw in her face and eyes as she approached. She held out her hand to Lynn. "Hello," she said, "I'm Sattva. Come on down and we'll have a look."

She had an air of quiet authority. For some reason Lynn trusted her immediately in this strange welter of events, people, and places she had suddenly become immersed in. She felt insubstantial and light as a ghost. Or maybe just light-headed, she told herself, as she hobbled downhill with the help of Akamu.

The huge black dogs barked and intricately garbed children watched as they walked through the lengthening shadows of the yurts.

Up close, Lynn realized that the yurts were more sophisticated than she might have guessed. Although from a distance they seemed made of heavy pounded wool, they actually sparkled with various filaments woven into the fabric. Smart-glass, with all sorts of communication capabilities.

She followed Sattva into the fourth yurt on the right, Akamu trailing behind.

Inside Lynn wondered what the funny smell was and then her eyes adjusted to the dim gold light bathing the faces of people sitting on layers of rugs around a low table. "Butter lamps," whispered Akamu next to her, looking around, his eyes filled with amazed curiosity. She was sure her face held the same expression. "That's what smells," he said.

"How odd," she murmured.

Swathes of azure, yellow, and red silk woven through the ceiling supports shimmered in the flickering light; two walls of the yurt were covered with permanent-looking shelving of heavy dark wood. These were filled with neatly stacked dishes and other household utensils. In the center of the shelves, on a low table jutting out with a yellow pillow in front of it, was a holo field. It manifested Tibetan characters, which flowed in and out of existence smoothly and swiftly. A variety of systems such as the one she had purchased for Akamu in Hong Kong lay scattered around, and even several of the faddish ergs that could be easily molded and remolded for the user's comfort. She glanced at Hawkins, but he was crouched next to the table, holding a cup of steaming liquid, chatting, and appeared not to notice her.

"Over here," Sattva said. To one side was a low bed covered with a rough blanket. "Take your pants off."

Lynn looked over her shoulder and saw that the group of people about ten feet away around the table were not paying the least bit of attention to her. What do you care anyway? she thought. Aware that the last time she had bathed had been god knows how many days ago, just a sponge bath on the lev and a quick dry-off, she tried to bend down and open her new cheap running shoes. The shoes brought back a hazy memory of Hawkins bursting into their compartment just as the lev left some station, breathing hard, tossing down an armload of stuff.

Sattva quickly knelt and unsealed the shoes for her. "Sit," she said, and Lynn gratefully sank onto the bed. Sattva removed Lynn's shoes and helped her pull off her jeans.

Lynn saw that her right calf had a nasty, swollen gash, which was mottled blue and yellow.

"A bullet?" Sattva asked, feeling up and down her calf gently.

Lynn winced. "So Hawkins says."

Sattva rose and pulled an aluminum basin from one of the

shelves. She walked over to the fire and poured some boiling water from the kettle that hung over it into the basin. She ripped open a packet and scattered white powder over the water, took a cloth from another shelf and wrung it in the steaming water. "This'll hurt," she told Lynn; it certainly did. She bathed the gash made by the bullet for several minutes. "Should have had stitches," she said. "Too late now." She looked up and grinned at Lynn. "No doubt you can have the ugly scar taken care of later if you like. Has it been imaged?"

"No," said Lynn.

"Okay. Let's go."

"Let's go?"

"Stand up."

Sattva helped Lynn up and wrapped a thin blanket around her like a skirt and tucked in the end. Lynn watched with amusement, as if this was happening to someone else.

"We have to go to the dome," Sattva said. "Mikhel," she said, raising her voice, and a burly man sitting with the group at the round table turned his head. "Think you can carry her?"

"I can walk," protested Lynn, but Mikhel strode over and swooped her up.

"I can carry you," said Mikhel, jouncing her up and down, "How many kilos? Probably about half my weight, eh?" He had very short brown hair, large, fierce blue eyes. Two earrings of complex geometric design dangled from each of his ears.

"Hundred and ten, last time I checked," she said. "Pounds."

In her strange post-opiate state, memories of her father carrying her rushed into her mind as they stepped out into the chilly afternoon. How caring he had been, so long ago! The surrounding peaks seemed to bob up and down with Mikhel's long stride as he and Sattva climbed the dirt path to the green dome.

Sattva opened the door for them, and Mikhel carried her in and laid her gently on the long flat imaging table that sat to one side. It was plain and smooth, just a cool slab about seven feet long and three feet wide.

Sattva stood for a moment looking at the panel at the foot

of the table. She pressed a few pads and they beeped. "Damn," said Sattva, "I can never remember my code." She pushed more pads then smiled. "Activate," she said, and a clear tube slid up and around from where it was stored in the base. Lynn looked through it at the rest of the dome.

There really wasn't much inside. Black cushions were stacked neatly in piles of three and four around the walls; the floor was composed of large, translucent hexagons that looked slightly yielding. A low counter ran around the perimeter of the dome, and she saw on it an object that looked like a halo, a head-sized, glittering circle. At every vortex of the dome itself was a crystal; the sun came out from behind a brief cloud and scattered tiny rainbows across the walls and floor and Sattva's face.

Sattva said, "Image right calf."

Lynn felt rather than heard the low vibration, and Sattva moved around to study the hologram that Lynn could see hovering next to her through the clear imaging tube. She couldn't remember when she'd last been imaged. Maybe when she had broken her arm when she was seven.

"Hmmm. Three-ex," said Sattva.

Lynn saw blobs of yellow and red and dark green enlarge fuzzily for an instant then focus sharply.

"What do you think?" asked Sattva.

Mikhel moved closer to the image. "Is that a cracked bone?"

"Yeah," said Sattva. "A fracture of the fibula. That's the small long bone in the lower leg. I guess the bullet just nicked it. Do you see a bullet in there, Mikhel?"

"I guess not," said Mikhel, shrugging his broad shoulders and frowning at the image. "I am not into these medical things."

"He's a gravitational lens expert," Sattva said to Lynn. "From Moscow."

"Oh," Lynn said.

"But I think that's what happened," Sattva continued. "See? That's the small bone. No big deal, but it probably hurts."

"It does," Lynn said. "It seems like a big deal to *me.*"

"Oh, sure," said Sattva. "Off."

The clear tube rotated back into the base. Sattva leaned over Lynn, bracing herself with her arms, and her hair hung down on both sides of her copper-colored, broad-nosed face. Lynn saw that it was filled with amusement and compassion, a strange but somehow appropriate and reassuring mix.

"What I mean is that I have some stuff here that will fix it, if it hasn't gone bad. Let's see here . . . "

Sattva pulled out a drawer and rummaged through it. "Mikhel, where—oh, here it is. Great, all ready. Hmmm—it expired last November. But it's probably all right. I love it when this stuff is already mixed." She held a shrink-wrapped package that consisted of a syringe filled with some sort of white stuff. She unwrapped it and paused. "Now, how?"

"That's mender, right?" asked Lynn.

Sattva nodded, frowning. "I know I'm supposed to inject it, but . . . do I have to touch the bone with the needle? Where *is* the bone? I mean how can I tell without the imager . . . "

"They used it to fix my broken arm when I was a kid," said Lynn. "If you just put it in the general area it migrates to the bone and bonds with it. Then it crystallizes and mends the fracture."

Sattva pushed the makeshift skirt aside and held the end of the needle against the side of Lynn's calf, about four inches below her knee. "Like here?"

"Looks about right," said Lynn. "Fire away." She gasped at the sharp pain.

"Okay?" asked Sattva. "I guess I could have numbed you with . . . something in here. Sorry." She tossed the syringe in a small can on the counter. "Anyway, I think you should wear a removable splint; that's supposed to be completely hardened in about twelve hours. She moved back and turned to her cupboard. "Here we go. Want some opium for—"

"No!" said Lynn, swinging herself around and sitting up. "I mean, Hawkins gave me some."

"Good," said Sattva. "It's the best pain reliever you could possibly have. I don't know where he got it—the Chinese are pretty anal-retentive about it, like most of the world, but that's kind of historical. It's not really addictive anymore if you don't want it to be. After the pain is gone we just give you some opivert."

"That's okay," said Lynn. "I'm foggy enough as it is. Maybe I'm at the opivert stage. Or just past it. Can you tell if that's infected? I think I've had a fever."

Sattva felt the wound. "It's cool."

"Hawkins gave me antibiotics too."

Sattva frowned slightly, then said, "Mind if I take a little blood?"

It *was* just a little; she touched a tiny vacuum pipette to Lynn's finger and released the drop of blood it sucked up into another machine on a console that was revealed at a touch of the panel.

"Ah," she said. "Hawkins said you were in Hong Kong, right?"

Lynn nodded.

Sattva brought up a holographic earth, about a foot in diameter, which turned slowly. Colors blossomed on its surface and spread, mingling with other colors, which faded as new eruptions spread and swirled.

"This is an epidemiology map," Sattva said. "All disease information from every clinic in the system worldwide is constantly updated and disseminated via satellite." She spoke a bit louder. "Hong Kong."

"I have something similar for mitochondrial tracking," said Lynn.

"Shhh," said Sattva, with a grin. "I haven't got this fully trained to my voice yet. *Hong Kong,*" she repeated.

This time when she said Hong Kong a small red dot enlarged to a circle around Hong Kong. Sattva said, "Fix, match, readout."

A calm female voice came from a small speaker in the counter. "This is a new virus that has arisen in the past two months, probably originating in Beijing. We project a seven-month trajectory that will follow the path you see." The globe rotated slowly, and purple areas multiplied rapidly, sometimes in seemingly unrelated places. "Fever, nausea, lasting five to seven days. Complications unusual in young otherwise healthy victims. Rest and fluid recommended."

"Thanks," said Sattva. "Off."

"I have a virus?" asked Lynn.

"On top of everything else, yes. But I guess it's run its course, pretty much. A bullet, eh? You and Hawkins will have to fill me in."

"Um—I guess you're not a doctor," said Lynn, as Sattva smeared the wound with ointment and bandaged it. She wondered how old Sattva was. Forty? Forty-five? Her long black hair was streaked with silver. But nowadays it was hard to tell. With the right treatments, she might be close to eighty and look like this.

"Not even close. Level-one mountain rescue training. Then I decided I wasn't cut out for medicine. I went into particle physics instead—about as abstract as you can get. One of us *is* a surgeon, but she had to go home to Benares because of a family emergency."

"So what are you doing here?" she asked, glancing at Mikhel. A particle physicist and a gravitational lens expert?

In the pale green light she saw their eyes meet.

"What's that over there?" she asked, pointing at the halo.

"Well," said Mikhel hesitantly. Sattva opened yet another low, wide drawer and Lynn saw that it was full of lightweight splints—Gore-Tex with aluminum ribs. She sorted through them.

"Arm—arm—wrist—there we go. Leg. Let's try a medium." She unsealed the wrapper, knelt, and Velcroed it around Lynn's calf.

"You don't have to tell me if you don't want to," Lynn said, but it came out sounding annoyed and definitely insincere.

"It's not that—," said Mikhel.

"It's not *only* that," said Sattva, standing. "I think that splint will do."

"You're some sort of religious cult, right?" asked Lynn, feeling more and more rude. This is what happens when you take opium, she thought.

Sattva's laughter was almost as deep and throaty as

Mikhel's; they were genuinely amused. "No," said Sattva. "I *hope* not, anyway. That's not what *I* want. The crystals have nothing to do with religion. Crystal lattice is an excellent storage and transmission material."

"What are you storing? What are you transmitting?" Lynn stifled a yawn in spite of herself.

Mikhel rose from his cushion. "The headpiece picks up, focuses, amplifies, and relays electrical impulses from the brain. And vice versa—it can be used rather like an MRI to cause the magnetic alignment of particles in the brain. And the crystals in the dome create a constant field that is ten to the eleven hertz." He moved to pick her up.

"But why?" she asked. "That's pretty low, isn't it? Not radio or satellite or anything, right?" She didn't know a whole lot about such things. Mikhel slid his arms beneath her legs and behind her back and picked her up easily; once again she felt like a child. As Sattva opened the door she talked to Lynn.

"That halo is just a sample somebody brought back from Hong Kong a few months ago. It's not much good to us. It was designed to initialize a brain to transmit impulses to a quantum computer." She laughed. "Benny forgot to pick up one of *those.*"

"Does such a thing exist?" asked Lynn.

"Well," said Mikhel, "We know of a few. At various universities throughout the world. They are all different, though. The artificial intelligence people have been working on them and these computers are supposed to be extremely fast and small and smart. And not very stable. But they are coming. They will be the next great breakthrough."

"Hmmm," said Lynn. The ache in her leg was subsiding to a numb throbbing. "So what's the dome about?" she asked, as Mikhel carried her through the door.

Sattva latched the door, then followed them. She said, "Some people used to believe that that particular frequency affects the microtubules in the brain and causes the brain to be in a quantum state that is unentangled with matter. During that time the wave function is suppressed," said Sattva. "These people believed that unentangled state was what caused the phenomenon of consciousness. The domes were just a way to finely control a particular state of consciousness. They're really kind of an artifact, actually. We bought this from Oxford; they still have a bunch of them, apparently, in some warehouse. I was excited to get it and see for myself what it was all about. It was even pretty interesting to *make* it—just a lot of bags of powder we mixed with water and some forms. It's come in handy."

Lynn thought that the temperature had dropped several degrees while they were inside—along with the sun. A strange place. At least she knew what microtubules were. All plant and animal cells were sheathed with a cytoskeleton made up of microtubules—long tubes only nanometers in diameter.

"Let's see," said Lynn. "The microtubules are made of . . . tubular dimars, right?" Tiny, interlinked peanut-shaped protein units.

"Yes," said Sattva, walking next to her. "Well, Penrose postulated that tubulin dimars actually control the synaptic connections of the brain in a way that is noncomputational—that is, in a way that can't be reduced to mathematical representation. Experiments *have* confirmed that the tubular dimars are capable of entering a Bose-Einstein state, even in a medium as warm as the brain, which is what happens in superconductivity, where a single quantum state exists in a large number of particles. The microtubules are actually full of a special kind of water, absolutely pure."

"Right," said Lynn. It was coming back to her now.

"When this relatively large-scale quantum coherence is reached," Sattva continued, "the strange effects of quantum theory that are true on a very small scale become possible on a larger, brain-sized scale. Quantum events cannot be computized—*measured*—yet they can be *communicated,* via the workings of what is called Bell's Inequality Theorem where it was proved that every quantum event has its precise twin nonlocally."

"Um . . . sure," said Lynn.

"There's more," said Sattva.

"You can tell me later. I think my tubular dimars just

knocked off work for the day. It's very beautiful here, isn't it?"

"That is one of the things I love about it," said Mikhel.

The sky was electric blue, so lucid it almost made her heart ache. A pale sliver of moon floated just above the Himalayan peaks, which receded in an endless series of random lines, brown and white when close, deep azure in the distance. She almost fancied she could tell that the earth was curved. She jounced toward the row of yurts in Mikhel's arms, where the vision of long shadows and blue sky darkened and she smelled the butter lamps as they reentered the yurt.

Everyone was eating dinner, passing plates around a table laden with large bowls of steaming food. The spicy smell nauseated her. She saw that Hawkins had a half-empty bottle of golden Scotch at his elbow. He grinned at her across the room, then returned to earnest conversation with a man next to him.

Akamu sat on the floor, cross-legged, in front of the big screen, holding a control sphere in one hand. Some preferred them to keyboards. The size of a tennis ball, they responded to complex combinations of pressures—which children learned easily when young. Every second or so he executed a new command by touching a different part of the sphere, emphasized by a slight forward jerk of his hand. She was at the wrong angle to see what he was doing. He seemed oblivious to his surroundings.

"Put her back on the bed," said Sattva. "Thanks, Mikhel. Hungry, Lynn?"

Lynn shook her head. She just wanted to sleep. Mikhel settled her, and Sattva said, "Put this foot up on a pillow. There." Lynn felt a blanket settle over her and sank into the warmth, the low murmur of the people at the table, the rush of wind pummeling the yurt, the smell of panting mastiffs and butter lamps, and then strange dreams.

When she woke the lamps were still burning but it was considerably darker. Small circles of golden light illuminated various areas of the yurt—the now-empty table, the shelves, what looked like several rows of bunks on the far side, above layers of the woven rugs that floored the place. What Lynn assumed was Om Mani Padme Hum rose and fell on the holo platform like waves, swiftly, in smaller script, as if infected with new urgency. A screen on one of the shelves blinked a frequency, but the picture and sound were not turned on.

The yurt itself was lit like a fairy tale; the delicate filaments woven into the walls glowed with a warm, dim, yellow light; Lynn assumed it was infinitely adjustable. She was relieved. Maybe the strange crew just used butter lamps, like the yurts, for atmosphere. She couldn't think of any other reason not to replace them with something more permanent. Like a bunch of kids playing on the edge of the world with crystals.

Just like you play at what you consider the center of the world with alleles, Lynn thought. Those small bits of the genetic code. There is no center anymore. Everything is everywhere.

She sat up and then rose cautiously, testing her leg. It still ached but held her weight. She felt clearheaded and ravenous. It was a relief to know that she wasn't dying, anyway.

She pulled on her pants and sweater, put on her shoes, feeling renewed.

In the kitchen area, the dinner dishes were drying next to a deep porcelain sink. Running water, even. Racked in front of a background of rough red and gold cloth, the simple white dishes looked beautiful. Lynn wondered if Sattva might not have slipped her some opium after all.

She sat on a large silk pillow patterned with golden elephants at the round slate table, where a bowl of small dumplings waited, with chopsticks. She popped one into her mouth. Inside was curried bean curd. She dipped the next one into the cool, sweet green sauce in another bowl. An iron teapot hung over a brazier set into the center of the table; she saw a pot holder and used it to unhook the teapot and poured herself steaming tea. She ate and drank until she was satisfied.

Outside she heard a distant deep sound, almost like a horn. Hurriedly she gulped the rest of her tea and stood, ignoring the twinge in her leg. It wasn't so bad once she was standing. She limped across the yurt and grabbed her jacket from next to the bed. Orange and black. Rather ugly, but probably all they had in whatever market Hawkins had raided. She shrugged into it, felt in the pockets, smiled. Thank you, Hawkins. Hat and gloves. Probably just as ugly. Next to the door was a bamboo cylinder filled with a variety of carved walking sticks; she gratefully removed one and pushed through the flap into the night.

She was hit by a wall of frigid air, and her ears burned before she pulled on the hat. Above the black jagged rim of mountains flamed a billion stars. Or so it seemed to her.

She had rarely seen stars so bright. The lights of the great cities of the world, where she seemed to spend most of her time, obliterated them. She gazed at them for a long moment, suddenly caught by the pure romance of the ostensible goals of Interspace: to travel there.

Then she laughed harshly. She believed in the here and now. Humans had the tools necessary to make the earth all anyone could ever long for until the distant death of time from heat or cold. And only human nature stood in the way of near-perfection.

She laughed again, this time at herself. The Japanese monks had tolerated her presence at the zendo, as they ought to have. But they must have been able to tell how very far *she* was from enlightenment! Petty, rude, selfish, pampered—who was she to grumble about humanity in general?

The very air here was cleansing, almost as if it blew straight through her, as if she were just loosely assembled particles with plenty of space between each speck. Lovely, lovely, despite the cold—maybe, perhaps, *because* of it. The intense, deep black of space; the power of the land, so different from that of Hawaii. So austere.

She looked away from the near-hypnotic heavens and tried to get her bearings.

Fires burned here and there on the plain, near the yurts, in containers that kept them from being scattered by the wind. But she saw no people, only a few dogs. Some of the windows in the tiny town half a mile away were lit.

Up on the rise, she could also see the dome. Was it—glowing?

She hiked up the hill, pushing herself with the stick. Her leg ached but the splint helped enormously. As she approached it, her interest increased. It *was* glowing, faint, light green through the translucent green panels. What the hell was going on in there?

She reached it, circled around until she came to a door. She knocked. No answer. She turned the knob and pulled. It swung open easily, and she stepped over the threshold.

There was no one inside. She closed the door behind her and stood in the glow, beneath the high center of the dome, again with the strange and even more intense sensation that she, herself, was made of particles, loosely assembled, held together by some amazing force. Of course, she was. She was a thinking sort of space, that was all. A part of space gathered together by gravity, informed by a complex code, that did things.

A part of space prone to strange thoughts after fever, she told herself. Would Sattva tell her more about this? Where was everyone? She turned and walked across the slightly yielding floor. Inside a lacquer box to one side she found a cloth helmet with electrodes inside. As she put it down she leaned on one of the floor panels; it beeped, and one of the wall panels came to life, empty of information. Waiting.

She could not resist. She slipped the helmet on.

The screen was actually a projector; in front of Lynn, the air filled with holographic images. Images of her brain. She saw a panel below that would vary the sections with a mouse.

She could cruise through her own brain. Interesting. But hardly novel. She wondered what they used it for here.

She removed the helmet and the images ceased. She carefully folded it and put it back in the box and closed the lid. She shouldn't be here. Then she smiled, realizing that she *really* wanted to try on the crystal halo. Yes! Put on the halo and *then* do some biofeedback with the brain imager. That would be fun. But Mikhel must have stowed it somewhere; she didn't see it.

The haunting, deep horn sounded again, as if it were the voice of the sky.

Electrified, she hurried to the door, stepped outside, turned.

There—at the golden-roofed temple. Now she could see that a few torches flickered on the terrace and along the steep walkway that led to the temple.

It wasn't far. She wished she had a flash but didn't know where to find one and so ventured out beyond the row of fires; her feet found a hardened path. All she had to do was head straight and hope there were no crevasses between her and the temple.

Buffeted and exhilarated by the wind, she hurried, feeling like a penguin with her stiff gait.

It didn't take her long—about ten minutes—to get to the ramp at its foot. Then it was easy going. She turned onto the smooth paving stones and held to the railing, limping but determined to get to the top. As she climbed she became aware of chanting.

Once at the top she turned toward the temple.

A vast balcony was empty but for two figures standing at the door. She recognized tall, thin Hawkins and chunky Akamu, staring through the open door from which flowed the sound of deep chanting. Above the lintel were two stone lions with fierce faces, and the flickering torchlight illuminated a frieze of inlaid turquoise. Crossing the courtyard, she stopped next to Hawkins and stared inside.

On a raised dais sat Sattva, in full lotus, swathed in heavy embroidered robes and wearing an elaborate headdress. About fifty people faced her, chanting. The chanting abruptly ceased, and in the rich silence Lynn's breath caught in awe.

She could not see the ceiling for it went beyond the light cast by the butter lamps. Behind Sattva was a huge sitting Buddha, smooth and gold, so tall—fifty feet?—that his massive head was lost in the shadows. Every surface of the room was covered with intricate design—carvings, inlaid mother-of-pearl, golden visions of demons and various grades of paradise.

How many centuries had this place been here?

She saw an empty cushion. As she moved toward it she felt Hawkins's hand tighten on her shoulder but shrugged it off. Not making a sound, she sat, carefully arranging her injured leg in a vague semblance of a lotus position, and watched her breath course golden up and down her spine for what seemed an eternity.

When Lynn opened her eyes the room was empty of people except for Sattva, who was once more wearing jeans, boots, and her bright jacket. Lynn blinked. She could not remember ever having been in so deep a trance.

Sattva was watching her, sitting on a cushion, her arms wrapped around her legs.

"I wanted to make sure you found your way back," she said, her voice low and resonant in the huge room.

Lynn could not speak for a few moments as she became reoriented. She didn't know if she should be here, in this sacred place. Finally, she straightened her legs and massaged them to bring back feeling. Sattva helped her stand, and they left the room. Sattva handed her the walking stick.

When they were in the vestibule, Lynn asked, "Was that you—?"

Sattva nodded. "Me." She stood still, as if awaiting more questions.

"I'm just a bit surprised," she said. "Zen roshis are almost always men, although there are a few women now. Maybe five percent. And from what I gathered about Tibetan Buddhism—which isn't much—it seemed that there weren't even any nuns at all."

"Pretty much true," said Sattva. "In the past, but not now. Things are changing. Everywhere. All kinds of things. Come on. Let's go. Pretty soon you'll realize how tired you are. I was really surprised you made it all the way up here."

As Lynn negotiated the many turns of the high stone ramp, she realized how right Sattva was. She looked across the plain. The dome still glowed.

Lynn woke the next day both puzzled and determined.

But, she realized, she also felt safe.

She dressed and stood, testing her leg. Sore, but much, much better, she realized in relief. The mender must be working.

A few people around the table were drinking tea, but about

five others sat in one corner conferencing heavily in German around the large screen, which had lost its mantra and instead had some sort of fractal display. It leaped from the screen and became three-dimensional. One of the women did something with her control sphere. Then she noticed that Lynn was watching, and the display vanished.

A digital readout on the wall above the screen said 11:57. So late! They must think she was a lazy slug. They fell silent as she passed them on her way outside. Lynn was mildly irritated. What do they think I am, some sort of spy? And if so, what are they doing?

The day was again exhilarating and incredibly bright.

"You'll need sunscreen if you stay out here too long, paleface," she heard, and turned to see Akamu.

Was it her imagination, or had he changed in the brief time she'd known him? He seemed taller—was he just standing straighter? His face looked thinner, more mature. His brown eyes seemed more aware, as if he were emerging from a deep sleep.

"I'll have you know I take quite a nice tan," she said. "What's up?"

Akamu looked around. "This place is weird," he said. Just a kid, sounding like a kid. She felt as if she'd had a glimpse of who he was becoming, not who he was now.

"Really," she replied. "How? Besides the obvious fact that they live in felt tents at an elevation of ten thousand feet?"

"Eight thousand ninety-four," said Akamu, pointing at his watch. "It's the people."

"What about them?" Whom had he known who had not been weird? she wondered. Even *she* probably fell into the realm of unusual, if not weird.

"Well, they all think that Sattva is going to save the world, for one thing."

"Oh?"

"Yeah. She's the new Dalai Lama."

"Oh." Lynn tried to digest this for a moment. It was too boggling, actually. *"The* Dalai Lama?"

"The. Javindi told me."

"Javindi?"

"Yeah, one of the . . . entourage? Is that the right word?"

"I suppose." She had been wondering what to call them herself. She had studied them for a while before getting out of bed. Young, mostly—her age. A few older men and women. Most of them looked Tibetan, but not all of them. Some looked Caucasian; Mikhel, of course; there was one Indian woman and one African man, at least. She certainly hadn't seen everyone. They had an air about them. Intense, but not frenzied. Focused and precise as they worked with their computers, as they conferred. And then there was the dome.

"You missed everything. They got up at four and meditated."

"How do they know she's the Dalai Lama?" She began to walk slowly back down the long row of yurts, favoring her leg. They were on a ridge that looked out over endless grasslands. Out in the sparse pastures she saw yaks and sheep grazing.

He smiled. "That's the best part. You know how they used to find the new Dalai Lama after the old one died? They believed the Dalai Lama would reincarnate immediately, so they'd go all over the country with things the old one had used. If a kid could tell which ones belonged to the old one, they figured that kid must really *be* the old one, reincarnated. At least that was one of the things they did."

"That's what they did with Sattva?"

"Not exactly. She got a bachelor's degree in Beijing and then got a scholarship at Harvard. The Dali Lama lived near Boston the last three years before he died and lots of Tibetans live there. She was friends with all of them and spent a lot of time at the center, the old guy's house. Anyway, she was at the center one day and went in the library and started pulling books out of the shelves; she didn't know why exactly. They bothered her, she said."

"She said?"

"Yeah, I asked her about it. What do you think, this is all on the system you got me in Hong Kong?"

"It was expensive enough," she said, in a teasing tone.

He smiled a bit smugly. She was glad to see he had a sense

of humor. "Anyway, she put all the books in a big stack and left. A few days later the people in charge called her."

"The people in charge?"

"Yeah. Whoever they are. People who knew the Dalai Lama. They wanted to know how she knew that those books had been added to the library since he died. She said she had no idea. But apparently she had removed every single one that had been put there, and none that had belonged to him. So they started to give her all the tests. They had pretty much given up on finding the new one, I guess. It had been a really long time since he'd died. She finished her doctorate and came back here to get her training. She snuck in. The Chinese don't know she's here."

Lynn found that hard to believe. She'd never heard anything about the Dalai Lama having returned to Tibet, but as Akamu had amply illustrated, she was woefully ill-informed about everything except DNA.

"Man, Sattva knows a *lot*," continued Akamu.

"No doubt," said Lynn. "People who want to change the world need to." They had that air here, she realized, that almost fanatic zeal of disciples, which she disliked. People like that always wanted to make you into one of them and couldn't relate to you if you disagreed even slightly with their dogma.

"I don't know if she wants to, but everyone here thinks she's going to. That's what Javindi said."

"A slight difference," conceded Lynn. "I wonder how they're going to change the world?"

"That's the best part. They're going to master time by changing the consciousness of the world."

She wasn't particularly jarred by the statement. She'd practically been weaned on the idea that IS would someday master time through faster-than-light travel. She felt like she'd heard every theory in the book and then some. "The consciousness of the *people* in the world," she told Akamu, in a correcting tone. "That's what they want to change."

"No! The consciousness of the *world,* dummy! All the *stuff.*"

"All the matter?" she asked, truly curious.

"I hardly think that Lynn is a dummy," came a voice from behind them, and they both turned.

"Hi, Sattva," said Akamu. "I was telling Lynn all about you."

"So I gathered," said Sattva, a slight smile on her face. She reminded Lynn of a Native American woman she'd once known—coppery skin, high, broad cheekbones. "I'm sure none of it is garbled."

"Oh, Akamu is pretty sharp," said Lynn. She realized she'd barely had a moment to talk to him, to decide what to do, to question him, or *anything*. That was the next thing to do. That and confront Hawkins. Who was he with, what were they up to? How had he known Akamu was with her, and where to find him? And then—was he telling the truth, part of it, or none of it? The very familiar feeling of anxiety returned full force. She had to get *going!* Whatever that meant in the situation she found herself in here.

"I guess you'd like me to run along," Akamu said, looking from one to the other.

"No!" said Lynn. "In fact I really need to talk to you—" She grabbed the sleeve of his jacket but he twisted away.

"That's all right," he said. "I've got a lot to do." He waved and hurried away, disappearing behind one of the yurts.

Sattva was quiet for a moment, but looked directly at Lynn. Her black eyes were amused. "Just what did he tell you?"

"That you think you're the Dalai Lama," Lynn said.

"Slightly incorrect. I don't know what to think. All the evidence says that, yes, and I'm enough of a scientist to be open-minded enough to believe the theorem until a better one comes along. I'm deep into the business of changing paradigms, actually."

"But others think you're the Dalai Lama? I mean, the reincarnation of the Buddha?" Lynn persisted.

Sattva shrugged. "They do. I certainly don't consciously remember having had other lives; they know that I don't. It's a bit disappointing, actually, but that's the way it goes. I'm not trying to pull the wool over anyone's eyes. I try to keep myself as demythologized as much as possible. I appreciate the spiritual training. It's very intense. Unique in all the world. They were quite chagrined that I put off beginning it until I finished my doctorate, but I felt I was learning some very relevant things. I don't blame them, though, especially now that I'm well into it." She grinned again. "Unless I get ahold of some sort of illegal long-term life-enhancement, I'll never reach the end of it! But I'm just kidding. Any change to my physiology would skew everything. Your body—your body-mind, I suppose—becomes very fine-tuned. The training has been kept alive here underground for almost a hundred years now."

She took Lynn's arm. She smiled, and her eyes became dark slits from which beamed amusement. The wind picked up her hair and pulled it around her head in long black tendrils. "Let's walk for a bit. It will be all right for your leg as long as you have that splint on, and you need to make sure your muscles don't atrophy. Let me know if I'm talking your ear off."

As they walked, Sattva waved her hand at the village, gleaming in the sun, half a mile away, before they took a path that led down toward a small grassy plateau dotted with grazing yaks. "We Tibetans are pretty persistent, and our philosophical system is too. This isn't the first time the Chinese have tried to smash Tibet, but Tibetan Buddhism is extremely hardy. It's survived other eras of Chinese domination, for longer than this one."

"What are they trying to do this time?" asked Lynn.

"They're trying to kill us with capitalism." Sattva's laugh was a brief bark of bemusement. "You know that they're trying to run China like a huge corporation? The problem is that this approach isn't a whole lot different from communism. Decisions are mulled over by committees who are usually pretty far removed from where the action is. The heart of true capitalism—the space for business start-ups, a healthy tax climate, and so on—is stifled by regulations. Or by violence—one of the side effects of capitalism seems to be a mafia. Hong Kong—the whole gung-ho entrepreneurial atmosphere—washed through the government when it was returned to China and really surprised a lot of people. Zhong Chau was elected—pro-*small* business and very Green—but of course was assassinated; her antitrust stance pissed a lot of people off. Anyway, they don't like me much; I'm trying to create a lot of independent primal societies in Tibet—"

"It does look pretty primal here," said Lynn.

Sattva seemed to do nothing but smile. "No, dear, not *primitive*. I can see what you're thinking, but there's nothing supernatural about it. Primal Societies, capitalized. True democracies. Total information access for everyone on a global scale. The ability to understand information on many levels— statistically, socially, even chaotically. Experts who are able to communicate information to their fellow villagers in a variety of ways, so that people with different learning styles can see what they're talking about." Sattva tilted her head. "To give you a simple example, some people get a lot of information from charts and graphs. Others don't. But once they have information they can try to make decisions about issues that will affect their lives. And once this is more widespread, I believe that the political situation in the world will change dramatically. It's very simple, but it depends on education. Now you can get a first-rate education just sitting at home. It's tremendous. What is the world doing about it? Nothing! Countries like China are actually holding people back. The idea of educating too many people is always frightening to those in power. It's a good way to lose it. Want to sit for a moment?"

They settled on a large sun-warmed stone. Lynn leaned against the rough lichened planes and put her arms behind her head, watched clouds surge across the sky as Sattva continued.

"As for me being the Dalai Lama, I certainly have a strong sense of duty toward humanity, in terms of feeling it necessary to help all people in any way that I possibly can. Of course the traditional role of the Lamas was to bring all people still living in the cycle of death and rebirth to enlightenment so that they could forsake that cycle. But in this age I feel that we're on the verge of uniting two disparate poles of human thought—not only the spiritual and the material, but the very small and the very large. Quantum theory and gravitational spacetime. Consciousness—and the matter of the mind through which it arises—is the essential aspect of existence. It arguably permeates the entire field of being."

She leaned forward and clasped her legs close to her chest. "I believe that we're coming very close to understanding the true nature of the physical universe—the very roots of matter, from the very small to the very large, from the quantum workings within the very brain to the nature of curved spacetime.

"You see, a famous mathematician once got this sort of intellectual bug. He believed that when we understand the nature of consciousness on a quantum level—or understand quantum mechanics in enough depth to explain the phenomenon of consciousness with it, same thing—we will have the tools and the information we need to understand the rest of the physical universe—including another of its mysterious manifestations, time."

"Are the two necessarily related?" asked Lynn.

Sattva twisted herself around so that she faced Lynn, crossing her legs tailor style. The sun was in her eyes and she squinted, but Lynn could still see the deep earnestness in them.

"Well, consciousness could be said to create time, since to think of time without consciousness is meaningless. Time is essentially a human construct, a somewhat slippery description of the relationship between ourselves—our consciousness—and matter. Is it so strange to think that consciousness will eventually be able to understand the physical nature of the universe, including itself? And then use that understanding to access, even *change,* the physical structure of the universe, much as we've been able to manipulate the physical structure of the human body?

"All forms of Buddhism have studied consciousness in many ways for thousands of years. Particle physics is necessarily concerned with not only the formation of the universe—and therefore, of course, time—but is concerned with the phenomenon of consciousness as well. It could be that we, as conscious beings, exist on the edge of a dynamical system. That time is a fractal."

Lynn breathed in the sweet smell of the waving grasses; stared at the sky. The heat of the rock was pleasant.

"What would that mean?" she asked. "If that's true, then we always have, right?"

"Well, that's like saying"—she cast Lynn a shrewd look—"that our genes have always manifested us, so what's the point in finding out more about them, using them in new ways?"

Sattva slid off the rock and stood with her feet braced and apart; she stuck her hands in her pocket; it seemed for a fleeting instant to Lynn that even if she tried very hard to push Sattva over she would not be able to.

Sattva's eyes were bright; her cheeks flushed as she spoke.

"Lynn, if time is a fractal, perhaps *consciousness* is the key to jumping between one area of the metauniverse to the other!"

Lynn politely repressed a sigh and did not roll her eyes. Her life had been full of such fanatics. Always wanting more, pushing in every direction—biological, mathematical, sociological. And what for? What for? So an innocent boy could be blown up in an old Nuuanu shack?

She sat up, ready to blast Sattva for—for what?

Lynn realized that anger was making her irrational. She took a deep breath; she *did* want to know what they *thought* they were doing here.

"The metauniverse?" she asked, trying to arrange her leg so it did not hurt. On a hill across a deep chasm, a herd of yaks trotted up a narrow path and disappeared behind a rock outcropping, their shadows short in the midday sun.

"Yes," said Sattva. "Vilenkin came up with the term back in the nineties. He postulated that thinking of ourselves as one of many similar civilizations in an infinite metauniverse—or metaverse, as we call it—is a much more fruitful approach than thinking ourselves as unique in a universe. He said that it's much more likely that we're *average,* an average manifestation of what is possible, and that therefore an infinite number of such universes exist in the metaverse. He called this the principle of mediocrity." She laughed. "Fitting name!"

"Ah," said Lynn. "So you're trying to *communicate* with them?"

"Communicate with, or travel to them," she said. "And according to the principle of mediocrity, that's probably what they're trying to do as well. I'm really in a unique position. The training I receive as the Dalai Lama is not just philosophy, not just studying the scriptures. It involves real physical changes. It's very exciting, actually." She paused. "Sorry. I shouldn't preach."

Lynn tried to say what she thought as politely as possible. "Maybe I'm just cynical," she said, "but I've lived my entire life around people who say they intend to change the world but all they really want is individual profit for themselves at the expense of as many others as it takes."

"You *are* cynical," said Sattva. "I'm about ready for lunch, aren't you?"

"Breakfast," said Lynn, sliding carefully from the rock and dusting off her pants. They started back toward the yurts.

"Cynicism is almost essential in a scientist," said Sattva, then hesitated for a moment. "I hope you don't mind him talking about you, but that's what Hawkins says you are. I gathered that when you spoke of mitochondrial tracking yesterday and asked him. He speaks very highly of you."

"Oh, he doesn't really know much about me," Lynn said as lightly as possible. She eyed the dome as they neared it.

Sattva saw her and smiled. "Later," she said. "I assure you that all our secrets will be revealed. In fact, that's what I wanted to ask you. I've tried to put together a multidisciplinary situation here. A sort of team that thinks about . . . well, everything. But in a new way, informed by fields of knowledge that might not otherwise interface because most scientists are quite narrowly focused. You're a geneticist?"

"Yes," said Lynn. "But I'm—" She paused for a moment. How to say this? I'm running away. I'm taking this kid from the corruption that science has been used for in IS and fleeing into the wilderness. I'm not going to do anything for a long, long time. Except . . .

Except.

She thought about the earring but did not touch it. Mao's genome could be the definitive factor, the information that, when compared to that of the other powerful figures she had, might crystallize all her painstakingly collected information about leadership—the evil and the good.

Sunlight washed in great bright sweeps across the mountains, interspersed with bands of shadow, as she stopped stock-still.

Why don't you be honest? she asked herself. It certainly won't hurt your research that the person you're trying to save is the clone of one of the world's great leaders. For his own good, of course . . .

She frowned and stomped forward for a few steps, but winced. She'd forgotten her leg.

Sattva took her arm gently. "Lynn, you don't have to decide this very minute. You hardly know us. Let's have tea."

Their yurt was close. It took a few minutes for Lynn's eyes to adjust inside the dark yurt. Again the people at the computers looked at her mistrustfully, but Sattva said, "She's okay," and they went back to whatever they had been doing.

"I'm surprised about the electric lines here," said Lynn, as Sattva whisked powdered green tea into a water-filled iron pot from which peered the tiny faces of frowning chimeras. "It's so remote."

Sattva said, "That was one of the first things the Chinese did here, actually. The Himalayas are the birthplace of some of China's great rivers. They came in and built small hydroelectric plants wherever there was falling water. That was what—seventy years ago? Of course, there was quite a stiff price for that help! For a while they tried to make the farmers grow wheat instead of barley, as if they could control the climate and soil as well as people. They failed in both efforts, of course. But eventually they got the monkhood pretty much busted up, by killing most of them off or sending them to China."

"Where's Hawkins?" she asked, as Sattva poured them both tea. She held the cup with both hands, relaxing into the small bit of warmth. "I thought he'd be here."

"He had some reconnoitering to do. It seems that he wants to get you into Nepal." She smiled, but her dark eyes were sad, and Lynn took the tightening around them, and around her mouth, for concern. "It's pretty rough there—a lot like here, actually, but without the Chinese soldiers." She looked directly at Lynn. "Hawkins is an extraordinary man. You can trust him with your life. I have. More than once. He speaks more languages than you can shake a stick at and seems to blend in everywhere. I met him at a faculty party at Harvard; he was wearing a suit and tie! He's a handsome man when he wants to be. Rough and urbane—but you know all that, eh?" Her eyes were pensive as she looked toward the door. "I hope he's all right," she said so quietly Lynn almost missed it. "He enjoys risk too much."

"I hope we're not endangering you by being here," Lynn said. She reached for some cakes on the table and tasted one. Meat inside.

"Take more," urged Sattva, and she did. "It would be nothing new," said Sattva. "I'm sure the Chinese know I'm here, though my crew seems to want to pretend that we're all invisible somehow. If the Chinese have any fears about me I'm sure they're remote. I haven't made any nationalistic moves, though I'm sure that I could. Probably a lot of people are disappointed that I haven't. The most I've done is try to get every family their own satlink; pretty radical, when you think about it, or at least, radicalizing. Of course they don't realize that at a certain point the Primal Societies, which they would find silly if they knew about them at all, will bring about enormous political change. The problem is actually one of information now, rather than religion. The Chinese still have a very tight, closely linked intelligence and scientific community. Of course they should be—scientific progress is the source of wealth now and, heavens, we can't just piss it away, can we! Let's use it to get richer than everyone else!"

Lynn glanced back at the small band of people. "So you're on the web?" she asked.

"Of course," said Sattva. "In fact, we have our own dedicated network. But we monitor various scientific work from around the world. In fact, I just sent a piece to *Physical Review*. I don't know if they'll take it yet." She smiled again, took another sip of tea. "It's rather strange, but exceedingly well pinned down."

"I wonder if you'd mind if I checked up on some things. I might have some mail."

"Depends. I'd have someone monitor everything you do, so you wouldn't inadvertently give out information we don't want anyone to have. And I wouldn't want you to send anything. We can keep anyone from knowing that you checked your mail. If someone was looking for you they might otherwise be able to trace you here."

"Oh—right." Why tell me anything then? Lynn wondered.

"Hawkins really gave me no choice," said Sattva, as if Lynn had spoken aloud. "He'd only come here in extreme duress. It's really quite bizarre. For some reason he thinks that you and Akamu are essential to what we are doing. Or that you can help somehow. He wasn't very clear. He was exhausted. And then he hurried off to make arrangements for Nepal late last night. He was suddenly in a great rush. But that's why . . . well, the lecture and the invitation. I trust him completely." She sighed. "And see him so rarely."

Lynn's uneasiness returned. She just wasn't sure who had tried to kill her. What *was* she doing, anyway? Two things— what was the important thing? Cataloging DNA, unraveling the evil shadow of eugenics from hard information insofar as that was possible . . . and perhaps it was not possible. Some parties believed that she was taking a tiny bit of Mao's DNA from China, to compare it with that of the other political luminaries in her library. And that was true, as far as it went.

But maybe Mao's DNA was supposed to have been just the icing on the cake to tempt her. Her brothers were certainly not above using her—it was quite possible that she was transporting something else for IS. What might that be? She stared at the flickering butter lamp, aware of Sattva's eyes on her face.

She also had Akamu, an illegal clone, created by IS or the Homeland Movement or someone else—a real, living, extraordinary boy who had certain human rights; he was not anyone's property to create and dispose of as they pleased. Perhaps the attack on her was related to him; perhaps someone had thought that he was with her at that time. Lynn felt her face growing hot at the thought of how he'd been treated.

And at her own proprietary interest. In which she would *not* indulge . . .

Each interpretation of events posed its own set of explanations.

Lynn started at an electronic beep from across the yurt. One woman stared intently at a screen for a moment, then pressed a key and ten feet away a paper slid into a basket and a light blinked. Sattva rose and went over to look at it.

Lynn continued her musing. As unique as Kamehameha's clone was, she failed to see how any aspect of Akamu's creation or of his life could further the wedding of quantum theory with Einstein's spacetime or expose Hawking's baby universes bobbing like so many soap bubbles all around them with flickering openings to other universes that, theorists postulated, *must* exist. Mao's DNA was a toy, really; not much more right now, because of all the international laws governing genetic research and use of research results. Still, for her own information, it would be fascinating.

But was she able, if need be, to let it go? If you're so idealistic, why not stop this right now? Throw away Mao, now.

No. Even hypothetically the idea was abhorrent to her; it went against everything she'd been working on all her life—understanding humans at the most basic level possible. She reached up and brushed the earring lightly, savoring its smoothness, imagining its content, seeing that information unfurl . . .

Besides. She might need it to bargain with her brothers.

Sattva dropped back onto her pillow. Lynn let go of the earring and put her hand back in her lap guiltily.

Sattva said, "I can see you're still skeptical. Look at it this way—we've mastered one dimension, physical distance, with fast travel and with telecommunication. Understanding consciousness is the next step for humankind, the next step in evolution—*mindful* evolution, for the first time on earth, at least. All of our AI models are basically attempts to replicate consciousness, to *create* it, and thereby understand ourselves better. First we extended our *physical* body with tools, and then mechanically and robotically. So what is consciousness? What is it good for? How and why did it come into existence? Is there some sort of evolutionary reason? Like everything else that exists, it's an integral part of the universe. Yet it is not matter, though it springs from matter and influences matter. Crudely, so far, just through humans thinking about what has to be done and then doing it—things great and small. Every action of daily life. The building of all cities. The hydrogen bomb. Space travel. They were all first only thoughts."

"So what's going on in the dome?" asked Lynn. "I don't think it's just an artifact."

Sattva smiled a bit. "You're not going to let that go, are you? Okay. We're using it to work on the ten-dimensional problem."

"String theory."

"Right. But with a twist. That of consciousness, of course. I mentioned Penrose. He wasn't the only one thinking about the body-mind problem in a scientific way. More and more scientists believe that understanding the evolution and nature of consciousness will lay the groundwork for a solution to the big question—how and where do the laws of quantum mechanics interface with the laws of space-time? Artificial intelligence is a big part of it too, because we need to know whether the laws governing the evolution of artificial intelligence—say, in self-replicating programs—can serve as a basis for understanding consciousness. And also of course whether anything that originates in that way and grows to be more complex can eventually become conscious. We have various intelligence modules working away, constantly, on calculations linking consciousness with spacetime. A long shot, to be sure."

"So—the dome?"

"Well, I mentioned quantum coherence, where the brain is in a state of superconductivity, and we are trying to pin down and prolong this state, using the dome, because when it is in this state the brain is not only linked to quantum events, but might possibly be able to influence quantum events *consciously*. But only in ways regulated by all our physical laws, of course—this doesn't mean that we can go out, say, and beam some sort of mindrays around and change things. But it *does* mean, perhaps, that we *can* predict the location of and travel to other areas of the metaverse. That ability would have to do with quantum-level oscillations and quantum nonlocality. We know a lot more that we *think* we know—for instance, the eye is sensitive to just one photon of light. So the human *eye* has information that quantum theory says is impossible to know—where one photon is at a particular specific instant. Can we make this information conscious? Can we use it?"

She grabbed a dumpling and stuffed it in her mouth. "Oh, Lynn, sometimes I drown people in gibberish. I have plenty of hard information to show you, if you're interested. It's the numbers that count, the theorems, the proofs, not these verbal descriptions. Words just don't do the job."

"So—all these people believe in you?" asked Lynn.

Sattva smiled.. "Well. I hope not *me*. They are each individuals. Some of them believe that they will be transmuted into pure intelligence, via computers, and they're working to make that possible. That doesn't sound too pleasant to me, but different strokes for different folks. Ingrid over there"—Sattva nodded toward a tall woman with a short buzz of hair fanning out around her face—"is an internationally known AI expert. She's building the various components she'll need in order to have her brain read into the web." Sattva shrugged. "It seems macabre to me, to tell you the truth, but she has the soul of a pioneer. She claims that there are already personalities on the web who no longer have bodies—I mean, not your standard AI personalities but former humans. We're just an odd crew, I guess. We each have something to put into the pot." She shrugged. "In my opinion, the answer to the burning question of consciousness and the exploration of the new frontier of spacetime will be physical and discrete."

Lynn looked at Sattva. "So what about you? Have you negotiated space-time? In a physical and discrete way, of course?"

Sattva didn't reply. This irritated Lynn. Then Sattva said, quietly, "Hawkins says that your father is the head of Interspace."

"Hawkins talks too much."

"Is it true?"

Lynn spoke carefully. There it was. The nugget that Sattva was after. The only reason they wanted her at all, probably, the reason Sattva was wooing her this way. An in.

"He used to have a lot of power, yes, though Interspace is set up as a board. But now . . . I think he's essentially been retired. Pushed aside. He's . . . kind of old-fashioned when it comes to the sort of decisions that IS is making now."

"There were rumors that twenty years ago IS was doing illegal nanotech experiments that made people think that they could travel in time. I wonder—do you know if they've been continued? Refined?"

"I need air," said Lynn, and rose rapidly. Despite sudden dizziness, she strode outside, grabbing a walking stick at the last minute before she went through the flap.

"Goddamn Hawkins," she muttered under her breath, infuriated. She glanced back. Sattva wasn't following her—good! What right did he have to tell a complete stranger, and a nutcase at that, all about her? And why would anyone assume that just because she was her father's daughter that she would know all sorts of secret IS information? That was what Sattva was really after. The hell with that!

She stumped along awkwardly, favoring her leg, for about five minutes, fuming. Then she looked up and realized that she was heading toward the temple. Fine. Good a place to go as any.

She was sweating by the time she reached the terrace. Panting, she turned.

Before her were jagged blue and white peaks. The highest mountains on earth, and growing an inch every five years. Here had lived a strange race of people for thousands of years, one of the most homogeneously religious of all countries, where virtually everyone believed that various miraculous feats such as the ability to control one's body temperature, changing matter just by thinking about it (but very hard and in just the right way!), and even swimming through time by living a thousand incarnations, were not only possible but a reality that overwhelmed the physical world.

She sat on a carved stone bench and became lost in the fantastic vista before her. The wind was more chill up here; she zipped her jacket.

Sattva's query had upset her. Why? Old nanotech experiments? Ha! So many!

In front of her, to the west, where the sun was beginning its descent, fierce winds moved clouds swiftly so that—by pieces and then in its entirety— a previously hidden range of stunning peaks was revealed beyond the ridge she had taken for the edge of the world. She inhaled sharply and blinked, for it was as if inner and outer united, and a long-ago day came into view much as the range had appeared.

Lynn grabbed her long black hair back with one hand to keep the wind from whipping it across her face. Swift sunset turned the blue Pacific steel gray far below, then fired it with red, gold, and rose. Within ten minutes, the sky was a deepening shadow filling with stars.

A good time for *it*—the music—to come. The gardeners were gone. Her brothers were not around. Her stepmother and her father often sat out here after dinner and heated sake on the little brazier next to the stone lanai, but tonight they were busy.

The forest in the gully next to her—a mysterious place of giant banyans and the sandalwoods environmentalists had planted—rustled in the evening trades that skimmed the top of Tantalus. The darkening bulk of the mountain sloped away swiftly, at the end of the lawn, down to the twinkling lights of Honolulu.

Then she heard the owl.

She stood very still, and the deep, hushed call was repeated.

Lynn stared at the forest, hoping to see a dark shape soaring over the treetops looking for rats and rabbits. But she saw nothing. The last light was gone and the moon wouldn't be up for hours. Still, she had heard it! She knew that the escaped snowy owl from Honolulu Zoo would come up here, where it was cool.

She rushed up the wide, flat stone stairs, through the open sliding panel into her room, flung some pillows off her futon— then remembered where her handy was. Probably still under the dining room table where it had fallen at lunch.

"Shit," she said, because she liked to, because it made her nanny mad, and ran down the polished hallway to the dining room, skidding to a halt in front of the door.

She put her ear to the door and heard the murmur of voices. Another important IS meeting. They were all important. Damn them! She tried to quietly turn the knob, but it was locked.

She went around to the side door where they brought the food in. It was open a crack. She peered inside.

A small blue-tinged fire crackled in the simple, elegant fireplace behind her father. The windows were open and it got chilly fast after sunset. He was seated at the end of the long ebony-black table. Six people were listening to him, four men and two women. One of the men was wearing a lovely yellow silk Chinese jacket that looked like molten gold in the flickering firelight.

She had seen one of the women once before and had figured out that Dr. Honsa was her name. Honsa was thirty-two and had a Ph.D. in genetics, just like Lynn's real mother. Lynn had ferreted her file out of the web for fun. Honsa looked furious now, her eyes slitted and black. Lynn could see beneath the table that she'd made her hands into fists in her lap.

Lynn studied the face of the man across the table from her. Long nose, pinched forehead, deep-set eyes. If she could remember it closely enough, she could composite it when she got back to her room and see if she could match *that* to a name.

Her father pushed a button and dimmed the chandelier. The liquid crystal screen between the tall windows lit, and the two people sitting on that side of the table turned their chairs around to watch. Now was the time.

She pushed the door as quietly as she could but her father said, "Who is that?" his voice angry, as it often was. It didn't bother Lynn, though she knew it made her half brothers, the twins, afraid. Lynn was pretty sure that Alyssa, her American stepmother, was afraid too, though her face was always expressionless, her voice low, smooth, and controlled.

"I need my handy," she said. "To record the owl—"

"We're having an important meeting, Lynn. You are ten. You should know better than this. Please leave."

"Okay," she said, then ran across fifteen feet of polished teak floor, crawled under the table between two chairs, and felt around until she had the handy.

She shoved herself back out, stood, bowed, and saw smiles tug at the mouths of a few guests as they inclined their heads in the flickering light coming from the wall. She retreated backward to the door, handy sandwiched between her hands at the center of her chest, gasshoed a few more times for effect, while the voice that went with the pictures on the screen droned on.

"Out!" yelled her father, and she slowly stepped back into the hall as he strode toward her and slammed the door in her face. She heard the lock click shut, laughed, slipped the handy into her pocket, and ran back outside.

Sitting on the lawn, she watched the Tourist Zone fireworks and waited to hear the owl. A froth of aqua, gold, and white rolled across the sky, stars peeking through like a part of it. That was The Wave. Copper for green, cobalt for blue. Fuses remote controlled, the whole thing precisely packed in clusters by computer.

While she watched, she heard the twins—still practically babies—yelling as the nurse got them ready for bed in their wing, and the night sounds of the mountain enveloped her: soughing trees, clicking palm fronds.

Then it began to happen. Notes gathered in her head, as real to her as the visible world. She allowed their harmonies to converge. A-flat; she visualized the odd, wild little riff as written music, then played it again in her mind to check and solidify. She rose as if holding something very fragile and moved toward the house carefully as a Zen monk in walking meditation.

Then she stopped. Her father had locked the piano room this morning because she hadn't finished her latest genetic segment of schoolwork. He'd pulled all dedicated music pads from her room too, the various-sized flat remote screens where she often doodled compositions, then touched the sensor to the screen to hear a synthesized version.

Her stomach twisted in anger and frustration. Of course she could write it down, but hearing it was important, and he had no right; he was always against her music . . . but before tears could burn her eyes she took a deep breath, pressed the handy button, hummed the idea, then relaxed. That would be enough to bring it back later.

The fireworks were over. The guests came out and got into the heli parked away from the house on its pad; it rose swiftly as a dragonfly, blue and red lights blinking, and ferried them away.

She'd lost the owl. But it would be back.

Her sliding doors almost always stood open, though her father complained that rain swept in. But the low, overhanging eaves kept all but the windiest storms out. She slipped inside.

A corner of the room was lit with the glow of her main screen, and one of the holographic genetic drills that she had to finish by tomorrow still hovered next to it, a foot-high rainbow DNA helix, each base a different hue.

"What is wrong with this person," she muttered, walked over, and dimmed it. She couldn't get rid of it till it was done. She saw that her nurse had straightened everything. She hated that.

She flopped onto the futon on her belly and slid back the small control door on the handy to play back her music.

But what was all this empty space? She realized that the record function had been activated when it fell on the floor at lunch. It wouldn't bother her bird collection, of course, which was permanently saved on the silver disk—except for the o-o bird she'd put in the buffer this morning. They'd released some of the previously extinct birds two years ago after cloning them from bones, and that was something she hated to lose.

Oh, well, might as well see what was on it. Nothing had happened for most of the day, and it was activated by sound. She bypassed the chatter of the maids setting up for the evening and found where the dinner started.

Dull grown-up talk.

Then they were talking about nanotechnology experiments. That interested her. They were illegal.

She got up and lit some incense, and a thin trail of spicy smoke hung in the air as she sat cross-legged and listened.

She'd heard rumors from classmates about failed experiments. She had just started a new scientific ethics class. It was interesting, especially since most of the kids were older than she was. "Is nanobiology ethical?" She didn't really understand it too well, yet, but according to one of her new friends the results could be extremely bad. She'd heard that often nan implants mimicked various kinds of mental illness, creating the grotesque people they would never be able to fix who lived in Honolulu, in the old downtown around Chinatown. Her father said those stories were nonsense. Someday, she'd decided, she'd just see for herself.

She recognized her father's voice. "Dr. Honsa—wasn't number forty-seven your responsibility? I've learned that this unfortunate woman was given experimental nans far in excess of what is legal. Both in scope and in function. Why did you allow this to occur?"

"Sir," the woman said, and Lynn visualized her metallic-looking black hair cut at odd, severe angles, the ugly green eyeshadow, that tiny tattoo of a single triangle beneath her right ear, on her neck. "The researchers—"

"*Your* researchers, carrying out your directions," her father inserted.

Dr. Honsa's voice lightened. "Yes. Exactly. They disobeyed my instructions—"

"That is not acceptable," said her father, his voice sharp and tight. "We are talking about a human life here. Furthermore, I see that there is evidence that this particular nan may have been transmittable, at some point."

"That window was very small," said Honsa, her voice dull and flat. "Please—it's not a problem—we kept no records."

"*I* know about it," said Mr. Oshima, quietly. "And an innocent person has died." After a silence, he went on. "But I didn't know about it soon enough. That was because you knew that I would have stopped this experiment. This all could have been done with animals, with simulations—"

"Mr. Oshima," said Dr. Honsa, "this is a very complex matter. We isolated a newly discovered bacteria that grows on electric eels and that facilitates transmission of their charge. I believe that if we properly introduce elements of it to the human brain, it will have precisely the focusing effect on the wave function we have been seeking. I do not wish to be disrespectful, but there is *no* way to obtain the data we need without—"

Lynn started at a sound and looked up. Her father was sliding shut the door from the hallway. "Lynn, I've told you never to interrupt—what's that?" He stared at the handy.

"You will have to take your questionable morals elsewhere, Dr. Honsa. Interspace has no use for you," it said.

Lynn's father was wearing a long blue silk robe that shimmered in the muted light. He walked across the room and grabbed the handy, flipped it open, and took out the silver disk.

"No, Dad!" She jumped up and tried to grab it. "My bird collection!"

Without a word he bent the small disk over on itself, back and forth, several times. His face was very pale, and there was sweat on his forehead.

"Daddy!" she shrieked, ashamed to be acting like her little brothers. "Remember? My bird collection!"

The first recording had been of squawking seabirds on Kaena Point. She remembered it well. Her mother's brown, smiling face, black eyes, and the smooth black hair that never seemed in disarray, even when blown by the wind. Long, slim fingers pushing the buttons saying to her father, "Nonsense, of course she can handle this. It's old, anyway, old technology, nothing to worry about. This will be our special project, sweetie. Maybe someday we'll go all over the world together, collect them all— loon calls, migrating ducks. Wild parrots. They squawk!" Her mother's words had always been there, her private litany, her under-the-pillow good-night kiss after she was gone.

"You didn't have a backup?" he asked, staring at her. At least he knows it was important, she thought bitterly. That's different.

"No," she whispered. Somehow she had felt it would never be right except on this old, obsolete disc, played on the battered handy her mother had touched and held.

"Well. I am sorry. I am very sorry. You didn't hear much, did you?" His face looked older than it had this morning, the wrinkles across his forehead and frown lines between his eyes deeper than she'd noticed before. His narrow eyes flicked down at her, bearing a hint of apology. She looked away.

"No," she lied. "I didn't hear much."

"Good," he said. "Please, never interrupt again like that." He left.

She flung herself across the futon.

She could still hear it all. Waves crashed into crystal pools filled with crabs, seabird cries swelled and faded; her mother's laughing voice said sweetie. She could almost smell the clean salt air of Kaena, lose herself in the wild, pure blue of sea and sky as she cried. "The old bastard!" she whispered. Her chest ached. She'd been meaning to transfer it all into crystals, where it would be safer. Now it was too late.

But finally she stopped crying.

She turned over on her back and stared at the ceiling beams in the dim light her unfinished homework still emitted. The wind rattled her bamboo blinds and dried the tears on her face.

She reached under her bed and pulled out the remote pad she kept there, touched it on. She couldn't do music on it, but suddenly that didn't matter. She thought for a moment about which web to access.

What kind of nan experiment had taken her mother's voice from her?

Twenty-five years later and thousands of miles from home, Lynn huddled inside her jacket. Those experiments—had nanobiology somehow stimulated the microtubules? Allowed the brain to remain in an unentangled state? Where a similar universe—or *universes*—could somehow be sensed, or even influenced?

It was very cold up here in the wind. She huddled inside her jacket. She had always known too much, perhaps. Maybe that was it. And now, with Akamu, she knew more. Fine, if you were an IS insider. But a threat to them if you were not. Akamu was, simply, valuable information. She smiled in spite of herself and sighed. She'd know a lot more if she ever got a chance to *talk* to the boy! Where was he now? He'd run off this morning. How long had she been sitting here?

Anyway, these people were nuts. She hoped Hawkins could soon arrange for them to leave. He'd stranded them here. She was fascinated by Sattva's vague premise, but that was all it was, a vague premise. Never mind that she knew that a fringe element in IS—one that was essentially invisible, even to the greater IS organization—was on that same time travel track.

Yes, there had been experiments. She had the expertise to access details that she would not have understood, back then. Some physiological effect, obviously. *It's physical,* Sattva had said. No wonder they wanted her. Lynn tried to remember what she knew about microtubules but felt tired. The tubular dimars existed in two planes, one rotated thirty degrees from the other. It seemed probable that elusive bionan extrapolated from the eels had something to do with the functioning of the tubular dimars of the microtubules . . .

She gripped her walking stick so hard that the carvings bit into her palm painfully; she laid it across her lap and thought about her father. What did *he* know?

She'd been out of touch with him for more than a few years, hurt but not surprised at the way he disowned her, emotionally, when she experimented with a music career. It confirmed the self-doubt that had grown since her mother died and he remarried: he loved the twins more. They were so perfect and good and obedient, driven by their just-as-good and just-as-obedient mother to succeed. Not like Lynn, with her independent and brilliant mother. Her father had offered to pay for her education when she tired of singing and went back to school, but she was too proud for that and of course did not need it, not with money coming in from her mother's patents. She was well-off enough; not wealthy, but quite comfortable if she managed things intelligently. He sent her proper holiday greetings, and she went to family functions but kept her distance. Now she wondered if she had not been, perhaps, too distant. Maybe he had changed. Maybe he wanted to make things up to her.

Despite his long-lived mother, he was frail. So far from him now, she felt as if she had been too selfish, too proud. The expansive landscape she found herself in, this strange unanticipated interlude, seemed to help her see things more clearly.

He still maintained his full board position at IS, but the twins seemed to have quite a bit of power. More than him? Most certainly. She remembered his outrage at the experiments. They were the kind of experiments, she knew for certain, that her brothers would not feel the least qualms about.

She could claim no moral high ground, though. She had not, she recalled, discarded James's invitation to benefit from Interspace's machinations, but had recorded the vital information in her passport in preparation.

Well, fine, she told herself impatiently. It helped you rescue Akamu. Quit giving yourself a hard time. Who are you to fight Interspace? One small woman fighting a many-headed monster. And it's not all evil.

The wind held the scent of snow, up here above the grasses, where she could better see the vast snowfields and glaciers that patched these amazing peaks. Her hands were chilled stiff. Best to get back. She hoped that Hawkins had returned and that they could get going, get away from this ethereal nonsense. When she meditated, she had no particular goal. She certainly had no thought of linking consciousness with quantum gravity, or saving humanity! She only knew that she got very restless when she didn't, just as when she didn't run. Like now. She would run, if it weren't for her leg. Except she was slightly short of breath up here. She held the stick upright and thumped the stones a few times. It would be good, wouldn't it, to trek out into those mountains! If Hawkins didn't get back pretty soon, she'd use their fancy system to get some fancy maps and get the hell out of here.

She stood up. She might as well take a look at the temple while she was here. What a tremendous gift, actually, to be deep in the heart of one of the essential branches of Buddhism. She wished she had it in her to feel humble but it wasn't exactly a part of her personality. So she would look at it, register it, marvel, and wish that she had the capacity to feel the awe that she ought to feel.

What a grump, she thought. Well, blame it on the altitude. She was starting to get a headache, too. The sooner they left, the better.

She hobbled toward the open door, dwarfed by its great height.

Inside, the butter lamps were all lit. She gazed up at the golden Buddha once again, marveling at the devotion of those who had built this gleaming edifice to—what? To a state of mind? To a state of being? To a symbol of a path to other universes? Corridors beckoned outward; it dawned on her that this was just the entrance to an enormous maze.

"Lynn!"

Startled, she turned. Akamu stepped from the shadows. He whispered, but his whispers were amplified in the enormity of the enclosed space.

"Hi," she said. Her voice lapped around the vast space. "Where have you been?"

"I fell asleep in the dome. Then I came up here to look around."

Ha. Sattva's secret dome. Used for a mundane nap. "It's beautiful here, isn't it?"

"Kind of scary, really."

"Are you scared?" she asked, and walked over to him. On impulse, she reached out and hugged him close, barely able to reach around him in his bulky jacket. He clung to her for a moment, then let go.

"I guess. A little."

Then the questions bubbled forth.

"What are we doing here? Why did the house blow up? Where are we *going?*"

She looked around and saw a little alcove with seats. "Let's sit down."

They sat facing each other. The lamps warmed one side of his face to the gold of the Buddha.

"I really don't know the answer to any of those questions, I'm afraid," she said. "It wasn't my idea to come here. Hawkins is—an old friend. Of my father's. He's taking us—some-where—" she faltered.

"But *why*?" he nearly shouted, then looked abashed as his outburst thundered back.

She decided, in an instant, that it was best to tell him every-thing she could. In case anything happened to her, he needed all the information he could get.

"You're a very special person," she said. "I believe that you're a clone of King Kamehameha."

His eyes narrowed. He looked past her for a moment and finally said, "I don't believe you. Cloning is illegal. My mother's name was Lelani. My father's name was Don. They died in an accident when I was real little. So little I don't re-member." He closed his eyes, then opened them and contin-ued. "I've always lived with my auntie. A few months ago John and Ellen showed up and my auntie said that they would take care of me while she was in the hospital. They wouldn't let me go out to play or anything. Then the house blew up. And you took me. *Kidnapped* me." His voice became more re-sentful with each word.

"Fine, so you're not a clone. Where did you live?"

"I'm not allowed to say."

"Who told you that?"

"My auntie."

"Why?"

"Well . . . just because."

"I'm telling you everything I know. You need to tell me too. You think it over, Akamu. I can understand you not wanting to think that you're a clone. But you know who Kamehameha was, don't you?"

"Of course," he said, raising his chin. "The first king to unite the Hawaiian Islands. Back in the late seventeen hundreds. That's the first stupid thing. I know that cloning of humans is possible. But that guy's been dead for over two hundred years. So what you're saying is ridiculous. You must think I don't know anything."

Lynn sat back. Of course, she wasn't telling him everything. How could she tell him that his two predecessors—maybe more—had been murdered? She didn't know who had done it. It was possible that the Homeland Movement somehow had the ability to create a clone, but she doubted it. In her opinion, it had to be IS, for their own twisted reasons. Maybe just to see if it was possible. That was reason enough, for them. And her own memories led her to that conclusion. There might have been something wrong with the previous versions, or someone might have found out about them, and IS had had them killed. Maybe they wanted to fool Akamu from the beginning, make him believe that he was being raised to be the leader of the Homeland Movement, then, when he was successful, control him and the movement.

Actually, her original theory, that the Homeland Movement had created the clones, made more sense—except that as far as she knew the only lab facilities with clone capabilities, and with knowledgeable personnel, belonged to IS. But the hard part was everything leading to a viable zygote. After that it was just a matter of implanting it in the surrogate mother.

And once they had one, they had many, which they could freeze . . .

The rumor that Cen Kalakaua had somehow left them the bones made sense, too. He had been pure Hawaiian. He also, she recalled, had apparently left them some sort of cockamamy "Kaiulani Proofs" that IS had been trying to get hold of for the past fifteen years or so, ever since Kalakaua had vanished. She only knew about the proofs because of her strong interest in the bones.

An involuntary shudder ran through her. It all ended, or began, with this kid in front of her. He was free now. Isolated, but free. He could live his *own* life.

Akamu pulled his legs up to his chest and leaned back, his head next to that of a stone goddess. He gazed into the meditation room. Probably thinking at a furious rate, turning over her outrageous assertion in his mind, trying to bash holes in it. She could see he was shivering, despite the warm-looking hat someone had provided him.

"Akamu," she said, but as she spoke he leaped up.

"Listen!" he said.

The deep horn she'd heard the previous evening began its haunting call, a subtle undertone to sunset.

"Now they'll come!" he said.

"Maybe we should go back to the yurt," she said. "You're cold and hungry."

He shook his head. "They start a charcoal fire on one side and they told me to sit there this morning. Sattva said that I could watch. My . . . auntie used to meditate." He jumped up and walked carefully though the rows of cushions and disappeared into the shadows beyond the Buddha.

A thin man walked onto the terrace and lit the torches. People began arriving. The man came to Lynn, and, smiling, motioned to her to sit on one of the cushions. She accepted.

She found that her leg was much better. As she settled onto the cushion, she wondered again if it might not be best for Akamu to be rid of whatever organization was behind him: Interspace or the Homeland Movement, what did it matter? He was obviously intended to be some sort of pawn for one or the other. He should disappear and be reborn. Learn to use his remarkable intelligence for his own self-formulated goals.

As for herself, she felt as if she were emerging from a long tunnel and realizing that the world was larger and not quite so closely curved around her as she had always thought.

In the middle of what she thought of as the sesshin the chanting was interrupted by a harsh whisper in her ear that she recognized as Hawkins.

"Where's Akamu? We have to leave. Now."

Instantly alert, she opened her eyes.

Around her were dark, chanting figures. The Dalai Lama was on her dais—behind her the Buddha shone.

She pulled on her shoes and rose.

Edging around the periphery of the room, Hawkins behind her, she passed three alcoves with braziers, but no Akamu. Fighting panic, she continued. With relief she spotted the boy in the next one. He saw them as well, for he rose and waited silently for them to approach.

Hawkins motioned for Akamu to follow but crouched back

into the alcove as they heard loud, demanding voices speaking in Chinese. He took a packet from one of his large pockets and pushed it into Lynn's hand. He looked around wildly. He leaned close to Lynn and whispered, "There's a door back there. Run."

Akamu, his face grim and much older than his years, yanked on Lynn's arm. He pointed down the corridor. He grabbed Hawkins's arm, but Hawkins pushed both of them, his eyes urgent in the dim light.

She heard running footsteps and then the sharp close report of gunfire and a shout that sounded like Hawkins's—

She turned without thinking and saw it all in a glance—the broad, low hallway rough-hewn at the top, damply gleaming in the light of some sort of lantern at a corner that branched into another corridor and the great hall; the floor, large blocks of grainy marble worn down in the center by centuries of footsteps—

And Hawkins, rolling on the floor, and two men in dark uniforms running toward him rapidly, still twenty yards away, holding their weapons in both hands as they ran—

Akamu grabbed her walking stick and shoved her into a dark shallow alcove. She thought he would join her there, but he turned and dashed back toward Hawkins, his bulk transformed to speed and strength. Lynn watched in terror as he ducked behind a column.

He brought the stick down on the first soldier's head; Lynn heard a sharp crack as the man dropped to the floor and sprawled, his weapon sliding into a corner. The other reacted by crouching and raising his weapon, but with a motion faster than Lynn could follow Akamu picked up the first soldier's gun and opened fire.

The soldier, with a cry, reared backwards, then fell.

Looping the strap of the gun over his head with a practiced motion, Akamu grabbed Hawkins's arms and began dragging him toward Lynn.

Her legs were shaking but she forced herself to run over and help him, pick up Hawkins's ankles . . . his face was bloody . . .

she looked behind but saw and heard only Sattva giving terse directions at the head of the corridor.

Then Sattva ran toward them, motioning one of the men to follow her, her robes billowing out behind her. She tore her headdress off and tossed it behind her; it bounced once, with a hollow sound.

"In there," she shouted. "To your right." She ran past them and there *was* a door, which had simply looked like a part of the ornately paneled wall. "Inside," she said. "Quick." She shut and latched the door behind them.

She had the man take Hawkins's ankles, and they hurried down the corridor awkwardly, Akamu and the man panting. The hall was plain and narrow, with a low ceiling and a floor lit by small phosphorescent lights set into it. The dampness smelled of sunless centuries.

Lynn strode behind, her leg forgotten, her mind burning with questions in the silent urgency of their flight. After about four minutes of mazelike turns, Sattva opened another door and motioned them inside.

The room was not very large—perhaps twelve by twelve feet. It held a high bed set in an alcove, surrounded by a frieze of wooden figures. One wall was lined with books—physics and mathematics tomes, Lynn saw, and rows and rows of what looked like disks of journal updates. Another was filled with shelves of crumbling ancient manuscripts, piles of ragged uneven paper that gave the room a musty smell mingled with spicy incense. The lights were electric rather than the ubiquitous butter lamps.

The bed was covered with red silk. "Put him there," Sattva said. Her face was streaked with tears.

Hawkins was breathing, though his face and shirt were covered with blood. Lynn was astonished when he opened his eyes. "Scalp wound," he said, his voice slurred. Sattva said something sharp to him in Tibetan, Lynn thought, and he replied to her gently, in the same language, with a brief smile. Sattva squeezed his hand.

"Akamu killed at least one of the soldiers, so there will be reprisals, unless we can think of something," she said. "But we will. We're used to taking care of things like this." As she spoke she hurried around the small room, her motions grave yet controlled. She opened a cabinet and got out an oxygen mask and hooked it to a tank in the corner. She filled a basin with water and washed Hawkins's face, her eyes fierce and tender. Hawkins looked up at her and spoke again. Sattva put her ear close to his mouth and listened for a moment, nodded. She shot a glance at Lynn after his next utterance. Then he lifted his hand to his ear and his head rolled to one side.

"He's out," said Sattva. "Just as well. He said he's sorry." She looked around distractedly and continued as if talking to herself. "The idiot. Sorry for what? For trying to save the heir to the Hawaiian throne?"

Lynn felt shock in the pit of her stomach. "What?"

Sattva grabbed a basin hung on the wall with a nail and handed it to Akamu. "Pump some water for me, will you?" She gestured at a small pump handle next to a stone sink in one corner of the room. "That's right, keep pumping. It'll come out." Water began to splash into the basin, and Akamu carried it carefully to Sattva.

"Set it on that table," she said. She bathed Hawkins's head for a moment then said, "Good. It *is* just a scalp wound." Then she went on, talking now to Akamu. "We Tibetans know what it means to have someone to look to, don't we? To have someone almost mythological to believe in, despite everything. It's the biggest responsibility in the world, young man. We understand what it is to live for centuries under the domination of foreigners. We understand what it is to long to own the land our ancestors owned, rather than work it for someone who pays you a pittance. We understand what it means to have someone to look to, someone to focus on." She then deigned to speak to Lynn, meanwhile opening and slamming cupboards. "You have a heavy responsibility as well. But it looks as if you may be up to it. Damn, where are those *scissors?*"

She knelt and yanked out a drawer, tossed clothing onto the floor, grabbed a pair of long scissors, slammed the drawer with her knee, and leaned over Hawkins. She pulled Hawkins's jacket open and cut his shirt up the middle. She sucked in her breath when she saw his abdomen. "More than a scalp wound here, I'm afraid." She drew a long, shuddering breath, and her shoulders sagged. She said to the man who had helped carry Hawkins, "Put in a call for Madhur. She can be here in five hours. But that will probably be too late. We certainly don't want the Chinese, though."

"I already called her," he said. "She's coming."

"Can I help?" asked Lynn. The air was stifling. Hawkins moaned. Akamu sat very straight, staring at Sattva. Lynn could tell that he was as astonished as she was.

Sattva continued cutting the shirt and then the jacket. "There's a first-aid kit in that cupboard over there," she said.

Lynn opened the door and found it behind some clothes. "I thought Hawkins was my *father's* friend," she said. "What does he know about the Homeland Movement? Why would my father tell him to help someone associated with it?"

"We're in the business of shattering paradigms here, remember?" Then Sattva's voice softened. "A lot of the pioneer mathematics on uniting various theorems that contain higher-dimensional space was done by a Hawaiian. Cen Kalakaua. I have studied his life, as I've studied the lives of all great mathematicians. I don't count myself in their league, of course. But I do know something about the Hawaiian situation because of him."

Akamu said nothing, but his eyes were fierce.

Sattva finished cutting and tossed the bloody clothes to the floor. Lynn pulled a wad of gauze from the first-aid kit and Sattva grabbed it and pressed it to the wound in Hawkins's side. "I wonder what's happened in there." She turned to the man. "Any sign of more Chinese?" she asked.

"Not at the moment," he said, "but I imagine they've been trying to reach the others."

"We'll have to risk taking him to the dome anyway," said Sattva. "We'll need a stretcher. Send Juan down here immediately and have him bring whatever he needs to set up an IV line." The man nodded and left. Hawkins was no longer conscious, but he was still breathing.

Sattva pushed her hair over her shoulder with a bloody hand

and said to Lynn, "It would probably be the biggest help for him to know that you've gotten safely away. He'd arranged for a heli to take you to Kathmandu, but it won't be here until tomorrow. I think that the best thing for you to do is walk to the Nepalese border. It's only twenty kilometers. With your leg it will be hard, but certainly possible. You can get there by morning if you walk all night. From there you can pay someone to take you to Kathmandu, perhaps further. The tourist buses stop there. You can just pretend to be a tourist. They won't be looking for you until sometime tomorrow afternoon, I think. The trail starts just behind the temple. Hawkins suggested taking the Chinese heli, but that would just make them more angry, I think. That will crash and burn in a crevasse, later on, with two unfortunate soldiers who got caught in a wind shear. Wait." She walked across the room and touched a panel. "Find a guide for them, and packs and flashlights," she told someone.

Sattva took a deep breath; she appeared to be collecting herself. Then she said, "Oh, we found some mail for you, Lynn."

"What do you mean?"

"Sorry," Sattva said, "but you are a security risk for us. Of course we had to know everything about you. This included searching your web record." She rose and opened another door, pulled out a jacket and shrugged it on.

"How could you possibly do that?" Lynn felt confused. Sattva had seemed so friendly. "You don't even know my password."

Sattva said, "Really, Lynn. Anyway, this was from Maui. Ever heard of him?"

"Maui?" She saw that Akamu's eyes had become alert. "Do *you* know Maui?" Lynn asked him.

"No," said Akamu quickly.

She let it pass. She didn't know who he was. "What did the message say?"

"Nothing," said Sattva. "It was just an address. You can get it yourself when you have time, somewhere. And Hawkins told me something about your father a moment ago, Lynn." Sattva paused. Then she said, "Apparently he died a few days ago."

Lynn rose then sat down, dazed. "How?"

"Hawkins didn't say." She washed her hands in the basin. She looked much older—perhaps, Lynn realized, she looked her real age. Fifty?

She turned to Lynn, drying her hands with her shirttail. "I'm very sorry. Sorry that it happened and sorry that you had to learn about it here."

Lynn nodded, numb, her eyes filled with tears that made everything look even more surreal than it actually was—glinting dancing goddesses made wavelike, distorted, as if they danced before her eyes. No death, no life. Enlightenment, samsara, reincarnation—which of course is failure except for bodhisattvas. All that Buddhist crap!

Akamu took her hand and squeezed it; her tears spilled over. How strange, she thought, that he should be comforting her! She squeezed back and wiped her eyes.

Sattva looked at Hawkins for a long minute. His eyes were closed and his face looked grayish, but he was breathing peacefully. "Silly man," she whispered, touching his forehead. Then she straightened, brisk. The door opened and someone came in—Juan? with a bag flung over his shoulder and three other people as well.

"The guide's ready," said the man.

"Thank you," said Sattva, and took a last look at Hawkins. "Come with me." She pulled open a heavy sliding wood panel that had looked like part of the wall.

They walked into a smaller room bathed in dim light; the walls were entirely lined with inlaid pictures done with gold and turquoise. A low dais was surrounded by a sort of carved wood gazebo. Sattva walked over to the dais and flipped up the pillow, pushed on several tongues of wood that formed the joint of the platform, seemingly at random. The platform swung upward and cold air rushed out.

A short man was waiting there, well bundled, carrying two packs. He handed one to Akamu and one to Lynn.

Sattva reached out and touched Lynn with her forefinger, between her eyes, then put her hands together in front of her chest and bowed. "Namaste," she said, and handed her a flash.

"Namaste," said Lynn, bowing, but Akamu rushed forward and hugged the Tibetan.

Lynn switched on her flash and stepped into the cold, dark stairway.

Cen

London 2014

11

Laughter-spiked lunchtime chatter rose and fell in the White Ox. The large room, rustic with exposed beams and wainscoting, smelled of meat pies and damp wool.

Cen, however, faced away from the convivial crowd and barely registered his surroundings.

He perched on a stool at a scarred, wooden counter fronted by thick, wavy glass down which twisted drops of rain. Small electric cars surged silently round the circus beyond like so many multicolored hamsters, a bright contrast to the grim stone buildings encircling the road.

Cen absently washed down the slightly burnt crunch of grilled sardines with a swig of warm, bitter ale. When he picked up his pen it activated the screen of his notebook, which flashed once, signaling readiness. Then something disturbing caught his eye; he glanced through the steamy window and frowned.

Yes, it *was* Smith, tromping up the hill with a crowd. Everyone in it carried dripping black umbrellas, which they folded in decisive unison as they approached the White Ox.

The heavy wooden door next to him creaked open and the laughing, chattering group rushed in with a gust of wind. Cen turned away and hunched over his screen, but it was no use.

"Cen!" Smith—blond, tall, and expensively tweeded—broke from the crowd and squeezed between some tables to get to him. She was panting slightly and Cen blinked; her perfume always made his eyes burn.

"Join us for lunch, Cen, all right?"

He gestured toward his empty plate, a sinking feeling in his stomach. "I'm about done, Judy. I really have to get back." He pushed back his stool and stood.

"Oh, nonsense," she said. She was very attractive, actually.

She had what Cen believed was called strawberry blond hair, slightly curly, which gave her bangs an unruly look. Her complexion was beautifully pale, her cheeks invariably flushed beneath large blue eyes. Cen had found that she was not at all used to having people disagree with her.

She glanced at the blank screen. "Thinking hard, I see."

Wouldn't you like to know? Nettled, he reached into his pocket and tossed some coins on the table. "I'm finished, I said." He swept the notebook into his bag and cinched it shut.

Judy tilted her head, nodded sharply. "Fine, Cen. We can do this your way. Please meet me in my office at four-thirty this afternoon. I'll expect a written report *and* your files for the last month. Unadulterated, please." *You're on thin ice,* her eyes said.

Hibritten was at the bar ordering their usual pints. Cen glanced over at the large round table where the rest of Smith's group was settling in. Silverstein yanked off her gloves and tossed them onto the table, leaned back, and, seeing Cen, smiled and motioned him over.

When he first arrived at Oxford, he loved these informal lunch gatherings. Every single one had opened doors in his mind, showed him new ways to look at the information he already had, seemed to be pushing him closer and closer toward Kaiulani, toward a way to see her again, toward a way to control that experience. Here at the center of the world of quantum physics and cosmology, Cen had found an undercurrent of quiet, yet powerful excitement, like the energy of a gathering wave. He began to compare his past meetings with Kaiulani to a surfboard, a vehicle holding information with which he could catch the edge of that wave and ride it with breathtaking speed, when the moment came, to an entirely new shore. There was a greater and greater consensus that existence was almost unimaginably strange. The question that had run through Heisenberg's mind, again and again, after his many talks with Bohr—"Can nature possibly be as absurd as it seemed to us in those atomic experiments?"—now had a definitive answer.

Yes.

Take just one thing—Bell's Interconnectedness Theorem,

which proved that physical reality can *only* exist in a milieu of faster-than-light information.

And that this milieu is the ordinary world of objects, which is . . . *created,* if you will, by information coming from somewhere *else* . . . superluminally. *Faster than light!*

This fact had not been in dispute for over fifty years. But what did it really *mean?*

Cen was convinced that this basic fact had something to do with his connection to Kaiulani.

During the first weeks after his arrival, an international conference had been taking place. Cen had been delighted when Judy, Dr. Judith Smith, had taken him under her wing and made sure that he tagged along. He could hardly believe that he was actually in the presence of people whose proofs and papers he had pored over, some of whom were Nobel laureates. He watched, thrilled, as arguments and discussions were punctuated by cosmological luminaries shoving their dishes aside and sketching on the tablecloth; after that he'd volunteered his spiral notebook whenever he could, and now one precious notebook was filled with wild speculation about tachyons and how time may have begun—if it ever *had* . . .

That was before he discovered that Judy worked for IS.

It had been an accident, really. He'd been in her office, waiting for her, when the tiny angled screen on her desk lit with a picture of a man. He said, "Dr. Smith, this is Ed Nicholman from London Interspace. Please return my call as soon as possible." In the middle of the message she entered the room; she pretended that nothing had happened, but she knew that he knew.

He had felt like an idiot.

He encoded all the work he did on what he called the Kaiulani Proofs, of course, but anything encoded could be decoded. Judy saw his course work, nothing more. He was "working" on a doctoral problem that he'd solved long ago; he fed her bits of it whenever she demanded something, but spent all of his time using the magnificent resources at hand to solve the problem the facts of his own life posed. He wondered if and when

Smith would explode and baldly remind him of the deal he'd made with IS.

He shrugged on his coat, waved at Silverstein, shouldered his bag, and walked out into the rain.

A cold wind whipped it into his face. Poor Kaiulani, sent from paradise to this dank climate. No wonder she was always sick.

She was constantly in his thoughts. He worried about her as if she were alive, as if worrying might do some good. She was homesick. She was asking for a bit more money, quite politely. She was writing about her course work—mathematics, languages, politics, history. She was asking about the situation at home, because the letters from Hawaii were so strange and cryptic, telling her to trust no one.

On impulse he turned and walked toward the Underground station. Oxford was for all intents and purposes a part of London now, linked by the Underground and taxed accordingly.

Cen mused as he walked, splashing through puddles heedless of his increasingly soaked feet. He had heard rumors that IS had other students at Oxford, too, and around the world, working on all sorts of problems. Genetic engineering. Nanobiology, nanotechnology. Every once in a while he relaxed enough to download some generic news, where something about the moon colony that was getting up and running again was invariably featured. The moon colony, and the generation ship that would be built from the moon base, was the prize of Interspace. There were many investors. And many naysaying alarmists. Some argued that it was too commercial, with its proposed pleasure and shopping dome; they were countered by those showing greatly enhanced revenue projections that could be used to speed up the progress of the generation ship. Only rarely were there investigative stories trying to hint at a dark side to IS. Try following the hypertext links on *that* and see how far you got!

At the station he changed his mind suddenly and punched the icon for a topside train ticket to Victoria Station.

"You ought to get yourself a nice warm hat," scolded the elderly woman in line behind him. "You're a fool to go out in the rain with a bare head."

"You're right; thank you, ma'am," he said. *I'm a fool period; you've hit the nail right on the head, old lady.* The British amused him. Always so bossy and sure of themselves.

He didn't have long to wait. He munched on a packet of spicy dried bananas from a machine and washed them down with a can of hot, sweet tea. After seven minutes the train arrived and he climbed aboard: a local, and very old. He could only tell that the worn holographic mural on its side was of Windsor Palace because the title below was done in stubborn blue paint. At this time of day only a few passengers were scattered through his car.

The train slid through the back gardens of the London suburbs, passed through the old stations; he liked watching the foreigners who lived in the various rings of settlement. They were a different mix than in Hawaii: Indians, Africans, Slavs, and the ghostly pale native Brits. In a neighborhood chiefly distinguished by astonishingly large piles of broken bottles in the streets he saw a knot of shiny-jacketed Plastic Lads hanging about beneath a gray awning. He stared with interest, but they were too far away for him to see if their bodies were as fantastically distorted via recreational surgery as the urban legend claimed. The train passed World Famous Mod Row—so proclaimed by a huge flashing banner—where illegal shops imitated in schlocky, often deadly ways, the various computer-human modifications that were spin-offs of the space program; where distant cousins of the bionan that had killed Mei, infinite generations ago, and in infinite variations, were sought by addicts. Beneath the gray sky, the holograms that shimmered in many languages, with accompanying pictures for the illiterate, were like beacons advertising joys and horrors that only religious promises could have matched in previous ages. A young woman danced in the rain, whirling as ecstatically as any dervish, wet face lifted to the rain, eyes closed, long red hair swirling about her, her abandoned shirt trampled beneath her feet. No one on the street paid her the slightest attention. Cen sometimes wondered if the previously elite apprehensions of the investigators of matter, which seemed more bizarre with each passing year, were now a zeitgeist seeping into society, one of madness, ecstasy, and fear.

As neighborhoods fanned slowly past, some drab, some elegant, the buildings became more massive; the streets more stately. Victoria Station swallowed the train at the end of the line, ushering it into the Industrial Age. The station was beautifully restored, though harboring its full complement of beggars and crazies. Housed here were shops of exclusive clothiers, restaurants catering to international tastes, vending machines that would charge your notebook with any written information in existence, in any language, translated to another if you so desired, at a speed dictated only by the size of your credit account.

Cen tried to ignore such things, preferring to try to see Victoria Station as Kaiulani may have, as a symbol of newness and speed at the apex of England's greatest power, when she was part of an elite group of people whose power was about to vanish—the young royalty of the world.

However, if his theories were correct, it would be far more difficult for him to ever see Kaiulani in London than it had been in Hawaii. Just mapping out the physical locations where she had been was more complex by many magnitudes; Honolulu was tiny compared to London, and Kaiulani had lived in Hawaii for years. She had not been in London all that long.

He paused for a moment before stepping down from the train. One of Kaiulani's names, Victoria, came from her mother's invitation to Queen Victoria's Jubilee, where she had met the queen. Of course, the Hawaiian court had been perfectly at home in London—for several generations Hawaiian royals had been making world tours. But they particularly liked the British and modeled the Hawaiian monarchy on the British. Not surprising considering that the British presence had been felt strongly in the islands well before the Americans arrived. How oddly amazed they had been to find that the Americans did not play fair. They trusted the Americans until it was too late.

The station was a cauldron of activity, as usual. Trains arrived and left constantly, the smells of five kinds of ethnic cooking mingled in the cool air; a thousand people milled about, forming constantly changing currents through the crowd, shadows from the complicated strutworks above falling across it all and train schedules echoing incomprehensively as ever in English, Japanese, German, Mandarin. If someone was following him, Cen certainly had no way of telling in this crowded place.

He stood still in the cavernous steel-strutted station, aching, short of breath. Kaiulani had most certainly been here, many times. She had been quite a traveler. How perfect a ruler she would have been—canny and worldly enough to be an effective stateswoman, at ease with many cultures, with wide enough vision to see just where Hawaii stood in terms of other nations, and how best the land could serve the people who had originally settled it. Just one visit to President Cleveland, in her Paris gown and smart ostrich-feathered hat, where she stated Hawaii's case with erudition and intelligence, filling the papers of the time with flowery paens of praise, had been enough to stave off annexation until his term ended. Cen thought of how the Hawaiians—*his* people, however much he felt removed from the Homeland Movement—now suffered under the heel of a new oppressor, IS. Funny how he was beginning to feel a kinship with Maui, so far from home. He'd expected instead to feel further and further removed from that turmoil, from those oblique demands.

A bagpiper under a stone arch next to Cen began the cacophonous prelude to music; his pipes bleated mournfully. His beard was long and filled with bits of food; his clothes were ragged. As the first skirl got up to speed and issued from the pipes, Cen turned and thought he saw her.

A woman in an elegant, old-fashioned hoop skirt was climbing onto a train. A dainty folded umbrella hung from a strap on her wrist. Beneath a sweeping, fanciful green velvet hat decorated with several peacock feathers was piled dark curly hair, and he caught a glimpse of a classic, utterly familiar profile—

"*Kai!*" he yelled, and darted down the platform. The door slid shut behind her and the train pulled away slowly. He ran alongside, tears streaming down his face, hoping to see if it was her, *really*—

Panting, he slowed. He watched the end of the last car recede as it left the station. Then he watched the vanishing point of the tracks for a bit longer and might have done so for an hour but for an obscuring fog that slowly gathered.

You are certifiable, he thought, as he trudged back into the station. Like a touchstone, he retraced the slim strand of memory that led back to his belief that he *had* seen her, long ago, not just imagined her. How long ago, Century Kalakaua? Soon it will be a decade. You're clinging to these beliefs like a child, aren't you? What's the point?

Yet his very presence here in London was proof that Interspace did not think his beliefs chimerical. They did not know the extent of his madness, of course, or his genius, whichever it might be, and he believed the truth might lie closer to the former. They did not think that he was searching for a passage to his lost love; they did not believe as he did that it might be possible to transfer from one manifestation of what Vilenkin had called the metauniverse to another virtually identical manifestation. They only wanted to know how to go very far, very fast, and how to predict the location of other livable planets.

But—was that so? This was the main goal of Interspace endeavor—of this Cen was sure. Yet—the memory of Mei arose, for an instant, the last time he'd seen her alive, *really* alive, not the frightened sparrow IS had turned her into. Her last true words had been of wormholes, of doors in space and time. What had become of those in Interspace who had believed such things were possible?

They had sacrificed Mei. And how many others? Where were those people now, and how much influence did they have? Were they somehow keeping tabs on him?

He passed the bagpipe man again, pulled his credit squirt from his pocket—an object the shape of his enclosed hand, fitting naturally with it, with a separate sensor for each fingertip—activated it with his thumbprint, and transferred a pound with his index finger to the thick bracelet on the man's wrist across a gap of a foot. A green jewel on the bracelet flashed and the man glanced down to read how much Cen had given him; nodded brief thanks. Cen walked on, past the ticket counters and the tourist bureau, and emerged on the street. Just as in Honolulu, no private vehicles were allowed in the city center.

At least I'm missing my meeting with Dr. Smith, he thought. One good thing. He smiled. A very good thing indeed!

As usual, the London air was chill and dank. The street was lined with granite edifices, and newer glass towers; a few blocks ahead a row of leafless trees traced dark lines against the sky. He set himself on *wander;* he had no particular goal. He sneezed several times as he strode along and pulled a handkerchief out of his pocket to wipe his nose. He couldn't remember ever having a cold before coming here, and now he was constantly sick. In sympathy with Kaiulani? He realized that his thin raincoat was soaked. Perhaps he should heed his fellow traveler and buy a hat. Hats! He laughed out loud, drawing glances on the crowded street. Yes, she had a hat or two, hadn't she? The finest millinery to be found, the exotic feathers fashionable in Thomas Huxley's time arcing above her head, curving around and drawing the eye back to her fine face, with those direct dark eyes, lively with conviction and intelligence.

It had not been the Hawaiians who resented the Victorian-like reign of the royal family, back there at the end of the nineteenth century, he mused, but the American businessmen. Iolani Palace, in which they'd isolated Queen Liliuokalani after having her arrested on trumped-up charges, had been a fitting royal palace of its time. He well remembered slipping inside with a tour group one time, marveling at the imported ornate furniture, the crystal chandeliers, the throne room. They had probably been the most benevolent monarchs in history and the most loved. Kaiulani's aunt Liliuokalani, he recalled, had agitated for a transpacific phone line and bitterly remarked after she was illegally deposed that it would not have been to the advantage of the American businessmen sharking after Hawaiian riches for her to be in easy contact with Washington when the fate of Hawaii was being decided. She had found it necessary to leave Honolulu and go to Washington herself several times, always traveling in state and staying in the finest hotels; her absences from her kingdom had not been beneficial either.

But—had he actually *seen* Princess Victoria Kaiulani, less than an hour ago?

Hands in pocket, head bent beneath cold drizzle, he walked farther, passing a large park of looping walks that vanished into hedges higher than his head. A man walking two Russian wolfhounds hurried past, looking away from Cen and turning into the park. Cen hoped the waterproofing on his bag was as good as the manufacturer claimed. He had nowhere to go, really; perhaps since he was in London he should go into a pub, turn on his notebook, and call up the maps that he'd painstakingly composed—maps that showed where Kaiulani had been, when, and for how long. The equation he'd derived from the curve of time and location, including the times and locations when *he'd* seen her, was there. But it was unfinished, hauntingly open, waiting for the addition of more variables before the chaos of it might settle into a predictable fractal. But once he *had* that information . . .

Heaven and ecstasy, for him, the byproduct of knowledge beyond the wildest dreams of most of the humans on this planet . . .

He shook his head as he walked, ridiculing himself. Why the hell should going to the places where she had once set foot make a goddamned bit of difference? The worlds had whirled through infinities of space since then. Despite that, he had traced her path—the theaters chronicled in her letters; the museums; even the royal anterooms available to him via tours . . . wildly searching faces in all these places, always with odd despair-tinged hope, black self-ridicule . . .

He stopped, suddenly utterly weary. Within his mind the world devolved into bizarre topologies, into vibrating strings whose evidence of existence was traces of electromagnetic force left over from the big bang. Now he had a phenomenon—his love, no less—that he wanted to jam into all the theories that had been floating around unresolved for almost a hundred years. Theories waiting for the unifying vision that would actually be able to use the information available at last to the conscious mind after infinities that lacked the singular, peculiar phenomenon of consciousness.

He realized that he was on a long, lonely, foggy stretch of wide stone walk punctuated at precise intervals by benches and ancient leafless trees that receded into mist. Oak, by the look of the brown leaves blown against the walk's border in a sodden line. It was utterly hushed here, as if far out in the country. No Londoners. The sky had come down to earth. He might be in ancient Londinium, laid out in the midst of bird-wild marsh, while vengeful red-haired Queen Boadicea plotted to storm the city and drive the Romans out.

Boadicea had failed. The Romans had won. The Homeland Movement, which he followed hopefully at a distance in spite of his skepticism, would fail. Conquerors conquered; that was their job, their goal, their drive. IS would win. They conquered and enslaved. It was the human way. And time went one way only; a good thing, actually. At least there was something about humans, about consciousness, that made it seem so. He, for one, would certainly not trade all the knowledge he had for the chance to live as an ancient Hawaiian.

But would he trade it for Kaiulani?

If he made it to her time . . . *what would he know? What would he remember? How would he be changed?*

A cold blast of wind hit him, sending a wild shiver through him. It had not been wise to thumb his nose at Dr. Smith. But what could IS do, anyway? They thought his mind was their cash cow. As long as they were nice to him, as long as they had something to offer, like the finest education money could buy, he would be around. If he came to any conclusions, though, he had no real reason to turn them over. Were they counting perhaps on his scientific vanity? Look at me, Cen Kalakaua—I've thought of this! I want the world to know; I want a soft drink or VR game named after me! He had no illusions about monetary profits in that situation; the subject did not interest him, but IS would claim any and all profits for their own.

Well, they would continue to be disappointed.

He paused—did he hear footsteps behind him? Some spy of Dr. Smith's following him? Then he almost laughed out loud. You *are* in a public place, idiot! There *might* be other people around.

Sometimes he felt as if he was on one side of a very thin veil, and that Kaiulani was on the other side, hands pressed against some membrane that he could dissolve with knowledge. Rain swept over him again. Now he was utterly soaked. He kept walking, ignoring it. Perhaps he was in some sort of trough in the unfolding of the complex system humans called time. Soon he'd be caught in a swirling vortex and all things would become clear, during the infinite instant before he was sucked into a black hole, unable to communicate what he knew.

Ah, shit, he thought, I'm *freezing*. Just give me a cheap hotel, a shot of whisky, and a hot bath. Where did this damned mall lead, anyway? Where had he wandered to?

Into some part of London he'd never been to, he found, as shadowy buildings came into view and he walked toward them. Not a bit surprising. After all, he'd only been to the center of what was practically the largest city in the world half a dozen times.

He should plan to go next to Brighton. After all, that was where she had spent quite a bit of her time in England, being tutored in languages, mathematics, and history. Yes, that was it. The information he needed was in Brighton. London was a dead end. She hadn't spent much time here, actually.

But his optimism was utterly shot. This was no way to go about things. He was trying to do two different things at once—work up a whole new theory of the nature of space-time and traipse around Europe searching for a ghost. But *location* was an important matrix. Fine, he told himself. And after Brighton you can head for Jersey, then Paris, Scotland, the south of France, various places in Germany, all the palaces and fine places where she'd hung out with the other royals of the day. Won't Dr. Smith be interested in that! Trips to London wouldn't arouse suspicion. But all those other places . . . that was what had been holding him back. Of course, if he and IS weren't playing a shell game he could probably ask for the funds to do these things and they would gladly pay. But they knew nothing of his real concerns, and he had to keep it that way. Now he had access to unlimited computer time, to luminaries in cosmology, physics, mathematics. The deal was that he would make all his thoughts available to them. He had no qualms about not keeping a deal with people he considered killers.

He felt so dense. What kind of information do you *need?* he asked himself. Your definition of the problem is wrong. You lack intelligence, the spark that will bring all this together. He wanted to weep. You're making yourself sick.

But—there *was* a clear record of where she had stayed, what she had done. She was forever having fine clothing made, but trying to stay within her budget. She had been shielded from the political events back home until it was revealed to her that her uncle David had died, and that perhaps it was best for her to travel to Washington and meet President Cleveland, to try to sway him against the annexationists lobbying the Congress at that time. Cen wondered, not for the first time, if through research evidence could be found for the poisoning of the *alii* of Hawaii. It seemed pretty strange to him that not just one generation but several—from a two-year-old heir to Kaiulani's mother, many of her cousins, and aunts, and uncles—had all mysteriously died within a ten-year period. She herself had been only twenty-three when she died—of what? Bright's disease complicated by self-inflicted pneumonia, as the stories suggested, brought on by a wild gallop through a cold storm on Mauna Loa's wintry slopes?

So *what,* Cen? She's dead. You can't do anything about all that now. If you could, now, just exactly what would you do?

A street of cozy-looking pubs resolved before him, their signs dripping. All bow windows, and dark wood inside, he knew, anachronistic as hell. He was caught by a sneezing fit and when it was over he was certain that to avoid pneumonia he *had* to have a hot bath and go to bed.

He paced more quickly down the wet street. Gas lamps flickered on, or at least good tourist imitations, and their lights shimmered on the cobblestones. He checked his watch. Well, it was pretty late in the afternoon. His stipend money should have been transferred to his account yesterday, and he certainly hadn't spent much money since he'd arrived in England.

He passed two small hotels that looked much too elegant for his budget and went inside the third. It was still costly but he realized that he'd better stop or he might become truly ill.

The room was small, almost stiflingly full of chintz with monstrous pink flowers. But the bathtub, with dull brass fittings he actually had to fiddle with to adjust the temperature rather than punching it in digitally, was large enough for him to stretch out in. He made tea with the kettle, put his wet clothes on the towel dryer, and passed out on the bed with the quilt wrapped round him. He dreamed, as always, of Kaiulani, and then the dream splintered into planes of white light, which changed to particles . . .

He was awakened by the sound of sobbing.

He opened his eyes. First, he thought someone in his dream had been crying, but as he lay in the bed, he realized that the sounds were coming from the next room.

He heard a muffled knock, the click of a door opening, a voice: "No, I'm not coming to dinner tonight. No, I'm perfectly fine. Fine! Yes, maybe later." The door shut.

He sat up, electrified. It was, without a doubt, Kaiulani's voice, now with a cultured British accent.

He began to tremble, his mind flooded with implications that had not occurred to him when younger. What if he saw her and it somehow changed history?

But he had seen her before, had he not, and as far as he could tell, history had not changed.

If it had, would he know it?

His clothes were still damp. Fine, he thought, pulling them on hastily. Does that mean I'm still in the same universe? What would *that* mean, anyway? Then his thoughts lost coherence, overwhelmed by immense joy that seemed to brighten all he saw—the mundane bed, chair, nightstand. Where *was* he, suddenly? Could it be true? After all these years?

He stepped into the hall, turned left. His footsteps made no sound on the flowered runner.

He stood in front of her door. He looked up and down the hall and saw no one. He raised his hand to knock. It was shaking. He heard muffled steps on the stairs and quickly rapped on the door.

There was no answer. The steps rounded the landing and began on the next flight. He knocked again, this time more boldly.

The door opened a crack, and Kaiulani looked straight into his eyes.

Her face was tilted upward, her exquisite golden skin a bit more pale than he remembered, her cheeks a delicate, natural pink. Dark curls fell across her forehead. "Yes?"

"Kai," he whispered and grabbed her; he held her close and before even thinking kissed her wildly, quickly, and she was kissing him back—

He pulled her inside and shut the door, then was filled with an instant's confusion—perhaps she had no idea of who *he* was—perhaps she thought him someone else? He was a man now; not a boy.

He needn't have worried.

"Cen!" Her voice was low and unsteady as she drew away. "What are you doing in London? Where have you been all these years?"

In another universe, of which there are an infinite number, he thought.

He let go and stepped back, looked at her.

She was wearing a fine black silk dressing gown wrapped tight around her tiny waist. Her black, kinky hair hung loose around her shoulders, and caught the lamplight in soft glints.

"How—how old are you?" he asked.

She looked at him strangely. "Seventeen," she said. "But you are *much* older . . . " She took another step back. "What is *happening*? Sometimes I've thought I must have imagined . . . I'm sorry . . . "

This was exactly what he had feared. "I'm not sure," he said. The truth! "How *are* you?" His mind did not seem to function.

A small coal stove in the corner of her room gave off an acrid smell that mingled with the scent of roses in a vase on a table next to the bed. A small card had been tossed down next to the vase; Cen wanted to open it. *Who . . . ?*

She thrust her hands into the large pockets of her robe and spoke; her voice a woman's now, deeper, more melodious.

"It's horrible here," she said. "I want so badly to go home. It's terribly cold and always raining. The people here are very kind, but I've gotten such strange letters from home from Uncle David, warning me to be careful and to trust no one. No one! Do you know how difficult it is to be suspicious of everyone around you, the people who are supposed to be your friends? And today we went to that wretched Tower of London. I've been there before." She walked across the room and stood by the window looking out. "I don't understand how these people can be so proud of it. Everyone trying to poison each other! Spies! Those poor princes! People were tortured there for years! Executed! Cen!"

She whirled, her eyes bright. "I know that Hawaiians sacrificed people. They've been cruel—utterly cruel and warlike, in the past. Kamehameha killed multitudes in order to unite Hawaii under his rule. But since him, because of him, things have changed. We all work together now, for our country and for each other. We've built schools and hospitals and fine homes—even a royal palace. Not as big as Buckingham Palace, but beautiful in every detail, as beautiful as some of those German castles that Ludwig built! These people *celebrate* cruelty. They're *proud* of it." Her tears spilled over and she wiped them away angrily. "And what are *you* doing here? Where have you been? I've wanted to see you so often . . . Cen . . . "

She dropped into a chair, leaned forward with her hands in her lap. He went and sat in the facing chair, in the window alcove. He wanted to take her hands but was afraid. He should leave. Now. She fixed her eyes on his.

"Cen, I remember. The towers made of glass, all around Iolani Palace. The fast carriages. The statue of Liliuokalani with some . . . some dates on it . . . " She took a deep breath.

"How is this possible?" She reached for his hands, touched them, and he swallowed hard.

"I—I can't say, Kai."

The strangeness of it was overwhelming. The little room swam before his eyes and only her face held steady. Only her great brown eyes. He rose. "I've got to go."

"No! *Please* don't go, Cen! I'm begging you!"

"I can't—I can't stay!"

Weird visions coursed through his mind—visions of IS people walking in through the very door he'd entered by—maybe even Dr. Smith, smirking, thinking about how to invest her money when she won the Nobel Prize in physics . . .

He was putting Kaiulani in terrible danger.

He tore himself from her, rushed to the door, and ran out into the corridor, slamming the door behind him. He heard the knob rattle, and running steps on the stairs, as he rushed into his door and locked it behind him, trembling, sick to his stomach.

He looked around. He was in his modern room.

He stood there for a moment. His clothes were still damp. She had touched them.

Could she walk out into the corridor and into *his* room?

He took a deep breath and just stood, silently. Something clicked deep in his mind.

At last, was all he thought, at least in English. For his mind was aswirl with numbers, ideas that were like shapes, like pure energy. . . .

He picked up the phone. He was surprised when a real person answered.

"Room service? I want a pot of coffee. No, not tea. Very strong coffee. Can you do that? A steak, rare. Yes, whatever comes with it. A bottle of single-malt whisky. I don't know. Is that a good one? Oh, of *course*—sorry."

He turned up the heat, took off his clothes, and donned the robe hanging behind the bathroom door. He sat down, took out his notebook, found it dry despite the rain. His food and drink came, and he ate absently. Two hours later he heard the door slam next door. He tensed.

"I *told* you that show would be a waste of money. But you never listen to what *I* say." A man's voice.

A woman replied. "I rather enjoyed it. I'm sorry you didn't."

"You know I hate musicals."

Cen let his breath go, filled with loss and relief. Then his fingers flew.

If he was right . . .

If he was right.

It was a fine line, the if-he-was-right problem, he soon realized. If he was right, he had to keep it a secret. At the same time, to fuel his work he had to learn even more.

The entire, exciting world of contemporary mathematics was open to him. He had never felt so completely alive.

He walked the drizzly winter campus, and then the delicately flowered spring campus, with increasing confidence, his mind filled with wonder because everywhere he looked it seemed that whatever he needed, in the next step of his proofs, appeared beneath his nose as if the entire world were just one vast field of information heading directly toward him, from all possible directions. It was just necessary for him to sit in the center and take the next bit of information, fit it in, fiddle and temper and stretch, then look round to see what was next. It all seemed as clear to him as if he were building an actual, physical edifice.

He haunted the web constantly, as if cruising down a long, fascinating street, stopping to enter first this building and that. He devised several disguises for himself, of course, though he was sure they did not deceive IS. Still, he wanted his search to appear like the work of a dozen different people, unconnected, and therefore of no significance. Like a bird building a nest, he took from every branch of mathematics and worked it in. And if he did not find what he needed he invented it. He did not want others to make the same links he was making, where everything formed itself so beautifully, as if the raw essence of existence were declaring itself to him in a relationship much like love. He did not question his feeling that the universe was alive, fluid and magnificent and possessed of infinite alluring mystery that he searched daily for clues.

He drew from a smorgasbord of twentieth- and early twenty-first-century mathematics as if each system were a discrete jewel with its own manifestation of truth, of the truth that was indubitably *there,* the bridge to Kaiulani, the exotic matter with which he would enter her world and save her.

For he did not doubt any longer that he would. Or die trying. But time was, in a crazy way, short. For in that world where she lived she would die in a matter of years. Even if he *did* manage to go there, though, how could he save her? That was the next problem. Evidently she'd been sick a long time. But he'd deal with that later.

His exotic matter—that which held this particular wormhole, or whatever it was, open for him was somehow generated by an emotional interaction within his brain, the very chemicals of love changing something within his brain. He knew that was crazy but there—he'd thought it. He didn't understand it at all on one level yet because of it he was able to forge the proofs that he knew were true. It was something new in the universe, a possibility that had just evolved, like the human ability to use tools or language. It was the conscious ability to affect the quantum wave function. Perhaps previous occurrences accounted for sightings of ghosts or for mysterious disappearances. But he was in the fortunate position of realizing the possibility, based on the deep structure of the universe and of time, and of having the tools, after years of growing proficiency, to be able to write it down.

Late at night when he was on the web he could almost visualize time as something with an ever-changing shape. Yet each change created a new, fantastic, incredibly intricate pattern, from one point of view, a fractal that repeated itself from infinitely large to infinitely small, but whose inhabitants would always think of themselves as . . . body-sized. He reworked the principle of mediocrity, first postulated by Alexander Vilenkin in a brief *Physical Review* letter.

Vilenkin, using only known facts about quantum cosmology, postulated that we "are one of the infinite number of civilizations living in thermalized regions of the metauniverse. Although it may be tempting to believe that our civilization is very special, the history of cosmology demonstrates that the assumption of being average is often a fruitful hypothesis." He had made the statement decades ago, in *Physical Review Letters,* volume 74, number 6.

Cen had the paper, with its careful reasoning, memorized.

Vilenkin dubbed his idea the principle of mediocrity. He said that the beauty of his theory was that, since it was well supported with known facts, if it could be disproved, the tools were there to do so. Have at it, he challenged—disprove the principle of mediocrity.

In thirty years, no one had been able to disprove it.

Assuming the Big Bang was true, and not everyone did, then the oscillating patterns within the fractal that was time were probably approximately the same age. Since Kaiulani's world was so similar to his, yet almost concurrent as she appeared to be a mere hundred years behind him, he gradually came to believe that the Kaiulani he knew was not from the past of his own timeline, but another, different one in which she had seen *him.*

And from that tiny difference would grow great changes.

Would a change in one pattern change them all? He tried to work out limits.

And always, he worked for himself only. Anything larger was exceedingly dangerous. He was constructing something entirely individual, based upon *himself,* an individual. He was digging a small gold mine on his own stake, and he intended to pull the shorings down over him when he left. He wanted the pathways of time to close behind him, like a healed wound. He took great pains to blunt any possible directions of thought that might help generalize it for use by others. Selfish, and yet not selfish. Protecting the metauniverse from Interspace and its insidious philosophy, which had killed Mei and Ross and who knows who else. Certainly there were pristine unpopulated earthlike worlds. He did not want to be responsible for their infection.

But, he wondered occasionally, surely the principle of mediocrity made it probable that someone else in the metauniverse was coming to the same conclusions as he was. He envisioned a sudden new crystallization, a leap in consciousness and ability in the living tissue of the metauniverse like the amazing leaps in evolution that seemed to show up in the fossil record. If physical bodies could evolve, could change in such sweeping ways, then why not consciousness itself, why not the metauniverse, why not . . .

Why not.

Despite his pains to disguise himself he became aware that he was gaining a reputation in the international world of mathematics. He received occasional E-mail with tidbits that frankly fascinated him; he received invitations to speak, which he always declined.

And once he got a message from someone that he followed like a seabird diving for a fish, for it had the flavor of home, and he broke through into the amazing electronic universe of the International Homeland Movement. It seethed with energy and conviction; the power of the place amazed him. He could walk through communities interacting with people dealing with problems, describing their community gardens, talking of new social paradigms and welcoming all people of the earth, indigenous and otherwise, to join their new society. Their logo was a Pacific voyaging canoe, of Hawaiian design though each island group had had their own. These had not really been canoes, but precisely, planked ships up to seventy feet long in which they explored the largest expanse of water on earth and mapped it in their minds. Their international community, where no one's name was revealed, was designing its own generation ship. They had come quite a long way, he saw, from the days when they had pumped their vision into the virtual arcades of Honolulu. This was the real thing, with real engineers, real social scientists.

But, he thought, not real money. Only Interspace had that, and they did a good job of sucking in every new independent start-up company that had a nifty new idea or materials innovation. Cen suspected that their spectacular buyout rate had more than a little bit of strong-arm action to convince these entrepreneurs to sell out. But here in the Homeland Web he found the sort of atmosphere that sparked new ideas—perhaps outlandish at first, before some genius figured out how to make them actually *work*.

Uploading consciousness was a hot topic too. Apparently some factions claimed they had the hardware to transfer the contents of a living brain into crystal matrices. Cen was amused to see that it seemed difficult for them to find volunteers willing to commit their still-living, healthy brains to the transfer—what, no faith? Your body would die, of course, but what would that matter? Your consciousness would live *forever*. Right. But the debate was lively and interesting.

Cen went there sometimes, to be refreshed, carefully avoiding direct contact, marveling at their audacity and inventiveness.

But mostly he mapped the strange attractor of the vast fractal humans called time. Sometimes he could only point in a certain direction, say, *"there,"* and that was enough, for him. His quest pulled him onward with happy, breathtaking speed, with as much intensity as he had dreamed of, when younger. He was here now, purely, doing what he was born to do:

Find Kaiulani—fragile, proud, intelligent—and help her fulfill her promise.

The rest of this world could go hang.

And for another year, he saw that it did.

12

C en!"
It was a day of rare blue sky, over a year after he'd seen Kaiulani. He'd spent the time since in a blaze of thought and research. He felt so close to knowing. Something . . .

The great autumn oaks burned red, gold, and yellow against the stone buildings of his college. Because it was so beautiful, the jolt of irritation that always struck him when he heard Dr. Smith's voice seemed more intense.

He heard her high heels click behind him; resignedly, he turned and waited. She always dressed in expensive suits. She took herself quite seriously. She seemed to have no sense of humor. Maybe, thought Cen, if IS wasn't breathing down her neck, she might. She had to be in hock to them, there was no other way to think about it. Her sleek, expensive steel gray car, the rumors of her fine country house, bespoke a deep hole in which she would founder without their dole.

Cen did not feel sorry for her.

She arrived next to him slightly breathless. "Mind if I walk with you?"

What difference would that make? Cen started walking and she did, too.

"Look, Cen," she said, "you need to tell me how you're doing with the data."

"I have no experimentally verifiable data," he said.

"I think that I've been too lenient with you," she said. "You're touted as some sort of genius, fine. I've seen no evidence of anything of the sort, but all right. You get free rein. But you're supposed to *produce* something. You're supposed to at least be *assimilating* something. For all we know you might be rewriting *Winnie-the-Pooh.*"

"We?" he asked.

"The cosmology department review board," she said, without a wink of hesitation.

He stopped, turned and faced her. She almost ran into him and stopped, flustered, her eyes angry.

He said, "You know and I know that you work for Interspace, so why don't we just talk about what's really bothering you. You're supposed to put the squeeze on me to perform magical feats of calculation that will create a whole new theory of everything, no less, an entire new paradigm. I can certainly understand why you might think me incapable of doing so. No one else has ever done this. There might be some vital calculations lurking in the history of mathematics that could clarify all this if only the right person put it all together. Who knows? I'm certainly not just doing rows of arithmetic problems, if that's what you want to know. But I may never have the answer. There may be no answer, at least not to this problem, at least not one that present-day humans can possibly imagine. So just lighten up."

Her mouth quivered. She brushed her hair back with one hand. After a moment she said, "I think you'll find, Century Kalakaua, that you can't blow me off quite so easily." She turned and hiked back the way they had come.

Always the diplomat, aren't you? Cen was not at all pleased with what he'd done.

But he was beginning to realize—and it was a big realization for him—that he could do what he needed to do anywhere. With web access to journals and mathematical texts, he could search to his heart's content. Of course, that did take money, and he was sure that his web time was monitored; he looked at a lot of totally irrelevant things to muddy the waters. The academic atmosphere had been wonderful here, the perfect catalyst to get him up to a certain level, a certain way of looking at things, to professionalize his outlook. But now?

He slung his bag down next to him on the library steps, pulled out and unwrapped a sandwich. He took a bite, put it back in the bag, rose.

He had reached a certain point in his calculations. He had put it off out of fear of being wrong and of losing his position here, but he had to face the fact: he was ready for a test.

It was something he didn't want to do with IS breathing down his neck.

Without giving it any more thought, his decision was made.

Walking through the cool shade cast by ancient stone buildings, crossing long-preserved green courtyards bright in the glorious autumn afternoon, he headed back through town. Climbing the narrow, crooked stairs to his tiny apartment, he was surprised to see the door standing open.

They wanted him to know that they'd been there.

The place was just one room, no more. His kitchen was a rice steamer, a hot plate, and a small refrigerator. IS probably would not have believed that he could live on so little money. He'd saved over half of every credit dump.

The place had not actually been ransacked. But he always

left his computer on; now the screen was dark. Damn, Smith had worked fast.

He tried to contain his rising panic and anger. Don't worry. They can't make sense out of anything they took. There were some parts of his proofs he knew by heart, important bridges that he'd never written down.

As he looked around the room, he realized that he felt light and free, rather than afraid and cowed, as they'd no doubt meant him to feel. He owed them nothing. A small shaft of sunlight came through the one high window, hitting, as it always did this time of day, one of the few personal items he kept, a photograph of Ross.

How hard it was to control someone who really had nothing more to lose, eh?

He walked over, folded the picture, and stuck it in his pack. He gathered the CDs of math and physics and chaos texts scattered about and put them into a carrying case; shoved a few items of clothing into his pack.

He closed the door behind him and went back down the stairs.

Nothing to lose.

An entire world to gain.

Several months later, rain streamed down the window of the M Street café Cen usually frequented. Washington, D.C., was even worse than London. Snow was predicted.

Cen's mood was dark. He stared at yesterday's *Washington Post*'s sketchy science page on his screen; for some perverse reason he had not only saved it, but looked at it every hour or so even though he had it memorized. Dr. Judith Smith at Oxford was quoted briefly; word had got out about her latest research. Which was, of course, his. And what a genius she was!

Genius. Kalakaua, what a genius you could be if this world was all you cared about. He snorted and ordered another beer. The beer here was very good. The marble bar shone dimly, the brass trappings picked up the light and glowed.

He wondered what he would do next. Smith would eventually be proven wrong—that is, if anyone could actually figure out exactly what it was that she was claiming. He was pretty sure she hadn't the foggiest notion of what the information she was parroting might really mean.

He knew that anything she'd ferreted out and cobbled together was wrong because the window *he* had calculated, the point on the jagged fractal he believed time might be, had come and gone. Nothing had happened.

He might have to start from scratch. But that was so depressing.

The darkness at his core seemed to be intensified by the relentless winter gloom and bad weather here. Sometimes he thought about his mother, and that made it worse. Stupid bones. He almost wished he hadn't found them. If she hadn't shown them to him, she wouldn't have been late fixing Dad's dinner that night . . .

He sealed his vest in response to the wave of cold air that eddied back into his corner as someone came inside, and he glanced up briefly, annoyed.

His glance turned into a stare.

The woman who had just entered had her back to him and was folding a bright yellow umbrella decorated with green and red parrots. She gave it a brief shake, then stuck it in the white plastic tub with the rest of the umbrellas.

She had attempted to gather her dark, kinky hair into a long braid, but much had escaped into a wild halo. Even though she was wearing a lime green canvas raincoat, it was highly tailored, showing a waist exquisitely slim. The long white dress with its ruffle at the bottom, and her boots, which probably required a buttoner to close the row of about a hundred tiny buttons, did not seem out of place in Georgetown.

Her face, when she turned and looked at him across the crowded cafe, was very dear. And, when she slid onto the stool next to him, her smile was decidedly impish.

"Bonjour," she said. And then, more softly, "Aloha."

Cen lifted his glass, but his hand was shaking. He set it down, and beer splashed onto the bar.

"Well," she said, "aren't you even going to say hi?" She

reached over, touched the hand holding the glass, and calmed him.

"Aloha," he said, and all his homesickness welled up in him at once.

His heart was so full he doubted that he could speak if he tried. He'd been contorting time and space into all sorts of theoretical shapes, trying to prove what he *knew* had happened *could* happen, trying to fathom why.

"Did you know that I was exiled?" she asked. "The queen told me that it was better if I didn't come home. That it would only confuse things for the Royalists and endanger the Republic and our constitution. But I'm here now. I'm doing all that's possible to prevent annexation. May I try some of that beer if you're not going to drink it?"

"Yes," he was finally able to make his voice say.

"I'm staying at the Arlington Hotel, to plead for my cause, for the cause of the throne and rights for my people. But I wonder—what *are* 'the people?' " She looked anxious, intense, and spoke as if they were continuing a conversation broken by her leaving to use the bathroom, instead of an absence of months. He had no idea whether or not she remembered their last meeting. He was afraid to press her, afraid that she would simply vanish. *Don't go, ko'u aloha, my love. Don't go.*

Then she looked up at him, her eyes lost and dark. "Cen," she whispered, "what am I *doing* here?"

"What do you mean?" His voice was high, and he had to force himself to speak.

She blinked, then he saw that she was making an intense effort to collect herself.

"It must be—so you can help me think. Or maybe it's a dream. I've been reading lots of philosophy. How would I know, really?" Her beautiful, well-modulated voice, with its British accent, grew in authority. *I'm going to ignore the strangeness,* it said, *because I need answers to a larger problem.* "So tell me this, dream person. When you plead for a people, for whom do you plead?" She looked down at her white-gloved hands, and Cen saw that the gloves were fastened by small white pearls that he was sure were real. "Do I plead for their—

our—bodies, which after all will die? Of course—for adequate food, clothing, education. But that's the least of it. Do I plead for our body as one entire body, one collection of characteristics that makes us unique? There are so few Hawaiians left now, since smallpox and venereal disease came to the islands. Do I plead for our old way of life, which was gone before I was born and, from what I can see of it, a good thing, too? It seems that I must plead for something intangible—the life of our soul, as a people—and I don't know what will ensure that life. I don't know what it even is. Everything is changing so quickly."

"I don't know either," Cen said. Hearing her clear voice, full of anguish and conviction, he felt deep shame at having abandoned the Homeland Movement and Maui. It had mattered so much to his mother that she had inadvertently died for it. What was wrong with him, he wondered? How could he be so cynical in the face of this wonder? Kaiulani had spent her life learning how best to serve her people as queen. Why did it seem so necessary to him to push those same people and their needs away?

Tears shone in her deep brown eyes. "It's not just that the land is being stolen from us by the haole businessmen," she said. "They did that everywhere they could in the entire world, everywhere they went where the idea of private ownership was a foreign concept. It's really a battle of ideas, you see. Do you know what makes us unique?" Her eyes blazed.

"What?" he asked.

"We set out for the unknown," she said. "And we did it because of ideas, and because the world was a different place for us than for the Europeans. We could navigate, you see. We latched onto the stars with our minds and they pulled us. Are you finished yet? Shall we walk?"

Cen could barely get his notebook stashed quickly enough, wondering how to begin to talk to her. Memes. Genes. The ideas she was talking about had no names in her time.

It was drizzling, but her parrot umbrella, as he held it over them, was quite large.

She was unusually tiny for a Hawaiian, but, after all, she was half Scots. He did not miss a single word she uttered, in her low, cultured voice. She had been tutored in the art of being royal from the time she was born. He had noticed it when she was a child, but he keenly appreciated it now. She was the only one of their people to go forth and survive, to tap the knowledge of Europe for those seven long years. It was her own land that had killed her.

Her hair frizzed more wildly around her face as they walked. The wind was sharp and cold and reddened her cheeks; it seemed as if the mist was getting more icy.

"What is it like here, Kaiulani?" he asked. He heard that his voice was desperate, pleading, and he didn't care. How did she *get* here? Could she even answer that question if he asked? He was sure that she could not. What had she called it? Friends of the soul. What sort of energy was *that?* How could it be defined, mapped, replicated, *used?* He was tired of strange geometries. He did not want to solve the mystery of space-time—except so he could see her. It was too terrible to see her so seldom. If only he could be with her forever.

Forever? She died when she was twenty-three. There wasn't much forever left for her.

"There are so many Hawaiians here that we're tripping over each other," she complained, in answer to the question he'd almost forgotten. "Washington is full of half-Hawaiians, haole businessmen, other *alii,* all trying to get things done their way through the newspapers and at parties with Congressmen. Some want the annexation voided, some want Hawaii to be a state, some want it to be an independent kingdom again. A lot of them are upset that I'm here. I met President Cleveland and his wife at a White House audience." He saw her jaw set. "I was bred and educated to think and to charm. I did both. The PGs—the Provisional Government, that's the name they've given their transparent plot—spread rumors that I was a *savage.*" Her laugh was beautiful as she tossed her head back; her eyes wickedly amused. "Unfortunately, now that I'm here, that's rather backfired on them." Cen had read the old papers. Her presence—that of an unexpectedly intelligent, cultured beauty dressed in the latest Paris fashion, discussing politics with reporters—had caused the *New York Times* to call for a complete investigation of the Hawaiian situation. "They could see for themselves that I am not a savage."

Easily, thought Cen, more dazed than he had ever been in her presence. Because something had worked. Something he had done had been right. Or *almost* right. He was suffused with waves of elation.

"I'm not sure," she said. "I could cause a revolution in Hawaii. I could unite my countrypeople, but to what end? I studied the histories of the European countries in great depth. They were the same as the history of the Hawaiians: endless wars both petty and grandiose." She sighed. "I will get them the vote. When we are annexed, we will at least have the vote."

"I'm afraid most Hawaiians don't vote," he told her, without thinking, for once, about possible consequences. "But then, a lot of Americans don't vote. Oh, of course, there are senators, college professors—a lot of kind, educated, and hardworking Hawaiians. But many don't participate in the haole society. They fish, they drink, they collect welfare. The pieces of land Kamehameha II deeded to them were pie-shaped, remember? To make any kind of a living you needed the mountain uplands and a stretch of ocean too. Some lucky people still have those old deeds, and they go to court and fight the big hotels that think they own the land now. Sometimes they even win. But not all of them . . . oh, Kai, I shouldn't have said anything . . . "

Tears ran down her face, and he put his arms around her, drew her close. She rested her head on his chest and whispered, "What can I do now? What *should* I do?" She shook with sobs and he held her tightly, rocked her back and forth, but she would not stop crying. "Kaiulani," he whispered, "I'm sorry."

"You're all I know when I come here," she said. "I see that things are different. I see that. It fascinates me. *You* fascinate me. I know you're not a dream." She held him tighter and he took a deep breath. "But I can never stay long. Never long enough."

When he released her, she looked dazed and said nothing. She walked another block with him, then said, "I must go now."

She whirled and stepped onto a bus whose doors were open right next to him.

Before he could follow, the doors slid shut, and the silent electric bus turned the corner and went uptown.

Stunned, he watched it go.

He felt someone rudely jostle him and turned. The man seized his upper arm with a hard grasp. "Who were you talking to?"

Interspace.

He didn't even think. He just laughed in the man's face, with a breath he hoped was sufficiently alcohol-laden from his earlier beers to knock him over. "Talking? I was talking to Ross Benet. I talk to him often. Ever heard of him? Heck of a guy! And my friend Mei!" He raised his voice, and passersby turned their heads and hurried past. He slapped the man on the back. "Hey, can I b-buy you a drink?" He hoped he was believable. The guy gave a look that was tinged with disgust. Then he let go of Cen's arm and walked away.

"Hey," Cen yelled after him. " 'Nother time, all right?"

Almost childishly pleased with himself, Cen began to spend a lot of time in bars. He found that he did not particularly enjoy getting drunk. It was necessary, though, at least once or twice, to cause a show. He even picked a fight and got arrested. He stopped washing his hair. He grew a beard and did not take care of it. He saw people on the street look at him with disgust and was glad. That's right. I've abandoned the world of thought. I'm in despair. At night he sat and thought, stretched out in a ratty old chair in his cheap room, the ATV flickering without sound.

And when the time was right, he left town.

Cen jerked awake and lay still for a moment, wondering what had startled him.

The faint, gray light of the Berkeley dawn flared beneath the heavy curtains.

Cen heard rain tap the window, reminding him that he was beginning to hate this sunless, squalid bay, rimmed by factories. The smog was a lot worse here than in the city. But it was cheaper to live here than in San Francisco. He rose and went into the kitchen; the counter was strewn with dirty dishes; a cockroach scuttled back to the stove. *Maybe you're carrying this derelict act a bit far.*

After arriving in California, he realized that he had some time to kill—how much, he wasn't sure.

He needed to see Kaiulani a few more times. Each time he saw her, he was able to predict more accurately the next window.

So he'd taken a menial job—loading for a moving company—and found the money good. It left his mind quite free. He was definitely off the grid. Once he had undone the code that was Maui's web address, intending to send him a message. The bones haunted him. Perhaps he should give them to Maui. Kaiulani would. But then he had not sent the message. He remained curiously suspended. He did not want to know what IS had done with the information they had. He was surprised that they'd allowed Dr. Smith to say anything at all to the press. No doubt she'd been cautioned by now. He was pretty sure that what he was really *doing* with this information was completely unknown to anyone except him.

Cen scrubbed the black stuff in the bottom of the frying pan with steel wool, then finally gave up. It was as clean as it was going to get.

He stood at the sink, wondering why he felt this strange lethargy.

Then he realized. It was the day. It was.

One single "day" floating in the bizarre debris of the big bang. The day that he'd looked forward to for months.

What if he was wrong? He'd been wrong before.

A moment's panic rose in his throat, but he grabbed his jacket and pulled it on.

He took BART across the bay and then walked up and down the hills of San Francisco. The sky was not clearing; in fact, it began to rain harder. He settled into trancelike motion. He allowed the usual thoughts about Kaiulani to filter through his mind along with his observations of the weather. It wasn't as if he could stop them.

The great puzzle was her death. Those curses and portents couldn't have helped! It just seemed that complete hopelessness had overtaken her. She was like a fine racehorse, tuned and trained for just one task: to rule a country and to rule it well and to do it with all her heart. She had simply felt powerless.

It took five hours of climbing hills to tire him. And there he was.

In front of the place he had ended up at more than once. Reconnoitering. Hoping. This was where Kaiulani had stayed when she returned to Hawaii from Washington via San Francisco after a second visit, after meeting with Liliuokalani, who was still fruitlessly attempting to change things via legislation.

A gust of wind made his teeth chatter. He looked at his faint reflection in plate glass while standing on the sidewalk and realized that, in this bedraggled state, he probably wouldn't be welcome in the upscale restaurant or bar, his usual haunts.

That was all right. Drinking wasn't in his plans tonight. This *could* be the night. He checked in, as he had done on several earlier nights. Each time, he had been disappointed.

But this time—

The room he walked into was filled with flowers—the orange spikes of bird-of-paradise; white, fragrant ginger blossoms; Chinese jasmine; and entire bushes of bougainvillea—yellow, pink, orange, red. The room was immensely old-fashioned, because the Occidental was supposed to be utterly authentic, but the wallpaper was fresh and new and bathed in the gentle glow of gaslights. Outside it was raining still. He walked to the window and could not see the spacebase lights, and felt a chill. Maybe they were covered by fog.

Yet, when he turned and saw her, she was entirely expected.

Kaiulani shut the door behind her and he saw that her eyes were filled with tears. She smiled and they spilled over. He couldn't speak. She walked to him and held him, pressed her cheek against his so that he could feel all her yearning, inexplicably focused on him.

She spoke little that night. Although he tried his best to be gentle, he was afraid that she didn't really enjoy making love very much, yet she insisted on continuing whenever he stopped and tried to talk about what was happening.

Of course, she was gone in the morning. Everything was in the present, the base had reappeared, and the bill was very much present-day.

But the sun was out.

Everything he owned, except his last two day's pay, was on him. But even if it hadn't been, he realized that he still would have taken the cab to the airport, as filled with hope and excitement as he was.

On the flight to Hawaii, he felt as if he'd been caught in strange patterns of energy that he didn't understand for a long time, as if he'd been serving some sort of sentence, and that now he was free.

Lynn

Asia 2034

13

The wind whipping up the pass was frigid as starlight, laden with snow coldness. Lynn's pack was heavy and swayed from side to side as she walked; she stopped, pulled off her gloves with her teeth, and tried to discover which of the many straps surrounding her body would remedy the situation. Ten yards ahead Akamu dipped into black shadow and out again onto the moon-drenched trail. Their guide, his smaller pack a hump on his back, rounded a sharp curve and vanished.

Lynn took one look behind. They had emerged from a door set in a smooth wall of rock reached by walking through a narrow damp tunnel. Just visible above the wall was the moon-gleamed temple; the roof tiles were dark, and ragged prayer flags flapped black with distant snaps. A place of death; she did not like it. Death related directly to her—death because of her and a message of death to her.

She turned away and hastened after the others. She gripped her stick firmly, well aware that one slip would send her flying into the darkness on her left, and tried to ignore the constant ache in her leg, remembering from the image how thick and sturdy the unbroken bone was. She told herself that Hawkins was not dead when they left him but that did not matter. Sattva could not work miracles. Odd, though—two old friends dying at the same time, her father and Hawkins. She realized how very little she actually knew about her father.

Despite her leg she felt fit enough; perhaps that was because of the exhilarating, knifelike wind.

In a moment she rounded a curve and saw Akamu and the guide waiting for her. Moonlight poured down upon a broken landscape of ridges and black valleys hinting of vast depth. The others turned and began to walk.

"Akamu," she said, when she had caught up with him. The trail widened into a saddle, where two could walk together.

"What?" He sounded preoccupied, annoyed perhaps that she had disturbed his thoughts.

"How did you learn how to shoot like that?"

"Like what?"

"Like good enough to kill people."

He was quiet for a few seconds. "VR games. I didn't think about killing anybody. Maybe I should have just tried to take their guns?"

"You thought quickly and you were very brave," said Lynn. VR games? It sounded semiplausible—most training, from surgeons to soldiers, was done with VR. Kids who played such games had demonstrably quicker reflexes.

But she didn't believe him.

She asked, "What do you think about what Sattva said?"

"About what?"

She gripped her stick more tightly. "About you being Kamehameha's clone."

"What about it?"

"You do know this Maui, don't you?" She'd never heard of him. But she was pretty sure Akamu had.

A huge bird let out a squawk and rose with heavy wingbeats from one of the scrawny pines in the protected saddle.

"What was that?" Akamu stopped and turned, searched the sky.

"Maybe an owl," she said. "Akamu, you can't sidetrack me. My father has died. Do you understand?" Her voice shook and she tried to control it. She stumbled over a rock and caught her fall with the stick.

"Careful!" said Akamu. The guide turned, saw that they were all right, and continued. She could not hear his footsteps for the wind though he was only ten feet in front of them.

"You're crying!" Akamu said, staring at her.

"Watch where you're going," she said, wiping her face. "What do you expect?"

"I don't know," he said dully. Then he added, so quietly that she had to strain to hear, "I guess I don't even have a father."

He trudged a few more steps and she heard a sharp laugh. "Or—I guess he's been dead a few hundred years!"

"Maybe you thought Maui was your father," she said.

"I never thought Maui—," he began indignantly, then fell silent again. "You tricked me," he said, finally.

"Look, kid, why do you think I ran into a building that was about to blow up?"

"How did you know it was going to blow up?" he demanded.

"Because I was watching. I have a condo on the forty-third floor of the Koolau House."

"The Koolau House?"

"That glass tower up the block from where you were."

"Oh." He trudged a few more feet. "What did you see?"

"I saw two men walk up to your house and leave in a big hurry."

"So? Why would you think anything about that?"

Lynn found that her heart was beating faster than it had been a minute before. He was sharp. You want to know about Maui? Tell him everything. Tell him all you know. With a name like Maui, it was a good bet her mysterious messenger had something to do with the Homeland Movement. It might even be someone notorious who used a code name. Most of them did. Fair trade, wasn't it?

Yet it was hard.

"Why, Lynn?" He stopped and turned to face her. His face was pure and smooth, a child's face despite his brave action and intellectual prowess. Children needed love and security and protection. Below them the guide too stopped and motioned impatiently. "Why?" he repeated.

Lynn took a deep breath and said it. "Because I knew that the other clones had been killed."

He didn't even blink. "I knew that too," he said. "I want to know how *you* knew."

"It's a long story," she said. "We'd better—"

"Fuck you," he said, startling her. His eyes glittered with tears in the instant before he turned and rushed down the trail. He pushed past the guide, who looked up at Lynn, back at Akamu, then took off at a fast trot.

* * *

After an hour the moon vanished and they got out flashlights. The guide had firmly put himself in the lead. Akamu refused to talk to Lynn, and the trail was too narrow to walk beside him.

The path twisted upward again and she labored, breath burning in her throat and her leg throbbing. Finally she could go no further. "Wait," she called, but the other two had rounded a bend and did not hear. She lowered herself onto the trail. Stones poked her butt and her muscles twitched as they relaxed; drenched with sweat, she began to shiver almost immediately as the wind gusted.

She thought she heard the roar of a river below, or perhaps it was just the roar of wind through trees. What sort of trees grew in this barren place?

She wished she could imagine the soul of her father but could not. The stars seemed to blaze brighter for a brief pulse of time; imagination, she said, but consigned him in that moment to those stars to which he'd devoted his life to reach— not for himself, but for humanity. Lost in thought, she was startled to feel Akamu shaking her.

"Lynn! Did you fall asleep? Were we going too fast? Here. Let me help you up. Sorry I got so mad."

The guide came back around the bend, frowning. "We have barely started. Twenty *kilometers* to go before dawn. Miss Sattva said soldiers might follow. I suggest we hurry." He swung his pack around and reached into it. "Here," he said, pushing something into both of their hands. He put his pack back on, turned, and hurried up the trail.

"Great!" said Akamu, ripping it open.

Lynn fumbled for her flash. "What is it?"

"A candy bar," he said. "Hey, put that wrapper in your pocket!" But the wind snatched Lynn's wrapper and pulled it into the dark void.

Somewhere in the middle of the night Lynn was searching through her pack for more candy bars, pointing her small flash at Hawkins's neat packet, and came across something she recognized from her hospital discharge—a packet of pain patches, mixed in with a mishmash of vials with directions on them. Gratefully she peeled one open and slapped one on her neck. Akamu was acting as if he was having the time of his life. Yeah, what an adventure, she thought. What an adventure. Then he was next to her, settling on the trail.

"Can you tell me now, Lynn? He said we could rest for five more minutes. Tell me how you know all this about me."

She told him. She told him, briefly, that her father had been the head of IS but that she didn't like them and when she grew up refused to get involved with them. Nevertheless she had access to everything IS did; her brothers were now pretty high up in the organization and besides that was how she'd grown up. She told him that she was an expert on all kinds of things concerning DNA and that that was the reason she knew about the clones. He was silent the entire time and didn't ask any more questions. Then the guide made them get up and go. She was beginning to not care who was chasing them. They were lower now and following a creek; there were trees and the smooth round stones she saw on the trail looked as if they would make comfortable pillows. She stumbled and fell once but waved them away, stood up, and kept walking. After awhile she put on another pain patch. She saw her father's face, wizened and concerned; heard his voice telling her to make sure to get in touch with Hawkins. What had he and Hawkins been doing? She itched for it to be daylight and herself rested, so she could look at everything Hawkins had given her. And she needed to squeeze the information about Maui out of Akamu. "Maui is my friend," he'd told her about six times. But maybe he'd tell her more now. He'd have to. But she felt helpless. She'd never dealt with someone his age before. He'd obviously been indoctrinated since young to say nothing to anyone. Well, he was alive, wasn't he, and the other Kamehamehas were dead. But he was alive only because of a lucky accident. Although he was obviously resourceful and had been trained in the use of weapons.

But why *had* he been in that house?

* * *

In the packet Hawkins had put together was money: Chinese, American dollars, plenty of yen, Thai bhat, and a good sum of the ubiquitous euros.

The Nepalese border official in the small hut on the south side of an incredibly green and fast river, which flowed a hundred feet below through a gorge of white cliffs, squinted at both their passports for several long minutes, looking back and forth first at Lynn's, then at Akamu's. Lynn was utterly exhausted. Their guide had turned back at first light, saying that now they would have no trouble.

Everything looked weirdly far away and seemed to be happening to someone else, someone rather unimportant. The wind whipped her hair back, and Lynn wondered if the fresh scent was that of glaciers. A few yards away buses even more derelict than the truck by which they had reached Sattva's village belched black smoke and disgorged tourists. Lynn couldn't hear anything except the buses and the bass roar of the river. She leaned on her good leg, wishing the guard would hurry. One of the drivers she'd talked to from the other side said two were going to wait for their passengers to do day hikes in China; another, filled with trekkers who had just finished a week's outing, was supposed to have left ten minutes ago and was waiting for her and Akamu.

"But hurry, miss," the driver told her after she'd talked to him as he ushered his group back into Nepal. "They have a plane to catch in Kathmandu." Akamu was sitting. He looked asleep, propped against an insubstantial railing.

The guard looked at Lynn once again. Lynn suddenly recognized the expression in her black eyes. Relief surged through her. Of course, the virus in the computer chip Hawkins had supplied, which straightened out vital information in each of their passports quickly and without a trace, had worked. One of the trekkers, a tall white man wearing high-tech trek clothing, got off the bus and gave the driver a dressing-down, waving his arms and shouting. The driver pointed at Lynn. The man shook his head. As the driver, standing in the large hard-packed patch of bright earth that served as a turnaround shrugged and hurried back toward the bus, Lynn pulled some bills from her pocket. If her mind hadn't been fogged by fatigue they would only have been here a minute. The guard was just waiting for her bribe.

The guard smiled, nodded rapidly. Lynn offered her local currency, a lot; she frowned. Lynn pulled out twenty dollars. The guard took it; still she held on to the passports and shifted her gaze to Akamu. Hastily Lynn handed her another twenty dollars. Lynn heard a faint thump as the driver closed the bus door. The guard handed her the passports. The bus shifted into gear. Lynn shook Akamu who at first scrunched up even more, then woke, and saw, and stood and ran, shouting and waving like Lynn.

Together they ran over the hardened lumpy mud of the turnaround as the bus vanished around the bend. Coughing in the dust Lynn stopped. She was too exhausted to maintain anger, but just stood there, amazed that the driver had not been allowed to stop. She realized that her leg hurt very badly beneath the overlay of pain medication. Akamu looked as if he might crumple onto the ground. The night trek had been grueling and dangerous; they might have easily slipped and fallen into a crevasse in the darkness after the moon had set.

Someone tapped her shoulder and she jumped. "Excuse, miss."

She turned and stared into the eyes of a man as tall as she with a red thika on his forehead. His black hair fell over his eyes and he pushed it back. He motioned toward a car even more derelict than the bus. It looked to be a gasoline car, which was good; they wouldn't have to stop in a few hours and wait for a charge. She was pretty sure this guy wouldn't have a spare battery for an electric car. This one had no bumpers and the door to the back was held shut with a rope.

"I can pass that bus for you, miss," he said. "No problem."

Indeed, the car rose with breathtaking speed out of the gorge on hairpin turns with no guardrails. Lynn fished out some old ragged seat belts for Akamu but found none for herself; he was out the minute he hit the seat. She locked her door but that was a joke. The car began to labor near the summit and the man, who had told her his name was Jehu and that he wanted two hundred dollars American for the trip, pulled over with a casual wrench of the steering wheel. He turned and grinned. "Needs adjustment."

Lynn had paid him seventy-five dollars, and promised him another seventy-five dollars when they arrived; he seemed very pleased about it. She blinked blearily; her side of the car was on the edge of a sheer cliff; if she opened the door and stepped out she would plummet into a gorge where the river was now just a thin green thread. Jehu reached under the front seat and withdrew his hand; he was brandishing a hammer. Lynn about choked.

Still grinning, he got out of the car and slid under it; she heard banging. "I adjusted it, miss, no more trouble now," he said, tossing the hammer onto the seat as he slammed his door.

Indeed, the car performed as if invigorated. They sped down the mountain into another narrow gorge where bare terraced fields rose on the left, and a river—the same one? A different one? flowed an appreciable distance below. Lynn saw a smashed jeep glinting upside down, tiny, where it had rolled to rest against a tree near the river. "We don't have to beat the bus," she said.

"It's okay, miss, I never let a bus stay ahead of me. A matter of honor." He unrolled the window and fished in his shirt pocket; Lynn shivered and zipped her coat. He lit a joint and turned around and offered it to Lynn. "Nepalese tobacco, miss?"

It would probably relax her. The road was so rough that she and Akamu bounced on the seat like popcorn. "No," she said.

Jehu shrugged and turned. She saw his narrowed eyes appraising her in the mirror. The bus was a small dot on a straightaway. He stepped on the gas; the car belched and spat acrid black smoke; Jehu carefully put his joint in the ashtray and leaned forward. He laid on the horn with one hand and kept it there; steered with two fingers of the other hand.

"Slow down!" Lynn yelled but he just hunched forward. The bus grew large very quickly. They were at the end of the straightaway. In the early morning a man was plowing a water-filled field with a white water buffalo; a woman walked down the road balancing a pile of sticks on her head. They passed them and a few bedraggled wooden buildings in a flash. Jehu wrenched the wheel and passed on a blind curve. "See?" he crowed, narrowly missing a head-on collision with a huge truck. He let up on the horn and reclaimed his joint.

"Let us out!" demanded Lynn.

Jehu looked abashed. "Sorry, miss. I won't do that again."

"You'd better not," said Lynn, but was unable to ascertain his compliance as sleep overtook her.

When she opened her eyes she didn't know where they were.

It was a small village on a rise. From her window she saw the vast, long line of the Himalayas. In front of her, Akamu was getting out of the front seat. She blinked. They must have stopped at least once and she hadn't even known it. Akamu stuck his head in the window. "Jehu's really cool," he said.

Jehu came around to her window. "Hungry, miss?" he rubbed his lean stomach. "I have to eat rice every day." Another happy grin.

Lynn slowly got out of the car. She felt as if she'd been beaten with sticks for hours, then thrown in a closet. She'd used up the pain patches. Akamu danced along, lightly for his bulk, with a skipping step. He followed Jehu toward a place evidently called Mustang. The faded sign had been painted ages ago. There were about six ramshackle buildings on each side of the dirt road, all with outside ladders leading to second floor openings. Across the road a somewhat mangled and bashed satellite dish was planted in the ground; it looked very old. A few people lounged on steps, watching her.

She staggered and grabbed the side of the car, wondering how in the world she had managed to walk twenty kilometers. She pulled up her pant leg and saw that her leg was swollen once again. Her stomach rumbled. She hurried after Akamu as best she could, carrying her pack. She caught up with him just outside the door. "Don't eat anything here," she said. She reached into her pack and pulled out some sort of bar that was wrapped in paper with Chinese writing.

"What's that?" asked Akamu suspiciously. "I want some rice. Jehu said the rice was good here."

"I'm afraid it will make you sick," she said. "Don't drink the water either. Here's some money." She pulled out a few bills. "Bargain for everything. One dollar here is about—oh—"

"I know what it is," he said scornfully. "Jehu told me. Besides, I can look it up." He pulled his pack around.

"And don't get that out here either."

"Don't do this, don't do that," Akamu mimicked. "I'm hungry. I'm going to have some rice." He stumped up the stairs.

"You'll be sorry," said Lynn. She turned and looked at the road. A sign!

She pulled out the map program Sattva's friends had put in the pack. It was just a cheap thing; she'd looked at it this morning while waiting in line behind the rude trekkers. The crude schematics showed roads that did not curve but always changed direction in sharp angles. It was good because it was easy to read at night. But the screen was dark; she flipped the switch back and forth. Damn. She must have left it on. She'd have to leave it out to recharge. She fished around in the pack. She hadn't had time to really look at what was there; she'd slept the whole way. She pawed through it, but didn't really see much that she hadn't seen before. Except—with relief she pulled out a paper map that crinkled as she unfolded it. A small crowd of children rushed up to her, hands outthrust.

She reached into her pack and gave them each a Chinese coin. A good deal of Asia was not linked into the web credit system, and she was quite glad to have real money. She didn't usually encourage begging, but felt reckless. When they ran off she unwrapped one of the bars Akamu had rejected. Munching on it, holding the map in her other hand, she walked to a small stand at the side of the road and peered inside, bought a strangely flavored soda in a clear container, sat in the sun and studied the map.

They were definitely on the road to Kathmandu. They had come fifty kilometers. Was that all? Amazing what a difference a little cheap technology could make—for practically nothing she could have picked up a satmap in Hong Kong that would have pinpointed their location anywhere in the world. But they had *something*—viable cleansed passports, apparently, and money, thanks to Hawkins. Sattva was right. He was an amazing man. She looked at her watch, the ornate old-fashioned beauty handed down from her mother's mother that her brothers made fun of and called stupid when they were teenagers. They were right—it was stupid. It did nothing at all but tell time. Their watches did everything but cook dinner. Well, actually, they could send a preset signal from their watches to start dinner cooking . . .

But at least she could use her dainty watch and the map to tell that Jehu must have slowed down after she fell asleep. Maybe he'd just been trying to impress her.

Then it struck her: her father was dead.

She lowered the map, stared into the bright sunlight unseeing.

She'd turned his death over and over in her mind for hours the night before. She again pictured the bright stars hemmed by black mountains, heard the trudge of their boots and the ceaseless thump of her stick on the trail. Her brothers. Were they capable of murder? Of patricide? How could she even think this? They would condone experiments that in an oblique way would allow them to satisfy their material needs, so much more refined than Lynn's: that necessary house of cool steel and glass on Black Point where monster waves smacked the cliff just below. That was James. Samuel preferred a tight high-tech compound in the mountains, with a view of half the island and as much of the blue Pacific as the eye could swallow. Those houses were just the tip of the iceberg. They both believed that they deserved these and the additional flock of domiciles in strategic countries. One couldn't go to Berlin or London or Perth to do business and endure the fatigue and distraction that even the finest of hotels might induce; besides, hotels were not secure. Add personal tailors, designer wives, spoiled children, staff and security, and untold accoutrements—it was easy to see why they might defend their positions no matter what.

Lynn's eyes were dry as she considered the situation. Despite their rift, she and her father had always been closer than he and the twins. Before he remarried they had gone everywhere together, around the world, as he conducted business. She dimly remembered the Louvre, snow out the train window as they sped through Switzerland, a steep, thrilling descent into Rio. But even more she remembered games at home, and what must have been his pain at the loss of his beloved wife, when he sat on the lanai for entire days staring out at the ocean. His second marriage had been different. More of an alliance. It had produced two Interspace warriors. Both lawyers.

Lynn tried to shake the horrible idea but could not. She had hoped that it might vanish like a nightmare in the light of day but instead was stronger. If Samuel and James had killed their own father they would kill her with a snap of their fingers. Maybe they thought they had; or maybe they knew that they had not by now.

She shivered in the warm sun, refolded the map, and stood. She wanted to see what else was in the pack, but the children standing and staring at her expectantly could almost be counted on to run off with anything she took out. She stood and started to walk back to the car; she'd look there, at least until Jehu returned. He'd probably run off the road watching her in the mirror if she examined anything while he was driving. As she walked, the children followed at her heels, chattering, with outstretched hands.

What about Jehu? Was it just a coincidence that he had been there? She couldn't question Akamu in front of him, no matter what—he was the type of person who would sell anything, including information. She shouldn't have let Akamu go off with him—

But assassins sent by her brothers would be much higher class. And, she thought, as Jehu appeared in the doorway of the bleak building, flung his arms out with, presumably, rice-induced exuberance, and smiled, he would not seem quite so silly. Jehu stepped down and Akamu appeared in the doorway; stretched and grinned like Jehu.

Jehu wanted to take them to the Hilton in Kathmandu, but she insisted that he let them off in the middle of town. She paid him and, as soon as his car turned the corner, hurried Akamu through a maze of alleys.

It was dusk. Akamu was whining about food again, and no wonder, being so large. People sat on the sidewalks, their various wares spread out on blankets. "I want one of those," said Akamu, pointing to a rough-woven wool hat.

"Later," she said, then stopped, annoyed, while he paid for it.

"Where did you get that money?" asked Lynn.

He just smiled.

"You don't have to pay them what they ask," she said.

"I thought we were in a hurry," he said, pulling it over his ears. "But where are we going, anyway?"

"I'm not sure," she said. "We need to rest and talk and decide." At least no one would follow them here. Or would they? If they followed Sattva's reasoning, this was the most sensible place to look.

Where to hide? She glanced over at him, and he looked absorbed in the sights and sounds. He was still enough of a kid, she noticed, to look longingly at the dark doors of VR palaces, undoubtedly low-res, where boys his age were hawking and hustling just outside, drawing in marks. But he didn't say anything and walked on by. Maybe reality was a bit more interesting than it had been—

Where?

"Akamu, how long have you known that you were a clone?" she asked.

"We shouldn't talk about things like that around all these people," he said, and ran suddenly through the crowd to a little table and bent over it. By the time she got there he was strapping something onto his wrist. "Look, a satmap!" he said, eyes gleaming. "Just what we need!" He walked, pushing buttons for five minutes, then said, "Guess what? We're on Fourteenth and K Streets in Washington, D.C."

"Needs calibration," said Lynn, trying not to smile. "Maybe something's interfering with it."

"It's junk, that's all," said Akamu.

The streets were mobbed. The air was filled with a cacophony of car horns, which did nothing to budge the brilliant white water buffaloes wandering at will. Vendors were everywhere; rich curry smells wafted from doorways. They emerged on a huge square and the temple before them was white, powerful, and had a face.

Or, at least, eyes.

Lynn was overwhelmed by; the brilliance of the flapping flags; green, yellow, red, purple; translucent as watercolors beneath the sky that was now deepening toward evening, intense and luminescent blue. The large eyes painted beneath the red tiles that served as a hat looked everywhere, uncannily, curling upward at the outer corners.

Shy mountain people sat on blankets with a few thankas, painted pictures of sacred scenes, all demons and Buddhas, death and dancing. Buddhists were a minority here, about ten percent of the population. The majority were Hindus. Lynn felt as if she was in a place that had not changed since medieval times, and washed as clean as if she'd deposited whatever was left of her mind and will and strength into the absolute whiteness of a water buffalo that stood in the middle of the street flapping his ears heedless of traffic, into the colors that seemed more important than the matter that they defined. There was barely an overlay of the present age. Even the stylized golden holograms of Kali, about a foot high, with which one vendor bordered her space, used technology so old it was practically from another age.

At a corner with three monkeys that a man had apparently trained to pick pockets while onlookers roared with laughter, Akamu was standing in front of a woman who was selling— what? Computers? Lynn realized she was starving and that she simply had to eat very soon. Enough of these silly episodes. She had to stay alert.

But she did not interrupt. Better not to draw any attention. Akamu turned from the small table where luminous laser chips were wrapped in plastic and laid out like candy on the rough wood and looked surprised to see her.

"Oh."

"What did you buy now?"

"Something."

"Like what?"

"Something to help me do my work," he said, his voice excited. "It's really weird to find this here."

"What?"

"Look, I'll tell you later, all right? I don't really need it now, but the system you got me in Hong Kong didn't have it and if I'm lucky this will work. She really didn't know what she had, but I think I figured it out."

They were walking away from the bright square, and dusk deepened the shadows in the narrow street. Small shops advertised hashish, rugs, thankas, cheap cotton clothing. The smell of incense alternated with clear cool wind. Then Lynn saw the place she wanted.

It was a small anonymous looking hotel, barely more than a guest house despite the sign: The Diamond Hotel. The owner showed her up a flight of stairs to a room with a linoleum floor, two iron beds, a bare bulb hanging from the ceiling, and a sink with the toilet down the hall. It was very clean. "I'll take it," she said, over Akamu's grumbles.

"Look," he said eagerly after the man shut the door. "Why don't we go for a plane ride?" He picked up a card that was sitting on the table next to some worn brochures.

Lynn glanced at it.

HIMALAYAN MARATHON
EXPERIENCED GUIDE * NEW PLANE
INDIVIDUAL OR GROUP TREKS
RM 7 DIAMOND HOTEL, KATHMANDU

"Right," said Lynn. "Wasn't the driver from hell enough for you?" she shuddered, tossed the card on the table, closed the window, and drew the flimsy cotton curtains.

Akamu looked several shades paler than a moment ago. "Where's the bathroom?" He rushed down the corridor.

When he returned Lynn handed him a pill from the kit they'd put in her pack. "Good for what ails you," she said. "I told you—"

"Shut *up*," he said, swallowing the pill. She grinned.

"So let's eat," he said, his hand on the doorknob.

"Resilient boy," she said. "Don't forget your pack."

They ate in a little café down the street with dirty walls and unmatched chairs. It was the closest place, and Lynn did not feel picky. She was perking up a bit and was ready to grill the hell out of Akamu after dinner. The place was full of Indians, Nepalese, and Tibetans. But since most of the Nepalese seemed to speak English, Lynn still did not want to talk here. Besides, she was ravenous.

She listened to Akamu's beep-beep-beep as he scrolled through the few offerings on the menu. Finally he held up a picture for the waiter. "Pizza."

"Maybe you should get something they know how to make here," she said. He glared at her as she ordered a curry and a Chinese beer. Then he yawned.

"I mean, I hope you like it," she said. "I hope the pill works."

"I'm hungry," he growled.

He wrinkled his nose when it came. She struggled not to smile. Maybe they used yak cheese. "Order something else. You don't have to eat it," she said. So, of course, he did.

She shoveled her curry down, finding it excellent. It was probably sheer luck that her digestive tract was still in order. But she was sure that the place where he'd eaten lunch was filthy. The life expectancy in Nepal was only forty-five; astounding! Why? Why?

Because of people like her brothers, and, she had to admit, people like herself whose silence and selfish concentration on their own lives amounted to compliance. Well, Lynn, she thought, blinking away tears from the fiery curry, exactly how would you start your program of worldwide social changes anyway?

Best to start small. She looked across the table at Akamu.

He was almost finished with what they had called a pizza. His large, expressive brown eyes were half-hooded and fatigue relaxed his features. His dark skin was flushed over his cheekbones. His black, curly hair was getting quite long, and almost covered his ears; the small ponytail he'd had when she first met him seemed about an inch longer. His T-shirt beneath his jacket was extremely dirty. Feeling her scrutiny, he looked up. "What?"

She reached over and shook him gently by one shoulder. "I was just thinking about how well you're doing."

"Yeah, I've got diarrhea, and I haven't had a bath in over a week. And I'm really behind on my work."

"What work?" she asked.

"Oh, you know," he said vaguely, waving a greasy hand in the air. "Work."

"That's what I want to know about. Among other things. Finished? Let's go."

Lynn paid and they stepped out into the dark, twisty street. A few beggar children followed them then dropped back. Lynn felt revitalized by the curry and beer but knew it wouldn't last. She looked around and saw no one; at the end of the street a bustling night market threw light across the pavement. Akamu would surely see something there he wanted. She took the next right. They'd go in the back way at the hotel.

"What do you think about it?" she asked.

"About what?"

"About you being Kamehameha's clone?"

He didn't say anything for a long time, and finally Lynn realized that he didn't plan to. She would be more aggressive. Tomorrow, when they were rested. She'd get the full story and they could make some decisions.

"Here we are," said Akamu, after glancing through a door in the brick wall bounding the alley.

Light spilled out of the courtyard of the Diamond Hotel. She was startled to see a black limo taking up most of it. Worrywart, she told herself. No one could find you here. Not unless there was some sort of tracer in . . .

She stopped. Akamu kept walking. Shit, she thought. We're both exhausted and dirty. We need a rest. She grabbed Akamu's arm and pulled him back into the alley.

She tried to turn the situation over in her mind. If someone wanted to kill them, would they arrive in so blatant a fashion? Probably just some . . . diplomat. Right. Staying here. All right then. A dealer in illegal nan. Advertising his wealth. That made about as much sense.

So, then, what?

She and Akamu were in the shadows. As she watched, a man she recognized as a colleague of her brothers got out of the car and swiftly walked to the door of the office and went inside.

Ah, yes. Of course he had come just to take her home. How kind of them, how thoughtful to follow her across half a continent.

Think, Lynn, think.

If they had found Hawkins, of course they could track her here. But how in the world could they do so this closely?

"What's wrong?" whispered Akamu.

"They've found us."

"The plane," said Akamu.

"How did they find us?" Akamu, she realized, must be bugged in some way.

He shrugged. "Who are 'they'?"

Room 7. She couldn't really think of anything else. What was some place really remote?

More remote than this?

Just a place to breathe. A place to buy a little time. Just a little.

The man came out of the office. She watched him climb the stairs to their room.

Fine, wait there. Wait there till hell freezes over.

Room 7 was just a few doors down. She went over and knocked on the door, then pounded.

A little man opened the door, a beer in his hand, dressed in underwear. Wild, tinny Hindu music issued from a small radio on a table.

"Can you fly us to Chaing Mai?"

He tilted his head. "Where, miss?"

"Chaing Mai. In northern Thailand." She'd been there years ago. It was one of the most remote places she could think of, the least developed, at least then. And it was closer, closer, to the place where they could truly vanish, a few days' hike into Cambodia, a Buddhist temple she'd visited once . . .

"Well," he said. The dome of his head was bald and the fringe of hair around it black. "I am really very tired. I have been giving tours for days. Everyone who came to the Festival of New Stars wanted to go flying. It was crazy."

"Can we come in?" She pushed forward and pulled Akamu in behind her, shut the door.

"Chaing Mai," he said again. "I have flown to Bangkok before. But not Chaing Mai. Perhaps we can follow a river? You have a satmap? I just do Himalayan tours. Same one, always."

"I have one," said Akamu, and Lynn just looked at him. He shrugged. "I do."

"Well." He took a few sips of beer. "It will be expensive. Take a lot of fuel for one thing."

"How much?"

"Let me think about it. I'll let you know tomorrow."

"We have to go tonight."

He smiled broadly. "Well. In that case you must pay double."

Double of what? one part of Lynn itched to ask, but she just said, "Can we leave now?"

"You have euros?"

She nodded.

"One thousand to start."

Nice round number. She counted it out in fifties. He disappeared into the bathroom and was buttoning his pants as he came out. He picked a shirt up off a chair and pulled it over his head, then sat to tie heavy boots. "It will be extra more than that because you are in some kind of trouble."

"We're not in trouble. My father died and I have to get home."

"To Chaing Mai?" he asked, raising his eyebrows. "Excuse, miss, but you do not look very Thai."

"My father was becoming a Buddhist monk. Are you ready?"

He pulled on a jacket and a hat. "I hope you have warm clothes. My heater is broken. Come, we will drive to the airport."

"I thought you had a new plane."

"Sure, new for me. I just bought it last month."

Lynn and Akamu waited in the shadows while he brought his vehicle around, a small old-fashioned plastic town car with many smashes. The limo was still there. She could not see who was inside, if anyone. She and Akamu could barely squeeze into the car. It was electric and accelerated silently.

The main street was even more lively than earlier in the evening. Colored lights glowed around the night market. Lynn's mind was a blank. This couldn't go on. She rested her arm on the windowsill and absently played with her black earring.

Her fingers paused. Then, without a conscious thought, she pried the back from it and undid the double chain which laced through the other hole in her ear as a safeguard.

She looked at it for a moment—smooth, round, and perfect.

With Mao's DNA she could achieve, she knew, important breakthroughs. Some of the assumptions the rest of her collection pointed to would be shattered; others would be reinforced; new—perhaps landmark—hypotheses would suggest themselves.

Lynn closed her eyes, saw a fleeting panorama of humanity's perfection; her dream—the full information the human genome could yield concerning qualities like intelligence, leadership, political vision. Information used responsibly, with goodwill, to liberate humanity, gathered and cataloged painstakingly by people like her. Used by people like—

Her brothers.

Who had of course included a tracer, one rather crude. But it had proven effective.

She rolled down the window. She hesitated a moment. If she

could smash it open—disassemble the components? Problem was, all the encoded information was most certainly embedded in the very configuration of the material.

It seemed to be burning in her hand: her life's work.

Her life's work, or Akamu's life.

They were crawling past a cart piled high with what looked like bolts of silk, across which streetlights danced in glints of yellow, azure, silver, and a stunning flamingo pink. The cart was pulled by a water buffalo that stepped into a pool of light as she watched. The animal shone for an instant, almost as if illuminated from the inside, a dazzling, pure, and intense white. The driver cracked his whip and the cart moved to one side.

As they passed, Lynn flipped the earring into the cart and saw it fall between the bolts of silk.

On the corner where they turned left, a little monkey in a suit danced to flute music.

"Too hot, miss?" asked the man, glancing in the mirror at the open window.

"No," she said. "I'm just fine."

His name was Hadid, and his plane was indeed old. The metal sides looked slightly out of kilter, as if they had beaten into shape. It had a propeller. One.

"This is really incredible," said Akamu in a worshipful tone, looking at it with wide eyes.

"It really is," said Lynn, thinking wryly about how Akamu had complained about the plane that took them from Honolulu to Hong Kong. Now look at him!

Of course, his personality *had* taken another turn in her mind the night he killed the soldiers. He was more enigmatic than ever. The more she knew, it seemed, the less she knew. But it made sense that he had such skills—he'd lived longer than the other clones and quick reflexes and training probably had something to do with it.

"This is an excellent plane. Entirely trustworthy, miss," said Hadid. "Excuse me. It is after hours. I have to pay my friend to turn the runway lights on—I hope you do not object but it is safer that way—and also pay a special exit tax." He held out his hand.

"Special exit tax?"

"Special exit tax for people who don't go through customs," he said.

"How much?" asked Lynn, wondering just how much money Hawkins *had* given her. I haven't even had time to *count* it, she thought. She certainly hadn't wanted to count it in front of Jehu's sharp eyes.

Hadid handed the money over to a man who had walked out to the plane with them; he counted it, nodded, pocketed it, and left.

Lynn was a bit relieved when she saw the inside of the plane. It was not as decrepit as she had imagined. It looked much better than the local cars. The seats were a soft gray, and the floor in the passenger compartment was even carpeted.

"Isn't it beautiful?" Hadid asked, beaming. "Have a seat. Any seat." He stepped into the cockpit and began his check.

"How old is it?" she said.

"That's the best part," he yelled through the door. "Only thirty-five years old. Like new."

"Hmm." There were six seats altogether, three on each side of the aisle. Lynn figured she could sleep on the floor. The cockpit seemed to have the requisite amount of dials. She supposed the propeller would twirl. What the hell.

It had been an exceedingly long day.

"It's a Piper Cherokee," said Akamu, excitement in his voice. "I passed on this one. In a virtual lesson. Can I fly it? Please?"

"Why not?" said Hadid, at the same time Lynn said, "No!" She reached into her pack and handed him the packet of paper maps. "Maybe this will help."

"Sit up here next to me, young man," he said, "and I will give you a lesson in reality flying."

"Just make sure you know where we're headed," said Lynn.

"No problem," Hadid and Akamu said together, and Akamu grinned.

"Smart lad," she said. "I give up. Don't bother me now; I have a lot of thinking to do."

She detached one of the seat cushions to use as a pillow. She fell deeply asleep on the carpeted aisle before they even taxied for fuel. She didn't wake until they had a bumpy landing and sat up, disoriented, among the dark empty seats. The sky was predawn gray.

"Where are we?" she asked.

"Somewhere in India," said Akamu. "We're getting more fuel. I'm glad you woke up. Hadid said I did so good that he's going to let me take off. Want to watch?"

"No," said Lynn, and promptly went back to sleep.

The mountains they flew over were high and green, sharp-ridged and covered in jungle. They looked fluffy and soft to Lynn as she dropped into one of the seats. She would have liked to lie down and sleep on all that green fluffiness. It looked a lot nicer than the floor of the plane.

Hadid had shared out some curried lentils, potatoes, and rice a vendor had been selling when they stopped in India, and Lynn felt rather sick now, her head pressed against the window. She opened her bag and poked her hand absently through the bag, searching for the nylon medicine pack.

Her fingers brushed a hard, flat object and she pulled it out. A small snap case. She opened it. Strange. Inside was just a small postcard, one of the two-by-one-inch cards you slipped into a computer slot to display on the screen. Iolani Palace. She looked on the back and there was no message. That she could see. She hadn't seen it before. It had slipped into the debris of candy wrappers and maps at the bottom of the pack.

She looked into the cockpit. Hadid and Akamu were focused on their chore, exhausted, no doubt.

"How much longer?" she yelled.

Hadid turned his head and shouted back. "Ah. You are awake, miss. No more than an hour, I think."

"Forty-seven minutes," said Akamu.

Lynn was stunned by the heat—damp, like a smothering hand—as she stood in the doorway of the plane.

"Let me help you down," said Hadid.

She looked around, feeling inexplicably safe and happy. She had no idea why. It was silly. Maybe they hadn't been following the earring. Maybe they were following something embedded in Akamu. She noticed that the mountaintop sloped off in fields of brilliant orange poppies. She was in a sweat. She ripped off her jacket, hat, two sweaters, and stuffed them into her pack. She turned to Hadid.

"How much?"

She counted it out and gave him a tip half again as much. He looked startled. "Thank you, miss, thank you so much. I think I must rest before I continue back. Your son is a good aviator. It is very good to give children lessons like that." He walked off toward the open wooden pavilion that served as a terminal to this airport, which was just a large, flat field on top of a mountain. The building had a high, thatched roof with a very steep pitch. Beer, read a sign over the stairs, and echoed the sentiment in a variety of languages.

Beer. Lynn mopped at her forehead. *Cold* beer? She looked at Akamu. He looked ready to topple over. She put her arm around him.

"Come on, your highness," she said gently, "I bet there's a great place somewhere here to take a nice nap." They headed toward the building and climbed the steps. Behind the bar was a thin, beautiful woman wearing a long dress, leaning against a high stool. Her black hair was cropped straight beneath her ears. Lynn silently thanked Hadid that there were no border formalities.

"Do you speak English?" she asked.

"Yes," she said, with a lisp so it sounded like "yeth."

"Do you know of a place we can stay?"

"In Chaing Mai," she said.

"Fine," said Lynn, somewhat startled to see her pick up a cellphone and push a single button.

She had two beers while they waited for a ride; they seemed to settle her stomach. Akamu took off all his clothes except his pants and put them on the ground, then lay down on top of them, covering his eyes with his arm. Hadid drank silently, bleary-eyed, and the wind blew through the open walls and rustled the thatch and bounced a wall hanging several times. Outside the brilliance of the sun seemed magnified a thousand times by the bobbing, dancing, infinite poppies.

Cen

Hawaii 2017

14

Cen slept away the Pacific crossing and was roused to fill out forms just before the islands came into view. He quickly denied shipping diseased plants or virus-laden computer chips and eagerly searched the blue sea for land. His heart lifted at the sight of his green islands strung out below in the intensely blue sea.

The Big Island of Hawaii was topped with snow and the observatories where he'd spent many happy hours with Ross awaiting a coveted minute of telescope time seemed to have multiplied to a glittering line of white domes before the ridge fell away to vast green and black slopes. Was that the Parker Ranch, where Kaiulani had spent her final months? The dry Kona coast showed the endless surf line white against the deepest imaginable blue. He gazed down upon a patchwork of legal victories. There was the Kohala Peninsula, a high-tech wonderland now owned entirely by the Hawaiian Homelanders. Legally, it was a bit like an old-time reservation except that they had written their own terms in exchange for ceding land rights to a single megaresort below. Monies from other resorts now owned by Hawaiians funded homebuilding and schools.

And, Cen suspected, something much more. If Maui's grandmother had anything to do with it.

They passed over Haleakala, laced with high clouds. Purple shadows swallowed miles of vast slope, then were chased by a rapid verge of sunlight beneath which the green and gold of forest and field were intensified to almost painful brilliance. IS had wanted the crater for launches; that had been completely denied by the U.S. government, much to the surprise of IS; they'd felt that even National Parks should be sacrificed to seeding the universe with humans.

In ten minutes the flight was over the island of Oahu, just off the coast of Kailua. Cen tried not to see the beach where he'd gone swimming the day his mother died, the little roads he'd run down, but his eyes were inevitably drawn to them, stark and real. His past.

But in a few moments the plane swept around to the other side of the island, the flip side of Cen's life: lapping around Diamond Head and far beyond was Honolulu, all the tight-packed ethnic neighborhoods washed with great sweeps of sunlight; the steep, uninhabited summit of the deep green Koolau Mountains above shrouded in fast-moving clouds.

Released from the dark image of his mother's death, Cen was free to wonder how long he would have to wait for the final, defining information he needed.

It might come today.

Or it might never come.

Honolulu proper surprised Cen with its smallness. When he was a child, the ten square blocks had seemed immense. Of course the metropolis of greater Honolulu, which had spread out from it long before Cen was grown, was measured in square miles, but this, his true home, was just one of a hundred neighborhoods and seemed so very quaint and old now. And much more sleazy than Cen remembered. I haven't been here since I was a kid, he thought. A kid. How did I survive? Holographic displays of prostitutes effervesced on building walls; one had only to touch a picture with fingerprint credit to receive an assignation; Cen thought of long-dead Mei and wanted to weep, but continued down Hotel Street. Customers spilled from the ramshackle wooden market with full baskets overflowing with exotic vegetables and plastic-bagged fish.

And the bones of Kaiulani rested five blocks away, at the Royal Mausoleum on Nuuanu where that broad avenue began its sweep upward to the Pali.

The thought sickened him. His stomach churned, and he felt faint.

Then he realized that he was probably hungry. The ever-present cloud of dead fish stink was overlaid by sizzling teriyaki strips skewered on bamboo cooking on a nearby brazier; he stopped and bought a few. After he ate them he felt much better. He could think of the mausoleum without pain: I will meet you previous to that fate, he promised her and knew himself to be obsessed yet completely sane in the midst of the street bustle, the roving hordes of tourists, and those who preyed on them. It seemed to him that time was pressing in on him like an ever-narrowing corridor, as if he was in a train rushing down an ever-steeper slope, and that he must steel himself to jump from the train at the last possible instance. And if his timing was wrong, they would both die.

I am counting on you, Cen. You're the only one I can trust now. I don't know what is really happening to my people, my kingdom, my life. I don't know who my enemies are, or my friends. I haven't even told my father about you and I tell him everything. You understand this? These were the words she had spoken that night in San Francisco.

"I do," said Cen, and the woman at the flower stand he had stopped before said, "What kind, sir, antherium? Bird-of-paradise? All fresh."

Cen rented a room, one not much different than the one he'd shared with Mei so many years ago—wood floors sagging with age, the bathroom down the hall. He was on the top floor, which just cleared the roof of an old abandoned customs building. Two large windows overlooked the bustle of the harbor and the market; below mobs of people, mostly Asian, filled the streets each day leaving little room for even bicycles. It was a relief to see this particular racial mix again; the faces of Koreans, Japanese, Chinese, and Pacific Islanders welcomed him home. The air was filled with the sweet salt smell that reminded him, this time pleasantly, of childhood. He supposed he should be afraid and cautious, because of IS, but he was not, particularly. His heart was filled with new strength, with a strange, unusual confidence. He did not know all he needed to know, not quite.

But he would.

The *Advertiser* and *Star-Bulletin* were both still publishing, and at the kiosk he did not customize them. He ordered the entire recyclable paper, which took almost a minute to print out while the customers behind him muttered impatiently, their category codes memorized, quite limited and always spit forth or transferred to their particular receiver in a split second.

Watching them, he was stunned by the oddness of it all. How and why had all of this—*conscious existence*—come about? He was trusting Kaiulani's life that he had some inkling, as much as it was possible for the human mind to grasp, much less predict and use. The people, the buildings, the very sidewalk beneath his feet—how insubstantial it all was, how frail and ephemeral! He could see right through the stuff of the world, or imagined that he could, its swarming tiny pixilated dots that might be the brain's take on a billion tiny wormholes opening and closing in less than an instant on another of the infinity of universes with which his place shared points. He felt a hairbreadth from completely comprehending the exotic mathematics that would permit him to vanish into Kaiulani's time and remain there; the information leading away would be an entirely new way of seeing the universe.

It was a sobering thought.

He ate at a lunch stand and reveled in the street banquet that cemented him in a growing feeling of being *home.* Filipino *adobo,* Japanese sashimi, strong Vietnamese coffee light brown with condensed milk. Poi and sweet, dried Chinese pork. The harbor was thick with boats—a New Zealand freighter; a research ship bedecked with electronics fresh in, according to the paper, from Antarctica.

The next morning he was awakened just before dawn by the cries of the fighting cocks that still rose from Honolulu backyards. He sat in the dark by the window, looking down at the pawnshop owner hosing his little piece of sidewalk, a cigarette dangling from his lip, and thought of Maui and that long-ago cockfight.

Streetlights turned off as he paid for Vietnamese coffee and a pastry at a window where no one inside spoke English. Thin, delicate Asians filled the streets, on their way to work, many of the women obviously lawyers, formally dressed, their high heels clicking. The young men wore suits and ties, doomed to sweat the day away, and the old men wore thin pale silk shirts that were not tucked in.

Cen found a bus board. All the island buses were driverless, smooth quiet electric cars equipped with audible multilanguage imprecations, running on tracks of light in dedicated lanes. He entered his destination—Makaha—and found he had only to walk a block and wait ten minutes to catch his bus.

It was strangely posh, with comfortable, upholstered seats and fake wood trim, stunningly clean. Two Japanese men dozed on the sideways-facing seat, their golf clubs in the luggage rack up front.

Pain and joy, loss and haunting nostalgia clashed with each new vista.

He saw that IS had built up Hickam Spacebase even more—mysterious windowless buildings, tiny satellite dishes bristling everywhere. The legendary Room That Could Control the World was there somewhere, not underground because Hickam was simply built-up coral, but a vast bombproof bunker inherited from the U.S. military. He had read in the paper that IS wanted to build a new maglaunch tunnel on the Big Island but that negotiations with the Homelanders were slow. There, at Kohala, the Homelanders had a thriving, somewhat enigmatic enclave; they also owned the land where the tunnel would emerge.

Cen knew, via the web, that the Homelanders were not isolated intellectually. For one thing, Kohala had exemplary schools that sent graduates to top universities around the world; many returned to teach. Cen was sure that the Primal Societies scattered like so many jewels throughout the web, virtual communities connected by a common philosophy, had their birth in Kohala.

It was understandable, though, that the upper echelons of IS were beginning to object at last to the moonbase launches taking place so close to their multimillion-dollar homes here on Oahu, particularly since debris from a recent failed satellite launch had taken out two estates. Yeah, let the burning junk fall on the Hawaiians, and their uppity pretentious school.

Typical. There were also serious objections to a Big Island maglaunch because of the precarious geophysical nature of the land, prone to frequent earthquakes. But the best engineers Interspace could muster—or buy off, Cen suspected—insisted that with new materials and construction techniques all would be fine. World-famous Kilauea, with its fountains of molten lava, had not erupted for ten years because the hot spot had found a new fissure under the ocean just south of the Big Island, and besides, was about a hundred miles from the proposed tunnel.

Cen was pretty sure that this maglaunch tunnel amounted to a pork barrel situation—some construction company had cozied up to the right people at IS and stood to make a lot of money.

Cen knew that Maui had a lot to do with the stupendous maturing of the Homeland Movement, though he'd had no direct contact with him since the night of Mei's death—since that same long-ago day when he'd leaned forward into the wind, weaving in and out of traffic, flattening the world with speed, along the very line the bus rode now, stodgy and sedate.

That was the day he'd met Maui's grandmother—ushered, he realized now, into the very heart of the Homeland Movement with no reservation on their part. Maui was completely underground now, having been the target of at least two failed assassination attempts; those who hired the hit men had never been uncovered. Cen had a vested interest in keeping up with the dark side of IS activities; there was no telling when they might turn on him.

The Homelanders had not pressured him in all the years since. He realized that they had believed he had totally sold out to IS.

He had taken a very different path.

Row upon row of homes, gridded with giant shopping malls every few miles, marched up the bare dry Waianae slopes. A gap in the mountains revealed another large valley, site of a dense U.S. military structure taken over by IS, mostly underground.

Then, on his left, he saw close blue flashes of ocean between the condos. Fountains of white foam, sparkling black lava leaved with bays of gold sand drew his eye and heart; refreshed him; recalled his childhood days of surfing and seaplay; touched him with Ross's memory so that his eyes filled with tears briefly. At every beach park he saw surfers bobbing far out on the swells, and the tents of Hawaiian ohanas, extended families, flapping in the constant wind, tangy smoke rising already from the huli huli chicken cooking on the grills. The sight of those hardheaded surfers made him feel better. At least one thing remained the same.

As the bus hissed along, the buildings on the sides of the road became more dilapidated. The Japanese men roused, pointed out the window, shook their heads in commiseration, and Cen's face burned. But they were right. Nothing much had changed here, except to decay even more. It might be the 1990s. No money had been invested here; *infrastructure* was a foreign word. There were the run-down sun-bleached shacks surrounded by smashed plastic electric car bodies, miles of them, and ominous markets with their barred windows, liquor ads, and seedy loiterers.

The bus turned into the majestic Makaha Valley and went right up to the gate of the club. A young man met the golfers, took their bags and loaded them onto a cart, then bounced off with the men in the back. The gate slid shut behind them with a decisive click, safely restoring them to the privileged side of the twenty-first century. Cen stepped down and stood in the cool morning air as the bus departed.

Surf half a mile away boomed in the otherwise still morning. Somewhere in those craggy cliffs that rose from the broad, emerald green valley floor, above tucked-away exclusive condos, wound a path steep and dangerous, where he had followed Maui to a place that had never left his memory.

Perhaps if he could find that haunting, spherical cave where he'd met Maui's grandmother, he could remember how it had been, that day. Perhaps the power of the path he'd not taken, the power of ancient seafaring Hawaii, would help him decide what his responsibility was toward the world he wished to leave behind. Kaiulani's passionate belief in her responsibility to her world and her people, a pact she had been unable to fulfill, had given him food for thought. He could not face her without knowing that he had done all he could, *here.*

He turned and walked past the gate, outside the wall of the club. After half a mile of searching the brush, speckled with empty beer cans and other trash, he found it—an overgrown trail—and began the hike. A hundred feet up the trail he felt drawn into another age, enfolded into the land. Unseen doves cooed, and the tall sun-heated grasses smelled sweet.

The hike did not take anywhere near as long as he thought it would, though he soon was breathing hard. He judged that he had climbed about three thousand feet, and gained a narrow red-soil ledge of doubtful footing, covered with crumbly rocks that made it quite precarious. Someone had bolted a steel cable along a hundred feet of cliffwalk; he clung to it gratefully. The tree-tops below him tossed in the rising wind, a forest of sweet-scented mimosa. A waterfall splashed nearby.

When he got across the cliff face, there it was.

The cave.

Holding his breath, he stepped inside.

It was empty.

He smelled the acrid remains of a fire, mingled with garbage. Should have brought a light. He fumbled in his pockets and found some matches he'd taken from a bar. Striking one, he saw several candles stuck to the floor of the cave; he bent and lit them.

He was sickened by what he saw.

Apparently it was being used as a drug lair. Nan drugs, or drugs that claimed to be nan-based but in reality were various pharmacological mishmashes guaranteed to have powerful effects, death frequently among them, were hot now. The method of ingestion was really up to the marketing ingenuity of the dealer. He saw a couple of plastic eyedrop squirts scattered on the floor in the flickering glow of the candles. Putting a few drops in the eye was popular, he'd read in the paper.

Obscenities covered the wall along with gang emblems, neon green and pink against the shiny black wall. A rat chittered away into a crack, abandoning a pile of garbage. At a sound behind him Cen whirled, but saw no one. Outside the world was green and fresh.

Deep within he felt this to be a sacrilege. Silly, he thought, as he blew out the candles and turned, stumbling over some empty drink plastics. Maui and his grandmother had made it into a holy place, where he had felt the power, the *mana,* which came from the land. *His* land.

At the cave mouth he breathed fresh air gratefully.

He moved downhill unseeingly, as if in a dark dream from which there was no escape. He had not realized how bright that single meeting with the still unnamed woman had been for him. Odd, since he'd rejected all their overtures. Then the true reason bubbled forth from long-quiet depths: she had known his mother, named her. She alone could tell him stories for which he was hungry, stories about his mother, her childhood, and the rest of his family. When he met her he had wanted only to escape from his past, from the blood and screaming, from knowing that his mother's heart and mind were forever silenced.

Now, he would treasure that connection, if he could find her.

But how to find Maui without direct web contact that might endanger both of them and the larger endeavors in which they were engaged? Cen was no good at cloak-and-dagger stuff. Any sort of veil he thought up would either not work or work so well that Maui would have no idea who was trying to contact him. He did not feel clever in that way.

And what could *he* do, what difference could *he* make, in the face of two hundred years of foreign rule in the islands? Pausing to look out to sea as he wiped sweat from his forehead, he gazed at a stunning panorama that made him feel almost as if he were flying. So easy to get lost in such a beautiful, infinite blue! How many islands had Tevake, the old navigator, held in his mind beneath the stars, his utterly precise field of reference? The cliffs of Kaena Point, Oahu's still-wild shore, were but a few miles away; after that, the nearest land to the north was Kauai, seventy miles away. Beyond, invisible, yet *there,* known by subtle signs that the experienced navigator could read from a hundred miles away, the *etak.*

As Kaiulani was his *etak*.

Cen was not sure anymore whether the lack of a written language was truly as backward as most people thought. The Polynesian memory was prodigious, filled with thousands of stories for which dance, in the form of the hula in Hawaii, was the framework for holding those stories in mind. And writing sprang from the necessity for documenting ownership and trade debts. Polynesian society had been communal and surely functioned better than any Communist regime of the 1900s, and for much, much longer. Their community had encompassed the entire Pacific Ocean.

As Cen gazed at his panorama he could almost *see* those great sailing canoes. He suspected that the *Hawai'i Loa,* the great canoe built by the Bishop Museum, in which Hawaiian children sailed the Pacific and learned the old navigational skills had made sailed starships *interesting* in the minds of IS engineers, who lived in Hawaii after all and constantly saw the the *Hawai'i Loa* on the news. That powerful visual image sparked their imagination, so that they began to brainstorm and add new technology to the old idea of solar-sailed ships.

Such a ship was now being built in orbit, its sails to lie dormant as seeds, then grow at just the right time to catch the particles of light which would push them after ages to the next galaxy. It would take, he had read, fifteen years to build, using the moonbase at last as it was meant to be used, a project that would involve all the resources and branches of IS.

Cen stood up and continued his descent.

Interspace with its grandiose yet hollow goals was simply an extension of colonialism. The children who used that cave behind him were exactly as he had been, left to their own devices, not believing that the future held anything for them, carefully kept from learning anything except how to swell the underclass and provide cheap labor.

And you, Cen, are just one person. What makes you think you can change a damned thing?

His sandals crunched on lava rock. He was almost at sea level. Next to him, inside an iron fence, the smooth precisely engineered swales of the golf course filled the valley. The open fence with its stylized art deco dolphin frieze was replaced by a brick wall, and then he was out on the highway where heat rose in waves. Several blocks away, through clapboard houses, he saw white foam; dancing sea. He crossed the road and headed toward it. Maybe he could wash this negativity away, for a time, at least, the feeling that he was running from a battle that was important to fight. But he didn't know how. What good could *he* do?

He stepped off the hot asphalt onto the even hotter expanse of unsullied golden sand. Wind-driven grains stung his face. Beyond was an ever-moving heart-stopping shade of aquamarine, edged with white surf. Not many people out here.

He took off all his clothes except his shorts, folding them neatly. He walked down the deep slope until the thundering waves curled overhead, translucent, shot with light, dove suddenly through the massive forces, and let the riptide he'd seen smothering the whitecaps to his left pull him out. He rode it until it released him about a quarter mile out. Someone on one of the huge old buffalo boards bobbed on the massive swells nearby; he waved at Cen and Cen waved back, was lifted and dropped in a soothing monotonous rhythm.

He turned and looked at the weathered cliffs patterned with cloud-shadows, and knew, suddenly, floating in this light-shot cool medium, what he should do.

Someone should know where they are, after I am gone.

His mother's words, the day she died, talking about the bones, still hidden in the Koolau Mountains, on the other side of the island.

He didn't think they were important. Not really, not compared to the things about which he thought. But his mother had died because of them, in a way. Her wish should be respected.

Cen had never burned with Maui's altruistic fire. He had kept to his own path, steered by the stars of his strange, private passion, had cultivated and fed his natural cynicism. Easy, with IS on your back.

Now, his entire body tingling in the life-giving ocean despite the cold with which he was beginning to shiver, he felt that fire

grab hold and warm him with a blaze he hadn't felt since before he could remember.

And was glad.

While the fan swirled overhead Cen sweated in his small room,
covering sheets of paper with numbers. He'd discovered a
strange predilection for the feel of pushing a pencil; it seemed
to help him think. He did this for three days straight but it was
no use. He scooted his chair back from the table abruptly and
pressed on his eyelids with his palms till the inner blackness was
light-shot. He rose and went to the bathroom sink, poured several glasses of water over his head, but it didn't wash the realization away.

He would have to log on. Retrace his way through the web,
to the glowing screen holding a particular juncture he'd worked
on in a London Underground station, at a web pay site, when
he discovered, in a panic, that his notebook was broken, and
that he was filled with what seemed like a minor rush of revelation. He'd made a copy of it, of course, but it seemed to have
been lost in the uproar of his leaving. Certainly, he couldn't
find it.

But it did still exist.

He cursed his ridiculous confidence, his certainty that if he
came to a conclusion once he owned it forever. If he'd ever published it, he could just go to the library and look up journals
on the computer. Instead, he had to risk revelation, use his
probably useless disguise, draw down the circling sharks of Interspace when they saw that he was not drinking but thinking—and even worse, show them that this chunk was of some
importance.

He locked his door and set out across Honolulu. None of
the web booths in downtown Honolulu were secure, despite
privacy laws. Some of the ritzier hotels claimed to have more
private web access; wealthy businesspeople had a way of making things unpleasant should their security be traceably
breached. He headed toward Waikiki, pretty sure that if he
went to the fanciest hotel he could find and used one of their

booths he would increase the odds of keeping the direction of his thoughts secret.

He took the route past Iolani Palace, past the golden statue of Liliuokalani, through the small expensive shops and large breezy restaurants of the tourist zone, past the Princess Kaiulani Hotel.

As the scene effervesced, he wondered if it was because he hadn't been eating right. A chill ran up his spine and then he jumped at the sound of a cannon being shot.

Ceremonial. Eyes closed, he saw a universe of internal stars. He wanted to *fix* this, somehow. He knew he had arrived at the nexus of all his thoughts. *Here.* Where was *here?*

Where, *exactly?*

How could he describe the passage and place mathematically?

How could he stay here forever?

A breeze cooled his skin. He heard reef-muffled surf and the wind-driven rush of a carefully imported botanical wonderland of leaves. He smelled ginger, heard the sharp cadence of marching feet and briefly snapped commands.

He tasted blood and realized he had bitten his lip quite hard.

The date? It had to be after August 12, 1898. That was the terrible day when Hawaii was officially annexed. That morning at Iolani Palace the Hawaiian flag was lowered and the American flag raised. At that moment, the Hawaiian musicians threw down their marching band instruments midsong and fled in tears, and a sudden storm washed over the festivities. That was the day Kaiulani's hopes, and the hopes of the Hawaiian people, were dashed forever.

He remembered seeing in the Bishop Museum so long ago the original invitation from the Provisional Government extended to Cleghorn and Kaiulani, an invitation to attend the Annexation Ceremony, R.S.V.P.; beneath that, the spidery handwriting of Cleghorn with which he "necessarily" declined the invitation for both himself and his daughter.

Cen opened his eyes. Ainahau—green, lush, filled with flowers and birds—was across the dirt road.

And there she was. He stared, heart in his throat.

A bit beyond the stone wall, Kaiulani's face was thin and pale as she bent over a bird-of-paradise plant. Slashes of bright orange bobbed as she cut several of them and lay them on the ground. She wore a voluminous black muumuu. A wide-brimmed straw hat shaded her face.

As he watched, she knelt and pulled a trowel from the basket at her side and began poking around in the dirt.

Behind her, the old mansion was half hidden behind mango trees and banyans. Her father had built her a new house in 1897, but Cen didn't see it—not surprising, seeing that the estate was ten acres. The raucous cries of peacocks exploded each time the cannon was fired.

He left the ruckus outside and walked in through the gate.

The clink of her trowel in the rich dirt mingled with the rustling of the leaves in the offshore trades. He glanced up once to see that American marines were there, dressed in uniforms from the past, carrying rifles. Guarding the public from her.

Oh, Kai, he thought, perhaps you should be more dangerous.

Kaiulani didn't look up, so he sat down in front of her, crosslegged, on the cool grass. She was only a foot from him. He reached up with one hand and brushed her cheek.

She looked up, and her brown eyes were flat and sad.

"You're much too thin," he said.

Her smile was derisive and did not reach her eyes. She gestured toward her enormous dress. "You can't tell," she said.

"Your face," he said. "What are you doing here?"

She knifed the trowel into the ground and leaned back.

"Don't you see the soldiers?" she asked. "I'm a prisoner here. I can't even have a charity event. They think I'm trying to raise money for the resistance." As she spoke he saw new hollows beneath her cheekbones; dark circles beneath her eyes.

"Then why don't you *do* something?" he asked.

She shrugged. "Lily—my aunt, the queen—surrendered. They held her prisoner in the palace. They uncovered some sort of plot—so they claimed, but it was only loyal young Wilcox, doing what was right. She had no knowledge of it. There was fighting on Diamond Head. Hawaiians were killed. They were going to try her for treason. They threatened to kill her. They have threatened to kill me."

"Isn't there anything you can *do?*"

"She keeps advising me to do nothing. The Provisional Government offered to make me queen, but she says they would only use me to bring the Hawaiians into line with annexationist plans. And she doesn't want me to take an opposition course and rally the Hawaiians. That would only cause more bloodshed. She's right." Her voice was bitter and old. "I never had any real power. I was never anything."

"You're something to *me,*" said.

She looked up, and he was surprised to see that her eyes were filled with gratitude. "Didn't you *know?*" he asked.

"I hardly ever see you," she said.

"I'm sorry," he said, and was suddenly curious. "Look," he said, "how do you think this happens? Us seeing each other?"

"I think," she said slowly, "that it has something to do with the bones."

"What bones?"

"Kamehameha's bones," she said. "Didn't I tell you? I'm sure I did. The kahuna used them to curse my mother and she died. He cursed me, the daughter, too. 'With vision,' my old Hawaiian nurse told me. When my father found out that she'd said that—I was very young, you know, but I remember it—he was very angry and let her go. From then on he only hired haoles to take care of me. He's Scotch, you know, and he doesn't believe in any sort of superstition. I used to laugh about it, too. And then I used to be so happy that I could see you that I thought, if this is part of a curse of vision, it's more of a blessing. Now I don't know. It only makes me terribly sad. Not only you. It's—other things too." She shivered. "Everything seems so dark. My life is over, the life I was meant to have. The life of my country is over. It's just a colony now, a place to be looted. And I can never see you if I want. It just happens. Sometimes. Hardly at all, it seems."

"It has *nothing* to do with bones," he shouted. "It has to do with you!" It has nothing to do, the subtext in his mind ran, with quantum cosmology, the metauniverse, "the observer," or branching time. Those were only *words*. The nexus that he'd sought so desperately, he suddenly realized, had to do with human consciousness, with will, with *love*.

Absurd.

Totally unscientific.

But then, since consciousness and all its attributes, including emotion, did exist, they must figure somehow in the vast equations with which he had so long and desperately struggled. Words flew from him, even while he cringed at how angry and forceful he sounded.

"It has to do with will! You're not doing what you were born to do!"

She stood, eyes blazing. "Are *you?*" she asked.

"You don't know anything about me," he said. "I know—"

"Oh, what do you know?" she shouted. "You only *think* you know. And don't tell me what to do or who I am! That's all anyone ever has done."

She ran off across the lawn. He followed, grabbed her shoulder, whirled her around, and held her. "Don't go, Kai," he whispered. "Please don't go. Please don't be angry with me. I need you more than anything. I need this time. I need *you.*"

"Then help me," she whispered, and he drew her close to him and stroked her hair, lowered his head, and kissed her.

A male voice called out from beyond a screen of green foliage, and she jumped away.

"Vicky! Where are you? Are we going to play cards? The others are waiting." His footsteps receded.

"Koa," she said, looking at Cen. "My cousin. He wants to marry me."

"You can't!" he shouted before he even thought about it.

"Who are *you* to tell me what I can and can't do!" she said, her voice filled with pain. "What else can I do, what else *should* I do, if he's willing? I care for him. We've always been close. And at least he's always here, and loves me no matter what! You have a lot of nerve. Who are *you,* anyway?" She pushed him away, and tilted her head to regard him with serious eyes that continued the question.

"Please, Kai," he said. "I'll marry you. If that's what you want. That's what *I* want."

"But—," she said, her expression one of stunned amazement.

"Isn't—isn't that what you want?" he asked, completely humbled. "If I beg you?"

"How *can* you marry me?" she asked, her voice almost scathing. "I hate this. I must be insane. You're not real. I've always told myself, you can't be real. But . . . " she glanced down at herself " . . . now I *know* you're real. What else explains . . . Cen, I am going to have your . . . "

And on the cusp of her declaration he fell again into darkness, then stood blinking in his own time.

People were staring at him, moving around him in a wide berth.

What had she meant to say? Your *baby?* How else could such a sentence end?

But she had never had a baby. He must have misheard her.

He turned and began the long run back to his room, his excitement growing. Maybe this last bit of information was all he needed, the where and when of this appearance. Late that night he fell asleep over his papers, trying not to be disappointed. All the pieces are here now, he kept telling himself. Don't worry.

But he was terrified.

The next morning, he faced the nature of his terror.

The vague records of the illness that had caused her death were quite mixed. "Bright's disease" was mingled with reports claiming that "rheumatism had reached her heart," or "she died of pneumonia."

If he actually *did* return, would it be only to stand at her deathbed?

He couldn't seem to think about his grand mathematical edifice with this hanging over his head. He had to find out more. And he had to think. He had to get out of his room, away from his papers.

The freeway he walked beneath was a dull roar of rumbling

wheels. Then he was in one of the neighborhoods above Honolulu, walking along Liliha Street.

He followed some inner magnet as doves hooted and filled the morning with primeval mystery despite the modern overlay. *I crave the past,* he thought; *I simply crave the past, and one woman in that past, Kaiulani.*

But he had to let the new information settle into some sort of coherence before he could fit it with what he already had.

He hardly dared hope that this meeting was the last point to fully define his vision of fractal time, and to predict the places where the fractals of the metauniverse might be jumped, transversed, when the particles that were *him* would be utterly translated . . .

But it was possible. Yes.

He bought a pack of cigarettes though he had not smoked in years; Ross had broken him of that habit. When he'd smoked half the pack he was in front of the Bishop Museum. He threw the rest of the pack in he trash and went into the gift shop. As good a starting place as any. After this he would go to the archives, see if there was any definitive medical information . . .

Inside was a short row of books about Kaiulani, mixed in with general Hawaiiana—genealogy, flora and fauna, navigational feats, recovered chants, and authentic hula videos. He pulled one of the books out, but he'd seen it before. He'd seen them all.

"Another Kaiulani groupie?" asked the man behind the counter. He wore a brass badge that said his name was Palea.

Cen turned, the book open. "I guess," he said.

Palea, a huge Hawaiian with a long ponytail, smiled. "They're in here all the time. Buying holographic posters of her. Got a whole society re-creating her clothes and stuff. Always making new virtuals. There's their latest. *Kaiulani in Jersey.*" He pointed at it, shook his head.

"Well, that's understandable, I guess," Cen said.

"Her granddaughter just passed away last week," said Palea. "Old times gone. Kind of a shame. Of course, she was less than a quarter Hawaiian. Stubborn old lady, too; she had a used-car dealership, so you can imagine. She wasn't at all interested in her ancestors."

"What do you mean, her granddaughter?" asked Cen, his voice sharp. "Kaiulani didn't have any children."

Palea shrugged. "Probably shouldn't say anything. My auntie would kill me—except she's been dead a long time. But you're Hawaiian, no? I'm surprised you don't know. Not that it's particularly important—but didn't you have any aunties? Didn't you grow up talking story with them?"

"My mother"—Cen's voice caught—"my mother died when I was pretty young. After that I was on my own." And I hated everything Hawaiian—I just didn't know why.

Except Kaiulani.

"Too bad," said Palea. "What the hell, all these old secrets. Not really secret, not to Hawaiians. You really missed out. Well, a lot of kids don't listen anyway. Yeah, she died a few weeks after giving birth. *Because* of it. It was all covered up." He turned to another customer. "Can I help you?"

Cen just stood there, the book open in his hand. Had he already moved, without knowing it, into another world? He was sweating. The cigarettes had made him dizzy.

Palea looked at him with concern. "Hey, brah, you all right?"

Cen grabbed at the counter. The shop swirled around him.

Palea's wooden kamaaina house, an old-timer's house, perched several hundred feet above the Nuuanu Pali highway. Traffic rushed past below, distance rendering the sound surflike, white noise that blended with the rustle of a huge banyan whose baby shoots were twining around Palea's precarious porch railing.

Cen stood on the edge of the wide wooden veranda, which was cantilevered out over a steep, jungled drop-off. Sisal mats covered the floorboards, and the outdoor room was furnished with an eclectic assortment of tables and chairs. Rain thrummed briefly on the roof, then the cloud passed. Orange, scarlet, and yellow hibiscus pressed against the screen. Cen moved to another corner and looked down at a precisely rocked pool where water paused only for a second before rushing over the lip and splashing invisibly far below.

Palea thrust a cold beer into his hand and flipped a switch that turned on an underwater light. "My koi. I've had most of them for years. See the white one? That's Ed Sullivan. Ever heard of him?"

"No," said Cen, opening his beer.

"The red one is Lucy. I love those old TV shows, man. Gotta hundred of the CDs. Sure you don't want something to eat? You still don't look good. I never saw a man faint before. Or a woman either, come to think of it." He unwrapped a vast sandwich he'd bought on the way home. "Here, take some."

Cen did not much care for salty lunch meat but he ate it to please Palea, who was a nice man. He felt like he'd fallen into a rabbit hole. "So tell me about Kaiulani," he said abruptly.

Palea sprawled into a deep bamboo chair, which creaked beneath his weight; Cen settled on a matching couch.

Full night had come, turning the Pali Highway to a half-hidden river of slow-flowing light. Sweet ginger scent came and went as the wind gusted, clacking the banana leaves in the darkness. Cen emptied his beer and set the can on a small round table.

"What you want to know?" asked Palea.

Cen wanted to ask him to cut the crap and speak correctly; he'd seen several anthropology degrees in Palea's name on the tamati-matted wall when they'd entered. He was always glad his mother had insisted on perfect grammar. He thought Palea's probably had, too.

"Kaiulani had a baby?"

Palea took a pull from his beer can. "Yeah, she did."

"Why doesn't anyone know? I never read about it anywhere."

Palea's face was in the shadows. His words came fast, mixed with Hawaiian, sweet as music to Cen's ears. He forgot his problems with Palea's way of talking and focused on what he said as if it were his very life.

"I'm only telling you this because you're Hawaiian, brah. Nobody cares, of course. She's been dead over a hundred years.

But yeah, she was pregnant. That's why she went to the Big Island, to get away, while she was pregnant. She gave birth on Moloka'i. You know, came back to the kahunas at the end. But too late to save her."

"What happened to the baby?" asked Cen, his voice a hoarse whisper.

"After she died, Kaiulani's father, Cleghorn, told the aunties that it would be known as his. I'd say that was probably the plan all along anyway. Probably nobody outside that room would have questioned it. Kaiulani grew up with a few half sisters Cleghorn fathered without being married before she was born, and I'd say he had more after Likelike died. But all those aunties were surprised as hell. That kid—could have ruled Hawaii, eh?"

"Could have been killed," said Cen. "Another threat."

He felt, rather than saw, Palea nod in the darkness. "Exactly," he said. "A threat to the new American government. It was pretty shaky. Can you imagine the riots—the bloodshed, even?—when the people found out that there was a new heir to the throne, the child of their beloved princess? And besides that, the kid was all the old man had left of Kaiulani."

"Boy or girl?"

"Boy."

"Who was the father?"

Palea did not speak for a moment but the night was alive with motion and sound—the shrill of insects, the hush of traffic, the roar of a million trees shouting the answer into Cen's mind.

Palea said, "Nobody knows. Best bet is Koa, her cousin. They were very close. He visited her in England once or twice, and when she returned they spent a lot of time together. But for some reason they didn't marry. They felt like brother and sister toward each other, I think. Just my opinion. The aunties said he didn't know about the child until much later, until after she'd died and he'd married another woman. She kept it secret from him all during her pregnancy. Maybe she—she and her father—always intended it to be a secret. The Hawaiians didn't have the haole hangup about ownership, about legitimacy. But Kaiulani wasn't really living in a Hawaiian world anymore. Maybe she cared."

"But *why?*" asked Cen, his throat aching. "Why did she die? She was only twenty-three. Did she hemorrhage? Have a problem with the afterbirth? What happened?"

"Bright's disease." Palea got up and went inside, continued talking through the open kitchen window. Cen heard the refrigerator open and shut. "They didn't really have Bright's disease pinned down too well. Alice Longworth, Teddy Roosevelt's wife, died the day she gave birth. She had it, too."

"Bright's disease."

"Yeah." A cupboard door slammed, then another. Palea muttered something to himself, then continued talking to Cen. "That's what they said. Basically some sort of kidney problem, maybe the aftermath of a strep infection."

All those colds, in Europe. "Why do some of the accounts say she died of pneumonia?"

"Part of the bullshit coverup, that's all. 'Oh, she rode off in the cold rain.' I guess they had to think of something. And who cares, anyway, eh? I think they told her son, when he got old enough. They lived in a world of high intrigue, those people. Backstabbers, you know? Always fighting over who's who. People still do it. I'm from a kahuna line; my cousins are all royals. Always lording it over us. Could be old man Cleghorn was tired of it. Just plain tired. And maybe he didn't want his daughter bad-mouthed by the Americans for having a child out of wedlock, especially since she was dead." He came back outside holding two beers and a bag of pretzels. Want another beer?"

"No," said Cen. "I think I've had enough."

"I think so, too," said Palea, his voice gentle. He peered at Cen from across the porch, his large, dark face highlighted by the citronella candle. "Who are you anyway? Why do you care?"

"Why do you?" asked Cen. "How do you know all this?"

"My uncle had a lot of old tapes he made himself. The old aunties used to have a club, Saturday mornings." Palea laughed quietly. "The old man said that his mother used to drag him down there and make him listen. A few years later when he was in college he realized that all those old ladies had *been there* and he started going around and taping them all, asking them questions. They were talking story about the old days. The last ones, you know? They all had American names because they'd married, but they were old aunties. The last of the royal cousins who'd been born in the late eighteen hundreds and early nineteen hundreds. Kaiulani's story was only one of them. Oh, the stories went way back. Way way back. She was always just a pawn. I'm sure Cleghorn realized that, at the end; there was just no point in telling anyone that Kaiulani died because of that baby. None of their damned business. Why should Cleghorn let another life—the child's—be ruined? And why should he have to give up all that he had left of Kaiulani to whoever the father was? It's very possible that Kaiulani herself made him promise not to say anything. They said she should have trusted the kahunas, had a Hawaiian-style healing, and then she would have lived. You tell everything you've kept hidden, get the poisons out. So who knows—maybe the secrecy of the pregnancy killed her, kept her from getting the care she needed." He sighed. "Or maybe it was what they said about her—she had no reason to live. She was not going to be queen, and now she even had an illegitimate child. She would be a disgrace in the eyes of her fancy European friends. She gave up. Ah, no wonder. She was only half Hawaiian. A wimp. Too pampered. Too damned *skinny*. But why do you care?"

Palea had asked a question—why did he care? Cen didn't turn his head. He told instead the stars, the stream, the river of light, and the overwhelming scent of ginger that came rushing from the night, his answer a whisper that Palea could not hear:

Because I love you, Kai.

"What?" said Palea.

Cen turned to look at the huge man with concerned liquid brown eyes that spoke to him of his people and his home. Of course he was the one to ask.

"You know somebody by the name of Maui?"

* * *

The next morning Cen bought a blank book, a spiral notebook that artists used for sketching. The notebook pleased him in some deep way, the white unlined expanse of paper. He bought a package of indelible pens because he did not want anyone erasing what he did nor did he want it to fade. It was not yet complete but he could feel its energy gathering and wanted to be ready.

What was in his head was a delicately structured edifice of thought. It would soon be complete, he knew; entirely whole and of a piece and satisfactory; sound as a bell that would ring loud as the peals of all the Honolulu church bells that had rung on the day of Kaiulani's birth so long ago.

He waited until the hour was right and went back to the museum. Palea ignored him. He saw the only copy of *Death of a Kingdom* and took it up to the desk, paid for it. When Palea raised his eyes they were full of questions but he just said, "Thank you, sir," and gave Cen his change. The night before Cen had finally convinced Palea that he was who he said he was and that Maui would want to hear from him. Palea had given him these spylike directions. The funny thing was that it was all so crude.

When he got back to his room he tore out page ninety-seven and held it over a lit match. A phone number, written in broad strokes, became clear. Cen smiled. Sometimes the simplest things were the best, eh? He memorized it, tore the page to bits, and flushed it down the toilet.

He was not quite ready to call Maui.

But soon, he hoped. Soon.

He was becoming increasingly polarized by hope, as if the one true navigation star was just about to rise above the night horizon and create a path across the dark sea. He'd known this rising curve of inevitable energy before, many times. He would work frenzied, for days, barely sleeping and eating, while the world seemed infused with light and pure purpose, filled with crystalline patterns that flowed through his pencil.

Afterward, he always plunged down the flip side into darkness; if it were not for his written record of when he had thought otherwise, he could easily deny that there was any reason to live.

This time he aimed to fly right off the curve, into the heart of the universe, into the truth of all matter and being.

Something fell into place that night in the live space between wakefulness and dream that always seethed with thought for Cen. He knew it when it happened; he sat up in bed. The sheet fell from his naked body, and he sat on the edge of the bed for a long time feeling as if he were the focal point of a vast field of information that had quietly manifested itself since the beginning of time and was only waiting with infinite patience for a target. He felt humble and deeply grateful while the breeze from the harbor cooled his body until he began to shiver; then he pulled the sheet back over himself and fell asleep, not at all worried that he would forget. When he put pen to paper it would all pour out.

At Ala Moana Park, just past sunrise, coconut palms cast long shadows across the soft green lawn.

Cen had spent an afternoon here with Kaiulani, back when he was so very young. Now he chose a concrete picnic table beneath a twisted tree, sat, and opened his notebook.

As the park filled with picnickers and the cries of children, he wrote, caught on a rising tide of joy. Doves cooed in their hidden owl-like way, each sound like a bubble that rose into the day and burst against his ear. Everything around him seemed to echo the truth of what his pen was saying.

When he finally looked up, finished, humanity had ebbed from the park and it was dusk. Light-limned tourist boats plied the sea on the other side of the reef and he felt as if all of existence was one thing, entire and whole: light and time, large and small, quanta and gravity, all forces and all of their results, one great wide open thing revealed by the existence of her, Kaiulani.

And on the path of her revelation he would travel.

He sat, dazed, for half an hour, drained and simply happy.

This was the place where she had lived, and within a few blocks was the place where she had died.

The lights of the boats glimmered on dark water, so close that across the stretch of reef-enclosed sea he could hear the band on one of them playing steel guitar. In the cool night he broke into a sweat.

It might not work for him. It might not.

But what did it matter? He could only try.

He realized now that it was not as precise as he thought it might be. It was like the difference between looking at a map of an intersection and actually being there: the richness of the description would vary greatly between the person looking at the map and the person standing in the very spot the map described. He could be a bit more precise than before, and now he had been able to broaden certain parameters so that once he crossed over he would not be able to return. Perhaps at some time, using his proofs as a basis, and with massive computer power, more precision would be possible. But this was enough for him. He could now make projections, and know within certain broad parameters the times and places where this would be possible.

He still had a few things to do, here in this life, before he was ready.

He had to do not only what Kaiulani would want him to do but what he now in his heart believed was deeply right.

And he had to do what he could to save her life.

He flipped back to the front of his book: in the light from a nearby bathroom he could see he'd left no room.

No matter. He flipped to the back of the book and wrote

THE KAIULANI PROOFS

He closed the book and gripped it tight, looking once again at the beautiful electricity. Pearl Harbor, the Waianae Coast, arced away from him in a great swoop of land, sprinkled with light as with so many grains of salt.

At a pawnshop Cen bought a long zippered bag large enough to hold several rods and reels. He considered two rods carefully and chose one, quite heavy, good sturdy ahi size, and went to another store before he found a fairly good reel and bargained for it, purely to give any IS spies who by the slimmest chance might be watching him a reason for his purchase of this bag. He watched himself do this from some detached place, savoring each detail. Each thing he did, every second, brought him closer to Kaiulani.

Besides, he thought, as he zipped up his new rig, it was pretty damned nice. He might just want to actually go fishing.

At first he had been deeply depressed about the truth of her death. Was he the father?

Given that he believed that he *had* been with her in San Francisco—yes.

In the Queen's Hospital medical library he looked up Bright's disease and found that it was a vague diagnosis and so was not sure exactly what she'd had or what if anything in that time could have cured it or kept it at bay after her dangerous birthing. Perhaps only dialysis might have helped. Perhaps antibiotics. Perhaps a new kidney. It all depended on what the problem had really been. He wished he knew some doctors who might help, might give him advice. Was abstinence the only answer? It was too late for that. What then should he take her? A birth control patch? Here, my dear, a present from the future?

He stopped into a free clinic for a while-you-wait vasectomy.

In the tiny room he sat draped in white paper, and questions spun in his mind. Could he possibly, possibly, change her life? Change her death to life? Could he—what if—

"Don't worry, this is an operation you can do on the kitchen table. In fact, I've *done* them on kitchen tables," said the jovial doctor as he pulled on his gloves with a snap. "You know, all the relatives want free jobs. Always the women want their husbands done. But you don't look worried."

"What?" asked Cen, jolted from his thoughts. "Oh."

"I said, never seen any man calm as you while you stare at these knives," said the doctor, as the nurse handed him one.

"Oh," said Cen again. "I guess that patch worked." He

didn't feel the least bit concerned. And he certainly didn't feel any pain. He felt euphoric.

"Guess so," said the doctor. "One last chance to change your mind."

Cen shook his head and closed his eyes.

He left with a year's worth of samples of a powerful antibiotic, because he told the doctor he was embarking on a long trip to remote parts of China. The doctor's physician daughter was there, too, he told Cen, doing volunteer medical work.

"I'll give you what she took with her to China, in case you have some emergency. Your medical history of kidney infections could be dangerous if you were in a remote area. Still have your appendix? That's too bad. Try and have that taken care of. The receptionist can help you set up arrangements."

The doctor emerged from a room holding an envelope filled with patches. "You would not believe how effective these are. These antibiotics are bacteria-sensitive. They're genetically engineered to respond to a broad spectrum of bacteria. Perfect for someone in your situation. They'll wipe out things so primitive we haven't seen them before, or things so hardened to assault that they're impervious to everything else. An entire new generation of drugs. Not FDA-approved yet, but they will be soon." He lowered his voice a bit. "Tell you the truth, they were developed by IS for their generation ship. If they didn't work, heads would roll."

He paused. "If you're worried about your kidneys, this is slated to be the kidney rebuilder." He went to a bank of drawers and pulled out a sheet of perforated patches, carefully labeled a plastic holder, and slipped them inside, along with some strips that when inserted in urine gave precise information about kidney function. He went over the indications for use with Cen, and said, "The way I interpret the research—I'm a urologist, by the way, so I've been following it closely—is that a regrown kidney might cause problems down the road. But not until the patient is pretty old anyway, a lot older than they would have been without them. Average old age, you know?"

Cen thanked him profusely, went back to his room, and put the packet in his fishing bag.

* * *

Everything he did now, every motion, every decision, reminded him of the lucidity of the special quality of light here in his home, above the sea and even below it, where the bustle of the world was gone and fish reflected light in slow-moving rainbows and where for fifty feet in all directions one could see through the alien medium of water. He was preparing to enter an alien medium now deliberately as a diver.

Cen got on a bus late at night so he would be alone, so he could be sure no one was following him. He hoped that IS had written him off at last, if they even knew he was here, deciding that the fragments they'd gotten from Smith were all that they were going to get.

With him he had his fishing bag with his new pole zipped inside.

As he settled into the back, and the bus moved steadily up the Nuuanu Pali Highway, he was reminded of the trip so many years ago on the same line when he had fled his mother's death, coming the other way over the Koolaus on this same road.

At what point had he locked the awful thing that had happened deep inside and sealed it into memory? At this block, where the lights of an all-night liquor store coldly fluoresced? Up here, a mile further on, where, looking back, he could see the panorama of Honolulu lights spread out below him like a shimmering dream of space? Each foot gained in elevation as the bus climbed the mountain seemed to bring him closer to some powerful, fearful place in his mind. By the time he reached the Nuuanu Pali—"the" Pali, though *pali* just meant cliff—he struggled to pull in each breath against the dark weight gathered there.

He got out. It was what—3:00 A.M.? He saw one couple silhouetted against some rocks, taking in the view, but otherwise the place was deserted.

Buffeted by the constant wind, which legend claimed you could sometimes lean against and be supported, suspended over the lush green rain-catching side of the Koolaus, where the valley below was straight down several thousand feet, he grabbed a wind-gnarled tree and perched dangerously close to the pali's edge.

Spread out below was the land of his troubled childhood. Kailua Bay, the maglev launch blazing with light, was fully defined by lights.

He raised his eyes to the glowing moon. The colony there grew apace. That was the logical place for the seed to spew forth, he presumed.

But he, Cen, could walk right through. Into another world. One person.

Perhaps some future mathematicians might extrapolate his results to a group of people, even to a field that included a ship, maybe even a planet. He might have himself, had he remained here.

But he did not intend to.

Kaiulani had gazed upon this view. Much darker at night, he surmised, and the stars much brighter, not drowned by land light. This had been her future kingdom. But Hawai'i had instead become the last shore on which Manifest Destiny cast its all-encompassing mantle, which had swept her away, into death, on its black tide of conquered indigenous peoples.

He thought of Maui as he looked out over the sparse lights below. How was Maui? What was he doing, really? Soon he would know. He looked forward to seeing Maui after so long. Kaiulani had awakened him to Maui's truth.

He was in more of a position now to appreciate Maui's grandmother's intimation that Interspace harbored within it Homeland Movement radicals.

He finally had what he wanted for more than half his life. He had all the pieces of the puzzle, he was sure. Just *understanding* how they fit was enough for him to be able to leave. And stay in Kaiulani's time.

Never to return.

It was odd, this having the pieces to such a very grand puzzle.

He would not do it for people like those in Interspace. There was no reason for them to know these things. Who knew what use they might put it to?

A great gust of wind blasted him, and he had to grab hold of his tree to keep his balance. He turned his eyes upward, with the great sweep of wind, and let the light of billions of stars fill them. Startled, he realized that he had completely lost sight of the ostensible, ultimate goal of the international Interspace consortium—to travel to the stars. Humankind's first concerted effort as a species, globally, to leave the planet. The data from tiny, distant robotic probes appeared in a box on page two of the *Honolulu Advertiser* every day. There were many probes, so the box was never empty. The huge scientific community living here noted it with interest.

But IS was a corrupt and immoral organization. As corrupt and as immoral as the Provisional Government, composed of American businessmen, the members of which had seen fit to quietly, gradually, and cannily take the land, the vote, and the rule from those whose right it was to have those things by forcing Kalakaua to sign what became known as the "Bayonet Constitution."

He should stay and fight, alongside Maui, in whatever way he could. He should. He should stay, and take the place he knew would rightfully be his in the annals of science.

But he would not. No, he would not.

He was surprised by the lightening of the sky. He had not realized the time. Hidden within the billowing forest, tropical birds greeting the dawn exploded with sound, suddenly, and the sky was a sheet of dark orange that changed in minutes to yellow and then blue and the vast ocean beneath was first a great metal-gray sheet that relaxed into blue and it was day, full day.

It was time to go. He picked up his bag, strangely untired.

The trailhead was only two miles away and he walked to it parallel to the road on a footpath through dense jungle. A shower swept across the roof of the forest, pattering against the leaves and freshening the air. It did not penetrate to where he walked among thick-trunked trees. It was quiet, away from the road.

His long bag was well balanced in his hand as he strode along the narrow trail. He could almost see his mother, a princess, a *priestess* of the *alii* kahuna class, walking in front of him, telling him not to eat too many guavas; he plucked a yellow, ripe one and bit into the sweet pink flesh, just one.

When he got to the pool and the waterfall he paused. How could anything be so pristine so close to Honolulu? Guarded by the spirits in which most Hawaiians still believed, eh?

He paid them silent homage and put down his bag.

This was a present to Maui, and to Maui's grandmother. He did not have to give them these things. But it was his duty to pass them on and it was quite clear to whom he should pass them.

For the third time in his life he climbed the cliff behind the waterfall and sat on the narrow ledge there.

Soaked, he reached inside and pulled out the packet of bones.

He stared at it for a long moment, relieved that it was actually still here. White birds flitted across the still green pool where the long waterfall fell straight as an arrow disturbing it as little as a perfect dive. This—*this!*—was what his mother had died for—to show him a packet of old bones.

Perhaps not directly. But if they hadn't been late getting back home . . . his father wouldn't have been in that mood . . . his mother would not have pulled out the gun over which they all, finally, struggled . . .

Absurd reasoning! But she had shown them to him on the day of her death, and because she had taken the time to do so, she may well have died, and his own life had changed forever. Because of the import of that day, because of the intensity of her belief in their sacredness, the bones were holy for him. Because of her belief, not because of his. He believed in the power of mind, and in Kaiulani, and in the truth of what he knew.

Balancing on the ledge, he unwrapped the bundle. The tapa crumbled and flaked away, stuck to his hands, as he hastily unfolded it.

The bones gleamed softly in the muted rain forest light. The musty smell of old tapa mingled with the scent of spray and the huge, mysterious white flowers that cascaded down one side of the waterfall.

He chose one bone for Maui, a long one that he thought might be a tibia. He didn't really know what they wanted to do with the bones, but something he faintly remembered Maui's grandmother saying was that it had something to do with DNA. So one bone was plenty, wasn't it? He would hold the rest back. He might need the bargaining power these bones could give him in some unforeseen scenario.

Because he might, he realized, with a chill that did not come from his surroundings but from his heart, be back. He might fail completely, in one of several ways. He might want to come back.

He might?

He turned that thought over in his mind.

So what if he *did* want to come back? He probably would want to come back, many times. Would he be able to?

He admitted to himself that he doubted it. He had no target here, in this age, nothing or no one that he loved. His *etak* lay beyond this horizon.

But still . . .

He ran his hand over the rough, pitted bones, thinking. If they fell into the wrong hands, or were simply lost, the Home-landers would have nothing, after all.

He needed both hands to extricate the skull from the welter of bones in the tapa. He looked into the dark, empty sockets for a moment.

Then he took a portion of the tapa cloth that had broken away from the large wrap, rolled the skull in it, and thrust it deep inside the cave.

Then he rewrapped the large bundle and laboriously climbed down, almost slipping into the pool several times. He edged around the water, trying not to trample lush ferns, holding tightly to the entire bundle. He unzipped the bag and put the bones in with his fishing rod. It was a very tight fit. He struggled with the zipper and finally got it shut.

Overcome with tiredness, he lay on a soft bed of moss clutching the bag like a lover and slept.

He woke several hours later, startled. Light had fled from the clearing; it was late afternoon. Soon it would be dark. He did not want to be on that narrow trail too late. Why had he slept so long?

But something within him had healed as he slept.

The bones were heavy and awkward on the return hike. He deliberately savored each spectacular vista, the sunset-colored sea, whenever the trees thinned. Once or twice he crouched as the roar of the wind rose, holding onto a rock or tree.

When he finally got back to his room, it was after midnight. He was exhausted. He put the key to the door but it swung open and inside was a tall man in the darkness bent over the table lighting his notebook—his proofs!—with a digiscan light.

All this registered instantly. Cen rushed the man while raising his bag and smashed him in the midsection with the bones.

The intruder cried out, dropping the camera, which clattered on the floor. He bent to grab it with one hand and reached for the notebook with the other, clutching the open pages.

Cen kicked the camera from his hand, grabbed the notebook and yanked it from him.

The pages the intruder held ripped. Cen raised the bones over his head and brought them down straight. The man rolled away, evading the blow; leapt up with one swift motion and ran out the door. Cen, breathing hard, heard him pound down the stairs. Cen smashed the camera with his foot; fished out the digicard on which the recording was done, held it under his lighter flame, and melted it.

What a fool he'd been, thinking them lulled. No doubt they'd been in here every time he'd gone out, trying to find evidence of his work, which they believed they owned, as if someone could actually own the history of time, the nature of the universe.

He grabbed the notebook with one hand and the bones with the other. Fierceness ran like fire through him and he almost wished, as he hurried down the uneven stairs, that someone was waiting at the bottom so he could kill them with his bare hands.

But the dingy foyer was empty, and Cen walked unchallenged into the night.

15

A brief, characteristic electronic burst told Cen that the encryption code was working.

Maui didn't sound surprised to hear his panicked voice. But he did sound rather cold. "I was told you might try and get in touch. We can talk safely for a short time. So make it quick. What do you want?"

Cen didn't blame him for being suspicious. "I have something for you," he said. "Something your grandmother wanted. I don't know if she told you—"

"Oh," said Maui. His voice grew thoughtful. "I know what you're talking about. What brought this on? You've been working for IS for years."

"I've never worked for IS," said Cen flatly. "I hate them."

"Fooled us pretty good," said Maui.

"I was trying to fool *them,*" said Cen. "But I didn't do such a great job. Who do you think paid for Oxford? That's where I've been. Look, how could I work for them? They killed Ross. They killed—they killed Mei. Remember her? You were going to try to help her out, that day you took me to Makaha. But it was too late. That night when you dropped me off I went up to my room and she was there. Dead. I guess I just went kind of crazy for a while."

Maui was silent for a moment. "I remember. She was missing from the hospital, it's true. Go on. Why didn't you call us? We would have helped."

For a price, thought Cen. The price of me remembering how my mother died. "It upset me to talk about my mother," said Cen. Damn Maui. It still did. His voice shook a bit; he cleared his throat and went on. "I'm just not very political. I'm a mathematician." He realized that that would have little impact on

Maui. *I've just been thinking all these years. You know. Thinking.*

"So what brought on this change of heart?"

Cen realized that he didn't even want to tell Maui about Kaiulani. "I've been . . . working on some proofs," he said, realizing that it sounded lame. "They're important. In fact, now they're after *me* because I won't hand them over. Look, if you don't want what I have, fine. I didn't *have* to call you at all!" He stopped just short of saying, The hell with you!

"Calm down," said Maui. "Can you meet me in an hour? I have to check on something. If I'm more than ten minutes late, leave." He gave terse directions, then hung up.

Cen paced down the concrete wall of the Ala Wai Canal in downtown Waikiki. He kept glancing behind him. He heard only the wash of boats bobbing on ripples. Get out of here, his adrenaline insisted. IS heard everything.

The bare aluminum masts of countless sailboats tangled in a linear puzzle that glowed in the tall lights lining the docks. A fish jumped in the darkness and so did Cen.

He about died of terror when a heavy hand clapped him on the back. "Hey, brah," he heard, a deep, rich, Hawaiian voice. He turned and there was Maui.

Maui embraced him briefly, stood back.

Cen blinked. "I thought—"

"We discussed the situation. We'll take a chance. In fact, we're very happy to hear from you after so long."

"We?"

"We," said Maui.

Maui was slightly shorter than Cen—still, of course, a very tall man, over six feet—and built more heavily. He might not become huge as Palea, if he was careful. He did look very fit. He wore shorts, a heavy sweatshirt, and hiking boots. His face was half hidden by a beard, and his hair was very long. He still had that white streak in it.

He looked at Cen's bag. "Perfect," he whispered, as if he knew what the bag held. "Let's go."

Their steps thudded on the wooden dock. After a few turns Maui motioned toward a boat. "There it is."

The *Lelani* was a long, low boat, a little longer and lower perhaps than might be good for fishing, though it had some of the trappings—outriggers to hold lines, though there was no fish-spotting tower, only a low, yachtlike cabin. And when Cen stepped down onto the polished wooden deck, he saw a glowing bank of digital readouts complex as those in an airplane. When he set the bag down in the cabin he saw a tiny black satellite dish behind the galley.

Maui didn't lose an instant, but began to cast off, motioning to Cen to untie the line from the forward cleat. Before Cen had finished coiling it onto the deck Maui had the engine purring and they were moving wakeless through the sleeping marina.

After a few turns as the canal passed through the streets and high-rises of downtown Waikiki, filled with the late night shouts of persistent partiers and glowing with randomly lit windows, they headed out through a channel toward the open sea. The white line of surf on the reef on both sides of the channel caught the moonlight. Cen looked back as the engine dug into the growing swells and saw lights sweep up the ridges of the university district, stopping suddenly on the edges of steep, deep gullies, black knives dividing lines of light. Red lights pulsed slowly across the rooftops of the high-rises. Above, even at this time of night, Cen saw planes stacked up in the sky, one after another.

Maui stood at the wheel, staring straight ahead. The waves seemed very large to Cen, occasionally breaking onto the deck, foaming at the top and spewing spray before passing on.

Maui's long hair flew out behind him. Cen shivered in the chilly wind and wished he had a jacket.

Maui turned. "You haven't changed much," he shouted over the engine's roar, after looking Cen up and down.

"You have," said Cen, just as loudly. "Where are we going?" It surprised him, but he felt no need to be chatty with Maui, or fill in the blanks. It was as if they had seen each other yesterday.

"Molokai," said Maui. "Your ohana's from Molokai, right?"

"Yeah, my family was from Molokai." The wind smelled good after his years in cities. He gestured toward the small splatter of lights ahead that marked the tiny town of Kaunakakai. "The harbor, right?"

"We're not going there," said Maui.

The outline of the island gradually grew visible as they approached. It was only twenty-five miles from Honolulu. Twenty-five miles and a hundred years. The residents had their small industries, such as fish and seaweed farming, that recognized the fragility of the small environment, an island only forty miles long and ten miles wide. It was quite different from Kohala, the more technological Homelander center on the Big Island. Molokai had never been wrested from anyone; instead, it had been firmly preserved.

Maui veered along the coast and headed east.

Now it was full day. Frame houses formed a rural string along the coast road; deep in the Halawa Valley, with its looming, dark mountains, one of the highest waterfalls in the islands fell, a long ribbon of water. This side of the island sloped gradually to a high plateau that finally rose to a plunging ridgeline that effectively isolated the northern cliffs.

Birds gathered ahead over a spot on the water, swooping and diving in a frenzy. Flying fish darted ahead, slicing the sea.

It took quite a while to round the end of the island. Maui struggled with the wheel and brought another engine on-line, but the wind and current from thousands of miles of open ocean buffeted the small boat.

Maui opened an ice chest at his feet and took out two sandwiches and two beers. He handed one of each to Cen and went to work on his, setting his beer in a gyroscopic holder.

It was a glorious day. The sun was bright and the sea around them was gray, turning blue in the distance where it met the increasingly rugged coast. Dark clouds sat atop Molokai's interior mountains, split by deep fissures—rain forest country, tropical, inaccessible jungle. After they had rounded the end of the island and the cliffs filled the horizon—the highest sea cliffs in the world, Cen recalled—Maui brought the boat closer to them.

The cliffs undulated to their left. Cen could not see the cloud-hidden summit. Crashing waves sent white fountains of foam upward forty and fifty feet where they met black lava. Four tiny goats leapt upward along the cliffs, almost vertically. "Shouldn't we stay farther out?" yelled Cen.

Maui glanced at him and smiled briefly, but didn't say anything. They motored along for fifteen more minutes while Cen drank in the beauty—the sea caves that honeycombed the coast, the white birds skimming the sea, two dolphins that swam along the side of the boat (with their strangely merry faces) before vanishing. The strong morning sun made black cartoon doors in the almost vertical wall of red-scarred green; deep in almost hidden valleys the green cliffs were laced with scores of waterfalls. Suddenly Maui shouted "Hang on!" and wrenched the boat directly toward land.

Cen was electrified by pure, absolute fear. Maui gunned the engine until they actually caught a huge wave and went surfing on it toward overwhelming black lava rocks, Maui laughing like a manic demon, fiercely focused on whatever he saw up ahead.

Cen wildly wished for at least a life jacket. This was madness. They rose out of the wave and slid down the face and Cen felt as if the bottom had dropped out of the world. With just a tiny loss of balance they would flip end over end and then they and the bones would be on the bottom of these cliffs, thousands of feet below.

The wave thundered around them and suddenly lost momentum. Their wave receded, swallowed by the ocean, and they coasted into a small cove.

Cen was shaking. Maui turned to him, an infuriating grin on his bearded face.

They were in a tiny pristine bay, a shimmering turquoise pool bordered by a half-moon of white sand fringed by palm trees. Waves rose and fell, muted, with a quiet slosh. This haven had been completely hidden by the surf breaking on the reef. Cen realized that the boat could leave only at high tide, when the rush of an outgoing wave could be precisely caught by a skilled boater, which Maui appeared to be.

He motored into a sea cave. Veins of light danced across the ceiling, and the soft slosh of water echoed hollowly once the engine was cut.

"Tie up over there," directed Maui, gesturing toward a lava knob. "We're home."

Home. Will I ever be home? wondered Cen. The target of his heart seemed so unutterably strange. But no more strange than this place, so far removed from the squalor, the garbage-ground-into-cement stench of Honolulu.

He handed Maui his bag, then accepted Maui's hand and stepped onto a narrow lava ledge that glistened anew with each wave surge, suffused but not suppressed by the cave wall.

Maui handed him the bag again, and he was glad to take it. Its contents were of infinite value to him.

This bag held not only bones, but light—light reduced to mathematical formulae; light's inception explored and mapped as one might explore these sea islands, with their exhilarating foam of constant surf breaking outside, where waves of energy, having passed through particles, smashed, reformed, and reversed to fan outward in their endless voyage of force.

A wall of lush jungle caught sunlight before them in ascending levels with leaves of almost infinite shapes, and back in a dark valley a waterfall fell several hundred feet without a break.

Maui edged along a ledge and Cen followed; they emerged in a miniature meadow of tall green and gold grass, bent by wind unhindered for thousands of miles. Spiked nests of sisal, mysteriously huge, their flowering stalks higher than Cen's head, stood like threatening guardians.

Cen felt at home, though he hadn't been to Molokai since he was a child, visiting his mother's relatives. But it went deeper than that, somehow. Cut free from philosophical trappings, separate from politics and rancor and history: this was the essence of his bones and the bones within his bag. Pacific wilderness.

He gazed out at distant whitecaps. Powerful wind cast back

spray frail as any lace finery he'd seen in England. Surf sounded, dissolving barriers between inner and outer for him; his essence effervesced into intense color: aquamarine, teal, deep blue where depth gained mastery. Salt tang filled his nose and black crabs crawled the lava rocks just below, giving them strange motion. The near-round succulent leaves of the one low plant whose name he knew, *naupaka,* billowed across the sea slopes, studded with small white flowers. Their green was almost fluorescent, as if the light they drank glowed in those fat leaves. The brain within the bones he carried had known this, and land's glory, too.

Maui began walking. Cen saw a narrow trail hidden in tall gold coastal grass. It led upward at a rather painful angle. With his load, feet slipping in awkward zoris, he soon was sweating in the powerful sun and wished he'd thought of a better way to pack his burden, but when Maui raised his hand to take it Cen shook his head.

In an hour they were high above the blue Pacific and the life-threatening monster waves were just wrinkles on the face of the sea. All sea sounds had receded. Instead he heard rustling grass and cries of birds he could not name.

Without warning they crossed the knife-edge of one of the ridges dropping directly to the sea and were within deep jungle. Cen let Maui move swiftly forward while he stopped and gazed in wonder.

The red path was just a mere etching on the steep side of a cliff where strange trees twisted in shapes fantastic and surreal. Their green canopy was far overhead, shielding them, suffusing light to dreamlike green. Their bark was shaggy, striped white and brown. Ahead he saw a clearing of tall golden grass deepened by striping shadows of a massive banyan tree.

Maui paused and was breathing hard when Cen caught up with him. He pulled a bottle of water from the small green pack he wore, gulped half and offered it to Cen. After a moment he squatted, staring outward, away from Cen, and began to talk.

"They made this a national park in the nineties. Hasn't been touched much since. It's funny. It's like space to me. I don't know why. Space is sterile and this is not. Anything in space will be something we put there. A million generations from now it will have mutated so much that it will seem as wild as this, just as much sprung from the forehead of Zeus." He brushed off his pants and continued upward.

Startled multicolored goats bounded from their path, black and brown and white bullets of startling speed, perhaps thinking them hunters. The trail laced through sucking black mud verges of fast-flowing streams.

Cen's life was a bubble of light effervescing from the center of his chest as he gazed outward. There was nothing but blue whitecapped sea, a curved indigo horizon line, and sky. As far as he could see. And this was good; infinitely, marvelously, powerfully good, past platonic Good in his human imagination.

This was perfection.

Had Kai seen this?

Would he be able to save her?

Though he tried to refuse doubt, it shadowed even this bright scene with fear. *He* might die as well. Yet he had no choice except to try.

He was as sure as he would ever be. Remembering his thought about the road map and reality, he hoped that he'd taken the right turn. Tonight he would plot out the final parameters as exactly as he could, and then . . .

He followed Maui to the next tier, drenched by rain that came suddenly and vanished just as fast. Then they followed a horizontal path that wove in and out of miniature jungles fed by plummeting streams. His legs ached. He wondered at the flowers he saw—flowering orange trees ranging down a hillside; tiny yellow flowers low to the ground; small streamside blossoms whose names he did not know, birdcalls exotic, haunting, providing an aural transition between what he thought of as his present and his past.

He hoisted his bag and followed Maui into a verge of enormous trees.

When he emerged from them he stopped.

Above him soared a thousand more feet of vertical pali.

Below him were black cliffs, blue sea, and birds weaving in-

tricate patterns, white, long-plumed, mastering air as he hoped
to master time. Imagine having the courage and knowledge to
dare to cross two thousand miles of this, he thought, and admired the hypothetical goals of IS that much more.

Will I remember IS? he wondered, as he pushed onward.
Maui had vanished. Before him on the trail a veil of hanging
vines with huge dark leaves filtered light. He parted them as if
they were a curtain and paused.

He saw a prosaic weathered-green clapboard house, set on
a flat bit of land, hidden from air and sea view by trees and
vines.

He'd seen probably thousands of houses like these, with
their squared oriental roofs and white-limned outlines. Two
large black dogs rushed out from the porch, barking, teeth
bared, till Maui, before him, knelt and they lowered their
heads, tails wagging furiously, as he petted and exclaimed with
soft words almost free of consonants.

A woman emerged from the doorway.

Of course he'd hoped; expected, but still—

Maui's grandmother. Funny. He still didn't know her name.

She wore a purple holoku, he could see the color even in
shade; it covered her feet. When she saw him she broke into a
grin. Her long white hair cascaded over her narrow shoulders.

"Cen!" she yelled, breaking the deep green silence of the
jungle, and jumped from the porch, stumbled, held up her
holoku and hurried toward him.

Deeply honored by her greeting, he felt like kneeling but
stood, straight and tall, lowering his bag in the tall grass. He
briefly registered a clear satellite dish in the meadow's verge,
then felt her impact, and her arms around his waist. She was
sobbing, and laughing, and strangely he was too. "Cen," she
said, "my dear Cen."

He just hugged her tightly as he dared, imagining the frailty
of her bones because her hair was so intensely white. He raised
his eyes and saw Maui's staring into his with immense sadness.
Cen pushed her hair back from her forehead.

"I don't even know your name," he said, and when she
smiled the corners of her brown eyes crinkled. "Lelani," she

said. "A very common name," and he hugged her again for a long, long time.

It was something she seemed to need.

"Thank you, my sister's grandchild," she murmured, her voice deep and throaty.

He was not even slightly surprised.

She let go, turned, and walked toward her house. When they stepped onto the porch, furnished only with bright green silk cushions and a low black table, she turned and said, "Sit down and let's talk story." Maui took his bag inside.

And then she told him about his family. "Kamehameha himself created the line from which you are descended, the *papa kahuna alii pule*—the class of royal, or chiefly, kahunas," she began.

The answers to his questions filled an hour, then two. He forgot everything else, for the moment. A shower swirled round them, almost like mist, glittering in the sunlight. Below arced close, intense rainbows.

"Tea?" she asked finally, and he nodded. On the deep porch she lit a Japanese brazier and hung a black cast-iron kettle from a hook attached to the ceiling. She gathered her wild white mane of hair and abruptly braided it in an inside-out pattern and tied the braid in a knot, then took cups from a small drawer. The dogs sprawled on their sides, asleep.

Rain pattered on the roof, its engendering cloud hiding all but the front yard of this strange abode. "This is a hanging valley," said Maui, legs extended on the porch steps. "Like a little scoop out of the mountainside. Vertical below and vertical above. Inaccessible, practically. Except for local boys," said Maui, turning and smiling briefly. Then his face grew sad as he glanced at Lelani.

The broad leaves of a banana tree clacked in the gusty wind. Cen heard the rush of many streams. The nearby cliff was laced with white intermingling etches of falling water.

Lelani poured from the black pot steaming water, which swirled into the iron-black cup, obscuring its smooth turquoise bottom.

Cen sipped bitter tea and finally ventured to ask Lelani, "Why? Why did you decide to grow old?"

She did not seem bothered by the question. "It was time. There was the possibility that I would lose my mental faculties if I continued. They are not yet sure why this happens, as with so much of this tampering, but it does happen—and quite swiftly after certain warning signs are observed—in about seventy-five percent of the people who have been enhanced for as long as I have been. They continue to live and look young, but their minds change." She leaned forward and wrapped her arms around her knees. It was raining in earnest now. The wind blew her hair back from her face. Raindrops danced on the boards at the edge of the deep, roofed porch. "But I'm not sorry for any of it. I've lived to do so much; lived to *see* so much." She paused for a moment, then said, "And it's not over yet."

Cen stood. He took off his zoris and stepped inside the door of the house.

The interior of Lelani's home was shadowed because of the storm. Sliding screens revealed a futon on tatami mats. A floor of highly polished red wood was beneath the mats, and the room was exquisitely furnished in a simple Japanese style. A computer sealed in clear plastic blinked on a low black table with cushions piled in front of it; next to that was a rack of CDs and the crystals a lot of people were using now.

Something that looked like a couch to one side of the room puzzled him. He decided it was probably an isolation tank, where visions of a new, revitalized Hawaii could unfurl in Lelani's mind. He went over and examined it more closely.

The soft indentation where one's head would go was a mass of sensors embedded in cloth. Hinged to the sides of this was a U-shaped screen that could be brought down in front of the user once she was lying down. It looked as if it had holographic capabilities. He ran his hand along the part that might hold the arms, then the back. It felt the same as the hollow for the head—silky—but entirely covered with, he felt now, those soft sensor nubs just as the head part had been.

A small, highly polished box of koa sat on the low table next to the contraption. Cen opened it and saw several crystals, recognizing the new lattice material that was becoming popular for read-once information, capable of holding the Library of Congress in a cubic centimeter. These were in the shape of the great seagoing canoes like the *Hawai'i Loa.*

He closed the box, carefully, feeling like a snoop, still puzzled.

Maui had left his bag next to a pile of pillows. Cen sat on them and tried to open it; the zipper stuck, and he struggled with it for a few moments, swore, then pulled out his pocket knife and cut the side, distantly surprised at his urgency.

His notebook was squashed onto the top; he pulled it out and set it aside. He stuffed the bag from the doctor into his roomy shirt pocket.

His breath catching in his throat, he gingerly reached beneath the tapa bundle and tried to pull it out but it stuck on both ends. He slashed the entire top from the bag and was dismayed at how much the tapa had crumbled.

Peering inside, he thought he recognized vertebrae, mixed with a hodgepodge of small bones. He took a handful of the smaller bones, several vertebrae, and a good-sized square of tapa—slipped them all into his shirt pocket with the doctor's packet. Then he carefully buttoned his pocket.

He stood and tried to scoop the entire bundle out at once, but it was quite awkward; some of the bones hung from the sides, and he had to gather them up.

He walked onto the porch, where Lelani and Maui sat, watching the rain.

"I've brought you something," he said, and laid the bones at her feet.

Lelani reached for them. Her hands hesitated over the bundle. She looked up at Cen. He nodded. "Except—I left the skull where it was—" He didn't say anything about the bones he'd taken for Kaiulani.

She unfolded first one side, then the other.

"Kamehameha's," Cen said, knowing that was unnecessary but feeling as if he should say something.

"Mahalo," said Lelani, laying her hand atop them. "Infinite thanks."

Until the sky cleared and darkened and insects shrilled and stars came out, Lelani sat on her knees and chanted.

Her deep voice filled the clearing, merged with the wind, rose and fell with hypnotic cadence. Cen, his Hawaiian rusty but quite functional, was chilled as she moved further and further back into time, made the jump to Tahiti, and continued on. Cen saw that, though the house had seemed hidden when they approached, it had a full, wide view of the sea, lit by the path of the moon, and the night sky filled with countless burning stars.

At the end Lelani lifted the bones with great difficulty and carried them out into the meadow and held them out to the sea, the stars, the moon. To time.

Past, present, and future.

"Kamehameha's birth was foretold, the same as Christ's," Lelani said later, leaning against the side of the porch, face drawn but dark eyes quite alive.

Maui had picked plumeria blossoms from a tree in the small meadow and threaded a double lei as she chanted—its fragrance was overwhelming.

"There were astronomical portents, like the Christians' star. The kahunas knew he would be born, and before his birth he had enemies. His mother bore him in a secret place for this reason, with the help of the kahunas and, of course, the royal midwives. Then he was hidden away and reared until he was older." She looked at Cen. "Your mother chanted that when she received the bones. As the guardian of the bones, the kahuna nui priestess, it was one of her great responsibilities. Did she teach you the chant?"

"She . . . only showed me the bones for the first time the day she died," he said, trying to make his voice clear and strong and failing. He'd never talked to anyone about her death before and it surprised him how keenly he still felt the terror of that night, and the darkness that had enfolded him for so many years.

"I am sorry," said Lelani, then was quiet. The hum of the night rose around them.

* * *

"I get pretty good service here," she said later, inside. Several candles burned on the low table that served for dining, but an electric light shone behind a glass sconce in the kitchen.

She took the iron lid off the rice cauldron, and Cen knew it was perfectly ready, to the instant. He hoped he understood time as precisely as Lelani comprehended the cooking time of rice. "Helis swoop in every now and then. I get vegetables, rice, bean curd. Plenty of fruit around here." She nodded toward a rifle in one corner. "Sometimes I shoot goats and pigs. There are mangos, papayas, breadfruit, just about everywhere. And I enjoy going down to the ocean and gathering seaweed."

"Don't let her kid you," said Maui. "Her nori comes straight from Honolulu. First-class stuff, eh? Kona coffee, too, no?" His smile was gentle, but his eyes were a direct, teasing challenge. "Wind, water, and solar power. Living off the land, right?"

She shrugged again, grinning, as she said to Cen, "So carry this soup to the table, all right?"

He picked up the steaming cauldron. "Lelani," he asked, "what are you going to do with the bones?"

A broad smile lit her face. "We're going to make clones," she said.

Cen almost dropped the soup. Even though he had suspected, to hear it so baldly stated was somewhat shocking. Even now, in this day and age, was such a thing possible? Apparently so. But it was surely illegal. He set the soup down carefully on the low table. "Why?"

Her smile became enigmatic. "You'll see," she said, and firmly declined to discuss it further.

After dinner they went back onto the porch, where a citronella candle burned. They each had small glasses of hot sake.

Cen leaned against some pillows. The night and day had taken their toll. He ached all over. He put his sake down and fell asleep. Maui woke him and showed him to his futon. Tomorrow, he thought, falling back into the rush of rain on the roof, the myriad night insects, the sensibility of the ocean so far below, the stars so far above. Tomorrow he would ask Lelani about those crystals.

Tomorrow he would map out the last bend in the road that led to Kaiulani.

And tonight, for the first time in his life, he felt utterly at peace, and knew he'd done something right at last.

The next morning Cen was refreshed but still sore, his mind quite clear.

It was chilly. He pulled on his shirt and buttoned it, patting the pocket with the medicines. He hadn't felt this way in years. Or maybe, he thought, as he accepted a cup of coffee from Maui, he had never felt this way.

Sunlight fell on the wide koa floorboards in angled patterns. Lelani was on the porch, sitting next to the low table. A bowl held slices of papaya and sweet bread. "Have some," said Lelani, and Cen sat, carefully balancing his coffee.

Far below them on the lush cliffside the tops of palm trees glimmered in the light, tossing in the wind. Everything moved—the sea, the forest, the clouds across the sky, and something within him, rushing as fast as the wind.

"I heard Kaiulani gave birth here, on Molokai," he said, his voice catching.

"It's true," said Lelani, looking at him expectantly, her voice low. How much did she know about what he'd been working on? After all, she did know a lot about Interspace, probably as much as anyone in IS knew.

She took another sip of coffee.

He saw that she'd been looking through his notebook. He reached across the table and pulled it close. He smoothed out the wrinkled pages. Three of them had been ripped in half. They were gone, clutched in the hand of the IS weasel. Only half-lines were left. Relief spread through him.

"I can rewrite this," he said. "I can complete it for you."

He trusted them, he realized. He knew their dream, he had eavesdropped on it when in London, via the web. They had passed through some sort of fire and would know how to use the proofs. That is, if they were expanded somewhat. Well, he could do that too, though the thought of legions of people fractal-jumping through the metauniverse still frightened him.

Maui and Lelani smiled at each other; he did not understand the look between them. Perhaps they did not consider this very important. Certainly it was not as important to them as the bones. He would try to impress them with the importance of his proofs later. He had already pleased them immensely. They would make a flock of Kamehameha clones. He was not sure how that would benefit Hawaiians, but they had clearly given it a lot of thought and believed in their plan with as much strength as he believed in Kaiulani.

And he had settled the ghost of his mother.

"Do you know where she gave birth?" he asked, half idly, since it seemed absurd that they might know. He turned the pages of the proofs, getting ready to find a pencil to write down what was already dancing in his mind.

"Of course," said Lelani, surprising him. "It's a very holy site. Has been for more than a thousand years. She asked to come here to give birth. It's really not far from here."

"Oh," said Cen. "Oh."

He stood up, stretched, shoved his feet into his zoris. The beauty of the morning seemed like a translucent veil—the cliff night-dark in shadow buttressing Lelani's meadow, the distant azure shallows deepening through shades of aquamarine to midnight blue, the countless trees tossing in the wind all around them.

"Can you tell me where it is?"

Everything around him seemed to coalesce; the sun rose above the cliff and struck him directly in the eyes so that he shielded them with his hand as he looked down at Lelani, her white hair backlit like a halo.

"It's not difficult to find," she said. "I've been there many times. It's a beautiful site. The ridge is almost five thousand feet above sea level. You can see all the islands except Kauai. Of course, she came up from the other side of the island. There's a gradual ascent on a wide trail. She was probably carried on a litter. Unless you know exactly how, it's very difficult to come back down this way; almost impossible. See the trail on that side of the clearing?"

A door in jungle, leading upward.

"Take it for a little over a mile. You have a watch? Good. Half an hour—it's a very steep switchback trail. You'll come to a waterfall and a pool. The water spills straight down out of the pool. There's an overhang for hundreds of feet above you, all along the ridge. It will look like there's no way up. Stay away from the edge of the pool. The rocks are slick, and it's a long way down."

"I will," said Cen obediently. When Lelani and Maui laughed, he was startled. He felt so solemn. But of course they did not know why, not really.

"The trail continues across the pool, on the stepping stones. But you want to go behind the waterfall. There's a small cave with steps inside. It's the mouth of a lava tube. The tube is about eight feet high and slants quite steeply. There are steps inside. Probably more than a thousand years old. I'll give you a flashlight, so you can check every once in awhile, but you'll need both hands to climb. I hope you're not claustrophobic. It's a very long tube. When you come out you'll be in another clearing, with a grandmother banyan."

Cen nodded again, seeing the banyan in his mind's eye— maybe fifty feet in diameter, an ancient matriarch of the forest, a hundred twining trunks all dropping new ones, constantly.

"Double back and you'll see another trail just beyond the lava rock formation. Follow that trail for ten minutes and you're there, at the birthing stones. There's the remains of a heiau. A holy place, a stone platform used for blessings, healings, worship. That's where she gave birth."

"That's all?"

"That's all."

Cen took another piece of nut bread and ate it but did not taste it. "I'll finish those proofs later," he said, gesturing at the notebook. Interspace would kill to get that information. Had killed. He would make sure Maui and Lelani knew all that. But they must know. They knew so much.

Lelani nodded but did not speak. She stood and hugged him, let go, and stepped back.

"Aloha," she called, after he crossed the meadow. Maui's deep voice echoed behind hers. He turned and waved. "Aloha."

Aloha.

Aloha.

He climbed through tiny exquisite meadows dotted with delicate flowers. Far below pines and palms gleamed in the sun, and the calls of strange birds rose around him. He climbed higher and higher, sweating, reached the pool, and stared outward at the ocean far below the narrow channel where the water rushed over the lip of rock. Soaked by the waterfall, he entered the long dark tube, flicked on his light. The steps looked well worn and seemed interminable; he felt as if everything was pressing in on him until he almost might have screamed and turned but saw the dot of light above and then emerged onto the knife-sharp ridge.

Set in the sea like green jewels, the islands of his home, the islands his ancestors had found and settled, spread out all around him, two large perfect volcanoes wreathed by clouds, Mauna Loa half hidden by Haleakala, each wearing leis of clouds low on their slopes. Joy surged through him like a bright tide, as if his veins were filled with light, as if he glistened and glimmered from within. How strong he felt, how fine. Maui and Lelani, and his past, his entire life, seemed distant as a dream. There was the banyan, the columns of its spreading trunk past counting, its leaves filtering sunlight in patterns that shifted constantly in the ever-present wind. The path was narrow but visible, flattening the ridge to a width of several feet. It was not quite like walking a tightwire, but almost.

But as if his mind was balanced on a tightwire, something moved within him. He saw that little notebook, on Lelani's table.

He had to go back. Not to finish the proofs. To destroy them. They were too dangerous. He'd been a fool to write them down.

He took the first step to return.

A familiar voice from beyond the veil of the banyan stopped him.

Realization rose like a translucent aquamarine wave, surrounding him, suffusing him, oddly surprising, comprised of shimmering intensity and a single amazing revelation:

Now.

He took a deep breath, suspended in time; then turned and stepped onto the ancient trail.

Lynn

Thailand 2034

16

Lynn sat on the floor at a low wooden table sorting things from the packet Hawkins had thrust at her.

The room was plain but beautiful. The varnish on the wooden floor was dark and worn to a satin sheen. French doors stood open to the balcony, a rickety wooden affair three floors off street level that quivered every time Akamu walked out on it. Beige muslin at the open windows turned light gold when the sun was out—which was not very often. They seemed to have arrived in the rainy season, for warm rain fell ceaselessly, just now a skein of sun-shot mist drifting across the close blue mountains. The night before she had sat on the balcony, watching the endless dissolution of old-fashioned green, pink, and orange neon reflected in the vast long puddle that was the street.

A gust of wind scattered the papers. Lynn reached over and picked up a wooden elephant, one of the ubiquitous tourist totems carved by the hill people, and set it atop the paper maps, which were crumpled but folded correctly. She had found more maps—almost a continent's worth of maps—in the packet from Hawkins. Clearly he had envisioned a far and erratic flight. She'd also found yet another light, wallet-sized electronic map that covered the same territory, in many cases better, in others, worse. It also contained instant translations of more languages than she'd had time to scroll through in her brief introductory foray. Backups. Hawkins had been into backups.

In the other room, Akamu snored. She could see him through the door. He rolled from side to side as she watched but did not wake. She frowned; he'd been sleeping for fourteen hours. Not surprising, she supposed, after their ordeal. She'd tried to wake him for breakfast, but he'd mumbled and rolled over.

Well. She went back to her sorting.

A magnetic key with no markings. Wonderful. What a cryptic old bastard he had been.

Their passports lay on the table next to her; nice pieces of work as far as she could tell.

The wallet, when unfolded, had partitions containing currencies that added up to about a hundred thousand dollars in various denominations. Someone had deep pockets. Her father, of course. In this country, she could use this to buy them food and lodging for years—probably forever. They could disappear.

Yes.

Well, why not?

She stood, and walked out on the balcony. The boards were warped and weathered beneath her bare feet; warm rain made the red railing she grasped glisten. Disappear, let this all die down, whatever it was.

A part of her said no. That she had to return, that she had to find out why her father had died. That if, as she suspected, he had been murdered, she should fight and expose the cancers at Interspace's heart.

But what proof did she have that Interspace had tried to kill her and had succeeded in killing her father?

That one of the stooges she'd seen around Samuel's house had shown up in Nepal, that's all.

So? Their father might have died of natural causes. The attack and pursuit might have come from elsewhere. She *might* have been tracked—for her own good, and the man in the limousine been sent to rescue her, inform her of her father's death, take her home for the funeral. And they might have even claimed that. There was also a good possibility that this was all being run by the shadow intelligence community within IS, and that her brothers had no knowledge whatever of her attempted murder.

Right.

The financial situation of IS was enormously cluttered. She

knew that the ship had cost many times what it ought to have cost. And that certain projects, like the maglaunch tunnel on the Big Island, had been built purely to pour money through crooked contractors back into the pockets of her brothers. Kickback city. She knew, or had access to, hard information about the details of all that. Yet another aspect of IS she had always conveniently ignored, along with the bioethical aspects of their endeavors.

Ah, yes, what can one small person do?

What can one *cowardly* person do?

You can get proof; you know how and they know that, whoever *they* are and whatever they may be doing.

She was certainly expendable. Though she was an expert, there was a small cadre of such experts who could do anything she could do and recreate the work she'd done toward growing more specialized humans. Infinitely more specialized than Akamu, who was, after all, just a replication rather than someone as predictable as possible. Besides, in her opinion, unpredictability was a key ingredient in that nebulous conjunction of inner and outer called intelligence.

Another strike against her was that she'd made it no secret that she would fight to the bitter end certain uses of some of the information she'd amassed.

But that wasn't really what they were afraid of. They probably acutely wished to silence the personal information she had on them—the dirt and where to find it.

Maui's message. It was somewhere on the web. "Maui"—whoever *he* was—had something to do with Akamu. But he had to know that if she contacted *him* IS would know all that was exchanged.

Should she, though, pick up the message? She didn't want to use Akamu's flat—once a link was initialized, they could be traced through that, and she knew Akamu would not jettison his precious flat. Somewhere, Chaing Mai was webbed, in a way she could access anonymously.

Not this guest house, though. She had chosen it for its utterly low-tech allure. Most business seemed absolutely local—food, clothing, necessities were all traded in the market. Except for the business having to do with poppies—it was the most likely to be webbed and absolutely high-tech. Though synthetics were widely available, and legal in most countries, many addicts claimed that "the real thing" was subtly different. Of course, the pharmaceutical companies manufacturing substitutes kept natural poppy products illegal in as much of the world as they possibly could, despite the availability of opivert. Just another game, rather similar to many played by IS.

Lynn did not fancy getting in touch with such people.

And then, there was the money in the pack. Such a large amount. It might have been her father's way of saying *vanish*. Forget Maui's message. Forget it all, for some very compelling reasons at which she could only guess. In certain countries she could buy a new face, cheaply; she could vanish and still, if she wished, make an excellent living.

On the other hand, it might mean *avenge my death*. Or, *it might be expensive but figure it all out and do something useful*. Without Hawkins, she didn't know.

The street she gazed down on was not wide. Electric tuk-tuks, small pods containing a driver and room for a passenger or two, flowed past below, obligatory bells to alert pedestrians to their approach a constant jingle. Just across from her, she saw a noodle shop, an ice-cream stall, a tailor, and a door with a cross above it. Most of the trade seemed to take place in the large green park down the road; she could see the border from here. Emerald green, its walkways were lined with stalls filled with produce and all sorts of clothing—traditional garb, piles of Hong Kong seconds, cages of chickens and ducks.

In front of the park, three monks folded umbrellas and boarded a bus, their thin orange robes sticking to them in dark patches. A vendor fished a floating coconut from a galvanized tub of ice water that he pulled about on a cart, lopped off the top, stuck a straw in it, and handed it to a woman.

Here, Lynn? You want to stay here?

Well, so far, at least no one had tried to kill them.

She heard an odd sound, twice; the second time she realized that it was Akamu, moaning.

She hurried inside, knelt at his bed. He was still asleep. She shook him. "Wake up, Akamu. You're dreaming." Poor kid. He definitely had material for some pretty intense nightmares. She shook him again, becoming frightened.

His brown eyes opened. They were full of pain. "Where am I?" he whispered. He sat up unsteadily. He was sweating. "Who are you?"

"I'm Lynn," she told him, a slight flutter of panic in her gut. "Remember? Your old pal Lynn. You flew an airplane from Tibet and brought us here. We're in Chaing Mai. Thailand."

We're a million miles from home.

To her relief, it seemed as if his fog cleared. He stared at his feet, blinking. "Lynn. Tibet. Right." But the blank sadness of his eyes when they met hers was shocking. Then, as she watched, his entire expression changed, to one of odd triumph. "Don't worry," he said. "I'll get over this pretty soon."

She sprang up, poured him a glass of cool water from a sweating pitcher. He drank it instantly; he drank three.

"What do you mean?" she demanded. "What's going on, Akamu? This has happened before?" She grabbed his shoulders and barely refrained from shaking him in frustration. "You have to tell me!"

He avoided looking into her eyes. "Don't get so excited. I just meant that it must be the food again. Where's the bathroom?"

She took him down the hall. "This is funny," he said, before he closed the door behind him. "No seat."

He muttered a little nonsense when he came out, and she hustled him down to the street, thinking that maybe he needed a little exercise to clear his head. He's not drunk, she told herself, but he sure acts like it—stumbling, laughing inappropriately. The rain had stopped for the moment and steam rose from the street. She steered him into the first shop, across from their balcony, sat him at a bare clean table. He was quite compliant, with a strange, musing look in his eyes.

The menu was all in Thai. She tried a few words. Noodles? She tried to remember how her translator, in the room, said noodles, one of the basic necessary words here. She thought she might also know rice, fish, meat, and curry, but she wasn't sure of any of them.

The woman behind the counter, her face burnished brown, broke into a smile from which several teeth were missing. Lynn's heart ached for how easy it would be to fix everything that was wrong with people everywhere, all over the world, then her mind screamed, *Stop it!*

The woman gave a brief quick nod, and Lynn saw that she was amused by her pronunciation. She sang it toward Lynn, at the same time moving a large lid from a warming bin and raising her eyebrows in question.

Yes! Lynn nodded, tried it again, until finally the woman nodded in satisfaction and doled out two bowls. Lynn took some chopsticks from the glass on the table that held many and handed a pair to Akamu. The noodles were bathed in a sweet, spicy peanut sauce.

"Don't eat those," she said to Akamu, pointing with her chopsticks at tiny black bits. "I think they call those mouse-shit peppers."

Akamu choked. "I think I already did!" His eyes filled with tears and his face reddened. The small woman rushed over with a pitcher of water and two glasses, laughing.

The pungent smell of coconut curry and sticky rice rose from the warming pans and steamed the inside of the glass counter.

She wrangled a glass of wine from the woman, too, after being put through her pronunciation paces. Condensation beaded on the glass, and she sipped the sweet pale liquid slowly and watched Akamu eat, slowly accepting the inevitable truth.

Whatever was wrong with him was not something they could hop a plane and leave behind. It had nothing to do with his digestive tract. He dropped his chopsticks as she watched. He had probably been using them since he was a toddler. He was having some sort of motor problem.

No, Lynn, I don't think you can stay here.

But where could they go? Death had followed them everywhere.

The hush of warm rain started again out on the street, glittering as it passed through the primitive hologram of a bicycle above a shop across the street. The road was thronged with people carrying umbrellas, along with bicycles and tuk-tuks.

"Feel better?" she asked Akamu.

"A little. Can we go back to the room now? Maybe I can get some work done. At last."

"Work?" she asked, as they left the shop. "What *kind* of work?" She tried to keep sharpness from her voice.

"Oh, just work," he said.

"Can you show it to me?"

"I guess." They climbed the stairs. He rushed to his flat, a small, elegant tool for thought, sitting alone on the low teak table. He had put it on to charge before collapsing; she'd noticed that in *his* pack he had several different adapters that she had not bought in Hong Kong. Odd; Hawkins must have provided them. Akamu flipped it on and got to his destination so quickly his keystrokes were a blur.

The rain had cleared and twilight was a glow of white just above the mountains. As she watched dark clouds lowered and then it was night. She unrolled the curtains and touched on a light.

"Akamu," she said, kneeling next to him.

He blinked but his fingers did not stop. She was used to abstraction, but even if she were a mathematician she wondered if she could understand what he was doing.

"Look," she said. "We need to talk. Please talk to me, kid. I want to help you. You know that, don't you? I think you need help, but I'm afraid to go back to Hawaii. If I knew what's wrong, maybe I could figure out what to do . . ."

"But I'm busy," he said, giving her just a hairbreadth of attention, a flicker of his eyelids.

"Akamu, people have tried to kill you. Right now they are trying to find us. This is because you are Kamehameha's clone, if I'm not mistaken."

"You are," he said. He looked up for a moment, and she saw an expression she couldn't fathom in his eyes. "Don't you understand, there's more than one of me. Why kill me when there are more?"

Lynn let the awful implications rush through her—his fatalism, his too-tough stance, the scope of what was happening—without reacting, for now. She pressed this breakthrough. It was the first time she'd been able to squeeze any information out of him. "How many?"

"I don't know." He kept typing, but his fingers faltered. "Why don't you leave me alone?"

"Akamu, I know you've been told and told not to talk to anyone. But—"

"You're from IS," he said, and swallowed hard.

"I'm not and you know it."

"I *don't* know it!" he cried out. "If you were, wouldn't you tell me you *weren't?*" His hands clenched. He looked as if he wanted to smash his computer. Lynn grabbed his wrists, held them gently. She felt him relax.

"I'm *not* from IS," she said. "Ever since I knew about the things they do I've hated them. I lost"—she paused—"I've lost my father forever because of that, because I couldn't forgive his involvement."

She should not tell him these things; he was too young. Then she remembered his easy facility in killing the soldiers.

So tell him.

"I think my own brothers have been trying to have me killed. I think that they might have sent someone to follow me. I think they killed our father. They *are* IS, at least an important face of IS. Do you really think that I could work for them?" Well, didn't you? asked a part of herself. Isn't that why you're here? "Akamu, I want to *help* you. But you have to tell me more!"

Akamu turned and hugged her suddenly—hot, sweaty, a child of thirteen who weighed more than she did. She hugged him back tightly, until he released his grip and wiped tears from his face with the backs of both hands. "I guess I'm—afraid. But I have to finish this. I have to finish it before I see Maui—"

"What is your work, Akamu?" she asked. "And who the *hell* is Maui?"

The curtains ballooned gently in the slight breeze, upon

which wafted the smell of sweet coconut curry. He ignored her and began typing again.

The screen glowed with tiny numbers and symbols packed together, their simple juxtaposition like some postmodern work of art. Here and there she saw a word or phrase but not many.

"Got that?" he asked. "Want to see more?" Without waiting for an answer he began scrolling through screens, stopping at each for a few seconds as if reabsorbing the information, nodding occasionally. His cheeks grew flushed as he read; she heard him began to breathe faster. Then there were no more numbers, only a blank screen and a blinking cursor.

"A couple of pages were missing from Kalakaua's proofs. That's what I'm trying to fill in."

Oh.

"Akamu," she said, her throat tight, "wasn't Cen Kalakaua some sort of genius? And a grown man, too? Working on a doctorate? I think that's what I've heard."

"Of course," said Akamu, without a hint of resentment. "I'm just a kid. I couldn't possibly start this from scratch." He pulled back from the screen, leaned against the bureau behind him, and pulled his knees to his chest. In the glow of the screen his eyes were contemplative. "You really *don't* know much about me, do you?"

"I've told you all I know," she said.

He took a deep breath. "I've never had any friends, any real friends that lasted."

Lynn tried to get past the first flush of anger and just listen. It seemed inexcusable. Like this kid was just some sort of intelligence module in the service of the HM. She was now sure they had created him, and they were no better than IS, it seemed.

"That's a shame," she said.

He gave his customary shrug. "I've been socialized. I guess that's what they called it. There was a bunch of kids I got to play with when I was little, but the problem was that they kept yanking me away. It wasn't their fault. They were just trying to keep me safe. I've mostly lived in Hawaii. But for a while they sent me to New Mexico. And to Alaska, too, and New Zealand. And somewhere in Russia. And I had a lot of month-long rotations so I could learn about my shipmates in real time. I guess one thing I learned was that Primal Societies really work. I felt at home in every one."

"Your shipmates?"

"Yeah. The *Hawai'i Loa* is going to have an international crew. We're all going to work together. It's going to be just like the ancient voyages. Only instead of finding new islands in the ocean, we're going to find a new world in time. You know," he said excitedly, "just like Maui—not the person Maui I know, but the god Maui, the legend. He snared the sun in the sky and made it slow down so people would have a longer day. We're going to be able to change time, too. And you know how the Maui legend goes, about how he pulled islands out of the ocean with fishhooks? That's kind of like what we're going to do, in the *Hawai'i Loa,* using the proofs. But I have to know the proofs. *Somebody* has to solve them." He sighed. "But I don't think *I* can."

"The *Hawai'i Loa?*"

"Oh. I guess it has another name right now. The generation ship they're building in orbit. In fact I think it's almost ready. That's why I have to work fast. We have to beat them."

"Them?"

"Yeah," he said, yawning. "IS." His eyelids drooped, but he forced them open again. "It has a shape, you know? The so-lution. It's like the answer is always pressing in on me, and I get little bits at a time. You know anything about string the-ory? It's really weird, thinking about it all the time. I wish I felt better."

He grinned a bit wickedly. "I got some stuff out of Sattva's system that helped a lot. Guess they didn't think a kid could find out anything. They thought I was just playing games. It seems like everything is falling into place, faster and faster. It's grand! It's so much more wonderful than I . . . thought . . . if only I felt like I usually do, and wasn't so tired . . . " His head nodded, and his fingers went slack. She was just about ready to rise and help him back to bed when his eyes snapped open again and he resumed his work, eyes seeming not to really look at the screen but within.

She walked out to the balcony, deeply disturbed. So much information, suddenly. And Primal Societies—hadn't Sattva called her little organization a Primal Society? She was beginning to feel even more out of touch. It seemed like everyone knew more than she did about what was going on. Even Akamu, and she was rescuing him.

Or was she?

And—hadn't he said something about taking over the generation ship? And rechristening it to boot?

Yes, Lynn. Taking the ship. *Just like the haoles took their land.*

She found her throat was tight; she was moved by the complete audacity of this boy's vision. Apparently that was the plan of the Homeland Movement. How grand!

And how absurd.

Or was it?

Steam rose from the street, blurring the green neon Buddha just across from their third-floor balcony, and the letters that Lynn imagined said Emerald Buddha Noodle Shop in Thai. Her thin clothes stuck to her as she stared across the steam-filled street that bustled now that it was night, cooler than day, a good time to shop. As Lynn watched, the Buddha sharpened in its endless blinking, so palpably that Lynn could imagine that it would go past mere sharpening and change to a new image altogether, grow a deity halo, or whisk the Buddha-pervaded inhabitants of the street, and her, and Akamu cease-lessly working in the hotel room behind her, to the pure land fixed within Akamu's mind. A sort of symbiosis between matter and mind, eh? Between light and bones, between faster-than-light, if Sattva was right, and the boy who had been grown from the DNA in a bunch of old bones.

She dropped into a frame chair and tipped it forward, crossed her arms atop the wet railing. Ubiquitous Thai music, phrased like the latest music, sling, but with a strange Thai twist that softened and transmuted, blared from the bar beneath her. She understood his passion; she had been the same at his age, and as stubborn and alone.

Akamu did not seem to mind being kidnapped, and that was what it was, she supposed, in the guise of protecting him.

Except, remembering the soldiers, and how resourceful he was, it seemed more like a decision he'd made. Yeah, I'll go with this lady because she just saved my life, and maybe I should get out of here, but I won't tell her a damned thing. If he'd wanted to, he could have left her long ago. Surely he could have gotten in touch with this Maui and been rescued.

So why hadn't he done so?

And what was Akamu here figuring out? He was trying to complete the Kalakaua Proofs?

It was a shame to set a child at such a game. She glanced inside, watched Akamu's earnest head bent over his computer. He was wearing only white shorts, and some sort of decorative plasticky-looking crystal that hung around his neck, light against the deep golden brown of his chest. Despite the whirling overhead fan, sweat sheened his body. She worried— did he have a fever? Maybe, but not necessarily. It was damned hot, that's all.

Her lurking headache flared, suddenly mature. Her right temple pounded with so much pain that Mr. Buddha seemed to waver but maybe that was just the heat. She was afraid for the first time in her life and, oddly enough, it was not for herself but for Akamu—strange, Hawaiian Akamu.

The Emerald Buddha was nothing compared to him.

If she were a Christian talking about Jesus, that might be sacrilege, but she was glad that she was what she was—some sort of quasi half-assed Buddhist—and that her inner vision of Akamu and his powers and his suffering could flare outward with such intensity and that she could feel such compassion and, almost, worship.

But even more, there was kinship, empathy.

Not that she was anywhere near as intelligent as he. But he was different, unique, alone, despite the other clones he spoke of, and she knew how that felt—though for her it had been more like teenage angst and for him it was utterly true.

"Buddha help us," she muttered, and stepped back into the room, her thin silk pants and shirt light as no clothing at all, even cooler when wet, a great boon in this incredible heat. She'd never felt anything like the heat.

Rain sluiced down in a sudden burst of sound, silver; and hot, quelling the steam, while umbrellas blossomed calmly in the neon-streaked street below.

The hell with the damned Homeland Movement, she decided. They apparently had some sort of vast plot and were just as willing to sacrifice individuals to it as was Interspace. This Maui should be imprisoned for child abuse.

Any danger contacting him might pose had been suddenly canceled, in her mind, by Akamu's strange behavior. She watched him for another minute.

It seemed probable to her now that the Homeland Movement had given him some kind of biological enhancement. Of which there were hundreds, including many strange neurochemical twists she couldn't possibly guess at.

Maui had a message for her, eh?

It was time to collect it.

And give him a piece of her mind.

Lynn hurried down the bustling late-evening street, concealed beneath a deep just-purchased umbrella, the guts of Hawkins's bag stashed in a small purse she'd bought this morning at the market. Passport, money, key, the mysterious postcard.

She'd passed two shop windows where thin girls posed, numbers on their shirts. Sinuous music emerged from several bars, always upbeat and in major keys. She passed a temple courtyard—smooth ancient paving stones, a fountain splashing, a serene oasis—and wished she could slip inside, just for a minute, and let timelessness infuse her.

She hurried on, afraid to leave Akamu alone for long. By now she'd hoped to find what she was looking for, a large, anonymous, modern hotel with some sort of business center where she could log on and collect messages.

One more block. She leaped across a puddle and landed in another, her sandals flipping water up on her legs as she jogged to get out of the path of a taxi. She stopped on the corner and looked in all directions. No hotel.

She stepped into some sort of all-purpose shop and felt inside her bag for her translator. She could just speak into it— *Where is the big hotel?*—and it would ask the question in whatever language she keyed in. Her fingers touched Hawkins's postcard, and she pulled it out instead.

Ah, yes, Iolani Palace, that Honolulu landmark, symbol of the lost kingdom. It was a holo, designed to project a three-dimensional image when inserted in one of the cheap, ubiquitous plastic holders just about everyone had. In fact, there had to be one here in this store. She looked around and spied the rack of postcards.

She spun it idly, dropped in one from the rack, admired a field of toppled stone Buddhas. The woman hovering behind her went to help another customer. She dropped in Iolani Palace.

Across the top of the palace was an address.

An address in Bangkok.

"Can I help, miss?"

Well, at least she didn't need the translator. Lynn's fingers shook as she removed the postcard with the address from the viewer.

"You want to buy that card?"

"Uh—yes. And this viewer."

"Three bhat."

"One," said Lynn automatically.

"Three," said the woman disapprovingly.

Lynn had partitioned off her bhat, and she handed the woman some coins, turned, and left the store. She did not run back through the streets, as she did not want to attract too much attention, but she walked quite briskly. She shook the water off her umbrella as she came in the door and the solitary woman at the desk gestured at a holder made of an elephant foot. Lynn shoved her umbrella in, hurried back to the room, unlocked the door with fingers that trembled so much that she dropped the key once because of the commotion inside. She kicked the door open, afraid of what she might find.

It was as she had feared. Akamu was lying on the floor convulsing, flopping around like a fish out of water. His jerks brought him near the bureau; Lynn rushed over and pushed him sideways so his head would not hit it. One foot kicked the table and his computer went flying; the table fell on top of it, crushing the frail flat. Lynn shoved the table aside and hoped the commotion wouldn't attract attention and hoped, hoped, that the electrical storm in Akamu's brain would be over quickly. When had it started? She shouldn't have left! She poured ice water onto a towel and tried to hold it to his forehead. He smashed the back of his head onto the floor, hard, twice, then went slack.

He was still breathing. He had just knocked himself out.

Waves of fear and anger passed through her body. She couldn't cope with this. An ordinary seizure would not bother her. But this was not an ordinary seizure.

Rain thrummed on the roof. Akamu lay sprawled at her feet.

She had no doubt now that this was some sort of tampering. Which had gone awry.

Twenty, thirty specific possibilities rushed through her mind, the ragtag ends of various illegal IS experiments done for myriad ostensible goals. Many of them had delayed results.

She remembered the Tripler Hospital glyph on her screen, back in Honolulu, before it had gone blank. So who *had* done this? Maui or Interspace?

She knelt next to him and pushed back his hair. "Akamu?" Foreboding almost overwhelmed her. What was it, what? Something that was supposed to make him solve those goddamned equations, that work he was always talking about? He was utterly still.

"Damn Maui!" she said, and jumped up, wet a cloth, and washed Akamu's face with it.

His eyes fluttered open. He didn't say anything. He just stared at the ceiling.

"Akamu," she said. "Listen to me. You must know what's wrong. You need to tell me. And if you know, I want you to tell me what to do about it, and then we'll do it."

He tried to sit up. She grabbed a pillow and stuck it under his head. He didn't say anything.

"No rush," she said. "Maybe I'll go get a doctor."

"No!" he said, looking alarmed. Then, "It won't do any good."

"Why not?"

"Because . . . I do know what's wrong. You can't help me. It's just starting to work, that's all. It took longer than I thought it would."

"What is it?"

His slight smile was ironic, much too old for a child his age. "I'm not sure. Don't you know?"

"No."

"It's okay. I feel better now." He pushed himself up. Lynn pulled a large soft chair close and helped him into it. She opened her mouth, ready to beat him over the head with questions, but he saw the crumpled flat and cried out.

"What happened?" He jumped out of the chair, muttering frantically as he felt it all over as if it were a small animal with broken bones. "It won't turn on!"

"You kicked the table," said Lynn.

He hugged it to his chest, collapsed into the chair, and began to cry. "Oh no, oh no, oh no," he keened.

"Did you back it up?" asked Lynn.

"Some of it," he conceded, calming a bit. "But not the last part, that I've done here. That was the most important. Because I feel—I feel—oh, I don't know." His face seemed thinner than just yesterday, and his eyes were burning, dark, and fevered. His hands trembled slightly.

Lynn sat in the chair opposite him. Obviously, she had to get him back to the world. To Maui, who had done this awful thing to him in order to squeeze the proofs out of him.

She rose decisively. "All I have is an address in Bangkok now. We'll just have to get there somehow. I think they have an overnight lev." Maybe once there she could figure out how best to get them back to Hawaii in one piece. She picked up the ragged Japanese guidebook and opened it to the schedule. "This is probably out of date but it says that one leaves about an hour from now. I want to get out of this place. You need help."

"I'm fine, I said," Akamu told her crossly. "I'm not ready to go back yet. I'll tell you when it's time. I feel better now."

"You're *not.* Let's *go.*"

He shouted, "I want to stay here and get this fixed! I have work to do! I'm all *right!*"

The transformation from a relatively pleasant boy to this furious screaming monster was somewhat shocking. But Lynn was not unfamiliar with such behavior; her brothers had occasionally performed this way, and she knew that Akamu had a much better reason. He was operating on some sort of biochemical edge. He was bigger and probably stronger than she, so Lynn just stood and looked at him with what she hoped were steely eyes.

"There's not anyplace here that can fix that, Akamu," she said. "Stow it in your bag, and let's get out of here. Bangkok is a big city. We can just get you a new one. A better one."

She did not like the slightly glazed look that came over his eyes, but it was better than loud defiance at this point. She helped him into his white silk short-sleeved shirt, but he jerked away and said, "I don't want it buttoned."

"Get your zoris. We're packed." Lynn stuffed the maps into the pack; they stepped into the hallway and went down the wide stairway past the check-in girl. Lynn stopped for a moment, holding onto Akamu's arm as she said, "I want to pay."

The girl turned to a computer and touched a pad. The printer whirred, Lynn paid the amount without checking, yanked her umbrella out of the stand, and hurried Akamu down the steps.

They were at the station in ten minutes and in their private compartment in half an hour.

Akamu passed out on the bed. Lynn stared out the window until the lights flashing by gave way to darkness. She checked the lock on the door and slept fitfully, waking after a few hours because of a nightmare, heart pounding. She sat up, turned on a tiny light. Akamu was still sleeping, breathing deeply. Who did these Homeland people think they were, anyway?

She curled up in a chair and watched him a long time before falling asleep again.

She woke with a jerk. Someone was brushing her cheek. She sat up.

It was Akamu, of course. "Lynn," he said. "I'm afraid."

She got up and moved to the bunk. She put her arm around him, thinking that the swaying of the train would lull him back to sleep again.

He began to talk, his voice husky. "I've never been away from my ohana—my family—for so long."

"I thought you said you went all kinds of places."

"They were all my ohana."

"Oh. That's right. You said something about Primal Societies, right?"

"It just means the way it used to be."

More Homeland golden-age nonsense. "How did it used to be, Akamu?"

"We all make decisions together. That's the way we did things for hundreds of years, before the Tahitians came." Lynn decided it was silly to point out to him that the more militant Tahitians, who arrived about A.D. 800, and the earlier Hawaiians were now seamlessly blended.

"Sometimes it's hard," he said. "There's lots of arguing. Maybe for days. But somehow it all works out. It works, I mean. Democracy. Look at all we've done. We're almost ready to go. I'm kind of glad it happened this way, really, even though I was so afraid when it happened. It's *working.*"

"*What's* working, Akamu?"

"You really don't know?"

"I do know that I think that you've been nan-enhanced by Maui."

"Maui!" Then he laughed.

"What's so funny?"

"You really *don't* know. Huh. I thought you were *smart.*"

"That's what I've been *saying.* I'm *not.*"

It was difficult to see him, but then they passed beneath some lights, his face was swiftly illuminated, and she saw that he was grinning.

"Well, actually, Maui's very angry with me."

"Why?"

"Because."

He started to laugh then, hysterically, choking and crying and making such a commotion that Lynn was afraid he was starting to have another seizure. Finally he dashed tears away, took a few sobbing breaths, and ended with a huge smile. "Yeah," he said. "Yeah."

How? Why? "So tell me about it," said Lynn, trying to keep her voice soothing.

"It's a long story."

"We've got time. *Plenty* of time."

He cleared his throat. "Well. Ever since I was little I've known that there was this *stuff* I could take that would help me do what I have to do. I don't even remember how I found out. One of the big kids told me, maybe, or maybe I found out about it on the web. Anyway, last year I started telling Maui that I wanted some, and he said that we didn't have any and that we wouldn't have any and that even if we did I couldn't have it. Then I found out that one of the other Kamehamehas died from it and that was why I couldn't have it."

Cold fear spread through Lynn. "Makes sense," she managed.

"Well," said Akamu, his voice rather singsong and distant, "I decided that I had to get it anyway. Because time is so short now. We can't fool around. I don't care what Maui says. He thinks he's so smart! So *bossy* is more like it. So I ran away and broke into Tripler and *took* some."

"What!" Lynn sat up abruptly. "How in the world . . . "

Akamu smiled sleepily, his eyes closed. "Pretty cool, huh? I planned it for a long time, all in my head. I took one of Maui's fast boats and made it to Kaaava on Oahu. It's on the opposite side of the island from Honolulu, still mostly Hawaiians—out country, you know? It's a real quiet place to land. Nobody noticed me at all. Then I took a bus to Tripler. The yellow line, and I knew the schedule. And I knew exactly what the stuff was, exactly where they kept it, what kind of security it had . . . "

"How?"

"Think I'll tell *you?*" he asked. His voice was teasing, yet firm. "Maui was totally pissed. I only talked to him once afterward and he was, like, extreme. But that was after they caught me, only I escaped . . . "

He yawned loudly. "Anyway, yeah, they poked me and stuff and took blood and did things like that for about a few hours. But I guess they thought I was just a stupid kid. It was pretty easy to get away from them. I've been worried because all this time it seemed like nothing was happening. I guess it took time to work and everything. After I got away I knew they'd be looking for me, and I got to that safe house on Nuuanu—the place where I saw you. I'd just gotten there. We have a network of them on all the islands. I wouldn't even let them tell Maui where I was for a few days, I was so afraid of how mad he'd be. But they told him anyway, I guess. They had to. Interspace decided that I was really important and they were watching pretty close for me. Maui was working out a plan to get me back to Kohala."

His voice became troubled. "I don't know what happened to John and Ellen. I guess IS figured out where I was and tried to kill me. Instead *they* were killed." He blinked back tears. "It was my fault they died. They were so nice to me."

Lynn was pretty sure the house had blown up because she had alerted IS with her night cruise on the Interspace web, but she didn't say anything.

"So what is this tremendously important thing that you *have* to risk death to do, Akamu?" And how will I save you from it? What are the parameters of what you've done? How can I get back into the system and find out without getting us both killed?

No answer. Try again. "How long have you been working on the proofs?"

"Since I was really little, I guess. It seems like everything I ever learned was a part of it. I had so many cool things to play with—computers, virtual stuff, special blocks and things when I was real little. We all have been working on it, I think. Even the ones that died. One of us solved Penrose's tile problem when he was seven. We like it," he said, his voice becoming more drowsy. "It's fun."

Well, Lynn told herself wryly, didn't you have similar plans for Masa?

Akamu leaned forward, his eyes filled with an earnest, happy light. "I only could figure out enough to know that . . . well, the only way I know how to explain it really is with numbers. But there's going to be a window sometime soon. Out there. Far out in space. And I don't think the next one will occur for at least twenty years."

"A window."

"A window for the *Hawai'i Loa* to make the jump. Lynn . . . there are *so many* places in the metaverse. But when you calculate where to find a place where the initial conditions were such that we could exist there now . . . it's like the way those old navigators could tell where land was, from hundreds of miles out on the ocean. It's almost like I'm sailing, and testing the swells, watching the birds, except it's all done with numbers that somehow tell me things about"—he grabbed the pillow and squeezed it with his hand—"*this*. Matter. Everything. How it flows. It's a fractal. The pattern repeats again and again, infinitely. I know *exactly* what we want—I'm *so* close to knowing how to get there! Ever since Tibet it's gotten stronger—and now Cen is helping me. He *is!* Maui told me how it happened to Cen. I guess he wanted to scare me."

"What happened to Cen?"

"Maui told me about some old records that he'd found. He knew Cen, you know? And he knew that Cen had been going to the hospital to see a woman he lived with, Mei. And Mei was given the same nan. She died from it. It was a very strong dose. But Cen had a very minor dose."

And you had, possibly, enough to kill you.

She pushed his hair back from his forehead. "We have to get you back right away." Her mind was racing, wondering who or what could stop this.

"I think . . . I *might* need some help," he said. "It's kind of scary."

"I'll do my best," she said, trying to keep grimness from her voice.

"Okay," he said, and closed his eyes.

"Akamu?" she said after a few minutes.

He was asleep again. She edged out from next to him, laid him down gently, found a sheet and covered him. She went back to her chair, but now she could not sleep, and watched the occasional lights from small villages illuminate his face from time to time throughout the night as she thought.

She was awakened by a knock on the door. Looking out the dirty window, she saw that they were pulling into a large train station. "Wake up," she told Akamu, shaking him until he roused. "Wash your face. We're in Bangkok."

"Bangkok?"

She handed him his pack as the lev hissed to a halt. "Come on."

She took his arm and led him down the corridor, following the other passengers as they stepped down into the platform. Akamu sagged against her. "I don't feel good," he said.

She fought panic. "I know. But we've got to get to this place. This address." She had visions of it. They would knock on the door. "Hawkins? Hawkins who?" Or the place would be empty. Or filled with rather nasty people waiting for them.

But if they returned to Hawaii the situation would be even worse.

Hawkins had been in touch with her father. He had given her this address. It was a slim connection, but something. If it didn't work she'd try something else. Check into a megahotel, the kind with the very best in-room facilities, go on the web, and really cook, fast and fierce, until she figured out what he had and how to stop its progress. Without killing him.

Akamu's forehead was covered with sweat. He pulled from her and sat on a wooden bench.

The train station was echoing pandemonium. Express levs were leaving within the hour for Hong Kong, Benares, Paris, Saint Petersburg, said a display above them. The huge scale of the rainbow arches of steel and darkened glass made humans antlike. She almost tripped over a blond beggar dressed in an impeccable Western suit, a line of tiny holograms running down his tie, sitting in lotus in the middle of an aisle, smiling madly, his credit receiver a small green Buddha he grasped in one hand, holding it above him in a triumphant gesture.

Lynn was feeling more and more like she had in Tibet: a mere collection of particles with nothing to bind them together. Coffee. There was a vendor. That would help her focus. Then they'd get a taxi.

A woman on the bench across from Akamu, who looked about sixteen, held a sleeping baby on her yellow-sari'd lap. Her own eyelids kept fluttering downward. Her oval, brown face was strikingly beautiful—the large, dark-fringed intelligent eyes, the long perfect nose . . .

For a moment, Lynn ached to hold the essence of her genes in the palm of her hand, the woman's entire explanation, the infinitesimal facts that guided her, that *grew* her. She wanted to trade places with her, to give her every fine advantage she'd been given, and hope that it would not be wasted as she had wasted it. She'd never made a difference. Her father had wanted her to, and instead she'd run off and performed for tourists. Then, even after she'd honored her own intelligence working on its growth as hard as she could, she'd turned her back on the implications of what she'd been doing, burying it all like a turtle buries eggs in the sand. Let someone else deal with it all.

In the echoing train station, just one limited collection of particles with a brilliant boy depending on her to save his life, she felt helpless, humbled by all around her. Sharp voices rose around her, trying to sell things; tiny holographic people danced or argued on pay platforms in front of rows of seats; the smell of strange spices from food kiosks rushed into her brain.

Information spilled in shimmering sheets everywhere. It spiraled in and out of existence as if sown by a profligate hand. Lynn saw generation upon generation of humanity in front of her, humanity that never changed, that never grew, but only presented itself and was acted upon. What had made her different? What lucky accident? Why did she have this knowledge, then, if not to use it for the good of everyone?

And perhaps, she thought, as the woman's eyes blinked open and she glanced across at Lynn and smiled shyly, this woman thinks of herself as just such a lucky accident. And pities me.

As if in confirmation, the woman looked directly into her eyes and her hand raised in a *mudra*, a Hindu religious gesture the meaning of which Lynn hadn't the slightest inkling.

Akamu was mumbling something. "What?" asked Lynn, putting her ear to his mouth.

He sat up, and his eyes were open wide, but looking beyond her. "I *know!* I'm *trying!*" He nodded his head rapidly.

"That's *it!*" muttered Lynn. Forget the coffee. She grabbed his arm.

He yanked it away.

The beggar smoothed his tie, his mad smile unchanged.

"Please, Akamu," she said, "let's go, okay. I promise I'll get you help soon."

Akamu slumped down in the seat, trembling. He blinked a few times. He was covered with sweat. He turned to Lynn, looked at her beseechingly. "I'm afraid now. Tell Maui I'm sorry. We have to hurry," he said.

"Yes," she said. "I know."

17

Akamu moaned in the backseat as the taxi jounced over the bumpy road and the driver turned back, frowning. "He is sick," the man said. "I do not like it."

"I don't either," said Lynn. "I wish you'd drive faster. I think you took the slow way."

"They are all slow ways. This is Bangkok."

They had just pulled out of a forty-five-minute traffic jam on a ten-lane-wide city street, out of a crescendo of honking and heat and steaming rain. Now a green, slow-moving klong was on one side of the road; on the other was an endless row of glittering high-rises.

Hot sun broke through the clouds as they turned a corner onto a quiet, narrow alley, bordered by white walls twenty feet high. Trees arched over the utterly clean brick pavement, a great contrast to the shacks of corrugated aluminum and cardboard they'd passed just five minutes ago. It was a strange oasis of peace.

"We are here," said the driver. "That will be two hundred bhat."

"You said a hundred," she said automatically, thinking, Stop it, Lynn, just pay the man. "Wait till they answer the gate," she said, "and I'll pay you two hundred." He scowled, but did not argue.

"Wake up, Akamu," she said. She shook him, then got out, leaving the door open, and pulled on his arm. With her foot she kicked at the huge wooden gate, wondering if indeed this was the correct address. There was a ragged unkempt air about the place. Her heart sank. It was deserted. Now what? She pounded again, harder, yelling, "Hello! Hello!"

After a moment the driver said, "There is no one here, miss. Can I take you somewhere else?"

Where?

She pushed vines from a brass plaque next to the gate and ascertained the address. Beneath it was a name: Colonel S. W. Hawkins.

The key.

She fumbled in her pack, found the key, inserted it into the lock.

She heard a click and tried the handle.

The door swung inward.

She saw a wild, green garden, overgrown with vast thick vines hanging from trees that spread over all like cooling umbrellas. Weeds grew between brick pavers. A hot breeze touched huge leaves to reluctant rustling, then they were still again. Two red and yellow parrots flashed through the courtyard, their colors echoed by flowers that twined in glittering rain-drenched jungle.

"Hello!" she yelled again, but heard only the wind in the leaves, birdcalls, and a monkey chattering from beyond the high wall. The tall Thai house on stilts towered above her; the surrounding balcony could be reached by several flights of stairs. A bony cat rushed up to her, mewing.

"Miss, you must pay me *now!*"

She took cautious steps further into the courtyard, ready to bolt. A dead frond crashed suddenly onto the bricks and she jumped.

Taking a deep breath, she chose stairs that looked as if they were at the back of the house—heavy stairs, solid. The ornately carved railing rippled beneath her hand. She ascended into the canopy of trees, and below in the alley she glimpsed the roof of the taxi.

She tried a door, and it swung open.

She walked through the large, spare house, beautifully appointed, with open shelves that held dancing Thai statues. The floors were highly polished wood, the furniture quite simple. She saw a living room, dining room, kitchen. Everything was as neat as if a maid had just left, though her finger left a trail in the dust on a low table.

She walked into a study—a large room with many windows between which were book-filled shelves. A low table served as Hawkins's desk; built into it was the usual keyboard that would manifest a screen and a holo platform.

She walked into the other bedroom and stopped suddenly, heart beating loud.

Hawkins lay on the bed and at first she thought he was dead. She stepped closer and it was even worse because he raised a complicated gun and pointed it right at her without opening his eyes.

"Stop right there," he said, then blinked.

"Lynn," he whispered, and the weapon fell from his hand.

* * *

"Where is the earring?" was the first thing Hawkins asked, after she paid the driver and got Akamu inside.

Akamu was doing a bit better and insisted that he was fine. She had left him lying on the couch. Lynn knew that he would worsen again in another hour, maybe two. She sat on a chair in Hawkins's bedroom, ready with her own list of questions.

"The earring?" she said, at a loss, then remembered. "There was a tracer in it. I threw it away in Kathmandu."

"Oh. Dear," said Hawkins, and frowned. He was wearing gray silk pajamas and looked tiny in the center of a huge futon set on a polished wooden platform. He had pushed himself up to a sitting position and was very pale. Lynn wondered how he had gotten here but decided to ask him later.

"I'm very sorry that I had you come here, considering the circumstances," he said, gesturing at himself. "I am much worse than I thought. Sattva did not want to let me go, but since I put all that information in the pack . . . " He gestured apologetically with one hand, but Lynn noticed he kept the other on the pistol.

"We had no place else to go," said Lynn. "I'm not sure what's going on, who to trust." She did not want to say that she didn't trust Hawkins; she was not entirely sure of him either. But he had been willing to die to protect them. "This is"— she had been going to say, better than nothing, but finished,— "a beautiful house."

"My father owned the entire block," he said. "My sister still lives next door, through the gate in the back wall, and a cousin lives on the other side."

"What are you eating?" Lynn asked Akamu as he walked through the bedroom door with a bowl of something.

"Rice," he said. "There was some in the refrigerator. I'm *starving.*"

"The house sets the cooker," said Hawkins.

"I'm sorry I threw the earring away," said Lynn. "But one of Samuel's stooges showed up in Kathmandu. I couldn't figure out any other way he could have found us. I guess they really wanted that genome information."

Hawkins's laugh was short and sharp. "They want the proofs," he said, his voice hushed as the rain that had started up again.

"What?" said Akamu, his chopsticks pausing on their way to his mouth. The rice fell back into the bowl. Lynn could almost see his eyes bulging.

"The Kaiulani Proofs," said Hawkins. "Perhaps incomplete, of course, but . . . "

"From *who?*" demanded Akamu.

Hawkins tilted his head. "Yes, you *would* be interested, wouldn't you? A private Chinese think tank claimed to have completed them, based on the Kalakaua Fragments that have been floating around in the web all these years. They put out feelers and IS was more than willing to meet their price sight unseen, after a few tantalizing hints."

"But I thought it was Mao's DNA," said Lynn.

"Of course, my dear. That's what you were meant to think. You had proven a reliable courier for your brothers in the past, but since you had refused, initially, they had just about finished alternate arrangements when they found that you were on your way after all. And of course they would put a tracer in it! Nothing is secure enough to transport information of such immense importance, with more potential power than atomic energy. I didn't have the capability to separate the tracer from the proofs. I just hoped we could stay a few steps ahead of them and get it through. The soldiers were not Chinese, you understand. After realizing that it was you who had rescued Akamu your brothers lost trust in you, for some reason." Hawkins smiled. "I did not count on such serious injury befalling myself. Which was very stupid, of course."

He shook his head. "Once I woke, and confessed the contents of the earrings to Sattva—well, let us say that her calmness makes the best case for her being the Dalai Lama. I was afraid that she would undo all her work by killing me instantly. What she had been working on all her life literally within reach! She insisted that I was not well enough to leave but I had no choice. I thought I would be well enough to make sure to intercept you before you came inside." He tried to sit up but fell back. "You must leave immediately. My sister will help you. I've done everything wrong. Now the proofs have surely fallen into the hands of Interspace."

"What?" said Lynn. "Then who—"

"My dear," said Hawkins, the ghost of a grin on his thin face, "have you not figured it out yet?"

"*I* have," said Akamu, almost gleefully.

"You don't work for Interspace. But I thought you knew my father."

"I did," said Hawkins. "We were very, very close. I would have done anything for him. He was one of the most honorable men in the world."

"We would tend to disagree," came a voice through the open window.

Lynn did not know that she had such swift reflexes.

She rushed Akamu and pushed him into the hallway as bullets splintered wood next to her head.

"*Run!*" she hissed at Akamu. "They must have been waiting . . . "

Damn this house on stilts!

She glanced out a window. A car was by the back gate where they had entered. And another, no doubt, at the front.

What was that about a sister?

Looking down, she saw several men rushing toward Hawkins's corner of the house.

It wasn't much of a chance, but they had to take it. She pointed to the house next door.

"His sister," said Akamu.

"Let's try it," said Lynn.

They hurried down the stairs at the opposite end of the house and twisted through the trees. Lynn was glad of the heavy foliage. If no one had seen them go down the stairs, then they could not see them now.

They ran down the wall, looking for a gate. Lynn was terrified. "Here it is!" stage-whispered Akamu ahead of her and pushed open a wooden gate that they slammed behind them. Lynn slid a heavy bar through an iron hasp and looked around, panting. "We can't stay here," she said. "They'll figure it out pretty fast." She had left the pack with all the money behind. All she had was some bhat stuck in her pocket, and they had no passports. Perhaps Hawkins's sister might help them but there was really no time to ask.

She saw an iron gate and through it a busy street. It was around the corner from Hawkins's place; they had nowhere else to go and could not dally. She grabbed Akamu's arm and ran into traffic amid honking and squealing tires that seemed barely to change the level of cacophony. She waved down an empty tuk-tuk and they jumped in.

"Where to?" asked the driver.

Lynn was completely out of ideas. "Take us to the Royal Hotel," she said. The name popped into her head from the guidebook. "Is it far?" she asked, when the driver started to laugh.

"Maybe a mile," he said. "But only government workers stay there."

She wasn't sure why he found this so funny but asked, "Only Thais?"

He nodded his head vigorously. "Yes. I could take you to the Intercontinental."

"The Royal is fine," she said. They just needed a lobby with a phone. As warm rain fell, Lynn closed her eyes. Hawkins was dead for sure now. And if he was working for, or with, her father, and yet not for IS, then what had her father been up to?

As she gazed at the side of Akamu's face, understanding dawned.

"Can't you *move?*" she asked. Traffic held them once again in its vise, and they were only a block from Hawkins's estate. A crowd had gathered, apparently attracted by gunfire. Surely the men would be looking for them—

"Come on," she said, grabbing Akamu's arm. "Let's get out. We'll have to go faster than this!"

But he was staring down the street.

"Maui!" he yelled, and leaped from the tuk-tuk.

Through the crush of traffic Akamu ran, threading through stalled vehicles. He crossed five lanes with the speed of a gazelle while Lynn watched in trepidation.

Then Lynn saw him.

A tall, bearded, well-muscled Hawaiian man, his long, kinky hair loose—black, with a white streak snaking down one side.

She had seen him before. In a younger version, in a brief news clip. The elusive head of the Homeland Movement, whose name was unknown, because it had always seemed to change. He was, she recalled, believed dead. There was probably even a death certificate filed somewhere. Certainly, he hadn't been sighted in—oh, ten years?

He leaned over and embraced Akamu, and his hair swirled around the boy like a sheltering curtain.

As she stared at him Lynn thought, incongruously, What a beautiful man!

"Miss?" said the driver.

She extracted the last of her bhat from her pocket, tossed it at the driver, and ran like hell before a new onslaught of tuk-tuks released by the change of a signal.

18

Maui seemed to know the twists and turns of Bangkok's back alleys well.

He never paused while leading their fluid flight. He rushed into the front of a garish electronics shop, then out the back door, always holding Akamu's hand, glancing over his shoulder at Lynn now and then encouragingly, including her in their effort.

When they were well away from the traffic jam surrounding Hawkins's estate they ducked into a closed cab with tinted windows and backseats that faced each other. Maui spoke to the driver in Thai. The driver nodded and Maui leaned back in the seat.

"How did you find us?" asked Akamu, breathing hard. He seemed not the least afraid of Maui's possible wrath, and Lynn could easily see why: Maui obviously loved the boy—treasured him, not for any "work" he thought he was doing, but just for himself.

"What do you care?" asked Maui. "You had me worried sick. I thought you were dead." But while he was speaking he held Akamu's face between his hands. "Are you all right?"

Did I get here in time? his eyes asked Lynn in a fleeting glance.

"How did you *find* us?" asked Akamu.

"Someone named Sattva got in touch with me," Maui said. "Which was lucky, as Lynn apparently did not think it important."

"*Akamu* didn't think it was important," she said. "Of course, I didn't know who you were, and he wouldn't tell me. He wouldn't even admit that he knew you. And we were rather out of touch for a long time after that."

Maui was wearing khaki shorts and a light green shirt made of rough, raw silk, the kind you could pick up at any street stall for a song. He had a scraggly beard. His face sagged with fatigue; his eyes were bloodshot.

He said, "Sattva told me that you might show up at Hawkins's place. I was afraid I would be too late."

"You were," said Lynn. "For Hawkins." She slumped back in her seat and curled up. Another death. And for what? She still didn't know. Not for sure.

"How are you?" Maui asked Akamu again.

"Fine," said Akamu, his limpid brown eyes disingenuous as he gazed at Maui. Lynn was amazed at these tricks. He had not used them on her.

Because he knew they wouldn't work.

"He's not fine," said Lynn. "He seems all right now, but I don't think it will last. He needs help immediately."

Maui looked at her appraisingly. "Do you think that you can help him?"

"Me?"

"I don't *need* help!" shouted Akamu, and the driver flicked his eyes across the mirror.

Maui held both Akamu's hands. His eyes became serious,

stern. Lynn was glad she was not the subject of this particular gaze. "Akamu, this is dangerous stuff."

Akamu stared right back at Maui. "There's going to be a window soon. Everything is ready, isn't it? By then I'll know the course. In my bones. Deep in my mind. I'll be ready to pilot the *Hawai'i Loa*. But I have to *stay this way!* I have to *keep going!*"

"I can't let you," said Maui, looking at him levelly. "Not if I have anything to do with it. It's not that important."

"It is and you know it!" Akamu's eyes filled with tears and he began to sob hysterically. "And Lynn threw the proofs away!"

Maui looked at Lynn. "You had the proofs and threw them away?"

"At the time I thought they were Mao's DNA," she said. "And I thought that we'd get killed because there was a tracer with them."

Maui's arms tightened around Akamu, and he looked at Lynn helplessly. "I imagine IS found them, then," he said, with resignation. "Another problem. But I'd say it was a false alarm anyway. Chances are they're incomplete. I'm most worried about Akamu. There must be some way to help him. If you don't want to, I'm sure I can find someone." His voice turned cold.

"I'll do all I can," she said quickly. "I have so far." She was rather surprised that he didn't have more questions about the proofs.

Because, Lynn, somehow he *knows* . . .

"I'm sorry," said Maui. "You have." The corners of his large eyes drooped; his dark brown face was furrowed. "Mind if I smoke?" he asked and before she answered he pushed the cigarette pad and an ashtray opened; a small fan whirled to suck in the smoke. It didn't work very well and when he lit his cigarette her eyes watered.

Maui rubbed Akamu's back and murmured, "That's all right; rest now, Akamu. Just relax." Akamu hiccupped a few times, and his eyelids fluttered downward. In a moment he was breathing deeply.

Lynn was impressed. "I'm not exactly sure exactly what it is that he *took,* there at Tripler," she said.

"Oh, I am," he said. His voice was grim. "I know precisely what it was. And so, apparently, did he."

"What was it?" asked Lynn.

Maui sighed. It was evening now. His dark eyes caught the light of an oncoming vehicle and shone for a moment; she saw immense sadness.

"It's rather convoluted, but apparently there's some sort of bionan that aligns these little—*things*—that are a part of the sheath of brain cells . . . "

"The tubular dimars," said Lynn.

"Hmmm? Yes, that's it," he said, and took a deep drag of his cigarette. "Well, if they are aligned to certain planes, is my understanding of the whole thing, they facilitate the brain's entry into a state of quantum superconductivity. Something to do with being able to precisely *know* what is happening wherever reality is formed before it comes *here.*" He drew on his cigarette again; in the dim light Lynn saw his mouth had a wry twist. "Right."

"So you don't believe this is possible," said Lynn, feeling relieved.

"Well," said Maui, "that's not entirely true, I'm afraid. But I'm pretty sure that whatever they cooked up is still not very refined." He sighed. "Some of this is my fault."

"I'd guess the whole damn *thing's* your fault," said Lynn.

Maui flinched. But his voice was grave and calm. "It's all been a risk, every part of it."

"People aren't just your pawns," she began, an angry edge to her voice. "Even if you've—you've just *made* them in a lab!"

"I agree," said Maui. "You've spent a few weeks with Akamu now. Does he act like your standard pawn?" He tilted his head and his eyes were questioning.

Lynn sighed. "He seems a bit—hardheaded," conceded Lynn.

"More than a bit," said Maui. "In fact it's entirely possible that we may be *his* pawns." A slight, ironic smile crinkled the corners of his eyes as he looked at Lynn. "So put that in your pipe and smoke it while I take a break." He yawned. "You must excuse me if I'm not making sense. I don't think I've slept in days. I've been doing nothing but trying to find Akamu. Well, that and trying to make a few . . . final arrangements, as it were. You'll be glad a bit later that I napped, believe me."

He leaned back into the corner of the seat, gathered Akamu to his side with one arm, and closed his eyes.

"Wait a minute," said Lynn. "I haven't even *started* with questions."

But she could not wake either of them.

Dawn above the Pacific was an intense, green, fast-moving verge of light that Lynn woke to, surprised to find herself lying on satin sheets in a tiny, wood-paneled bedroom. Then she remembered.

After Maui fell asleep there was a ride through darkening Bangkok alive with lights; a detour around a Buddhist Festival of the New Moon—a sinuous line of thousands of candles snaking through the streets surrounding Wat Po, where the famous Reclining Buddha reposed, enormous and sublime. So the driver told Lynn. "They had last week a festival they've never had before," the man said. "They called it the Festival of New Stars. It was much louder than this one, with a huge dancing of millions."

"Millions?" asked Lynn.

He shrugged. "It seemed so. They blocked up all the streets around the palace and Wat Po with their wild dancing. I had to drive for many blocks out of my way and my passengers complained."

Once they were out of the city, Lynn must have dozed, too, for she was wakened when they left the pavement and bumped along and she heard Maui giving directions and then she opened her eyes and saw a small airport surrounded by many private planes.

Lynn made a remark about the opulence of the one they climbed aboard and Maui only said, "It's not ours. I've been wanting to fly it for years and finally had reason enough to ask."

Now, the small jet chased the edge of morning. Lynn sat up in the bed and looked around. She was not unused to private jets but this was really something: High-style postmodern decor; subtle waves of wood and metal. And although the fluffy white tops of the clouds were bathed in pink and gold, their night had been quite short. She was still tired.

She took off her clothes and had a shower; searched through the drawers and belted an enormous pair of someone's shorts around her waist. She found a large T-shirt that said Ono Restaurant and put it on.

"Just in time!" Maui said, when she slipped into the seat next to his in the cockpit. Akamu was sprawled behind them on a couch. "We'll land in about twenty minutes."

"Where?" she asked.

"Ah," he said. "Top secret, you know."

"Kohala." The northern peninsula of the Big Island ceded to the Homeland Movement decades ago.

"Exactly."

"And how do you think I can help Akamu from there?"

"If anyone in IS knows how to help him you can find out from there."

"That's a rather interesting assertion."

"I think you'll find everything about Kohala immensely interesting."

"How could he get away so easily?" asked Lynn. "Doesn't anybody keep an eye on him?"

Maui leaned forward and made some digital adjustments. "Hell no, we just let him do whatever he pleases. If he'd told us he wanted to rob a bank, why, we would have helped him out. What do you *think?*"

Lynn's rude streak was beginning to surface. "But why weren't you more careful? What about the other children—the other *clones*—who died?"

He nodded and a muscle in his jaw twitched. "Why don't *you* think about who killed them," he said roughly. "We didn't want our *clones* brought up in some sort of cold assembly-line way. It could be that we gave them too much freedom, made them too vulnerable, but what's the alternative? We wanted them to be a part of a larger community. Otherwise what would they care about their fellow humans? What would they know? How could they choose to take a leadership role?"

"Could they choose not to?" Lynn asked, her tone acid.

"Well, one of them shows all the signs of becoming a very successful investment banker in Hong Kong, actually, despite his age. We've learned an immense amount about humans, about cloning humans and the aftermath, from this program. We wanted them to grow up as normally as possible. There have not been that many."

But more than Lynn had known about, she realized. After a moment she felt incongruously bad about upsetting him. She could see a muscle twitching in his cheek.

"Akamu talked about Primal Societies," she said, to divert his thoughts.

"Yes," he said, as the jet sliced through the cloud layer on its descent. "Primal Societies will allow us to successfully leave this planet and survive in a wide variety of circumstances. There is no hierarchy. It's a true democracy, but people have to learn how to function in one. They have to trust that it will work. They have to learn to trust themselves, they have to know how to access information, true information, not just what's been handed them. They have to learn how to compromise, how to forge a new path, how to formulate goals, how to think of a community as a true community and not some sort of top-down dictatorship, however benign. It's a huge responsibility for the individual. And I have to admit that for somebody like—me, for instance—learning to listen is one of the hardest parts. But I think it's the only form of government that will really work in the long run. And that's what we're thinking of—vast amounts of time."

He banked the jet sharply over the Kohala coast.

The sea was translucent turquoise, fringed by a thin, distant line of wavebreak, white against black lava. Steep rain-forested cliffs were fissured by vertical narrow valleys. Most of the Big Island was relatively young, geologically speaking. As the tectonic plate on which the Hawaiian Islands sat rotated northward over the hot spot, each island in its turn had been formed.

Kohala was the northernmost point of the Big Island, much, much older than the southern part. Now, a new island was forming deep under the sea south of them.

Lynn pointed at a distant plume of smoke. "Is that Kileauea? I thought it hadn't erupted in years."

"It hadn't," said Maui. "But that was a mere blip of time to a volcano, of course. It started up again a few weeks ago. Its supposed 'dormancy' was one of the reasons the IS investors could be talked into financing a maglaunch tunnel on the Big Island." He grinned as he stared out the window, focused on landing. "That's bad and good. Bad for IS, because they literally poured their money down a hole. The Big Island is the least seismically stable of all the islands, naturally. They've never used this maglaunch, even though it's pristine, complete, ready to go. It's too risky. They continued using the one over on Oahu for all the generation ship work."

"But good for the Homelanders," said Lynn. She knew exactly why the tunnel had been built.

Or thought she had. To funnel money to her brothers and others like them. Now—she wondered. "Akamu told me about your plans. And his—to be the pilot."

"What do you think of all that?" asked Maui.

"I think you're crazy. And you've driven Akamu crazy, too."

"Maybe you'll change your mind."

"So where is the maglaunch?"

Maui pointed out the window. "The entrance is behind the mountains, near Kailua-Kona, where the coast slopes down to the sea gradually. About thirty miles away. The tunnel angles upward from there, so the vehicle can gain momentum. Then it shoots up through the mountain and leaves from that hole, over there," he said, and she saw it, surrounded by glinting black lava, the spun glass of the land, fenced and guarded by tiny doll-like soldiers. It belonged to Interspace, but the exit bordered on Hawaiian Homeland.

Maui brought the jet to a delicate landing, and taxied to a halt. His eyes were Akamu's, deep brown and large, but quite grave, as he turned to her. "As important as this project is, I've just about lost heart over this last thing. IS is afraid of us. As indeed they should be. I guess this has driven them to use desperate means." He sighed. "And I guess it made Akamu think he had to use desperate means as well. When you're young, you don't think about the downside. You think that you're immortal. But time *is* short. We have to win through soon, I think, or maybe miss this opportunity forever. Not only for ourselves, but for everyone." As he spoke he unconsciously grasped a crystal hanging around his neck on a thin, clear filament—fishing line? Like Akamu's. Yes, that's where she'd seen it before. She looked at it more closely. It was a delicate representation of one of those Polynesian canoes that could sail thousands of miles.

"You see," he said, "if it weren't for Akamu, I'd be ecstatic. All our plans are coming to fruition now. What I have worked on for a lifetime. Only a few pieces of the puzzle are missing." He looked at her directly. "And one of them is you."

"Me! After Akamu is better I'm through with this stuff. I'm going to become a hermit." She rose as he did, followed him to the door.

He turned and put his hand on her shoulder. "Wait and see," he said, a bit sadly. "I'm not sure you'll really be able to. In fact, I hope not." He spun the wheel that opened the door. "You first," he said, and went back to gather Akamu.

As always when she returned, Lynn was stunned by the intensity of colors, the cool purity of the air, as she climbed down the stairs from the jet. Palms bobbed tumultuously in the morning wind, their fronds shadowy blue-green, in a row that bordered the lower verge of a cliff. Vast fields of mountain grasses filled her eyes, backed by steep rain-forested mountains where, high above, the flowering canopies of trees, streaks of brilliant yellow and red, tossed in the breeze. Lynn heard only the rush of wind through billions of leaves.

At the end of the airstrip was a deep country lane overlaced by the branches of trees centuries old. They were probably about a thousand feet above the ocean, and she had seen the vertical cliffs that plummeted downward from here—completely unscalable. Across the blue channel was the massive slope of Haleakala, purple in the distance.

This world hummed with life. How could anyone stand to leave it, to agree to enter a lifeless suffocating spaceship—no matter how grand—for the rest of their days? She did not know; she had never understood that urge.

An open electric jeep waited. Maui carried Akamu with seeming ease and laid him in the backseat, got behind the wheel, and flicked a switch. They moved silently beneath the great trees and birds swooped across the lane before them.

She didn't know exactly what she had expected—grass shacks? Instead she saw, with a slight shock as they emerged from the lane, several domes similar to Sattva's, out along the high sea bluffs that drank light from the wide sky. Further inland, near waterfalls, were many fascinating houses built of glass, wood, and black lava rock, utterly modern, blending with the land.

Maui did not take her toward those, though. After speaking briefly to those who had greeted them he took her arm and led her toward a neat shed. She could feel his exhaustion, see it in his eyes, smell it emanating from his skin as they crowded into the elevator inside the shed. They descended for less than a minute.

She expected the same coldly gleaming underground corridors of Interspace but was happily surprised.

The door opened onto a cathedral-like space that looked natural. Whatever had been caught in the lava flow and created this space had long since vanished. Tile and polished wood were interspersed as flooring, marking areas of use in the vast, lobbylike nexus, which was filled with palms and other tropical plants, flourishing beneath subtle lighting. A small waterfall splashed into a pool. Quietly lit corridors with luminescent flooring radiated landward from the central atrium, and toward the sea was a great open place flooding the interior with sunlight. A woman who was clearly a guard nodded at Maui, and a man disappearing down a corridor turned and waved.

"Have Dr. Konapai come immediately," he told the guard and she nodded again.

Maui walked them over to an open balcony and Lynn leaned against the railing, breathing deeply. The balcony was set in a deep curve of pure black lava that echoed the curve of water hundreds of feet below. She looked to the right and to the left. Even though she was so close, the glass set into the cliff on both sides of her for hundreds of yards was almost invisible, blending with the lava's natural glitter.

The scent of seaweed drying on the rocks, mingled with salt air, the solid, distant smack of massive waves on rock far below, welcomed her. She had missed the intense Pacific blue.

"Home sweet home," Maui said. Akamu, lying where Maui had deposited him on a wide couch, opened his eyes. "I want my flat," he said, reaching out. Maui caught his hand, held it tightly for a moment.

"Rest," said Maui. "Dr. Konapai will be here in just a minute to take care of you." Lynn was amazed to see Akamu close his eyes and snuggle into the cushions.

Maui turned to Lynn. "Come on. Time to get to work. I have something to show you."

She followed him to a spacious apartment at one end of the complex. She glimpsed a bedroom off to one side, nice, but impersonal as a hotel.

In the center of a wall of glass was a spare, elegant virtual system.

The console was a curved flat, and in front of it was a chair that looked something like an insect, swooping lines of thin round metal with a cushion in the center. It was on wheels. Maui motioned her into it. It was surprisingly comfortable. He pulled its twin chair close and sat next to her.

"Welcome to Interspace," he said.

She looked at him.

"Go ahead," he said. "Try it."

The helmet was just two curves of crossed metal that sat on her head; an eye panel lowered when she pushed a pad by her ear. She twisted in the chair to get comfortable and pushed the button on the arm console.

Lynn Oshima lived in Koolau House. She rapidly bypassed the guard and the elevator and walked inside.

"I took the liberty of putting you right at home," said Maui.

"Oh, many thanks," she said, rather shaken.

Using the control that nestled beneath her right hand she began to cruise through her own system. She saw her latest work, several weeks old, where she had wiped the genescan of Akamu clean. She tried not to be disturbed. It was rather ironic. This was what *she* had been doing since she was very young.

"You've been *spying* on me!" she said, feeling enormously predictable.

"No, actually, no one has." She couldn't see his face, only hear his voice, quite deep and somehow reassuring. "You haven't been of great interest to us, until this. But you see, we can." He scooted his chair over to a cabinet and pulled out another helmet, put it on. "Now watch."

And then they were at IS headquarters. She could actually hear people speaking. He moved them to a warehouse, ordered an extra zodiac boat for a backup rescue launch.

In the next twenty minutes he walked her through the heart and soul of Interspace without a trace of gloating. He was absolutely calm and at home.

It was quite easy to see how Akamu had made his plans to invade Tripler Labs.

"Think you can find what you need?" asked Maui. "He took that stuff—here—" He brought up a calendar, touched a day about a month ago.

"If it's there, I can find it," she said. "It's another question as to whether I can do it in time."

"Well," said Maui. "Time *is* very short."

"That's what I said."

"No," he said, "I mean—how much did Akamu tell you about our plans?"

"Well—not a lot. Just that you were going to take over the generation ship. It sounds kind of outlandish, actually."

Maui leaned back in his chair, his face grim. "I hope anyone else who has an inkling about what we're doing thinks the same thing. But we have to do it soon. They've christened the ship. They're planning on leaving within the month. Right now"—Lynn thought she could hear his heart beating with excitement—"right now is our best chance." His voice became an intense whisper. "In the next few *days.*"

"Days?" she asked. "But I thought—I mean, I think the official schedule is another year or so—"

"No," said Maui. "It's all been set in motion. What we've been planning for fifteen years."

She motioned toward the screen. "How long have you been doing this?"

"Ages," he said. "Ages." He stood. "I'm going to check on Akamu and get some rest. They know how to get him stabilized, at least for a while. Everyone here knows who you are and why you're here. If you need anything just ask. You saw the international doorway?"

She nodded.

"There are many people there totally willing to help us. The Homeland Movement is worldwide. I'm sure you can figure out the icons. Oh! I forgot. You'll probably want something to eat."

She leaned back in her chair. "I don't understand. You can obviously control Interspace. What are you *doing?*"

"I hope it's not obvious," he said. "We don't want to tip our hand too soon. We just keep tabs, and any changes we make are absolutely necessary, and very small, even though with such a large organization no one would even notice substantial changes—they'd just think that they were authorized. Let them do all the work. We're just a bunch of scruffy stupid indigent people all wrapped up in old legends. With a silly pretentious underground facility that they think they know everything about." His voice was cool, but the expression on his face was fierce. "I just want you to heal Akamu, for now."

"Look," she said, "we're dealing with very subtle changes in brain chemistry."

"So take that away. Make him normal again. Make him what he was."

"He never was normal."

"He was a perfectly normal Kamehameha, and Kamehameha lived to be pretty old. Lynn, I'm not a fool. I understand the things people like you can do, maybe better than you think. I just can't do them myself."

"I don't think you're a fool."

"Maybe I am and I'm just desperate. We have so much to do, very little time, and I love Akamu."

"Maybe he likes the way he is."

"Do you like the way he is?"

"Of course not. I'm just telling you that it will break his heart if he loses the capability to finish working on those proofs. He'll hate us."

"That's worlds better than the alternative," Maui said. "Aren't you afraid he might die, Lynn?"

"I was," she said. "I still am. But . . . think about it, Maui. What if one day you understand these things? They're like the air you breathe. The next, it's like you're a clod of dirt. You can't even imagine what it was you were thinking about. Can't you see how painful that might be? I'm just not at all sure that such fine control as you are talking about is possible. I'm saying that I might make things worse. That's very frightening to me, too. He *looks* very bad, but rapid brain growth is a phenomenon that upsets the entire organism. All sorts of new neural connections are forming."

"I don't know about that," said Maui roughly. "I just don't know. And the proofs *are* important, but we're making headway using a lot of other sources. I think the proofs are kind of like inevitable knowledge, in a way. It's information that exists that we're finally capable of discovering and using. We never were counting on the revelations of just one person, much less a child. He's taken all this on himself."

"Maybe knowing that he was Kamehameha has given him some sense that he is rather important to you," she couldn't help saying, with some force. "It can't be easy knowing that you were created only because you were identical to some wonderful, fabulous, powerful figure from the past. And what for? What *for,* really?"

Maui spoke slowly. "Cloning Kamehamehas was Lelani's idea, really. My grandmother's." His hand dropped to the crystal starship, and Lynn remembered *their* name for it—the

Hawai'i Loa. "She was a Hawaiian priestess, so this was sacred for her. She had a vision of a perfect Hawaii, of moving to an entirely new world, of having the leaders necessary to assess a completely new situation, the way Kamehameha did when the Europeans showed up, and use it to their advantage. We did fine for a hundred years, until the last of the Kamehameha line died. But diseases, like measles and smallpox, depleted over half our population in twenty years. Furthermore, the missionaries made it clear that women should not have children unless they were married, which was a completely alien idea in Polynesia. Marriage existed, but children . . . children were special. They were shared by the community. It was a common practice for a couple to give their child to a sister or brother to bring up, and for them to in turn bring up others' children. It cemented the community. Children were not 'owned'; nor was the identity of the father of great import—not, anyway, in the sense of 'legitimizing' children. After the missionaries came and foisted their philosophy on everyone, abortions and infanticide by women made to be ashamed of their own culture depleted the population even further.

"I think that for Lelani it was kind of like, here is something preserved from the days when everything worked, and these children will be a symbol of everything working for us again. But it was much more poetic than that, I suppose. And she was right. Having these children has meant the world to the Homeland Movement. They've brought it all together. *We* can use the technology of the modern world, just like anyone else. It's a kind of *mana,* power. We've brought three generations of Hawaiian children here for education, the education the state never gave them. Our own private schools. Having the Kamehameha children—*clones* if you will, though I'm sure that's not at all the way you think of Akamu—has given it all a real touch of magic. When Hawaiian children leave here to go to college they are confident and proud, working to the best of their abilities. Many have returned to work here, others are working for us in various capacities internationally, and many are happily pursuing their own normal lives in every imaginable profession and capacity. Really, Lynn, who would mind being born!"

Certainly not an optimist like you, she thought.

He kept talking. "I grant you that cloning has brought problems which we didn't foresee, but we'll all have to cope with them eventually, so why not now? Now, while we're on Earth. I've been here for all of them, every last one of them. They're my children. It's been absolutely amazing to me that this kind of thing actually works! It's like a miracle. A miracle," he said more softly.

"And now it's all falling into place." He sighed. "I know you're tired, and I've given you a lot to do—"

"I'll do everything I possibly can." The files of Dr. Honsa, she was thinking even now. That would be the first place to look—long closed . . . she picked up the helmet.

"Oh—wait." Maui pulled open a drawer and took out a small silver disk. He hesitated for a moment, then handed it to her.

"I've been saving this for you," he said. "If you think there's time, maybe you should look at it first. It won't take long. And if you want more information press the newspaper icon in the information corridor." He patted her shoulder as he left. "You got a great write-up."

She held the small disk in her hand when Maui left, almost afraid to look at it.

She walked to the bank of windows and was pleasantly surprised to find that they opened. The wind rushed in, so strong that it blew her hair back from her face.

Hardy green *naupaka,* with its stubby ovate leaves and delicate white flowers, glowed bright green just outside the window, growing from gnarled lava. She could not help but think, as she watched it shake with each gust of wind, that it was like the ancient Polynesians, pushing the limits, living on the edge, colonizing every bit of possible land. She heard the hush of surf hundreds of feet below; drank in the very blueness of the sea, like a balm; breathed sharp salt air. How she had missed it! And she hadn't even realized it.

She stepped back from the window and looked at the disk.

She rather knew what was on it. She returned to the chair.

But she dallied, accessed the news. Read her own obituary. A tragic freak fire in a Hong Kong jewelry store. Her accomplishments—rather few. Her community involvement—scanty. Her brothers *would* be disappointed if they had to give her inheritance back to her. She saw videos of congratulatory parties celebrating the completion of the generation ship, by-passed the doorway that would allow her to mingle virtually with a more nuanced record of the tremendous celebration.

Finally, she could put it off no longer. She went back and slipped it into the player in the bedroom. She sat on the edge of the bed and watched her father speak.

19

Lynn," he began, and she froze it instantly, studying his face.

His dear face.

It was more wizened than she remembered, though she had seen him less than three months ago, at a formal dinner given by Alyssa, the twins' mother. She remembered how he asked her to stay late and talk, and, when she refused, to call him. She felt very bad, remembering. She had never called. She was newly pregnant, euphoric. She did not want to listen to the same negativity she had gone through when she had taken her first job as a musician. Time enough for him to know when she could show him his granddaughter.

What a difference those few months had made.

A date blinked in the upper right hand corner. The day she had fled with Akamu.

It was odd, she thought, that his old face glowed with happiness. It had been years since she had seen it so. His smile touched memories to life; memories of happy days, before her mother died.

She released the freeze, and he spoke.

"Lynn," he said, "I am making this to give to Maui, of the Homeland Movement. If you see this it means that I am dead. But do not grieve. I wish to be buried in the Nuuanu cemetery, next to my father and my sister. Your brothers know this; and I am sure that they will obey me in this matter. I have received threats, but I refuse to be intimidated. I know that you will understand.

"For many years I have become more and more uneasy with the direction taken by Interspace. I was so proud of the organization when it was formed! There could be no greater endeavor, I believed, than to take humanity to space. But one by one those with ideals have mysteriously resigned or died. Interspace has been gutted from within. Not just by one person, but by the complicity that comes from a subtle sort of blackmail. Huge profits are being taken without keeping enough to do what needs to be done, is the simple way to put it.

"I know that you think the worst of your brothers, but they are truly not as bad as you believe. They have refused to listen to my warnings about Interspace, but they are not bad people. They have their families to protect and care for. And they do not understand that the intelligence branch of Interspace is ruthless. It is a ruthlessness for its own sake. These people do not care about me, they do not care about you, and they do not care about your brothers, nor will they listen to them. Your brothers will be bitterly shocked, I think, at how little power they have in some matters." He shrugged and looked deep into Lynn's eyes. Impossible that he was dead. He was right here in front of her.

"Perhaps any large organization like this where secrecy is involved engenders a class of spies, who believe that they are above the law," he continued. He took a sip of water.

"I have for some time been in touch with the Homeland Movement, Lynn. I suppose this will, unfortunately, surprise you. I say unfortunately because I realize what has caused you to draw away from me, and I believe that if you knew these things about me you would not . . . hate me so much. But I did not want to endanger you. I certainly hope that your brothers are surprised, otherwise my sacrifice is in vain.

"Those in the Homeland Movement are good people. It has eased my conscience to supply them with all the information I possibly could. I like them. They are everything I hoped Interspace would be. And you know what, Lynn? I think it quite possible that Interspace might send this great ship into space knowing that it will end up nowhere, and everyone aboard eventually dead. They have painted themselves into a corner. To save face—and profits—they *must* go.

"But the Homeland Movement has other plans. I have helped them, I hope, add the necessary components, unbeknownst to Interspace, that will actually make the ship *function!*" He struck a table out of the viewing angle with his fist. His eyes narrowed, as filled with glee as a small boy's.

"Lynn! If all goes well, this ship will *jump the fractal!*" He laughed. "Oh, I have had great fun with Maui, during our few meetings. He has told me all manner of outlandish things, like jumping the fractal, and he's given me strange things to think about and I believe in him.

"If you are seeing this, it is because my old friend Colonel Hawkins has helped you. You can trust him." Nostalgia rushed across his face. "He would do anything for me, and I for him. I would not put him at risk, Lynn, except for you. But he undertakes it gladly, I know. He is like that. I died a thousand times when I found that you were in such danger, but by then it was too late to do anything except call Hawkins."

He cleared his throat.

"Lynn, I have tried to tell you many times how much I admire you. I know how difficult it was to lose your mother." He cleared his throat again. "I do not regret marrying Alyssa, but I do regret not understanding that just making her my wife would not give you a mother." He sighed. "It is hard to raise a girl! You must admit that you were very wild." He smiled into the room at her. "I have all the music you ever recorded, my dear. I listen to it quite often. It is beautiful. I wish I had helped you more. You might have been a great composer."

Lynn froze the image, rose, blinked back tears, and stomped around the room a few times. She wondered why she felt so angry. She grabbed a tissue and blew her nose, then sat and continued the disk.

He paused for a moment, shifted in his seat. "This is kind of a funny thing to do, you know. Nothing I ever told you made any difference. So I certainly can't give you any advice. I can only tell you that I love you."

There was silence for another moment. Then he said, "Good-bye," abruptly, and the screen went dark.

Lynn threw herself down on the bed. She heard great fountains of foam splash again and again through the cries of the seabirds while the wind washed over her.

So. The Homeland Movement and Interspace were closer than she had imagined. Her heart lifted for some reason. Was the vision of which Akamu had spoken in that little room in Chaing Mai actually . . . *possible?*

Hawkins had no doubt meant to deliver the proofs as well as Akamu back to the Homelanders.

The proofs of brilliant, unstable Cen Kalakaua.

Which Akamu claimed would help him pilot the generation ship—the *Hawai'i Loa,* no less—across interstellar space.

To another world.

How?

She removed the disk from the player and put it back in its case. She realized she had nowhere to put it so left it in the middle of the bed. The news, Maui had said. But she was in no mood for more emotional intensity. She was keenly aware of Akamu's suffering, now. She dropped into a soft chair, pulled up her knees, and thought.

There was a way in which a virus could carry new DNA into his brain—his own normal DNA. She would have to take a good look at the nan he carried. Access the records and find out exactly what he had. Yes. Only then could she know for sure if anything could be done.

Anything? What a thought! Of course *something* could be done. At least some sort of stabilization.

She hoped.

Someone had left a black lacquer box on a table. She lifted the lid, drank the miso soup, polished off slices of sweet grilled eel with a flash of chopsticks, and finished with a pickle and cold rice.

Then she sat at her elegant machine and went to work.

She soon fell into the rhythm of investigation, almost forgetting the angst engendering her quest. She welcomed the soothing glow of the virtual corridors but soon forsook them impatiently—they slowed her down—and entered the realm of pure information.

Date, time, place. Tripler Labs, last month. She narrowed it down quite quickly: the Hawaiian male, thirteen years, two months. Healthy and hostile.

Caught with a retscan jammer and a tiny vial of bionan in his pocket by a mechanic who had to tackle him. The mechanic had suffered a broken rib for his trouble.

Stealing fire.

Apparently he'd already ingested half of the bionan. One milliliter was missing. They took the vial back.

The stuff had no name, only a number. It had been refrigerated for years, along with thousands of other solutions, each of which induced highly specialized changes in brain chemistry for which there were no particular uses. That anyone knew of at the time.

It took them fifteen minutes to figure out who he was. Of course, the computer found a quick match with the blood from the dead clones. No hint of the elation they must have felt or the puzzlement either—what the *hell* was this particular kid doing here, of all places?

They left him alone with a guard who underestimated him.

He escaped and they didn't know it for forty-five minutes.

Heads had rolled.

Lynn smiled within her helmet.

Now. What was it that he had taken?

Shelled within the report were old records unearthed during the investigation related to actual human experiments done years ago. Many years ago.

MRIs of subject's brain changes; a movie of blossoming color and shifting activity. A list of questions the subject was asked, the tasks she performed; the concurrent movie, the delicate, lovely responses of her neurons, of her . . .

Lynn stopped it, shifted back. Opened a window.

Marveled.

Here information had been collected that fell into the realm of which Sattva spoke, high on that windy cold Tibetan plain. The microtubules. Questions. What do you see *now?* A steady state of ten to the eleventh hertz, the oscillation at which Sattva claimed that, possibly, the wave function could be kept collapsed.

No data. No data. No data.

For five minutes the subject was dead. Right?

They gave her back her brainwaves. Test over.

What had happened, then? What had she *seen?* Where had she *been?*

And what had happened to her?

There was no record of that.

And why had Akamu gone to all the trouble to get this stuff, anyway?

Years of research into what made people exceptional flashed through her mind. She knew how to *make* people special, yes. That was all highly classified information. Eugenics pure and simple. To tamper, even with the highest of motives, even when shooting for great things—great intelligence, in one area or another—was not right.

But was it really wrong to create, or try to create, those who might in turn pull us all farther, faster? Those who might by God come up with the Grand Unified Theory, with the chaotic calculus . . . with the truth about time? What was the answer? Allowing adults to make educated choices about how to change themselves? But by then it was too late. Brain growth was over by then.

What Akamu was doing—solving the proofs—was deeply human, entirely natural. From what he had told her, his education had been such that he could not help but resonate with mathematical genius. It was very easy to create an environment in which children could reach their full potential. They appeared to be geniuses when compared to children who had not had their advantages, that's all.

But true genius *did* exist, and she knew it. Had seen it—the vast leaps some children were able to make, the way they seemed to absorb the ability to read, when three years old, to do complex mathematics by the time they were seven and to revel in it. These were the children she had studied. Exceptional children and exceptional adults. Kamehameha, by all accounts, had been such an exceptional person. And Akamu *was* Kamehameha, at least biochemically.

The nan program at Interspace had not been exactly hit-or-miss. Massive research had been done with rats, not very well hidden because no one really cared about rats. She could access that; look at Honsa's work—and who knows what had happened to Honsa, after her father had fired the woman. Lynn could track her down. But first . . .

Maui had seen to it that blood was drawn from Akamu as soon as they arrived, and she was grateful, for it meant that his genome was available, along with a library of other vital information.

With expertise drawn from long-honed skills she isolated the nan in his blood. That she was able to do so meant that the nan had settled in his bone marrow and was sending out a constant stream of modifiers. It seemed that the nan was bumping up the production of certain hormones.

One effect of this was to cause subtle changes in the shape of the tubular dimars, which in turn affected the angle between their planes.

There was also in this cocktail a bacterium it took a while to find a match for. Eventually, she found that the research that created a slightly changed version of it had actually taken place in Copenhagen years ago. They presently had one of the prototype quantum computers Sattva had mentioned.

This bacterium, isolated from the skin of deep-sea electric eels, lived in a symbiotic relationship with the eels. Its presence on the skin of the eels evidently facilitated their electrical charge. Now the Copenhagen subjects were taking a suitably manipulated version in order to facilitate their connection with the quantum computer.

Lynn's eyes were burning. She fiddled with the lighting and continued to search, frantically, for information—*any* information—she could possibly use.

After more sleuthing through dead ends, accessing long-sealed records, she found the Honsa work and compared it to the more recent Tripler experiments. They were dovetailed onto something called the Human Navigator Project. She marked that as something to return to after getting to the root of the immediate problem. She was becoming frantic—Honsa's data were filled with generation after generation of dead rats.

She started over, systematically accessing any and all leads that grew out of the data. It was all so dull that she was in despair, afraid that she might be missing something of importance, lulled by the dryness of it all. She would probably have to do the work herself—go down into the minute structure of the bionan and see how she could disable it without further damaging the delicate tubular dimars. She thought that she probably could do it, though, and decided to abandon this approach and just start with the nan she'd isolated.

Lynn stood, cleared the helmet for a moment, and poured herself some coffee from a pot someone had left—she did not remember when. It was cold. She gulped it down. She was exhausted.

When she returned to visual mode, she saw a tiny icon she hadn't noticed before blinking in her upper right hand field—a Hawaiian sailing canoe. She punched it up.

HUMAN NAVIGATOR INTERFACE INITIATOR ACTIVATED

What?

She quickly ran through the informational sidebar.

It told her that the human navigator interface of the generation ship had been undertaken and completed in just the past two years. It linked a human to a quantum computer. This quantum computer would translate the quantum-level brain function of the pilot to the actual, constantly changing coordinates of high-level space as swiftly as the pilot was able to think. With it, the ship would be able to . . .

Jump the fractal.

Her father's signature on this project seemed very clear to her.

And of course there were no experimental data to indicate the state of the pilot once this was accomplished.

However, only someone who had participated in planned sustained biofeedback during certain phases of enhanced brain development, which had to be begun when they were very young, was a candidate for such a role.

Bleary-eyed, furious, Lynn ripped off her helmet.

She tossed the helmet onto the chair and got up.

She ran out into the main nexus beneath the high, rough lava roof. Many plants rustled in the wind; flowers scented the air. She was chilly. Now, where had his apartment been?

There was a woman sitting near the door, quite awake, at a console; obviously a guard. She waved at Lynn and Lynn went past her, right into Maui's apartment without knocking. It was dark; she went into the bedroom where he was asleep in the moonlight, naked. She shook him.

"What?" he said.

"Wake up," she said. "There's something you're not telling me."

They walked out into the windy, tropical night. Dark haloed clouds scudded across the face of the moon then freed it to brilliance again. The constant rustle of leaf upon leaf was kicked to greater volume by each gust of wind, growing and subsiding, and there had to be mimosas somewhere as their sweet cloying scent was here, too.

"Where is that dome?" Lynn asked, looking around.

"About a twenty-minute walk," said Maui, moving so quickly down the moonlit path she practically had to run to keep up.

"Can't we drive?"

"It's a twenty-minute walk up a cliff face," he said.

"And why did you build it, again?" she asked. "Are you sure he's there?"

"Pretty sure," said Maui, his voice grim. After Lynn woke him breathing fire and demanded to know where Akamu was, Maui had sparked a panic in the infirmary. The monitoring machines said that Akamu was there.

But he was gone.

Sensors in a dome showed movement, but there was no answer when Maui tried to contact the person inside.

"You didn't forget; I haven't told you," he said. "They're really almost a kind of artifact. I'll try to explain, but this isn't really my field. My grandmother was deeply interested in it, though. She's the one who set this whole program up, really." They had reached the foot of the cliff—black, looming, alive with night sounds. Lynn was surprised to find that when Maui set foot on the first step, the path illuminated with lights set into it.

He spoke rather breathlessly and coughed now and then as he climbed. Lynn had to stay right behind him to hear. "When all the research was being done on consciousness about thirty years ago, one of the theories was that the understanding of consciousness and the linking of gravity with quantum theory would turn out to be one and the same. I'm not sure why—just perhaps that it was pleasant wishful thinking to think that we'd solve two great mysteries at once. You understand that the collapse of the wave function is supposed to admit all possibilities at once."

"Yes," said Lynn. "I don't know all that much about it either. But I do know that a lot of physicists rejected that premise with the Copenhagen Interpretation. Or at least, they asserted that we couldn't create what was not already there. That is, just *thinking* can't make it so. But it was a question of access. Possible universes exist all around us—within this one—here, now. I think that just about everyone agrees on this now. The problem is, though, that the initial conditions of all of them are such that they are so physically different than ours that we can't possibly comprehend them. They're meaningless. They're certainly not possible destinations."

"There are other theories, Lynn," he said. "One of them is that we exist in a *meta*universe, rather than a universe. The creation of the metaverse is, like everything, a chaotic process that solidifies into order at certain points in its evolution. During the times when this fractal, if you will, crystallizes, there are infinitely repeated identical patterns existing. Then, as you said—it's a question of gaining access. *Wormhole* is a rather antique term, but it's one that people are able to relate to.

"Your father was very open to these ideas and helped initiate work on the generation ship that might possibly enable it to access the metaverse. Of course, we were helped by some of the top scientists in the world via the Homeland Web. You see, even if Kalakaua actually did prove the existence of the metaverse, higher mathematics such as these are noncomputational. That was proved by Gödel. Only a *human* can truly understand them. But the tremendous speeds required to access the metaverse, and the constant stream of decisions that must be made, mean that the quantum computer in the ship must be directly linked to the mind of a human who understands the proofs. That person doesn't have to necessarily be the one to *solve* them—he or she only has to be able to understand them on a deep level. That's what this is all *about,* Lynn. The generation ship was ostensibly built as a faster-than-light ship—still exploring *our* cosmos, and what lies beyond. But the quantum computer interface your father helped create for the ship will enable navigation of a fractal jump. However, we have *no* idea what effect this effort will have on the human involved. That's why I wanted to avoid it. And that's why I absolutely forbade Akamu to pursue this."

Lynn was glad when he paused to rest for a moment. He turned to her and said, "He overheard us talking about all of this more than once. It didn't take much to get him terribly curious."

"What is your alternative?" asked Lynn. "I presume that you were planning to do the same thing, with someone?"

Maui shook his head. "We have done something analogous, from an AI approach, and we've been racing against the clock to try to develop some sort of safe way for humans to interface, because our deadline is whenever IS decides that the generation ship is ready to go. Once they found Akamu, I think it tipped our hand. I think—I think they killed your father because they figured out what he had done with the quantum computer and the human navigator. Obviously, *they* have no one who can navigate such a ship. Best to try to kill the only one who possibly could." His laugh was wry. "It's kind of funny—the larger the organization, the easier it is to hide things. Now that they're suspicious, they're rushing away, in a matter of weeks. So *our* plan has been set in motion, too. Our crew members have been arriving in droves. I can only hope that IS still doesn't really know how ready we are."

"Your crew?—never mind. We're in a hurry. What about the AI interface?"

Maui said, "Well, you could find plenty of people who would argue that what we will be using will be conscious." He paused for a moment. "In fact, I certainly hope that's true. But if we had decided to go with a living human, he or she would have been an adult, someone capable of making the decision to be initiated, knowing the risks."

"I think that Akamu knows the risks," said Lynn slowly. "In fact, that's why he wanted to stay away from you until he finished figuring out the proofs. He didn't want you to be able to stop this process. But it sounds to me that if you are using an artificial intelligence, you're back to a computational basis," said Lynn. "I don't understand."

"Maybe you will later," he said. "What about Akamu? Have you figured anything out that will help . . . ease this transition, or stop it completely?"

"No," she said. "I was just getting ready to start on it when I saw this Navigator Initiation thing. I think I've got my breath again. Let's get going. If something *else* is happening to him then all bets are completely off."

She forced her legs to move, and continued talking to Maui as they climbed. "Why didn't you tell me that you have a quantum computer *here?*"

Maui stopped suddenly and turned. "How do you know?"

She pushed past him. "I said we have to hurry. I didn't. I know now. My father talked about it on his message."

"I didn't listen to your message, of course," said Maui.

"He talked about it being on the ship, not here. But you see, in addition to the nan, Akamu has apparently ingested something developed much more recently than the nan, something I think he could only have gotten if you were in contact with the people developing the quantum computer. Which, according to my father, you are."

"Right," said Maui, huffing and puffing behind her. "We've had this latest prototype for over a year. Hell, Lynn, if you can figure *that* out, I think Akamu's in good hands."

"I'm no genius," said Lynn. "I'm afraid that's what he really needs. And he told me that he fell *asleep* in the dome in Tibet. Ha! I wonder what he was *really* doing?"

Maui's footsteps quickened behind her. "There was a dome in Tibet?"

"Yes. Sattva—the Dalai Lama—is a particle physicist. She has one of these domes, too."

"No kidding." Maui was silent for a moment. "She seems very nice. We didn't exchange much information. We were rather in emergency mode."

"I would *hope* so," said Lynn. "But yes, I would have to agree. She is very nice."

"And very brilliant, apparently."

"Hawkins told me that she was furious—in her way, of course, very calmly—that he had not told her that the earring held the proofs. Apparently she's been working on them all her life."

"Really!" he said. He sounded quite excited. "That's another problem. If Interspace got hold of those Chinese proofs, and if they were any good . . . your father was going to pass over the Chinese version of the Kaiulani Proofs to try to help us. We had no idea, of course, of the true worth of their attempt. Kalakaua made many sheer jumps of reasoning and left out the scaffolding to begin with. It's quite possible that he didn't even know that others couldn't follow his reasoning— I think that he believed that it was all crystal clear. Some of his math is just being reinvented. We of course have most of his final proofs—"

"You *do?*" asked Lynn, amazed.

"Yes," said Maui. "Someone from IS had ripped out some

of them, half pages. I have to hand it to them, it seems to me to be an impossible endeavor to re-create the proofs from a few ripped pages and whatever he left on the web, but they've tried very hard."

"If Kalakaua was the great genius," said Lynn, "why the hell didn't you clone *him?*"

Maui shrugged. "Sheer shortsightedness, I guess. He was gone before we realized exactly what he was doing. He kept it very close to himself. Lelani—my grandmother—really wanted the bones of Kamehameha, and thought he knew where they were. He did, and eventually gave them to us. We simply had no idea of the tremendous import of his life, his work."

"So. The dome? Are we almost there?"

"Just about. It was built a while back. Basically they put a human in an environment where they're exposed to a constant oscillation of ten to the eleventh hertz. This is to help the human mind, which is *noncomputational,* link with quantum events. Without the interface of *reasoning.* Simply on a level of *knowing.* When humans are in this state—if the theory is correct—they *understand intuitively* the very nature of the quantum universe. And they are *conscious* of it when they're in that state. They can see the openings. It's like—well, it's like holding a sphere in your hands, feeling it, seeing it. Instead of knowing it through mathematical formulae, an abstract picture that only a few people can relate to. Bear with me!"

"I'm trying to," said Lynn. "Sattva told me about the same thing. What I really want to know is whether or not Akamu spent a lot of time in here when he was little."

"Trying to pin me with child abuse again, I suppose. Well, I'm guilty. Akamu did spend time here. All the kids did. After the first few years when it began to seem kind of silly, they weren't even supervised. That's right! Shocking as that sounds! They could just come in here, use the biofeedback, and watch MRIs of what was happening to their brain. They all seemed to find it great fun. I tried it and it didn't do much for me. I mean, it was relaxing, but it didn't seem harmful, and they liked it. So we just left the domes here."

"It probably didn't do anything for you because your brain was too old and ossified," said Lynn.

"Thank you very much," said Maui.

"No, it's true. All of the incredible informational fields and connections are created during the first ten years of life or so. And the most powerful are created during infancy until the child is five or six. When will we *get* there?"

"Just over this rise," he said.

They turned a switchback and walked about a hundred more yards. Gradually, the roof of a gently illuminated green dome became visible, and more of it with each step. Black palms were silhouetted in front of it. A wash of moonlight lay across the tiny, high meadow. Far below, swells looked like ripples on the pale, glowing face of the sea.

As Lynn ran across the meadow, the door swung open.

Akamu stood in the doorway. He seemed to glow in the soft golden light.

When she was just a few feet away from him, she stopped.

He was wearing only a pair of black shorts. The small *Hawai'i Loa* shone against his chest. A halo of crystals sat on his head.

There was a small, illuminated inscription panel right next to him; Lynn's eyes involuntarily went to it, absorbed it in a second.

Consciousness would be some manifestation of this quantum-entangled internal cytoskeletal state and of its involvement in the interplay between quantum and classical levels of activity.

—Penrose, 1995

She looked back at Akamu. Her heart sank at the unmistakable triumph in his eyes.

"You're too late," he said, utterly calm. "Nobody can stop me now."

He looked out past them, toward the stars.

"At last I'm ready to take us *there.*"

20

Maui grabbed Akamu by the shoulders and stared into his eyes for a long, grave moment. Lynn thought she could see tears in Maui's eyes for an instant, but then they were gone. Akamu's gaze was steady and calm. Maui let out a long sigh, dropped his hands, and stepped back.

"Akamu," he said, "there was no need for this." But his tone of voice held respect as well as anger, as if he realized he was no longer talking to a child.

"I've become who I want to be," Akamu said gently. "It's all right." He looked up at Lynn. "If you knew it was possible, isn't that what *you* would do?"

"I'm afraid I'm nowhere near as brave as you," she replied.

"I bet you are!" he said, with great conviction.

She shook her head silently and walked past him into the dome.

"Is this where you did the biofeedback?" she asked, standing in front of a familiar screen. "This projects a hologram of your brain, right?"

Akamu and Maui came and stood next to her, watched "completed" flash a few times on the screen.

"Isn't there *anything*—," began Maui, his voice agitated, the possible consequences of Akamu's actions apparently striking him anew.

"No," Akamu and Lynn both said at once.

Maui wheeled and stalked out of the dome.

"Wait!" called Lynn, and started after him.

Akamu grabbed her arm. "He'll get over it. Leave him alone. You don't want to talk to him now. Believe me."

The night swallowed Maui as Lynn stood in the doorway.

She turned back. "Did you get that bioelectric facilitator when you were in Sattva's dome?"

"The stuff from the eels?" asked Akamu. He shook his head. "I got it here. It came with the rest of this—the prototype quantum computer and the headpiece. I talked a long time with the people in Copenhagen about it. Maui didn't know. He's pretty busy."

"But the quantum computer alone wasn't enough, right?"

Akamu shook his head. "I need to understand the Kaiulani Proofs, too. I thought the bionan at Tripler would help. I want to be just like Cen Kalakaua. In every possible way."

"Why would you want to be just like him? Didn't he end up a drunk, a bum?"

"A drunk!" Akamu glared at her. "Cen Kalakaua was the most brilliant man in the world!"

"Well, I just heard—"

"You heard the story he wanted Interspace to hear. Ha! Guess it worked. Lynn, Cen Kalakaua *jumped the fractal.*"

A month ago, Lynn realized, she would have laughed in Akamu's face, had she understood his assertion. Now, she said, "How do you know?"

"We know by studying his proofs, of course."

"You mean, nobody saw him do it."

"Not directly. It was on Molokai. He left Maui and Lelani—Maui's grandmother—and hiked up to see the place where Kaiulani gave birth, in the International Biosphere Park."

"Now, I don't know all that much about Hawaiian history," she said, "but I don't think Kaiulani had any children. Didn't she die young or something?"

"Forget that," said Akamu. "It's not important for now. But he hiked up to see this place and never came back."

"So? Isn't that rough country?" asked Lynn. "Couldn't he have fallen off a cliff?"

"He might have," said Akamu. "Except that it's pretty clear from the proofs that there was a window right at that time and place. In fact, until the past few weeks there was room for doubt. But I'm positive now." His face flushed with excitement as he spoke.

"Is that why you called them the Kaiulani Proofs?"

"That's what *he* called them. I've *seen* them, Lynn," he said, with a touch of awe. "I've held them in my hands. They're just in an ordinary notebook. He wrote the title on the back page."

He sat in the low chair in front of the screen. "Here," he said. "I'll show you what my brain looks like now."

Then he looked up at her and his eyes blazed with unmistakable joy.

"Lynn," he whispered, "It's working. Everything's *working*. It's like—it's like long streets of light. A lot of them, that I can't see the end of. Like—oh, I don't know what! But, Lynn, I'm *so* happy!"

Kohala erupted into a maelstrom of activity as the sun came up—frantic, yet controlled. Large trucks kicked up dust from old cane roads; the airstrip received one small jet after another at intervals so close that Lynn was afraid she'd see a collision any minute.

She perched on a rock at the edge of the meadow where the dome sat. Small planes were in a holding pattern out over the ocean as far as she could see. A large fleet of enormous helicopters was added to every fifteen minutes or so.

Akamu was asleep in the dome, his head on a round zabuton, one of the pillows used in Zen meditation. Lynn felt strangely at peace concerning him. He had made his own decision, and now it was irrevocable. He was a strange new creature now, taking hold of his destiny with both hands no matter what the risk, in order to lead humans to a new homeland.

Lynn stood and stretched. A narrow waterfall plummeted into a pool on the meadow's edge. She walked over to it; chilly mist filled the air and settled on low hummocks of impatiens. She undressed and carefully climbed over the slippery rocks to plunge, gasping, into the pool. She only stayed in for a moment. As she climbed out she noted that only a puckered scar was left from her bullet wound.

She waited on a sunny rock until she was dry, then dressed. She looked in at Akamu but he was deeply asleep; she pushed his hair back from his forehead with her hand and closed the door behind her. As she turned she saw a nurse she recognized from the previous night's furor coming up the path.

"Maui sent me to stay with Akamu," he said. "I left my moped at the bottom of the hill. Maui said you can use it if you like."

"Where is there to go?"

The nurse looked at her in disbelief. "Everywhere!" he said, flinging out his arms expansively. "It's gorgeous everywhere you go. But I'd stay off the cane roads. They're moving lots of supplies today."

She descended the riprap trail, which was wet and somewhat slippery.

She told the moped to take her back to her station.

She had more work to do.

No one seemed to notice her as she walked through the corridors. Everyone was rushing around like mad.

She sat in her chair.

It took her twenty minutes to set up the bounce. Her message would appear to come from Germany. She punched in the code she knew so well.

In a minute James's face, somewhat bleary, appeared on the screen. His eyes widened when he saw her.

"Lynn! Where are you? We've been looking for you. You have to come home soon. Father is dead."

"I know," she said. "That's what I'm calling about."

His eyes narrowed. "How did you find out?"

"How did he die, James?"

He took a deep breath. "It was a heart attack, Lynn. You know how we kept telling him to get that new—"

"Bullshit!" Lynn said and thumped her table. She jumped up and leaned over the screen. "He was murdered! He was killed, James. I want to know what you and Samuel had to do with it."

"You're not in Munich," he said. "Where are you?"

"Why don't you tell me the truth?" she asked.

"Why don't you?" asked James hotly. "You were in it with him all along, weren't you, you little—"

She severed the connection, switched off the whole system, and sat breathing hard for a few minutes.

Then she switched it on again and began collecting and storing data as fast as her fingers could fly.

What could one person do?

Plenty.

When she was done it was almost noon. Sleep was out of the question. She'd never felt more awake in her life. And she was starving.

She stood and slipped the small silvery disk she'd created into her shirt pocket and buttoned it securely. She glanced out into the corridor and it was even more busy. Clearly no one had time to serve her a nice little lunch today! She went up top and climbed on the moped.

"I want to eat," she told it. "Take me to the nearest place. And stay off the cane roads."

The computer digested that, probably fixing on a few key words and ignoring the rest. Finally it said, in a tinny voice, "Take the next right."

The moped climbed a narrow road that ran along the cliff, apparently a former state highway, though now in terrible repair. She steered around the potholes and tried to ignore the flutter of fear she felt, seeing how far below the ocean was now and how steep the cliff that dropped into it a few feet from her right side.

Then she rounded a corner and saw a weathered sign: Ono Restaurant.

On a picnic table beneath a thatched roof she had some teriyaki mahi and a beer. The only other person there was the cook, and he sat reading the newspaper at the next table.

"You going?" he asked, as she stood and set her dishes on the counter.

"Yes," she said. "Thanks. That was good."

"No," he said. "I mean *going*. On the *Hawai'i Loa.*"

"Good lord, no!" she said. "Are you?" she asked, jokingly.

"I hope so," he said gravely. He rose and held out the paper. "See? It's ready. I'm nervous. And excited. Nervously excited."

He laughed tremulously, sat down, ran one hand through his hair. "I look around and every day I think about how beautiful it is here. But the ship is beautiful, too. And where we are going, and what we will be doing—that's very important. More important than me staying here and cooking fish."

"I suppose," she said.

"Oh, without a doubt! Where would we be if we'd stayed in Asia, eh? Where will the earth be if we all stay here? Humans are meant to explore, to expand. The earth is getting used up. Some of us have to leave. Overcrowding leads to war. Innocent lives lost."

Lynn found his premise oversimplistic but didn't argue. She held out her hand. "I'm Lynn Oshima. I'm a friend of Maui's. I just got here."

He smiled and shook her hand. "My name is Ken. Maui is a good man."

"So you've been on the ship?"

"Oh, of course. In virtual. It's kind of like being in the army reserves. We have to spend so many hours a week on the ship with our ohana. The members are international, and we rotate constantly so we have experience with many different kinds of people. It's been very exciting this week—more and more are arriving here, and I've met many people I've only seen virtually before. We have emergency simulations and things like that. It is incredible there. So much information, so easy to access. Amazing gardens—acres of them. An infinite food supply—an ark, really. And very Hawaiian." The little man gestured toward the billowing green crevasses of the rain forest that covered the mountain behind them.

"We've stocked a lot of the birds from here that were thought to be extinct at one time. Around the millennium many species were found in very remote bioreserves. Eventually we were able to get the population back up. A lot of bones were found, too. Some of those birds were our first success at cloning from bones. So many species of flightless birds, plants that had lost their thorns—such a defenseless place! This is the most isolated land on earth. Without predators, without diseases."

His smile was shy. "Sorry. I hope I'm not boring you. I'm an ornithologist; that's how I got tapped for the ship. I've been working out just exactly what to take. Can you imagine a more wonderful or scary thing? But sometimes"—he waved his arm in a large arc that took in the cliffs, the sea, the distant village— "I just want to stay here the rest of my days." He laughed again. "There are others who would be happy to take my place! In fact, I think they're arriving now, all the time. They've been coming all week, from around the world."

After leaving the bird man Lynn motored silently through deep green lanes draped with sun-dappled vines, rising along the cliff face on a narrow rutted road that did not connect to the rest of the island. The moped told her, when she figured out how to ask, that since Kohala was internationally recognized as an independent political entity, they did not have to comply with U.S. immigration laws nor were arrivals and departures on record with the U.S. government.

Far below, green and golden headlands reached fingerlike into the ocean, divided by small bays inaccessible by land because of treacherous cliffs. She was turned back at the maglaunch parameter by Interspace guards who told her that it was private property. One of them was surveying the peninsula with a powerful telescope that she thought probably translated information into several different broadcast mediums. She wondered what they thought of all the activity and turned the moped around.

She descended through a golden afternoon. The sea was aquamarine near the shore, reefs clearly visible through the crystalline water. White seabirds flurried around the tiny islands near shore, catching the sun. She took the short road back to the village on the advice of the moped, which told her that it had just enough charge to do that, in a rather scolding tone of voice.

She drove back into the melee. It had not abated; in fact, it was even more intense.

Vehicles were flying to and fro, at a great rate. Computer terminals had literally risen from the ground, on heavy posts, completely weatherproof, and she saw a woman press her hand against it and apparently receive an assignment, for she hurried off purposefully.

Lynn wasn't sure where to go, though the place wasn't very big. Then she saw a red-roofed pavilion with several picnic tables—Akamu was standing on one of the tables, waving at her.

The moped rolled reluctantly toward him, filling the air with resentful messages.

"Lynn!" Akamu called, when she got closer. "Lynn, we're leaving! Right away!"

"What?" she asked, bringing her moped to a halt. "You don't mean—you don't mean the *ship?"*

"Yes, yes," he laughed and her heart went dark. *No more Akamu.*

"You can't go!" The words burst out of her, even though she know he *had* to go.

"Lynn," he said gently, as if he were much older and wiser than she, "it's what I was born for. I feel wonderful now. That's the only place I can really live, I think, the way I am now. On the ship. The ship is set up for me—or someone like me—to interface with it."

"I know," she said, without enthusiasm.

She saw Maui coming up the hill. He waved, but she didn't. She was too upset. About everything. So *soon!* She thought of the disk in her pocket. At least she had something to occupy herself with after they left.

Maui looked tense and calm at the same time. Alert, aware, and capable, as if he were holding many threads at the same time, ready to reweave them at a moment's notice if necessary.

"Lynn," he said. "I was just getting ready to message that moped. I'm glad you're back. I didn't think you'd be gone so long! We sent our part of the proofs to Sattva this morning." His voice was filled with tremendous excitement.

"Now you've sent them over the *web?* I thought this was top secret and all that."

"You wouldn't believe the people she has over there. Their encryption changes second by second. Every burst of information was in an entirely different frame. At this point, it's worth a try." He seemed like an eager boy, not a middle-aged man.

"I hope they do it," said Akamu. "There are so many of them. There's only one of me. I think I've about reached my limits. I only need to be able to *understand* it."

Maui said, "Interspace is getting ready to send up their crew, Lynn. They're actually getting ready to *go.* For nothing. They're making believe that they have some sort of destination in mind when they don't. They're just not ready. But they're afraid of us. Since your father—well, they certainly suspect that we're going to make some sort of move soon."

He squinted at the sky. "But they don't know how or when. They might know *what,* though. So we've got to get out of here right away. In fact, the first helicopter over to the maglaunch is leaving in about ten minutes. We have a crew of five thousand to load."

"Five *thousand?*"

"Oh, the launch is capable of carrying the weight. The one on Oahu has taken a lot heavier loads for construction. We have pretty sophisticated shielding on the way up, and we have Homelanders in various sensitive positions throughout the world who'll prevent any sort of nuclear strike, though I think that's a very remote possibility. Once we dock, there's nobody there capable of putting up any resistance—mostly mainte-nance people."

"They must know you're getting ready, Maui," she said. "Those guards up at the launch—"

Maui laughed, shortly. "You could call them double agents. They're with us. They send faked reports to the surveillance satellites. The people over at the Kailua-Kona site where we'll board the maglaunch are with us as well. We haven't left any-thing to chance. We have a plan. Interspace doesn't, not really. And they're going to sacrifice all those people. I think they're just going to send them on their way with the promise of an eventual breakthrough. They can coldsleep their way into eter-nity. Without that breakthrough, they'll be out on the edge of nowhere with their clones, their information banks, forever, a ship of fools."

"They don't have *me,*" said Akamu.

"That's right," said Maui. "Without precise information

about the nature of spacetime, they'll never, ever get to a livable environment. The odds are simply totally against it. And even if we got all that information and sent it to them, they wouldn't have a pilot. But *we're* ready. Our whole crew is ready. We know *exactly* how to run this ship. Trainees have been doing it virtually for years. All we need is that final information about where to go and how to get there. Lynn, we're ready to *take over the ship!*" His voice shook with excitement.

"Yeah," she said. "Well, it sounds easy enough."

"You'll see," he said. "And we're not quite ready to *go*. Yet. To pilot the ship once we get up there. But Sattva was stunned to get all of Cen's proofs, except for the torn pages. She said it was like a dream."

"Yes, shouldn't take her long to work everything out," Lynn said in her driest tone. "Maybe an hour or two."

"I think she can do it," said Akamu. "I saw a lot of what they'd done already. There are a lot of smart people there, Lynn."

Maui turned and looked out at the ocean, his hands on his hips. He sighed. "But once we're *there,* on the ship, no telling what will happen. The world isn't going to look too kindly on us stealing it, particularly not with Interspace raising the battle cry. They need to have their feet kicked out from under them somehow. We'll be like sitting ducks for at least a day or two; there are a lot of shakedown details to take care of. We don't want a bloodbath. There are bound to be soldiers sent up to get rid of us *unless* we can explain our position and our motivation in a worldwide arena. Quickly." He cleared his throat. "Your father was going to give the world our side of the case, but—"

He put his hands in his pocket and remained with his back to them, studying purple Haleakala, across the narrow channel.

Something clicked in Lynn.

For a moment, though, she didn't say anything.

Visions of earth swept through her, beautiful and green, a *planet*. Her home.

Only here could she make her pilgrimage, to that monastery in Cambodia, down a dusty sun-dappled trail that led through a vine-draped forest to the place where she could learn who she really was.

But maybe she needed to learn a lot faster than that.

Like right now.

The turmoil of the past month roiled about her, shot through with the question *What can one person do?*

Well, here was the answer. Staring her in the face. *It's simple. Sever yourself forever from all you've ever known.*

If she didn't do this, now, she knew that no matter how long she lived, and no matter where or how, all the white water buffaloes in the world couldn't save her.

But it was so damned *hard.* Her throat seemed to close in claustrophobia just thinking about it.

She glanced at Akamu. He was looking at her expectantly.

I've been set up, she thought.

Never mind. She took a deep breath. Maui turned toward her.

"I think I can help you," she said.

To her surprise, Maui took a step and embraced her tightly for a moment, then moved away, still holding her shoulders, his face strangely happy.

"I was hoping you'd say that," he said.

"I know," she said.

They went in a series of huge helicopters around to Kona. "You'll see," said Akamu, holding Lynn's hand so tightly she thought he'd break it. "There's a beautiful compartment on the ship just for you! Maui showed it to me this morning in VR." He had to shout over the din.

"Oh he did, did he?" she muttered.

She hadn't had much time to ponder her decision.

Yet it felt right. She'd had trouble staying one step ahead of those who wanted to silence her. This was the best way to gain an effective forum.

And she was pretty sure that "her" compartment was to have been occupied by her father.

That thought steadied her.

Amazingly, it was as Maui had said, after they swept around

the mountain and landed. The double-agent Interspace guards hurried them to the maglev, down long escalators that made Lynn feel a bit crazy with claustrophobia. Maui was not with them but this had all been planned out forever, Lynn guessed, as everyone filed into assigned seats one after the other with an excited low murmur and the sweat of fear that Lynn smelled despite the air system. There was an excellent chance that they would be blown up at any point.

But maybe Interspace hadn't planned for anything quite as audacious as this, despite the evidence beneath their noses. Lynn remembered, and smiled at, the many parties she'd attended when the Homeland Movement was the butt of hilarious jokes. Last laugh, she thought, as Akamu patiently buckled her in, saying, "What's *wrong,* Lynn? You don't have to be so nervous."

She blacked out during the great rush upward and was terribly sick during the rest of the flight. Akamu squeezed her hand anxiously from time to time saying, "Don't worry, Lynn, you'll feel better once we get there."

This is crazy, she was thinking, this is just plain crazy.

21

Lynn looked at the prompter, which was ready to go. The satellite link had been negotiated, and she had spent the time accumulating even more information; at least enough to send the top echelons of Interspace to hell for several thousand years.

It was as Akamu had said. The ship was beautiful.

The crew had settled in instantly, going right to their places. Maui told Interspace that the ship would depart instantly if there were any threats; all was in complete readiness to do so.

Except for the proofs. Maui didn't tell them that.

Lynn had not been there nearly long enough to tour the entire ship. That would take months. But she had seen a lovely small apartment labeled hers, and that was where she had done all of her information gathering. It was absolutely incredible that all possible information from earth had been replicated aboard the ship, but data compression and backups and alternates made it possible.

Maybe Maui was right. It was time. The technology was here, anyway. And he totally believed in his new/old social system. Maybe it would work.

And according to him, they would only be cruising for two years at the most.

"The idea is," he told her, taking a moment to drop into a chair next to her, "that we will be far in the future. So far that we understand exotic matter and can send at least messages back to earth. We can tell them where we are, how we got there, if we choose to. That's part of the treaty I'm making with them right now."

Lynn stared at the blinking red light; as she stared it turned yellow and a voice said, "Thirty seconds."

She pressed the pad that brought up a screen of the points she would cover. She glanced at herself in the monitor.

Was that her? That thin woman with the pale face and shaggy black hair? She was going to be televised internationally looking like this? It hadn't occurred to her until just this second, and then it was the next second, and she was ready to speak.

Interspace relinquished all claim to the newly named *Hawai'i Loa* shortly after her speech.

Sattva sent them the finished proofs two days later, with a congratulatory note, which included thanks for having given her group the opportunity to complete one of the most important proofs in the history of mathematics.

The proofs were transferred to the quantum computer and Akamu studied them; excitement infused the crew and increased with each passing hour.

Lynn was surprised at how free she felt.

Her only regret was leaving Nanà. Somewhere down there

beneath the swirling clouds was a tiny island, and on Nuuanu Avenue in a small frame house was an acerbic old woman who had just lost her son and who would now lose her granddaughter.

Lynn called Nana, and as they spoke pictured her sitting in the special chair she used in the hallway just for calls, using her old-fashioned cellphone without video.

"I am going into *space,* Nana," she said.

"What is wrong with here?" Nana's voice was deeply irritated, scathing. "First you left without telling me. I was *so* worried. And now—I always *said* you were a silly girl." Her voice turned pleading, suddenly, and Lynn felt a pang hearing the old lady's deep loneliness. "You are all I have left now. Please write to me!"

"Nana, I can't write to you where I am going," she said, wrenched. "But I'll think of you."

Akamu, newly infused with purpose, seemed to mature before her eyes in the final days before departure. They were only waiting that long for Akamu and the ship to go through the final stages of initialization.

During the departure ceremony, Maui removed the *Hawai'i Loa* from around his neck and set it into place on his console. Akamu's, Lynn had learned, was a backup. Lynn was there when he did it, as was Akamu.

Everyone on the ship was standing, waiting, watching a video of the event from atriums, bridges, and gathering rooms.

Maui slid the panel shut, paused. Then he said, his voice rather shaky, "Initiate AI interface."

There was a moment of silence. Maui's hand, resting on the panel, trembled.

Then a woman's rich, gentle voice filled the air.

"Hello," she said. "My name is Lelani." There was a long pause, and when she spoke again, her voice was filled with wonder.

"I guess . . . it *worked.*"

TOR
BOOKS The Best in Science Fiction

MOTHER OF STORMS • John Barnes
From one of the hottest new nanes in SF: a shattering epic of global catastrophe, virtual reality, and human courage, in the manner of *Lucifer's Hammer*, *Neuromancer*, and *The Forge of God*.

BEYOND THE GATE • Dave Wolverton
The insectoid dronons threaten to enslave the human race in the sequel to *The Golden Queen*.

TROUBLE AND HER FRIENDS • Melissa Scott
Lambda Award-winning cyberpunk SF adventure that the *Philadelphia Inquirer* called "provocative, well-written and thoroughly entertaining."

THE GATHERING FLAME • Debra Doyle and James D. Macdonald
The Domina of Entibor obeys no law save her own.

WILDLIFE • James Patrick Kelly
"A brilliant evocation of future possibilities that establishes Kelly as a leading shaper of the genre."—*Booklist*

THE VOICES OF HEAVEN • Frederik Pohl
"A solid and engaging read from one of the genre's surest hands."—*Kirkus Reviews*

MOVING MARS • Greg Bear
The Nebula Award-winning novel of war between Earth and its colonists on Mars.

NEPTUNE CROSSING • Jeffrey A. Carver
"A roaring, cross-the-solar-system adventure of the first water."—Jack McDevitt